Praise for Stephanie Marland

My Little Eye is an enthralling, intriguing and twisty tale for all of us armchair detectives who think we know it all.

Liz Nugent, author of LYING IN WAIT and UNRAVELLING OLIVER

The first novel in what promises to be a riveting new series, *My Little Eye* is a one-sitting read: gripping, clever and worryingly plausible. *Mick Herron*

Ingeniously plotted and perfectly chilling, Marland knows how to ratchet up the tension and keep her readers balancing on the edge. A dark, mysterious thriller with characters you can't wait to meet again. I loved it.

Susi Holliday, author of THE DEATHS OF DECEMBER

A masterclass in pacing & such an original take on the serial killer thriller

Eva Dolan, author of THIS IS HOW IT ENDS

A clever, twisting, nightmare-inducing read, I couldn't put this one down

Chris Whitaker, author of ALL THE WICKED GIRLS

This is a multi-layered, gripping read steeped in authenticity that will keep you up at night.

Catherine Ryan Howard, author of DISTRESS SIGNALS

My Little Eye should be a contender for anyone's book of the year - it's certainly one of mine. It's fresh, original, has a rip-roaring plot and is totally addictive. In Clementine Starke and Dominic Bell, Marland has created intriguing lead characters to rival the best in crime fiction.

of STASI WOLF

Stephanie Marland has worked in the university sector for over ten years and published research on how people interact and learn together in virtual environments online. She's an alumni of the MA in Creative Writing (Crime Fiction) at City University London, and an avid reader of all things crime fiction, blogging about books at www.crimethrillergirl. com. Steph also writes the Lori Anderson action thriller series (as Steph Broadribb) for Orenda Books.

You Die Next

Stephanie Marland

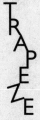

First published in Great Britain in 2019 by Orion Books,
an imprint of The Orion Publishing Group Ltd
Carmelite House, 50 Victoria Embankment,
London EC4Y 0DZ

An Hachette UK company

1 3 5 7 9 10 8 6 4 2

A CIP catalogue record for this book is
available from the British Library.

ISBN (mass market paperback) 978 1 4091 7199 7
ISBN (eBook) 978 1 4091 7200 0

Typeset by Born group

Printed and bound in Great Britain by Clays Ltd, Elcograf S.p.A.

www.orionbooks.co.uk

For my Mum – Jill Jones
An inspirational woman, a great friend, and a wonderful mother
With love and thanks for everything

PROLOGUE

It's streaming. Quality's good, not HD, but clear enough. On screen, top left, are the words: *JedUrbXTM is LIVE*. Could be that he's the guy in the balaclava.

He's close to the camera, holding it out like he's taking a selfie, his face oversized from the weird angle. The tight woollen hood obscures his features, reducing him to two irregular-shaped eyeholes and a gash for a mouth. There's light somewhere below his face, illuminating his lips. It makes him look ghoulish.

He's talking. The balaclava shifts, the material skewing a few centimetres to give a hint of stubble around his mouth before the hood slides back into place. The sound has a minuscule delay, as though he's lip-syncing out of time. His accent is northern, from Manchester perhaps. 'I'm Jedx, and for me this is all about the rush . . . the massive adrenaline hit. The risk . . .'

As he speaks, hearts and thumbs-up emojis float across the bottom of the screen; the viewers of the live-stream are showing their appreciation.

He grins and gives a thumbs-up. Then the camera swings away from his face, plunging the view into darkness, and the autofocus struggles. The picture is grainy, impossible to make out, but the audio remains clear; there's a sound like running water, as well as loud rustling, muttering with a few swears, then hurried footsteps on gravel.

A picture morphs into view. Three people, silhouetted by torchlight, march ahead of Jedx. The camera rocks from side to side as he follows them. Trees hang over the pathway, their gnarled branches clutching at his jacket like deformed bony fingers. The undergrowth is dense.

Jedx's voice, disembodied this time, says, 'It's tough getting in, but no surprises there. We've found a virgin site . . . unclaimed. We need to tread careful. We didn't see any on-site security when we reconned the place, but there are loads of "Keep Out" signs. If there's a patrol, we don't want them to know we're coming.'

Comments are appearing under the live-feed:

DavidSees: Where are you guys?
Optxxxx: Dope!
UrbexFan984: Loving this feed
FunLeapExp: Bravo
VulcanD86: Where you at?

The camera wobbles and closes in on the three figures ahead. As it reaches them it pans right, to the closest one.

'Hey, Sass. Tell the viewers where we are.'

'Hendleton Studios.' The woman's voice is quiet, breathy. She half-turns to the camera but all that shows is that she's wearing red lipstick, and tiny diamantes glitter around the eyeholes of her balaclava. 'Famous from the black and white era until the end of the sixties . . . the hit movies *Die Happy*, *Marriage and the Man*, *Lola's Journey* and *The Fourth Way Down* were made here. So was the cult horror classic *Death by a Thousand Daggers*. The studio closed after owner Joey Oakenridge died unexpectedly—'

'In totally dodgy circumstances,' a new male voice cuts in, higher pitched and younger-sounding, with a London accent. 'Well suspicious if you ask . . .'

'Beaker's right.' Jedx turns the lens back to himself. The angle's crooked once more, with only his mouth visible. 'Wikipedia says it's haunted.'

'Fucksake. I'm trying to give the facts here.' Hands, with orange-painted nails emerging from fingerless gloves, grab the camera and yank it round to face the woman, Sass, again. 'The verdict was death by misadventure.'

There's a shout to hurry up from another voice, an older-sounding guy. The view shifts forward and the image sways as the trio jog towards the fourth person. He's standing in front of a high wire fence. Although he's a half-foot taller than the rest of them, the fence must be a good two feet higher than him.

The camera focuses on a sign. It's weathered and faded with age. NO ENTRY. TRESSPASSERS WILL BE PROSECUTED. The taller guy throws a rucksack over the fence, followed by a crowbar. It hits the top and the wire jangles.

Sass pulls the camera back to her. 'Mortgaged several times over, the studio stopped production and closed its gates for the last time on 24 January 1972. It's been lying dormant ever since.'

'Until tonight,' says Jedx. The view returns to him. He's smiling beneath his balaclava and puts on an American accent, movie voiceover style. 'Because tonight, folks, we're breaking our way in.'

The on-screen counter beside the word *LIVE* is at 28:03. The viewer tally beneath it stands at over four hundred. A doorway comes into view, boarded up with plywood. Tattered 'Keep Out' notices are pasted haphazardly across it like badly hung wallpaper. The arched stone doorframe is green with algae but still impressive. Carved into the stone over the top of the door is HENDLETON STUDIOS: SOUND-STAGE ONE.

Jedx swings the camera round to face him. 'We're gearing up to gain entry. As you know, this is kind of illegal.' He grins into the lens. 'But you guys won't tell anyone, will you?'

Pinnyhip078: Do it!!
DavidSees: Oh this is epic. Let's see what's in there!
Upyeah99: Hmmmmmm.
Koso: Don't go inside.
LiveWildRock: Your secret's safe with us!
UrbexUncovered: Googling Hendleton now!!

Thumbs-ups and hearts stream across the bottom of the screen again.

Jedx laughs. 'Looks like you're as keen to see inside as we are.'

The camera moves to catch the tallest guy taking his crowbar to the boarded door. The plywood splinters, rotten chunks of wood crumbling away as he levers off the board. He flings the pieces out of his way and steps through the mouth of the building.

'Come on,' he says, not looking back. Two paces in and the darkness swallows him whole.

The lanky guy – Beaker – follows, pulling a pair of night-vision goggles into place as he steps through the doorway.

'We're entering the sound-stage where all the biggest hits were filmed.' Sass's voice is hushed, excited. She climbs over the discarded wooden board as she talks.

'Let's check it out,' says Jedx. The view swings left to right as he navigates the doorway. 'This is such a rush. My heart's going mental. Ready for anything. Bring it on!'

Inside, the only light comes from their torches. The hall is narrow. Old movie posters hang in tatters from an ancient noticeboard. The ceiling has caved in, spewing wires and debris onto the floor below.

They move quickly.

'It stinks in here,' Jedx narrates. 'Really bad.'

Beaker, in the camouflage jacket, turns towards the camera. 'Like somebody died.'

'Shut up.' Sass's voice has more tension in it now. 'You're creeping me out.'

There's a clatter as someone kicks something.

'Fuck.' Beaker stops. Curses some more under his breath.

The tall one calls from the front. 'You OK?'

'Yeah, Cap. I just . . .' Beaker shines his torch onto the ground. 'Shit.'

The camera zooms in. At his feet is a wooden box. It's filled with clown heads.

Jedx laughs, but his voice sounds nervous as he swings the camera around and addresses the viewers. 'Freaky, yeah?'

Laughter emojis float across the screen showing that those watching the action are still enjoying the show. The comments keep coming.

DavidSees: How does it feel being inside?
LiveWildRock: This is crazy!
Upyeah99: It's too dark. More light needed.

Pinnyhip078: Woah! Awesome!

UrbexUncovered: Great work. Lovin' your channel.

FunLeapExp: Great explore. Can I join you? DM me.

Jedx is nodding as he reads the comments on the live-stream from his phone. He looks into the camera lens. 'David, it feels awesome, totally pumping. We've got torches, Upyeah99, that's all the light we have. FunLeapExp – sorry, man, we're a tight group – no vacancies.'

'Come on,' Cap calls from off camera. 'Keep moving.'

Jedx gives a mock salute and the view rotates. He follows Sass along the corridor, manoeuvring around the piles of broken ceiling tiles and mouldering boxes that litter the route. The floorboards creak beneath their feet.

They move faster.

At the end of the corridor they stop. There's a door. On the wall is a large beacon covered in decades of dust. The sign beside it says: NO ENTRY WHEN RED LIGHT IS ON. RECORDING.

Cap turns to the camera. The whites of his eyes look artificially bright against the balaclava and gloom. He's talking fast; high on the thrill. 'This is it, nirvana for this site. Abandoned over forty years ago. Now we're about to breach. You ready?'

Sass holds up her SLR camera. Grins.

Beaker takes out his mobile. 'Ready, Cap.'

'Streaming live every step of the way,' says Jedx. He looks into the camera. 'You guys ready to see inside?'

Hundreds of thumbs-up icons flit across the feed.

DavidSees: Get in there now!

LiveWildRock: Hell yeah!

UrbGold300: This is so fascinating.

Upyeah99: Show us! Can't wait it see how it looks.

Koso: Don't! Go home.

Pinnyhip078: Dudes, go for it!

Optxxxx: Wooohooooo!

*

Jedx nods as he reads them from his phone, then grins at the camera. 'I'll take that as an affirmative.' He pushes his phone back into his pocket and nods at Cap. 'We're good to go.'

As Cap pushes down the door handle the other three crowd in close. The camera tilts, and as it moves it looks as if the dusty red light blinks. Then the view is blocked, and only Beaker's camouflage jacket and Sass's black fleece are visible.

'It's stuck,' Cap says. 'The wood must have warped.'

There's a thud and the camera view jerks upwards, showing Cap shouldering the door. The hinges squeal. Cap exhales hard. Then it finally starts to inch open.

Sass turns to the camera, just one of her crystal-ringed eyes visible, and whispers, 'We're in.'

They move into a small space, like an anteroom. Floor to ceiling curtains hang across the opening to the main sound-stage, obstructing their view. As they look around, their torchlight illuminates a row of dust-covered chairs and a low table with a pile of decomposing magazines. On the wall is a shooting schedule from forty years ago; the daily running order for a film titled *Dark Pleasures*.

Sass grins towards the camera. 'This would have been the waiting area, the twilight zone between the real world and the fantasy of whichever movie was being filmed.' She steps towards the curtains. 'I'd have expected velvet curtains like in a theatre but—'

'It's black plastic sheeting.' Beaker sounds nervous. 'The velvet's piled up in the corner over here.'

The camera moves to a heap of material in the corner, then Jedx swings it round to face him. 'There's no dust on these curtains, they can't have been here long.' He moves the camera closer to the plastic. 'Yeah, these are pretty clean. The colour hasn't faded and the plastic is thick, heavy-duty stuff.'

Sass appears. She runs her fingers across the black plastic. There's confusion in her tone. 'It's been cut precisely to size and carefully hung, completely filling the opening.' She looks past the camera, towards Jedx. 'We're not the first here. Someone did this recently.'

'Wow' emojis appear on the live-stream. Questions are being asked in the comments.

DavidSees: Why replace the curtains?

UrbGold300: Who did that? If the place hasn't been touched for forty years . . .

Upyeah99: Plastic curtains?? Weird as!

ExpoDisW: Don't like the look of that. Get out of there guys!

For a moment there's complete silence. Then Cap steps alongside Sass and slides his hand between two of the plastic sheets. A chink of light appears.

Sass inhales hard. 'Why's there light? This place was cut off years ago. There shouldn't be any power.' She reaches towards Cap. 'Wait, we ought to . . .'

But she's too late. He's already pulling the plastic aside.

The light is blinding.

'Fucking . . . what the . . .' There's a tremble in Jedx's voice. 'That's . . . that's . . .'

The camera swerves sideways, the autofocus struggling. Silhouettes seem to morph into each other in the haze. Then the view stabilises and there's a glimpse of a wooden frame, before it shifts again, focusing on an old Arriflex movie camera, its body and shooting reels covered in dust. The view tilts, revealing a second camera behind the Arriflex. This one is tripod-mounted and modern. Focused on what's in the centre of yet more plastic sheeting, spread out across the stage floor.

Someone retches.

Sass cries out.

Beaker turns towards the camera, his eyes wide. 'We need to move. Fucking move.'

'Go.' All the bravado's gone from Cap's voice. 'Get out before they—'

There's a noise like an angry roar. It sounds half human, half animal.

Cap shoves Beaker and Sass backwards into Jedx, blocking the camera's view. They jostle against each other, panicking. Jedx twists round; the camera's view is a blur of light. He pushes the others ahead and, for a brief moment, the camera finds colour – grey rope, brown wood, and a long river of crimson. Then it's gone.

'Quick, come on.'

'Move!'

'Shit.'

They scramble back through the plastic curtain. Barge through the door into the hallway.

The camera jerks side to side. Angled down, it films three sets of feet; black Nikes, maroon Converse, some kind of leather hiking boots. They're sprinting. Leaping broken floorboards. Swerving round debris. Something falls from Cap's pocket, no one seems to notice.

'Hurry up.'

Loud breathing. Panicked cries.

There's a crash. Swearing. The camera drops to the ground, landing at a right angle to the floor, and the lens fractures.

Jedx is on his knees, clown heads scattering around him. He scrambles to get up, the heads rolling in his wake, but they bring him down again, his face inches from the lens.

Loads of 'wow' emojis and hearts are flooding across the live-feed.

Jedx's gaze is focused past the camera. He's shaking his head. Eyes wide. Mouth open. Fear obvious.

Footsteps thud along the floor in a slow rhythm. Confident. Deliberate.

'Oh fuck.' Jedx lurches forward on all fours, his arms and legs paddling wildly. His expression desperate. His foot catches the camera and it spins, sliding along the floor, out of reach. Jedx crashes over the clown heads, crushing their skulls beneath his feet. Disappears.

The camera lies still.

The image is grainy. The view split into three by the broken lens. Rotten floorboards. Upturned prop box. A clown head with its smiling face caved in.

The footsteps come closer. Black Doc Martens appear on-screen. Halt. There's a sigh, just audible. A gloved hand reaches towards the camera.

The image cuts to black.

JedUrbXTM live-stream terminated.

SUNDAY

1
CLEMENTINE

I would rather be anywhere but here. The headphones make me feel claustrophobic and I itch to rip them off. But I won't. After over two months of media attention, I know what's expected of me, so I do what I've become used to; hide my true feelings and force a smile.

The balding man sitting opposite me on the other side of the desk talks with the over-bright tone all radio presenters have. 'Good evening, and welcome to W5X Radio. Tonight on *Crime World*, I'm joined by Clementine Starke, the young woman who solved a serial killer case before the police could.'

I twist the butterfly ring faster around my index finger. Lean towards the microphone and lie. 'It's a pleasure to be here, John.'

He glances at the paper on the desk in front of him, then back to me. 'So, Clementine, you've become the poster girl for armchair sleuths everywhere . . .'

I know what's coming. They all ask.

'. . . tell me, what was it like to catch the Lover?'

I launch into my rehearsed media lines. Try to sit still. Fight the urge to fiddle with my headphones. 'As I've said before, it was a group effort. I was part of an online collective – True Crime London. Initially, my interest in getting involved was more from an academic perspective, my specialism is online behaviour and I was studying—'

'A lot of people have said it was always going to happen, with the rise of all these true-crime shows and podcasts and whatnot.' John waves his hand dismissively. 'They predicted amateur detectives would get bored of looking at cold cases and try something in real time.'

'That's what my PhD was—'

'Exactly, and then you went a step further, you actually tracked down a killer rampaging around London.'

Media people sensationalise everything. *Rampage* sounds over-dramatic. The Lover killed four women and one man over a number of weeks; it was a binge, a splurge, or a spree rather than a rampage. But I know how this works, and the university requires me to play this media game to their advantage if I want to stay employed. Which is what I want too, for now. So I keep my expression neutral and wait for this over-excited idiot to ask me another question.

John leans forward over the desk. 'Tell us more about how you discovered the Lover's identity.'

'We used a lot of social media sources.' I stick to the truth, just a limited version of it. 'And talked to people who knew the victims.'

'Now, the victims, wasn't one of them a friend of yours?'

I frown. 'Yes, he was.'

John's nodding, encouraging me to say more.

I twist the headphone cable around my fingers. John knows I don't want to go into details about this. I speak sternly. 'He was stabbed to death in his home.'

'That must have been tough. And, of course, you yourself were almost murdered by the Lover when he broke into your apart-ment.' John's words are sympathetic, but his eyes are wide, his expression almost manic, as if he's getting off on this. He leans forward across the desk. 'I'm going to open the phone lines in just a minute for our live phone-in, but first, tell me, when you managed to get free and kill the Lover, what went through your mind? How did you feel?'

I can't tell him the truth; that it felt like I was reborn. That on that night my ability to feel emotion returned in an overwhelming, suffocating, glorious flood of feelings, after the twelve years of numbness since my father's death, since his murder. So again, I lie. 'I was terrified, fighting for my life. In fact, if Detective Inspector Dominic Bell hadn't arrived at that moment, creating the distraction that allowed me to grab the syringe, I don't think I'd have survived.'

John licks his lips. Nods faster. 'Well, it's great that the detective barged in when he did, and that you're OK.'

I stare at John. He's grinning, oblivious to my real feelings. Things are not OK. It's been two months and six days since I watched the life fade from the Lover. Now, rather than the numbness, I battle duelling emotions which fluctuate moment to moment. It's overwhelming. Exhausting. And try as I might, I haven't learnt to control them. I've almost given up thinking that I ever will. 'I was the one who caught the Lover. But I owe my life to Dominic Bell.'

Ignoring what I've said, John looks through the glass of the recording studio into the control booth beyond. A woman in a red jumper holds up her hand, her index finger rises. He nods. 'Let's go to the phones now. Line one, what's your question for Clementine Starke?'

'Hi, John. I'm Mary from Biggleswade and I'm a big fan of *Crime World*. I wanted to ask Clementine if she's working on another true-crime case at the moment?'

'I'm still part of True Crime London and we have a few cases we're interested in.' I think about my longest running case, my father. 'So, yes. I'm still very much interested in true-crime.'

The woman in red holds up three fingers. John nods. 'Caller on line three, what's your question for Clementine?'

'This is Mark from Watford. Clementine, what are you doing next Friday? Fancy going out for dinner?'

I shake my head. What a dick. There's always at least one in every phone-in or live appearance. 'Mark, I'm flattered, but no thank you.'

John raises an eyebrow. There's a smirk on his lips as he says quickly, 'Let's go to line two.'

'I'm Jody from Brentwood. I saw that you've been awarded your PhD – congratulations – and wondered what research you're doing now?'

I smile. At last, something interesting that I can talk about. 'Hi, Jody. Great question, thank you. I'm just starting some new research that focuses on thrill-seeking versus voyeurism. Why do some people live their lives on camera and other people watch them? The rise of YouTube and camera phones has spawned this phenomenon, and technology enables narcissistic tendencies to flourish in all of us. But it makes me wonder, how much danger will people put themselves in to get the most followers, the highest likes, and how extreme would things need to get for the voyeurs watching to turn off?'

Jody starts to reply, but the call is cut off. The woman in the red jumper holds up her left hand and makes a winding motion with her right. John nods. 'We have time for one more question, let's make it a good one. Line five, you're on with Clementine Starke.'

'Clementine, this is David Ender.'

Shit. I feel cornered under the spotlight.

'I've tried calling you at the university, but you've not returned my calls.'

John raises his eyebrows. I shrug and, trying not to look bothered, take a sip of water. I know David Ender's been calling me; he's left over twenty messages in the last two weeks.

'After I read that interview you did in the *Metro* I knew I had to speak to you. I'm a huge fan of urban explorers, urbexers, and they'd be a perfect subject for your research. They explore abandoned places and post their adventures on YouTube or live-stream direct on urbex sites. They're the ultimate thrill-seekers.'

'They sound interesting, David.' I keep my tone friendly but not too keen. 'I'll look into them as a potential group.'

'There's a huge community of viewers watching this stuff.' David is speeding up, his tone urgent. 'I know people, I could help you get access to all the best—'

'I'm afraid that's all we have time for tonight.' John cuts across David, as the producer fades him out. 'You've been listening to *Crime World* here at W5X Radio with me, John Webly, and my special guest tonight, the ultimate armchair detective, Clementine Starke.'

The woman in the red jumper gives us the thumbs-up and we're off air. I pull the headphones off and rub my ears. It unsettles me that David Ender called into the show. I know he's been trying to get hold of me for weeks, but to ambush me live on air is a bolder move. Why is he so desperate to introduce me to these urbexers?

John takes his headphones off and collects his notes. He leers at me. 'Don't think I've had a caller ask a guest out for dinner before.'

'Really? It happens to me all the time.'

'Nice for some.' There's a strange expression on his face, and I get the horrid feeling he's about to chance his own luck.

I shake my head, making it clear there's no sense in him asking me out either. 'No. It's really not.'

There's only one person I want, but right now he refuses to speak to me.

MONDAY

2

CAP

Cap isn't going to tell them about the missing wallet. What good would it do? He must have dropped it at the studios, and if he says that it'll only freak them out. They don't know his real-life identity anyway. That's part of the group rules – aliases only, no personal details shared other than the numbers of the unregistered pay-as-you-go phones they use to arrange each 'exploration'. What they do is highly illegal, so the fewer things to connect them the better.

He checks his watch – it's ten to twelve. If they're going ahead with tonight's planned exploration, they need to do it now. The CCTV system used by the owners of this location gets updated once every six months. Tonight is one of those times. If they're not in and out within the next hour, they'll have missed their chance.

Cap glances along the street to the junction. The traffic on the main road has thinned out but there are still loads of cabs and the odd bus around. Beyond the road, the lights twinkle, reflected in the surface of the Thames. Picture pretty but damn freezing. He's thankful that Surrey Street's quiet. There's no one to notice the four of them talking in the shelter of the doorway on the corner, their scarves pulled up high, and their balaclavas rolled up to their brows. Lit cigarettes provide their alibi for loitering outside at this time, in this weather. No one questions a smoker's motivation.

He nods towards the red-tiled frontage of the old tube station's second entrance and exit. 'We doing this then?'

'I can't.' Sass's voice has a tremble to it. Her eyes are blotchy from crying. Her usually sleek blonde hair is greasy and tangled, sticking out from the bottom of her balaclava. It's the first time Cap's seen her not wearing lipstick. 'Not after last night, what we saw—'

'But what did we see?' Beaker says, shifting his weight from foot to foot. 'It was dark. We were high on adrenaline. When I watched back our live-stream there wasn't a clear view of anything, just some boots and a gloved hand before the camera switched off.'

Jedx, usually the joker of the group, is more subdued tonight. The dark shadows beneath his eyes are the tell-tale sign that what they witnessed has taken its toll. 'We should go to the police.'

Cap shakes his head. 'No police.'

Sass frowns. 'But the woman . . .'

The image he's been trying to forget all day flashes in his mind's eye; her white-blonde hair, the pale skin splattered red, a growing pool of blood. He blinks the image away. Hardens his tone. 'Because we'll get arrested. We were trespassing, breaking and entering. Do you *want* a criminal record?'

Sass looks unsure. 'But what we saw was—'

'Already done. Telling the police won't change that. In this world it's survival of the fittest. We managed to get out of there, but we can't change what happened to her.'

Jedx looks solemn. 'Thinking about it, I'm with the Cap on this. I can't get busted. What if they lock us up for all the breaking and entering we've done? Surely none of us want that?'

'But . . .' Despite the cold Sass's cheeks flush red. 'What if she wasn't dead . . .?'

There's a pause. When Beaker speaks his voice is low, almost a whisper. 'No one could live after losing that much blood.'

Cap shudders and wishes that the others would shut up. 'If we tell the police we'll be suspects. We could get charged with murder. Think about it, it'd be all over the papers. Our lives would be ruined. Do you want that, Sass? Do you want to ruin our lives?'

'But if we do nothing we're leaving them free to do it again,' Sass says. 'What if they come after us?'

Jedx tries to calm her. 'They can't, they've got nothing to identify us, and they can't trace me through my camera or the live-feed. We're safe.'

'I can't do this. I . . . go without me.' She turns away, her shoulders shaking. As she looks back at Cap, then at Jedx, tears are streaming down her face. 'I'm done for tonight. I'm just done. And if you're so cold-hearted you can ignore that woman . . . then . . .' Sass shakes her head. 'Then you as good as killed her yourself.'

Cap watches Sass stride away until she turns the corner onto the main road. He doesn't mention the wallet. Tries not to think about what she said. Tells himself she'll come around, that it'll be OK, that it's not his fault. He didn't kill that woman, doesn't know who she was; they didn't even see her face. But there'd been someone else there too, most likely her killer. He shudders, then looks back at Jedx and Beaker. 'What about you?'

Jedx speaks first. He ignores Sass's departure and sounds more determined now. 'I'm in. Our USP is posting regular adventures. We're at over ten thousand subscribers – way over UrbGold, and catching up with ExpoJunkieUK. The audience loved the intensity of last night's stream and they don't really know what they saw. We shouldn't do anything unusual or go blank. People could start asking questions. If we miss the gig promised tonight, we'll get labelled inconsistent. Start losing viewers. And we'd probably kiss goodbye to the chance of sponsorship deals.'

Beaker nods. 'We can't lose everything we've worked for. The explore last night was *good* for our stats – we got an extra two hundred followers from that live-stream alone. And they want more.'

Two hundred followers, thinks Cap, and a murder on his conscience.

They cut the padlock on the secret exit door at eight minutes past twelve and crowbar it open. The CCTV should be off and there's no security patrol. They slip through the metal grille and the second door, while the street outside remains empty.

'Bodycams on,' Jedx says. 'Check now. It's a shame we can't live-stream from underground, but your cameras will wirelessly transfer footage to my master-cam. I'll edit it all together and post it as soon as I'm home.'

Cap nods. He wonders about the camera that was lost last night, and who might have it now. He knows how precious it had been to Jedx. He brushes the thought away to focus on the job in hand. He switches on the beam of his head-torch first, then presses record on the small black box clipped to his jacket. A red light shows it's working. He looks at Jedx and Beaker. 'Ready?'

They nod, the beams of their torches tracing light across the passageway.

'Let's do this then.' Cap sets off, jogging along the passage with the others behind. He's studied the station layout and knows they should be able to get to the other side of the foyer, and access the tunnels, through the old lifts. On the wall to his left, his torch illuminates a tube map, grubby with age, and a 'Way Out' sign above it. Glancing right, he sees the lift doors are open, and feels relief. He looks over his shoulder at Beaker and Jedx and points to lift number one. 'Through here.'

The old dual-exit lift, with its wood-panelled sides painted dark green, is big enough for forty-five people, and still in good nick. They run through it, their feet echoing off the slatted wooden floor, then take a right, past the ticket office and the steps leading up to the station's other entrance via the Strand. There's no natural light but in the beam of his head-torch Cap catches glimpses of old-fashioned signs – Exit, Booking Office, Telephones – sees chunks of plaster on the walls that are brown from damp, and a section of the ceiling above that's been patched with yellow plastic sheeting. Behind him, Jedx is narrating what he sees for the camera.

'. . . hope you guys at home are getting this. Sass can't make it tonight, but we've still got something totally fresh for you – a three-way bodycam split. We can't live-stream from underground, but although it's not in real-time you'll get footage of what each of us sees, three viewpoints on how this old station looks. Should be pretty cool . . .'

They reach the stairwell and start their descent. He read that it's a hundred and forty steps down to the platforms. The stairs are steep, twisting, and the bottom of the wall around them seems to glow.

'Spooky,' says Beaker. 'What's that?'

'Transport for London trialled luminous paint here as a possible safety feature for all underground stations,' Jedx says. 'It wasn't used anywhere else in the end, but it's useful for us. Makes it much easier to see the steps.'

'There's a hell of a lot of them,' says Beaker.

'Yeah,' Jedx says. 'It's kind of weird, the way the spiral staircase and torchlight makes your eyes go funny. I feel like I'm going cross-eyed.'

He's right. Cap's glad when they make it to the bottom. He feels anxious, can't get what happened at Hendleton out of his head. Up ahead there are metal grilles screening off derelict areas of the station. He peers through one of them and sees a dark void, a huge pit, with some kind of rusted machinery. Shudders.

'Which platform?' Jedx asks.

Cap turns to him. 'Let's do two first, it's the one that's been out of action the longest.'

They run through the tunnel and down onto the platform. The air is mustier here. Beaker doubles over, coughing. Cap can taste dust in every breath he takes. He shines his torch around the platform. On their side there are old posters on the wall for Madame Tussauds and the London Planetarium, and some of the original tiling says Strand rather than Aldwych. But on the other side of the tracks the walls aren't as good, with tiles gone, and a lot of the panelling stripped away. At each end of the platform the access tunnel has been bricked up.

'Fancy a closer look at the tracks?' Jedx says, for the benefit of the viewers who'll watch the video once it's uploaded. He pauses for a moment, as if waiting for an answer, before jumping off the platform onto the rails with a whoop. He strides along them towards the far end of the platform, still narrating. 'This is so cool. You see these tracks? If they were live, the combination of the positive and negative charged rails would put six hundred and thirty volts through me.'

Cap checks the time and feels some urgency. It's almost half-twelve. They only have thirty more minutes before the security cameras come back online. 'Come on, we need to hurry, let's go to platform one next.'

Platform one looks almost as if it's still in use. The Aldwych sign has the same look as modern Transport for London signs, and the platform is neat and clean. There's no dust in the air like there was on platform two. And the tunnel here remains serviceable.

Jedx is narrating again. 'So this is the place used to film underground scenes for loads of movies. *Patriot Games*, *V for Vendetta*, *Sherlock* and a bunch of others.' He gestures to the posters on the walls for the Imperial War Museum and announcing the extension of the Piccadilly line to Heathrow. 'These aren't original, they were probably put here by the last production company that used the platform for filming.'

Cap walks down the platform. He feels tense and jumpy. The buzz he usually gets from exploring now seems to be morphing into a creeping fear. Every time they go into a new part of the station he braces himself, ready to see something awful – the blonde woman in the contraption at Hendleton keeps flashing into his mind. He checks his watch again; it's 12.39. He really wants this to be over.

He hears footsteps running up behind him. Flinches as a hand touches his shoulder. 'What the . . .?'

'I thought I could add some clips of the movies made here at the end of the piece before I upload it,' Jedx says. 'What do you think?'

Cap doesn't care. They can talk about it when they're out of here. 'Yeah, sure, whatever you think.'

'Cool.'

He reaches the end of the platform. Standing still, he switches off his bodycam and stares into the tunnel. The wall lights are on, illuminating the track. He'd read about this safety feature – if those lights are on it means the voltage is switched off and technicians are safe to go onto the tracks to work.

'All right, Cap?'

He turns and sees Beaker approaching. Am I all right, he wonders, but he knows he's bloody not. Beaker and Jedx don't seem as affected by last night, or the fact that Sass had been so distraught when she walked off earlier. Their reactions seem off to him, weird. Still, he nods and says nothing, then looks down at the grimy, disused tracks. A soot-covered mouse scurries beneath a rail and disappears. He used to wish he could disappear and put an end to the pressure of the financial shackles he'd got himself into; the houses, the cars, the children's expensive schools, his ex-wife's cosmetic surgery habit. But after last night, after seeing what had been done to that poor woman, he wants to cling onto his life with everything he has.

'What we saw last night, I reckon it was a prank.' There's faked bravado in Beaker's voice and Cap can't tell if it's disguising fear or something else. 'It has to be.'

'Does it?' Cap thinks about his daughters – Poppy and Daisy – and a punch of emotion slams into his chest. He swallows hard. If one of them had her life drained from her in the same way the woman at Hendleton Studios had, it would break him. But he'd still want to know what happened. He'd want to be able to see her one last time.

He'd need to say goodbye.

Cap shakes his head. The woman deserves to be rescued from that contraption. Her family should know where she is; have the chance to get what happened to her investigated. Sass was right. They can't hush this up.

He looks at Beaker and grimaces. 'We should go to the police.'

3
DOM

Death by tube is always bloody messy, but this one's something different. Dom drops the phone back into the receiver and looks across the desk at his team; Detective Sergeant Abbott and Detective Constable Parekh. 'There's been a death at Holborn.'

Abbott turns away from his computer screen. 'That's not usually our thing. Why aren't the British Transport Police handling it?'

Dom doesn't look at his sergeant, and doesn't hide the pissed-off tone in his voice either. 'This isn't a jumper. The victim didn't die on the rails.' He gestures to Parekh. 'Get your coat.'

'Died not murdered, guv?' Parekh's already out of her seat. She wraps her maroon scarf around her neck and pulls on her woollen peacoat, knocking a stack of files off her desk in her eagerness. Leaning down, she scoops them up and dumps them onto her chair. 'Where?'

'On the road outside the entrance, they said, but it's not a straight traffic accident, their CCTV is showing some strange anomalies.' He flicks a glance at Abbott. 'Hence the call.'

'Makes more sense.' Abbott picks his phone off the desk and starts to stand, but Dom catches his sergeant's eye and shakes his head.

'You can stay here.'

Abbott grimaces and looks like he's going to say something, but Dom turns away before he can. He doesn't want a discussion. And he doesn't want Abbott along on this job, or any job for that matter. Not after what he did.

Grabbing his parka from the back of his chair, Dom turns towards the exit. 'Let's go, Parekh. You're driving.'

*

The morning rush-hour traffic is at a standstill, but Parekh uses a portable blue light to force her way through the crush in pretty decent time. It's 7.45 when they arrive at Holborn, and Dom's relieved to see a good job's been done cordoning off the crime scene. Uniforms have shut off the road and, as well as the blue and white police tape corralling a yellow-liveried hackney cab, a forensics tent has been erected around the body, shielding the victim from the prying eyes of the damn rubberneckers who are already lining the barriers.

Ducking under the tape, Dom heads towards the inner cordon with Parekh alongside him. He pauses, observing the dent in the nearside of the cab's bonnet, the shattered windscreen, blood tinting the remaining shards of glass red. He runs his gaze along the drag of blood from the bonnet to the tarmac.

Taking a breath, Dom looks away and gives their names to the officer for the scene log. He steps into the tent and isn't surprised to find pathologist Emily Renton already inside.

He turns to Parekh. 'While I have a quick word with the doc, can you find out what we've got so far?'

Parekh nods, her waist-length black ponytail swinging from the motion. 'I'm on it, guv.'

Usually he likes to be alone with the victim for a few minutes, to get a sense of the scene, a *feel* for it, but in a situation like this there's no point. The tent gives an artificial perspective to the scene of the crime. And outside it, the closed road changes the usual dynamics of the street.

He looks down at the victim. He's male, but it's hard to tell more as the body's lying face down on the tarmac. Poor bastard, Dom thinks. The man's arms are outstretched, his bloodstained hands clutching air. On his left wrist the face of his silver Breitling watch is smashed. Its time stopped at six forty-one.

Pathologist Emily Renton is crouched down, examining the victim's torso. Her unruly brown hair is pulled up into a high, messy bun. The white paper CSI suit is a size too big and has wrinkled around her hips, waist and elbows, giving her the air of a partially deflated marshmallow man; it's almost comical.

Almost. But there's nothing funny about death. Not for Dom. He's pleased it's Emily on this job. He has the utmost respect for her opinions and they've always worked well together, even if she can be inclined to try and mother him. 'What can you tell me?'

Emily turns to look at him. Grimaces. 'Well, there's not much I can say about the actual cause of death that you can't deduce for yourself.'

'So, humour me.'

'Fine.' She stands, and as she straightens up he sees that her paper suit is blackened at the knees, and there's a smudge of dirt across her left cheek and down the side of her left arm. Her voice is confident and unemotional as she says, 'Our victim is male, around six foot three at a guess, and middle-aged. The cause of death is obvious given where we are, but a road traffic accident isn't the only thing that happened to him today.'

'Meaning?'

'I need to turn him to show you.' She checks that they have all the pictures needed with the body in situ, then beckons over a CSI and together they move the victim onto his back.

'Shit.' Dom now understands why they've been called in.

'Exactly.' Emily crouches next to the body. 'As well as injuries consistent with a collision, this man suffered multiple stab wounds within the last few hours. As you know I don't like to guess, still it's safe to say he'd lost a lot of blood by the time the car hit him.'

'But the stab wounds didn't kill him?'

'No, but given the depth and number of them, if this man had had a little more time before the cab finished him off, I think they might well have done. Not that I can say for sure. For that you'll need to wait until I've got him back to base and had a proper look.'

Dom nods. 'Appreciate it.'

'Pleasure as always,' Emily says. Her voice is heavy with sarcasm, but there's a smile on her face. 'Now, can I get back to it?'

Dom smiles despite the gruesome surroundings. Emily's one of the good guys. 'Course.'

'Guv?'

As Emily gets back to work, Dom turns to see Parekh heading towards him followed by a stocky bloke with round glasses and a tight-fitting fluorescent tabard. 'This is Jeff Timber, he's the BTP Area Supervisor.'

Dom recognises the name of the man who called him in earlier. 'Where's the cabbie?'

'He was pretty cut up from the accident, and having some trouble breathing so they blue-lighted him out.'

Dom nods, and turns to Parekh. 'Get Abbott onto it. Find out where they took the driver and when we can speak to him.' He looks back at Timber. 'I've seen the victim, the doc tells me he'd been stabbed before the RTA. On the phone you said you had footage that made the death look suspicious – did you record the stabbing?'

Timber shakes his head. 'Nothing as conclusive as that I'm afraid. We've got footage of him making his way through from the platform to ground level, and the remains of a blood trail for those movements.'

'So he was stabbed on a tube, before stepping onto the platform?'

'There's no evidence of that. The platform he came from opened late this morning due to overnight track maintenance further along the line. No trains had stopped at that platform at the time he appeared.'

'Appeared?'

Timber rubs his forehead, frowning. 'I can't think of a better way to describe it. Your guy just appeared in the tunnel leading from platform four. There was no sign of him before that anywhere in the station. It's like he came out of nowhere.'

4

CLEMENTINE

Sometimes I fantasise about murdering my colleagues. Monday mornings are one of those times. Professor Wade insists we do a weekly show and tell, a peer discussion about our ongoing research projects. For me this has no value. I prefer action to debate, but I am in the minority.

We're squeezed into the glass-walled meeting pod that's only really designed for two. On the other side of the glass is our faculty's open-plan workspace. Our department's desks are closest to the pod; a bank of desks set in a row three by two; six in all. I wish I was sitting at my desk now. Instead, I'm forced to satisfy Wade that I'm making an effort to engage in faculty life, following the required collegiate protocols, and justifying my existence. He's threatened to block me from continuing my research if I don't comply.

So it's my turn to stand at the whiteboard and present my work. Getting up from my seat, I squeeze past Wade as I step towards the front. I hear him inhale deeply. Feel his hand brush against my bum, the pressure too firm to be accidental. Turning, I glare at him, warning him off. His expression is one of feigned innocence.

He needs to be more careful.

Using a blood-red dry marker I write the word OBSESSION across the top of the whiteboard in ten-inch-high capitals. I turn to face the group. There are fewer of us than normal, just Wade plus two of my fellow researchers; Jan with her bad breath and habit of always wearing pink, and Otto, sharply intelligent, whose eyelashes are so pale they're virtually translucent, giving him a rather alien look. I tap my pen against the word and introduce my subject. 'Obsession – an idea or thought, or in this case an activity, that continually preoccupies a person's mind. My research focuses more on the genesis of the obsession; what it is about the person, their characteristics, drivers and experiences, that brought them to the world of voyeurism or thrill-seeking in the first place. What do they experience when they are in its thrall that sparks the obsession and keeps them coming back for more?' I force a smile at Jan and Otto. 'Basically, what gets them hooked?'

From the back of the pod, Wade scrutinises my words. Immaculate as ever, he wears a grey suit, checked shirt and no tie. His black hair, unnaturally dark for a man of his age, is swept up into his trademark quiff. He watches me, sitting with his elbows resting on the table in front of him, hands clasped together, his fingers forming a steeple under his chin. Our eyes meet. He purses his lips. 'How are you progressing with the case studies?'

I hold his eye contact. 'I've completed my initial litera-ture search and have begun selecting my sampling frame and conducting preliminary interviews.'

Wade nods, but there's something in his expression that makes me think he's unsatisfied by my answer.

We've clashed over where and how I should work. He thinks that because he's made me a Research Fellow I should become more of a team player, but I disagree. To make his point he's enforcing the rule that I spend a minimum of fifteen hours in the office each week. As a subtle 'fuck you', I've made it my mission to do most of them outside the hours other academics work. But since I started coming in early, so has he. He's also increased the number of compulsory meetings I have to attend. He's trying to keep watch over me and I don't like it. Just because I slept with him sometimes when I was his PhD student, it's as if he thinks he owns me. He hasn't realised that I can't be controlled. It's not in my nature.

'From my first voyeurism subjects, I've found that although the urges driving them can be sexual, often linked with impotence or feelings of inadequacy, mostly they stem from the desire to fill a void. They're trying to create meaning for themselves or to be a part of something bigger.'

Jan waves at me, her usual precursor to a question. 'How do they get to feel part of something bigger?'

'Technology. Social media lets them learn about the exploits of others, and they get involved in discussions online.' I write the words 'impotent', 'inadequate', and 'meaning' on the whiteboard. 'They get instant gratification. It's something I'll be studying further by monitoring their physiological and mental reactions in a controlled computer laboratory environment. I anticipate results will show a release of adrenaline followed by endorphins. In short, voyeurism validates them and makes them feel good.'

Wade runs his hand across his jaw. Licks his lips. 'And the thrill-seekers?'

'I'm still compiling my sampling frame, but my focus will be on individuals who take part in group outdoor pursuits and have a significant online following. It's important their activity has an element of danger.'

Wade closes his eyes a moment. Shakes his head. 'You've been working on this for several months, I expected you to have interviewed *all* your subjects.'

He's being unreasonable, and it has nothing to do with my work. I'm progressing faster than all the other researchers, a fact he well knows. I've been observing his body language; the deep inhales, running his hand over his face as if to wipe away emotion, and briefly closing his eyes are all signs of frustration. And then there's the times when he 'accidentally' touches me. We haven't slept together for two months, and I know he can't understand why I've not been interested. He doesn't realise how I've changed. 'I'll complete the first phase within the next month.'

He holds my gaze. 'No, no, that's too long. I want the initial results put into a paper for the Psych2019 conference. Expedite the timeline. Have this phase completed and written up within two weeks.'

I clench my fists. My claws dig into my palms. 'I don't have any thrill-seeker subjects yet.'

'Then find them, quickly.'

Two weeks is barely long enough to find and screen potential subjects, let alone conduct interviews and complete the preliminary report. Wade knows that. I'm about to tell him to go to hell when Otto speaks, seemingly oblivious to the tension between us.

'I am intrigued.' Otto blinks slowly as if his mind is still contemplating what's been discussed. 'What inspired you to study obsession?'

I inhale hard as the object of my own obsession appears in my mind before I can block him. A riotous surge of emotion pulses through me; desire battles with anger, protectiveness duels with regret. I push away his image before the memory of our last interaction starts to play out, but my physical responses continue; the prickle of heat raw across my skin, the acceleration of my pulse, the need, the yearning, deep within my core. But I tell them none of this. Instead I count to four and then exhale, before faking a smile. 'It's just something I find intellectually stimulating.'

Jan and Otto nod, satisfied with my answer, but Wade narrows his eyes and continues staring. He knows me better and can tell that I'm lying, but I will never tell him the truth.

Detective Inspector Dominic Bell is my inspiration, and I am research subject zero. I have violent thoughts, impassioned feelings, and they are increasing. Often it feels as if they will overwhelm my rational mind and compel the wolf within me to act.

I fear a loss of control would be fatal.

5

DOM

Holborn station looks like the set of a post-apocalyptic ghost train. Dom glances across the foyer, at the discarded copies of the *Metro* by the turnstiles, and the fast food wrappers drifting along the floor towards the escalators like tumbleweed. It's weird seeing the debris of rush hour without the people. It makes the place feel oddly desolate.

Parekh seems unaffected. Efficient as ever, she flips open her scratchpad and runs a magenta nail along the page before reading the details. 'We've got a provisional ID. Our victim was carrying an unregistered Oyster card and a bankcard in the name of Thomas Lee. I've called Abbott and asked him to follow up with the bank. Also, uniform say the driver was taken to University College Hospital so I've asked Abbott to get onto them about his condition.'

'Good work.' Dom doesn't want to think about Abbott. He looks at Jeff Timber, the transport police guy. 'Let's see everything you've got. We'll do the physical evidence first, then the CCTV, yeah?'

Timber clears his throat. 'Actually, there's a witness. She—'

Dom stops, turning to face him. 'And you didn't think to mention this before?'

'I thought you could see her after we've been in the tunnel. Closing the whole place is clogging up the rest of the tube system . . .'

Shit, thinks Dom. Here we go. He doesn't doubt that closing off the station during the morning rush is a nightmare for the transport network. He looks out, through the metal grilles that have been pulled across the entrance, to the forensics tent beyond. It was a nightmare for the poor bastard smeared across the tarmac, too.

'Control want us to be as fast as possible,' Timber continues.

'And it's my responsibility as Area Supervisor to take decisions around cleaning and reopening.'

'You think?' Dom glares at Timber. He doesn't want to get drawn into some jurisdiction-related bullshit, but he can't keep the frustration from his tone. 'A man died here this morning. We need to find out why. And as he died topside on a public street, overseeing this investigation is very much *my* responsibility.'

A muscle twitches above Timber's right eye. He looks away first.

'Guv?' Parekh calls from over by the furthest turnstile. She's leaning down, gesturing towards the ground as she snaps on a pair of latex gloves. 'He came through there. The trail leads back towards the escalator.'

Dom strides over to her. The blood is already dry, but there's no mistaking what the splashes of red-brown are on the pale cream floor tiles. He looks back at Timber. 'You should tell your people the station will be closed a good while longer. You know our CSIs are going to need to work through every point along this route.'

Timber pales, but his expression is compliant enough. 'I'll make the call.'

Dom gives him a tight smile. He tries not to be too bad-tempered with the bloke. He's only doing his job after all. And, to be fair, Dom can see they've tried to preserve the evidence, but on a Monday morning in rush hour it was always going to be a big ask; especially as they only realised the strange circumstances after the vehicle hit the victim. By the time the TfL staff had started closing off the tunnels, hundreds of commuters had already trampled along them. It's a miracle that any of the blood survived, but it has, probably because the victim seems to have stayed close to the wall.

They follow the trail to the escalator, go down using the stairs, and then pick it up again at the bottom. It continues along the tunnel, and in many places the blood splatters have been smudged or rubbed out. But from the ones still intact he can see that they're getting smaller, the drops less frequent, the further underground they go.

'The bleeding was getting worse as he reached ground level,' Parekh says.

Dom nods. 'Yeah.'

They keep walking; Parekh in front, Dom and Jeff Timber behind. The Grimms' fairy tale, the one with the kids leaving a trail of breadcrumbs as they go into the woods, comes to mind. Only this trail is far more macabre.

And then the trail ends; on platform four, the eastbound Piccadilly line, near the gap to the exit tunnel.

'Guv?' Parekh points to a dark red smear on the white-tiled wall a few feet away. Fingermarks are clearly visible. 'He used the wall for balance here. His hands must have already been covered in blood.'

'So he arrived on the platform bleeding, or was attacked here.'

'There's no CCTV of him being attacked on Transport for London property,' Timber says. 'Like I said, the first sighting on camera was of him staggering along this platform. I had our local control room analyst go through the footage. We're a hundred per cent certain.'

Parekh frowns, cocking her head to one side; something Dom's noticed she often does while thinking through puzzles. 'So how did he get here?'

Yeah, thinks Dom. And why was the victim down here in the first place? He looks towards the tracks. 'You said the platform opening was delayed because of engineering works. Were the rails electrified at the time he appeared?'

Timber nods. 'They were live from about an hour beforehand. And anyway, we'd have seen if he was on the tracks, we have a clear view straight down the rails from the CCTV.'

Dom nods and keeps walking along the platform. If he didn't arrive on a train, and he didn't walk through the tunnel, he can't see any other way for the victim to have appeared down here; but he can't have manifested out of thin air. Dom turns back to Timber. 'Where are your CCTV blind spots?'

'They're—'

'What's this door for?' Parekh interrupts, pointing towards a pair of metal double doors.

'There's just storage through there,' says Timber. 'And the doors are kept locked, he can't have—'

Using her gloved hand, Parekh pushes the handle down. The steel door opens. She peers inside. 'The blood continues through here.'

'Good work, go and get the CSIs down here,' Dom says to her. He looks at Timber. 'Who has access to this area?'

'Transport for London staff only. It shouldn't have been unlocked. We always—'

'*Should* doesn't matter right now. What matters is where this leads.'

'Like I said, it's a storage area.'

Dom steps through the doorway and into a tunnel. The lighting isn't as powerful in here, and the walls are poorly maintained. A cluster of tiles are missing from the lower part of the wall, exposing blistered and cracked plaster. On the inside of the door blood is smeared in layers across the metal, concentrated thickest around the lock. Dom looks over his shoulder at Timber. 'It looks like he spent a while trying to get it open. Could be he picked the lock.'

Timber frowns. 'But why would he have been in the storage area anyway? It's generally for old stock. Rarely used.'

Good question, thinks Dom. The blood trail leads along the tunnel straight ahead. As he walks down it, he notices another one branching off to his right. He glances along it, and sees a set of stairs leading down into yet another tunnel.

He carries on following the trail. The air gets staler, mustier, the further he goes. Wall tiles laid in rows of brown, white and green guide him like go-faster stripes until he reaches the end of the tunnel. The blood continues through the archway and into the bigger space beyond for a few more feet. Then the walkway ends.

Dom swears under his breath, pissed off at Jeff Timber for holding back the true facts or not knowing them. Because this place isn't just a storage area, it's another platform.

Timber answers before Dom prompts him with the question. 'This is the original platform five. It's been decommissioned for years, since the early nineties. Like I said, it's just used for storage now.'

Dom grits his teeth. He doesn't say the obvious – that a platform with exit and entrance tunnels has far more potential for being the way the victim got into the station than a four-walled storage room. 'Where does it go?'

'To Aldwych station, but that's decommissioned too.'

'Is there still access between them?'

Timber looks uncomfortable. 'Well, yes, but Aldwych is locked down, so it's not like this guy could just take a stroll between the two.'

Dom crouches on the platform edge and looks down. Sees dried spots of dark liquid among the grime on the rails. He turns back to Timber. 'You one hundred per cent sure about that?'

When Timber doesn't answer, Dom turns to his right and strides along the platform following the blood he can see below. The old platform is piled with storage crates. In one section a collection of oversized ironmongery is laid out in neat rows, a pile of huge chains and a metal sawhorse beside them.

The station signage is still on the walls, but most of the far wall is concrete, some of it stripped bare, other sections painted deep blue. There are a few posters dotted along the wall that are recent, advertising modern brands and websites.

Timber notices Dom looking. 'It's not about to be put back into service, they just do practice runs with some of the new posters down here from time to time.'

Dom nods, and moves along to a narrower section of platform where the original depth has been converted into storage cupboards. At the mouth of the tunnel he switches on his phone's torch and peers into the gloom. 'How far along that tunnel is Aldwych, how long would it take to get there?'

'Hard to say. If a train was going full tilt then—'

Dom scowls. 'How long to walk? Like our victim might have.'

Timber purses his lips, looking flustered. 'Well, I . . . it's just over half a mile, but it's pretty dark in there – only basic safety lights. So, what, fifteen minutes if they had a torch, probably slower if they were feeling their way.'

Whether he'd had a light or not, the victim had certainly been bleeding. That would've made him slower, but the distance wasn't far, he could have walked it. That was the most likely explanation for him appearing inside Holborn the way he did, but it also raised an obvious question.

What the hell was Thomas Lee doing in the abandoned Aldwych tube station?

6

CLEMENTINE

Back in the open plan, I sit down at my desk and check my emails, wishing as always that I could smoke in here. Around me, my colleagues have filled their workstations with photos and trinkets. They pin telephone numbers and reminders to the faded blue divider boards and collect free conference pens in cups. From their displays I can see that Jan, who occupies the desk to my left, has two children, and Otto, sitting to my right, enjoys football with an amateur team.

My desk is devoid of anything personal. I have no hobbies and no family, and a strong reason for not wanting to draw my colleagues' attention to my background. My father is dead, and my mother may as well be. These differences in our workspaces are another sign that I do not fit.

Wade sits opposite. He's staring at me over the divider between our desks. His watching makes it hard to concentrate, not that my emails require much concentration. They're the usual nonsense, a few academic conference adverts and invitations to submit journal papers, but mainly fan mail. I regret doing those press interviews and appearing on breakfast television in the aftermath of the Lover case now, but it had been my first amateur case. The serial killer, the Lover, had been murdering young women in their homes, and leaving their naked bodies surrounded by rose petals and candles. With the help of the online group True Crime London, I tracked him, but when I got close to discovering his identity he targeted me, breaking his way into my flat. I fought back, and with Dom's help I won. The media went crazy for the story, wouldn't leave me alone. So I did the interviews, had my face all over the news, and told the truth – or as much as I was willing to tell – about what happened.

The fame is what the university wanted, what Wade wanted, but being a celebrity (of sorts) comes with its own problems. It's ridiculous how familiar people get when they believe that they *know* you.

Most of the emails are from men. They range from polite to crude, from well worded to semi-illiterate. They're better than the online messages, though. Those usually come with a dick pic. I've become a target for freaks that get off on the idea of sleeping with the woman who killed the Lover. They disgust me, and they need to keep their distance. I'm more likely to bite their dick than suck it.

I'm irritated by the emails. Perhaps that's why I answer the phone this time when it rings, despite the number that comes up.

He sounds surprised that I do. 'Clementine Starke?'

'Yes.'

'It's David Ender.'

'I know, I recognised your mobile number. You think I should study urban explorers as part of my research.'

'I . . . yes. That's me. I really think they'd be—'

'OK, let's talk. Convince me.'

'Can you let me in first?'

I frown. 'What do you mean?'

'I'm outside your faculty building. I didn't think you'd answer the phone so I thought I'd come in person.'

Although his behaviour seems desperate, I don't tell him that. I've learnt that sometimes it's better to hold back my thoughts, people can be rather over-sensitive. Plus I'm on the clock now; Wade wants my thrill-seeker interviews completed within two weeks. David Ender says urban explorers would make the perfect subjects. Given my timeline it's worth considering, whatever David's strange motivations might be. I hang up the phone, and go to let him in.

David Ender isn't how I imagined. He's tall and slightly awkward, yet his floppy blond hair and strong cheekbones make him almost attractive in a nerdy kind of a way. He's smart too, doing a PhD in Pure Maths, or so he tells me. Now we're in the meeting pod together his flushed cheeks and constantly jigging leg make it obvious that he's nervous. I can feel the anxiety radiating from him and it's getting to me, making *me* feel restless.

I look at his jigging leg. I want to stick my claws in and still it. I fight the urge though. I need him to tell me more about his fascination with urban explorers, and maybe introduce me to some. 'Why are you so keen for me to research these people?'

He frowns, like he doesn't understand the question. 'Why wouldn't you want to? They're the ultimate thrill-seekers, far more exciting and progressive than BASE-jumpers or whatever.'

'Really? Don't they just break into places?' I'm being deliberately provocative, but I don't understand why this is so important to him. It's not as if *he* is an urban explorer, by the sound of things. 'Why should I include criminals in my research?'

His cheeks flush a deeper red. His leg jigs faster. 'They're explorers, not criminals. You don't . . . look, it's probably easier if I show you.' He pulls a laptop from his messenger bag and sets it on the table. 'This explore was done at the weekend by one of my favourite groups. They're a bit more theatrical than average urbexers which is helping them build a massive following.'

A popular group would make good subjects – I could explore the psychology of these thrill-seekers alongside that of the voyeurs watching their exploits. The symmetry is appealing, even if David's tunnel-vision obsession with me researching them is rather creepy. 'OK.'

David presses play. The video starts and he stares at it, fixated. 'This opening part is just preamble, really. Them talking about the place and what it used to be, then they break into the site and the exploration starts for real.'

On-screen four balaclava-clad figures run through woodland. It's dark, but the moon is high and there's light from their torches. From the shape of them, I'd say three are male and one female. When the smallest turns to the camera, I see that she's wearing red lipstick and has what look like crystals sewn around the eyes of her balaclava. The group climbs over a high wire fence with faded 'Keep Out' signs tied to it, and head towards a collection of buildings. I glance back at David. 'How often have you watched this?'

He blushes. 'Maybe a hundred times.'

From the date and timestamp, I can see that the video was streamed live via the website on Saturday night, less than forty-eight hours ago. David's level of viewing is extreme compared to the voyeurs I've already interviewed. 'Is that normal for you?'

David mumbles something and looks down like a little boy who's been caught stealing biscuits. He shrugs. 'I can't help myself. I'm addicted.'

Addiction is the bedfellow of obsession. That David self-labels as an addict is interesting. 'Why does this group especially interest you?'

He pushes his glasses up his nose. 'I don't know . . . I like all their videos. I guess it's the way they film. It kind of makes it feel like you're right there with them. They talk to the camera like you're one of them, it makes me feel part of their group.' He fiddles with the cuff of his jumper. 'Plenty of urbexers record real adventures, but I know the popular groups like this often manufacture horror showstoppers to lure a bigger audience. It's part of the fun – you never know what you're going to see.'

I nod. It's clear David's an armchair adrenaline junkie who gets off on watching the exploits of others – the more dangerous the better – just as long as he's safe behind his computer screen. 'What's the horror element in this one?'

He gestures back towards the screen. 'It's best you watch it for yourself.'

So I do. I see the tallest member of the group crowbar the door to a building. I observe them entering – the excitement in their voices as they narrate their progress, the gloomy decay of the corridor they find themselves in, and their surprise at glimpsing light through the plastic curtains in a room they believed abandoned for many years. Moments later they're running from what they've seen, fear in their voices, panic in their actions. For an amateur video, the suspense is very well done.

Even more interesting is David's reaction; his pupils are dilated, his face more flushed. 'How are you feeling?'

'Excited. Fearful. Half wishing I'd been with them, but also knowing that's fantasy and I'd rather watch.' There's a rasp in his voice that wasn't there before. 'Rationally I know the horror stuff is set up to shock viewers, *Blair Witch Project* style, but it still gets me each time I watch.'

I've heard this from other voyeurs. That mix of fear and excitement is their ultimate thrill. David gets off on this, no question. 'How do you think they did it?'

He shakes his head. 'I don't want to know. Seeing behind the curtain would ruin the experience.'

David wants to suspend reality. That's what this is to him, little more than a real-time feature film streamed live. But there's something in the video that makes me wonder. 'Can you show me the point when you think it changes from standard urbex exploration to faked horror?'

He nods and slides the bar at the bottom of the video along to the left. His movements are slow, deliberate, searching for the precise moment. He stops it at 38:13 and clicks play. On-screen the view is blocked by the guy in a camouflage jacket, then the camera pans right, and a bright light flares across the screen.

'Tell me what you see that makes you think that.'

'Spotlights. Fake blood. Knives of some sort.' He presses pause. Keeps staring at the screen. 'In their intro, Sass mentions the cult horror film made at the studio, *Death by a Thousand Daggers*. I checked it out over the weekend, and it's obvious this is a homage.'

I lean closer to the screen. There's a splash of red against the white light, but it's too out of focus to see what it is. In the corner of the picture there's a glint of silver, but again the movement of the camera distorts its shape. It's open to interpretation. If you take the silver to be a knife, the red could, from association, be assumed to be blood. But there's nothing concrete there. It's too jerky and blurred, like modern day smoke and mirrors. I shake my head. 'It could be anything.'

He looks disappointed. Presses play again, and the video continues forward. The group running from the room, the clown heads scattering across the corridor, the cameraman – Jedx – dropping the camera as he falls. He turns to the camera, and that's when I see it.

My breath catches in my throat.

7

DOM

They're still in Holborn tube station, heading towards the transport office to see the witness when his phone vibrates. Pulling it from his pocket, Dom sees it's a text from Abbott: Driver conscious. UCH have admitted him for tests but he can be interviewed briefly. Shall I go?

Dom catches Parekh's eye. 'You got any mobile signal down here?'

She looks at her phone. 'Yes, one bar.'

Good. 'Abbott says the cabbie's OK to be interviewed, although it might be a small window of time as they're doing more tests. We're going to be here a while longer so give him a call and tell him to get over to the hospital, would you?'

Parekh raises an eyebrow but doesn't comment on Dom's obvious unwillingness to communicate directly with his sergeant. Turning away, she makes the call.

Dom looks at Jeff Timber. 'I need copies of the CCTV footage from inside and outside the station. And find out if Aldwych was opened for filming, or anything else, in the last twenty-four hours, yeah? I need to know how our victim got to be in that tunnel.'

Timber nods. He's been quiet since they discovered the blood on the rails of platform five. All of his earlier self-importance has evaporated. 'Will do.'

Dom knows Timber's anxious to get the station reopened. There's always time pressure on anything that involves shutting down part of the transport system. So far Dom's managed to keep the place locked down, but DCI Jackson won't like it if Transport for London start chewing his ear about the closure. Dom needs to get the scene processed efficiently and avoid a situation. 'When I've interviewed the witness, I need to go back down there and see exactly where that trail leads. Get us some decent lighting, and make sure we can access Aldwych. We'll be as fast as we can.'

As they stop outside the office, Timber murmurs agreement and scuttles off to the local control room. Dom hopes he won't take the opportunity to bitch to his bosses.

Parekh taps Dom on the shoulder and points at her phone, mouthing, 'Abbott wants to speak to you.'

Dom clenches his jaw. Shakes his head.

Parekh fobs Abbott off, then ends the call. She looks back at Dom, frowning. 'He's going to UCH now.'

'Good.'

'Guv, what's going—'

'You ready?' Dom cuts her off. He doesn't want to talk about Abbott. 'Let's see what our witness has to say.'

Being hit by a car is a shit way to die for all concerned, especially those who watch it happen. Alice Klevie has worked for Transport for London for less than a month, and this is the first fatality of any sort she's been involved with. It's boiling inside the transport office but even though her padded coat is draped over her shoulders, and her blue and orange TfL bodywarmer is zipped up over her jumper, she's still shivering.

Dom hates it in this place. The air is stale, and the light is yellow-tinged and depressing, as if they're in constant shadow. He wonders if that's just his imagination playing silly buggers with him, because he knows they're deep in the bowels of the city. Either way, how anyone can stand working underground for hours every day, he doesn't know. He reckons it'd drive him crazy.

Putting that from his mind, he leans towards Alice Klevie and makes his voice as calm and encouraging as he can. 'Take as long as you need, OK. I know it's tough.'

She nods and clutches the mug of tea tighter.

Dom has never got the whole tea and sympathy thing. It makes no sense. Since when did a cup of tea help anything? Time is the only thing that helps, and even that has its limitations.

Beside him Parekh shifts in her seat. She's eager to get answers, to find out what the woman saw, and he can sense that she wants to jump in with a question. He meets Parekh's gaze and gives his head a small shake. She needs to wait. Sometimes the most revealing answers come from the longest silences.

Behind him, a clock on the wall ticks away the seconds. A computer over on the far desk displays rows of continuously updating numbers. Train arrivals and departures, Dom assumes, even if it does look like something out of *The Matrix*.

Alice Klevie sniffs and blows her nose on a ragged tissue. She rubs her fingers under her eyes, wiping away black mascara. Her nails are short and unpainted. The two gold rings on her wedding finger are the only jewellery she wears. She sniffs again. Her voice is shaky when she speaks. 'I saw him as he got off the escalator. He stumbled, and I thought at first he was drunk. He got a few annoyed looks from people around him, but no one stopped, I mean, they wouldn't, would they? At that time, they're all in the zone – rush-hour mindset – no one takes any notice of what's happening around them.' She wipes her eyes. 'It was only after he'd gone through the turnstile that I noticed the blood dripping from him.'

'Whereabouts were you?'

'On the wide-exit gate, the one for pushchairs and luggage.'

He nods. 'What happened next?'

'I . . .' She bites her lip. Colour spreads across her cheeks. 'It's not . . .'

Dom can see she's feeling conflicted. He needs her to be honest, not cleanse the truth. Everything, every tiny detail, is important at this stage of an investigation. He leans towards her. Keeps his voice gentle, encouraging. 'Whatever you're thinking, it's OK to say it.'

She hesitates, sighing. 'It's just, well, he looked kind of dodgy. Really unkempt, you know?' She looks down, lowers her voice a fraction. 'His eyes were unfocused and he was hunched over in a weird way, like he might be concealing a weapon. So, I . . . I was afraid . . . I didn't act immediately.'

'It's natural to be afraid of the unknown,' Parekh says. 'Don't beat yourself up over that.'

Except Alice Klevie should be beating herself up over it, Dom thinks. Looking for potential threats and taking action was in her job description. 'What happened then?'

Alice raises the mug of tea to her lips, and then lowers it without drinking. She meets Parekh's gaze rather than Dom's. 'He passed me, and I saw the blood on his clothes.' She wrinkles her nose. 'I smelt it, that strong metallic smell? I've never . . . it was . . . I called out but he didn't respond. Like I said, everyone else seemed either to avoid him or be oblivious to him, just rushing to wherever they had to be.'

Dom keeps his eyes on her face. 'You didn't feel afraid of him any more?'

She looks down. 'No, I . . . I thought he was in trouble.'

Dom glances at Parekh and sees she's making notes. He looks back to Alice and smiles as encouragingly as he can. 'What happened after you'd called out to him?'

'He didn't stop. So I called again, louder. That time he glanced back over his shoulder, just once, but it was like he didn't see me. It looked like he was searching the crowd around him for someone else.'

'Do you think he saw them?'

'I don't know . . . maybe, because he speeded up. Started doing this strange kind of lope across the foyer to the exit.'

'And you followed?'

She tightens her grip on the mug. 'Not immediately, but within a few seconds, yes.'

Parekh jots down the information. Frowns. 'Why didn't you go immediately? Why the delay?'

Alice looks tearful. Passes her mug from one hand to the other. 'I checked my colleague was at their post before I followed. We're not allowed to leave the turnstiles unattended.'

'It's OK. You did great.' Dom gives Parekh a warning look as she says this. They have to keep their personal views hidden during interviews and avoid showing any judgment on the witness's actions. They can't afford for Alice to start feeling guilty about what she didn't do and clamming up. 'Tell me what you saw,' Dom continues.

Alice shakes her head. Gives a little sob. 'I didn't see what happened on the road. I was too late. But I heard him.'

Dom frowns. Jeff Timber had said Alice watched the crash happen. 'Heard him?'

Alice gulps at the air and looks as if she's going to be sick. 'The noise as the cab hit him – a wet thud, like a beefsteak on a butcher's block, only louder. And his scream, like an animal bellowing . . . cut short.'

8
CLEMENTINE

A loud rapping noise makes me jump in my interview with David. Looking up, I see Wade standing on the other side of the pod's glass wall. He holds up his hand and taps his watch. I glance at the booking sheet on the back of the door and see that the pod was booked out to him, starting ten minutes ago.

I turn back to David. 'You've convinced me. I'd like to study these urban explorers as part of my research, and the people that watch their videos too.'

David grins. 'I knew you'd love it. Ever since I read that you were studying thrill-seekers I knew they'd be—'

'Sure.' I don't have time for David's gushing monologue and I'm still not clear what he's really getting out of this. I glance out through the glass wall at Wade. He's gesturing for me to wind up my meeting. 'The first thing I need to do is to speak to the members of this group. How do I contact them, is there a forum or something on their website?'

David shakes his head. 'Most urbexers use fake identities. What they do is illegal. You can't just barge into their world and expect to be trusted.'

'So you're suggesting what?'

He smiles, nervously. His leg jigs faster. 'That I help you.'

I stare at him for a long moment. After what happened with the Lover, I remain highly suspicious of offers of help. Trust makes you weak. I do not trust David, but I need to get my sampling frame agreed and the preliminary interviews done in two weeks. 'Fine, then I need you to get me a meeting with these people, fast.'

*

I'm starting to understand what David meant when he said these urbexers guard their privacy fiercely. For the past hour I've been searching the web for their live-stream site and I've still not managed to locate it. The link David wrote down for me isn't working, and I wonder if he gave me a fake link on purpose just to force me to get in contact with him again quickly. Pulling up my email, I type a message to David asking him to forward me a link to the site, and the video. I don't tell him that I really need to watch that video again, to check if my mind is playing tricks. That something I saw in it has unnerved me.

'Clementine?'

I look over the divider. Wade's standing there, fresh out of his meeting. His jaw is clenched, his brow creased into a frown. His quiff is perfectly symmetrical as always, its jet-blackness at odds with the hint of grey stubble across his chin. He's hot, there's no denying it, but I can't afford to lose focus. I know he's waiting for me to apologise for staying in the pod when he'd booked it, but I don't.

He clears his throat. 'Was that boy a potential subject?'

I shrug. 'Maybe.'

'What does that mean?' The jealousy is thick in his voice.

'It means maybe.'

Irritation flashes across his face. 'I need you to be honest with me.'

'Why, because you're my *boss*?' I put the emphasis on the word boss and let the rest of the question hang in the air unspoken. Our relationship has always been complicated, mentally and physically. Right now, I'm not in the mood for mind games.

He gets the hint, and changes tack. 'Did you see the invitation from HUMTEC Chicago? They've asked us to do the keynote address at next year's conference.'

'I deleted it.'

A muscle twitches in his jaw. 'You've deleted an invitation to give the keynote address at the most influential conference in our field? Presenting at HUMTEC is huge. It'll be a pivotal moment for you as a researcher, it could springboard your career to—'

'And your career.' I know it's not just for my benefit that he wants me to accept.

'By association, yes, and there's nothing wrong with that. I supervised your PhD, my name is on those papers too. It's a great honour, you should . . .' Wade rarely loses his cool, but I can tell he's close to that now. His voice is raised, the pitch an octave higher than usual. 'I just don't get you. Why aren't you excited about this?'

It's too hard to explain it to him.

I can't stay here. In my heightened state of emotion, his angry words feel like punches and I'm not equipped to block the blows for long. Switching off my computer, I grab the red parka from the back of my chair. 'I have to go, I've got an appointment.'

'HUMTEC. Just think about it, please,' Wade says. His voice has an edge of desperation. 'That's all I ask.'

I nod but know I won't change my mind. Conferences and symposia are what Wade thrives on, not me. He has to have the adoration of the masses to prove over and again that he's the brilliant man he needs everyone to believe. But standing in front of an audience, hypothesising and pontificating, is not my idea of fun. For me it's only about the puzzle, and the resolution.

I enjoy the hunt for truth. I'm good at it too, and don't need the glory afterwards.

As I push the door release and step out into the frigid January morning, I banish Wade and the conference invitation from my mind and think instead about the emails I trawled through earlier; the fan messages, the marriage proposals and the filth. To these people I'm a celebrity, but I never wanted that. I only ever wanted justice.

Killing the Lover was self-defence, that was the official verdict, and it was true. I stopped him murdering innocent people and of that I'm proud. But how killing *felt* shocked me. I felt powerful. Incredible. More alive than in any other moment of my life.

Feeling that way isn't normal, I understand that, and I know it makes me far from innocent, but I'm not evil either. The police and the public, though, if they knew the truth – that I enjoyed the power – would lock me away. And I do not want to be caged.

If I want to survive, to fit into this world, I must suppress my base instincts and retreat out of the limelight. I've come so far; I mustn't expose myself now. But, although I try to resist it, what I saw on that video – the moment the camera lens fractured and Jedx scrabbled among the clown heads – repeats over and again in my mind.

I think there is a puzzle to be solved.

This wolf smells blood.

9

DOM

The tunnel would be pitch-black without the safety lights, but even with them Dom, Parekh and Timber have to tread carefully, using their torch beams to scan the rails for signs of blood. Back on platform five, the CSIs are working their magic. Once Dom's established the route taken by Thomas Lee, they'll start work on the tunnel as well. They need to move fast, find leads as to what the hell happened here. This has to be one of the most bizarre crime scenes that Dom's attended.

Timber glances at his watch. 'We should be close to Aldwych by now. Another couple of minutes maybe.'

They keep walking. The blood trail has stayed close to the wall most of the way, as if Lee had been using the side of the tunnel for support. He was lucky the rails weren't live; several times the blood has been scattered across the rails, as if he had tripped and fallen. If the track had been operational, Thomas Lee wouldn't have made it as far as Holborn.

Dom hasn't found any blood smears on the walls, but with the limited light and the layers of sooty grime coating everything down here, it's impossible to be sure. Forensics will need to be all over this place.

From some way behind him, he hears the rumble of a train. The concrete floor seems to vibrate beneath his feet.

'All the tunnels are interconnected and the sound travels long distances between them,' Timber says, his voice overly loud with forced confidence. 'There's no train coming along this line.'

Dom doesn't respond. Timber's told them something like that every time they've heard a distant train. At first, he thought Timber was trying to reassure him and Parekh, now he thinks it's more that he's reassuring himself.

The noise grows louder, and Dom feels the chill of cold air blowing on his neck. Then the rumbling fades, and they're left with the echo of footsteps and the sound of their breathing in the silence. At least so far there's been no sign of rats.

'Guv.' Parekh hurries forward, focused on a dark object up ahead on the track. 'Could be Lee's.'

She's right. The small black rucksack looks clean, so can't have been in the tunnel long. The top is unzipped. Parekh uses her torch to peel back the material. Looks up at Dom. 'Bolt cutters.'

'Guess that tells us what he was doing at Aldwych.'

Timber swears. 'What is it with these people? Always trying to break into stations, it's bloody stupid.'

Parekh stands. 'Big problem, then?'

'Like you wouldn't believe, we get—'

'We'll leave it in situ for the CSIs.' Dom catches Parekh's eye. 'Get onto them with the details.'

Parekh taps a note into her phone, and they continue along the tunnel. A hundred metres or so later, Dom sees a white marker plate fixed to the concrete floor in the centre of the track. He reads the signage: *ALDWYCH STATION.*

Timber exhales loudly. 'Here she is.'

Dom nods. Up ahead, the platform is in sight. From this distance it looks like a regular station – the platform is clean and well lit, there are posters on the walls. It's only as they get closer he realises the posters aren't modern, and that the fixtures are old-fashioned. Aldwych is a time capsule buried beneath the city.

He sees it as they reach the start of the platform. A smashed head-torch, the bulb broken, the safety glass in pieces around the elastic strap. There's blood, a lot, on the glass shards and across the rails.

'Up there, guv.'

Dom follows Parekh's gesture and sees more blood splatter on the platform. He vaults up onto the platform alongside her, taking care not to get too close to the blood. 'From the spray, I'd say he was looking up the platform and, given this void, facing his attacker.' He points at the arc of blood across the tiles. 'Then he twisted away and fell onto the tracks.'

Parekh peers over the edge. 'Or he was pushed.'

'Yeah.'

'If the head-torch broke when he fell, he could have hit the rails with his head. He might have been knocked unconscious a while before he started stumbling along the tracks to Holborn.'

Dom nods. 'It's possible, and that would explain the amount of blood on the tracks. But this is all guesswork, we need the CSIs in here, and the post-mortem results, to know more.'

'What about cameras?' Parekh looks at Timber. He's still on the tracks, crouched over the blood, his face ashen. 'Do you have CCTV down here?'

'I'll have to check. We have it above ground, not sure about this level though.'

'Find out, yeah?' Dom says. 'We need everything you've got for the past twenty-four hours.'

He looks back at the patterns of blood. In the middle of the arc something catches his eye, twinkling beneath the fluorescent lighting. He leans closer, squinting until he sees what it is; a tiny diamante, half submerged in the blood.

'Guv?' Parekh's tone is serious, with an undertone of excitement. 'You're going to want to see this.'

Straightening up, he strides over to join her at the archway of the platform's exit tunnel. Lying just inside the tunnel, the weapon is smeared with blood.

Shit. What the fuck was Thomas Lee messed up in?

The weapon isn't just a knife, not like the sort you'd expect to find. The stubby, jewelled hilt and thick blood-crusted blade are unlike any knife Dom's seen before.

This isn't a knife; it's a ceremonial dagger.

10
CLEMENTINE

Albert is standing by the front entrance waiting for me when I arrive home. Pushing seventy, he has perfect deportment and an understated yet classic style; pinstripe suit, black woollen overcoat and brown brogues that match his briefcase. He nods and the corners of his lips lift into a smile. He's my father's lawyer, and is the only person from my childhood with whom I have contact. I want that to change, which is the reason he's here.

He greets me as he always has done, with a formal handshake, and follows me into the hallway and up to my fourth-floor attic apartment. I unlock the door using the Yale key and close it behind us.

'I don't know how you can stay here,' says Albert.

Wade also thinks it strange that I've continued living on St John Street after what happened. The Lover attacked me here, but I beat *him*. That makes me feel strong, not weak, the victor not the victim. This is my home.

'It was Father's apartment. Being here makes me feel closer to him.' I gesture for Albert to take a seat on my new teal sofa with a purple throw over it. 'Tea?'

'Thanks, that would be nice.' He glances towards the door, frowning. 'If you insist on staying here, I hope you have good security in place.'

'Of course,' I reassure him, but the truth is the four bolts on my door I used to lock and triple-check stay unfastened these days. I don't see the point any more. I know what I am capable of. I can fight my corner, literally. And so I stay, and the bolts remain unlocked. 'Earl Grey?'

Albert sits poker-straight, his hands on his knees. 'Great.'

I busy myself in the kitchenette preparing the tea, thankful that Albert isn't one of those people who insist on filling every silence with chatter. He's old-school and so I use leaves and a pot rather than tea bags straight in the mugs. I set the tea-making paraphernalia onto a tray and carry it across to the coffee table. That's when I realise why Albert's so quiet.

He's staring at the back wall of the living space, the wall behind my desk. 'What's all this?'

I open the window a few inches, then light a cigarette and take a long drag. The wall is where I've mapped out all the elements of my research. Red strings connect information – photos, documents, website references, subject interviews – giving the effect of a spider's web, laden with flies. I need to see things graphically to make sense of them, and there isn't enough room to do this at the faculty. 'It's my work.'

Albert frowns. Standing up, he strides over to the far side of the web and taps his finger against one of the photographs. 'If it's your work, why is *his* picture here?'

I take another drag on my cigarette. Exhale. The man in the picture is in his forties, dark-haired, and although he's smiling there's a jadedness in his eyes, dark shadows beneath the heavy lids. I've written the relevant questions that haunt me, taunt me, across the top and the bottom of the picture:

Who killed my father?

Why?

Moving to stand beside Albert, I trace my fingers along the red string. It connects the pin holding the image of my father to a spoke leading from the word in the centre of the web, the core theme of my research: *Obsession*. Each spoke has a number and leads out from this central word to a different research subject; numbers one to eight are the online voyeurs I've already interviewed. I am subject zero; a picture of me is pinned to this spoke, and a red string connects my photo to the picture of my father. 'Because that's how I work – I'm a participant in my own research. I want to understand obsessive behaviour in others and myself. Especially myself.'

Albert looks concerned. 'Aren't you researching thrill-seekers and voyeurs? Which are you?'

I think for a moment. Shrug. 'Probably a combination of both.'

He shakes his head, gesturing to the web. 'Doing this, after everything you've been through, is it wise?'

I hold his gaze. I don't care whether it's wise. I have to know. I won't rest until I've found the truth. Everything in life is interconnected; my history, my work, and all that lurks between the cracks. For the last twelve years, ever since the fire, I believed my father was a dirty copper and that I started the fire that killed him, and almost killed me. I was dead for three thousand and six seconds, and when I woke I was numb and emotionless, with partial amnesia of that day. But, as the Lover tried to choke the breath from me, my memory returned and I remembered what happened. My father had been set up to look like a dirty copper while he was working undercover. Someone else was in the cottage, *they* stabbed my father and started the fire. Then they locked the doors so Father and I couldn't escape. I watched him die, the flames burning the skin from my arms, as I tried to revive him. As soon as I remembered, I vowed I wouldn't rest until I found who was responsible. 'I have to do this.'

Albert nods. He steps back to the sofa and sits down. 'What you've asked me to do won't be easy.'

I pour our tea and pass him one of the china teacups that I keep especially for his visits. 'I didn't think it would be.'

'As you know, your mother lives a transient lifestyle.' Albert takes a sip of tea, nods approval, and places the cup back onto its saucer. 'She has a habit of changing husbands and names on a semi-frequent basis.'

'I understand that, but I have questions.' I glance back at the web, along the string from my father's picture to one of him with my mother. It was taken around the time they got married. They're smiling, leaning against a sports car; a green MG. 'I want to ask her if she knew any details about Father's work.'

'And if she doesn't want to speak to you?'

I stub my cigarette out in the ashtray beside my teacup. I haven't spoken to my mother since just after Father died. He left me everything – his London flat, the Oxfordshire cottage, or what remained of it, and the money in his accounts. When Mother discovered he'd cut her from the will, she contested it and lost. I haven't seen her since the day she stormed out of that courtroom, discarding me again, as she had done so many times in my childhood before my father was given sole custody. She never wanted me. All she ever wanted was the money. I bite my lip, trying not to let the hurt show. 'I have to try.'

Albert nods. 'So be it. As I said in my correspondence, I'm happy to undertake this search on your behalf, but as your mother is proving troublesome to locate, you'll need to exercise patience.'

I light another cigarette and inhale deeply. Patience is not one of my strengths, and anything involving my mother makes me anxious. Albert has been looking for her for over a month already. I hate the waiting. 'She's not my only potential source of information.'

'You're still associating with those true-crime people? Is that a good idea?'

Yes, it is. I have come to rely on True Crime London, they are helping me with those questions that haunt me, scrawled under my father's photo. He had been found guilty of dishonourable conduct, fraud and criminal activities after his death. But he was framed and then murdered, and those responsible have never been brought to justice. I will not let it go. 'I think it's necessary.'

'And this person?' Albert gestures to another photo that leads from my picture with a different thread, this one of another dark-haired man. 'How does he connect to all this?'

I take a drag on my cigarette and try to keep my expression neutral even though my pulse starts racing and emotion swells in my chest making it hard to breathe. Feeling vibrates through my body, jolting every nerve until I think I'm going to break apart. The physicality of my emotion scares me.

Albert frowns. 'Clementine?'

The nothingness where feelings should have been had lasted twelve years, since the day I was pulled from that burning cottage. The skin they grafted over the burns on my hands and arms will last a lifetime. The Lover almost cut that time short. But Dominic Bell helped me stop him. 'Dom saved my life.'

11

DOM

Back at base, DCI Jackson's face is getting ruddier by the second. 'A ceremonial dagger?'

'That's what it looks like.'

Jackson runs a hand over his head, smoothing imaginary hairs back into place. 'I thought this was a simple one, that the boys in Transport had got all over-excited about some drunk wandering out in front of a car.' He shakes his head. 'And now we've got break-ins and stabbings at tube stations and a ceremonial bloody dagger?'

Dom waits for the DCI to finish his rant. He's learnt from experience that there's no point trying to interrupt, so he chooses a chair and sits down. The office has a gloomy feel to it. Even the glossy family photo of Jackson with his four daughters, wife and their Yorkshire terrier looks jaded surrounded by the mud-coloured decor.

Jackson swivels in his throne-like chair, facing him across the desk. 'At least tell me you've got some decent leads?'

'A few, and there's a lot of stuff waiting for forensics.'

'Good, good, so you're hopeful then?'

Dom doesn't answer. He never says he's hopeful – he hates to guess how long things will take, and always waits for a successful conviction before considering a case he's worked closed – the DCI knows that.

Jackson gestures to the open file on his desk. There's a complicated-looking spreadsheet topping the stack of papers inside. 'Well, the violent crime stats are up, and I'm taking the beating for it. We need a bit of hope and some quick wins to get the suits in Whitehall off our backs.'

The tabloids too, Dom thinks. They credited Clementine Starke with solving his last case rather than him. Even if she almost got herself killed in the process. Shit. He doesn't want to think about Clementine right now. If she'd been straight with him about her involvement with the group of true-crime nerds that were trying to beat him to catching the serial killer, he might have been able to stop the killer before he got so close to claiming her as his last victim. As it is, she's now some kind of celebrity academic, appearing on chat shows and giving magazine interviews. He hates all that nonsense. He's kept away, and tried to forget her, but somehow she always pops back up to unsettle his thoughts.

Jackson's voice pulls him back to the present. 'Dom? A bit of hope needed?'

'Noted.' Dom starts to get up. 'I'll get back to it, then.'

'No, sit. There's something else we need to talk about. There's been a development in the internal investigation into Operation Atlantis.'

Dom clenches his jaw. Operation Atlantis was the failed multi-agency operation he'd co-led a few months previously. 'What is it?'

'Holsworth at the IPCC isn't telling me much, but he said there's new evidence come to light that's going to break the case wide open.'

Dom grimaces. The experience of being grilled by the IPCC lead investigator, Holsworth, and his two attack dogs is still fresh in his mind. The Operation Atlantis team had been strong, or so he'd thought. His ex-girlfriend, DI Therese Weller, and a colleague he'd come up the ranks with, DI Simon Lindsay, had been key players, along with Darren Harris – his sister Chrissie's partner. But the raid had failed, and Dom and Therese had been injured. The IPCC believed it was because at least one of the team was in league with their target – Russian gang leader Marcus Genk. Maybe now he'd finally get to know the truth. 'Like what?'

'Look, Holsworth wouldn't tell me the specifics, but he said it's pretty damning – phone calls, money transfers and the like.'

Dom can tell from Jackson's voice it isn't the news he's been waiting for. 'Tell me.'

'I'm sorry, Dom. I know this isn't what you want to hear, but all the evidence is pointing at Darren Harris.'

Dom tenses. 'That's fucked up.'

Jackson softens his tone. 'I know, son. Betrayal's hard. Harder still when it's family.'

Dom clenches his fists. 'He's not my—'

'As good as, then. Has your sister been in touch?"

Chrissie hasn't spoken to him since Darren got suspended two months ago. It feels like a lifetime. 'She thinks I should be able to persuade the IPCC that Darren is innocent.'

'You can only say what you saw.'

'And that's the problem, isn't it?'

Dom had been knocked unconscious. When he came round, he'd seen a man wearing boots like Darren's talking to Genk, but he doesn't believe it was Darren. The whole team is under suspicion and one of them is lying. From the way he's behaved since, Dom's money is on Simon Lindsay being dirty, but he can't prove it.

Jackson gives him a sympathetic look. 'I know it's tough, but you can't tell her about the new evidence. You need to sit tight, let this take its course.'

Shit. The only contact he's had with Chrissie was one text at Christmas: I love you but I can't forgive you. He'd thrown himself into work, taken every extra shift over Christmas and New Year, and worked out at the gym for hours in-between, just to escape going back to his flat and staring alone at the blank walls. Even the gym had closed on Christmas Day. It'd been a miserable time. 'I think Lindsay's involved.'

'And you've told them that. Now you need to let them do their job. Holsworth might be a pedantic son of a bitch but he's thorough and doesn't give up easily. He'll find the truth.'

'And if he doesn't?'

Jackson gives him a warning look over the top of his glasses. 'He will.'

Dom recognises from his boss's manner that the subject is closed, so he changes tack. 'Any news on the vacancy in my team being advertised?'

'Well . . .' Jackson makes a steeple with his fingers and looks thoughtful. Dom's pretty sure it's a stalling tactic, his boss is always thinking several moves ahead. He was a detective back in the day, and still likes to think of himself in touch with the sharp end. 'I was thinking a trainee Detective Constable might work.'

No, it won't, Dom thinks. Those coming through the straight-to-detective graduate programme needed a good two years on the job before they'd be useful. 'I thought they were only based in boroughs, not specialist teams.'

'As a guideline, yes, but I was talking to my counterpart over the river and they've already taken two into specialist units.'

Dom rubs his jaw. Tries to look like he's considering the trainee as a serious proposition. Shakes his head. 'I don't think it'll work for me. I need someone with field experience. I've already got Parekh, who's green.'

'But you said she's doing well.'

'And she is, but she needs mentoring, support. I need someone who's been around a bit and can fly straight off – it's a sergeant's role.'

Jackson fiddles with the papers in his in-tray, lining them up perfectly. 'Can't do that, I'm afraid, Dom. Budget cuts are biting us in the arse. You need to drop the rank to Constable.'

Damn bean-counters; endlessly squeezing them to make cuts, then shouting the loudest when there aren't enough boots on the ground to respond in emergencies. 'I'd rather have a career constable then, someone solid, with years on the street.'

'We'll see.' Jackson's tone implies he's still set on them getting a trainee. 'Anyway, you said you've got some leads on this case, so you should be fine with just Abbott and Parekh for a bit.'

Yeah, thinks Dom as he gets up to leave, except Abbott's been lying. Dom's been cutting him out of his cases, trying to keep him at arm's length, but he can't keep doing it forever. He needs to tackle what Abbott did.

Fucksake. The way things are going it could soon be just him and Parekh.

12
DOM

The victim's ID has been cross-checked and confirmed as Thomas Lee, matching the credit card that the victim was carrying. He was a banker. Thirty-six years old with two kids. Married but legally separated. His wife is listed as next of kin. According to the electoral roll, they still live at the same address.

Dom takes Parekh with him to do the death knock. It's a shit job, but important to get right. He couldn't have Abbott there and risk the tension between the two of them messing things up. But, as they've been driving to Thomas Lee's address, Dom's sensed something not right with Parekh. She's unusually quiet and has a constant frown on her face.

As they pull up outside the house, he decides to clear the air. Undoing his seatbelt, he turns towards his DC. 'You all right, Parekh?'

She pauses before answering. Keeps her gaze straight ahead through the windscreen. 'Guv, I'm grateful for the opportunity to be working the case with you like this. And I'm loyal, I hope you know that, but please don't ask me to lie for you again.'

Dom keeps looking at her. Remembers how he'd asked her to fob Abbott off on the phone when they were back at Holborn. He doesn't respond.

She glances at him. 'I don't want to get caught in the middle of whatever's going on between you and Abbott. We're a team, and the thing between the two of you is making things awkward.'

'Yeah.' He runs his fingers through his hair. She's right. Getting her to act as his intermediary isn't fair. He needs a permanent solution; he can't keep putting off tackling Abbott about what he did. A detective who can't keep his mouth shut is a proper liability, everyone knows it. Everyone, it seems, aside from Abbott. 'I'll sort it, OK.'

*

Thomas Lee's wife can't be more than thirty-five, but she already has the over-tight features of someone who's had plastic surgery a few times. She allows them inside her home, an imposing white-fronted townhouse near Marylebone station, but her body language and tone are decidedly frosty. Dom reckons that, if she were able to, she'd be frowning at him.

As it is, she shows them into the lounge and gestures to one of the huge chesterfield sofas, before sitting down stiffly on the one opposite. The room is straight out of a glossy magazine, beautiful but lacking in any character or soul. On top of the piano are several photographs in silver frames; a portrait of Mrs Lee and two little girls in matching white linen dresses, the three of them picnicking in a meadow, the two girls riding a donkey on the beach. Thomas Lee isn't in any of the pictures.

She stares at Dom. 'So, what is it?'

Dom looks at Parekh. They'd agreed she'd take the lead on this.

Parekh clears her throat. 'It's about your husband, Mrs Lee, he's—'

'My *ex*-husband.' Thomas Lee's wife glares at Parekh. 'The decree absolute is due any day. And, anyway, I go by my maiden name, Coles.'

'My apologies, Ms Coles.' Parekh takes a breath. 'As I was saying, we've got some bad news about your ex-husband.'

Ms Coles makes a hurrying motion with her hand. Given the situation, Dom tries hard to hide his irritation at her rudeness and keep his expression neutral.

Parekh continues, her voice a little less confident now. 'I'm afraid he's dead. He was—'

Ms Cole jerks backwards as if she's been slapped. 'Dead? How can he be? I was talking to him just yesterday. He was being weird, arguing about having the girls and trying to change his weekend with them to later in the month. He's never done that before. He got all jittery when I said that it wasn't acceptable. I called him some awful names. I . . .'

'We're sorry for your loss,' Dom says. 'Is there anyone you'd like us to call?'

Ms Coles looks from Dom to Parekh and back again. 'No . . . I . . . no it's OK.' She presses her hand against her forehead for a moment. Takes a deep breath, then looks at Parekh. 'How did it happen?'

Parekh speaks slowly and clearly, keeping eye contact with Ms Cole. 'He was hit by a cab outside Holborn station this morning. We're investigating the circumstances and—'

'Oh God.' She clasps her hands together. Her eyes search their faces for more. 'Hit by a . . .? Poor Thomas, he . . .'

'Do you have any idea what he was doing in the Holborn area this morning?'

'No . . . I, we lead separate lives now. Apart from when he comes in to see the children, I don't see him and he doesn't tell me his movements.' She looks confused, thoughtful. 'I can't imagine why he'd be around Holborn though, he works over at Canary Wharf.'

'It looks like something happened to Mr Lee while he was down in the Underground. We're investigating at the moment to see if that and the traffic accident are connected. We're treating his death as suspicious.'

'I . . .' Ms Coles gets up. 'I think I'd like a drink now.'

'Please.' Parekh motions for Ms Coles to stay seated. 'Let me.'

Ms Coles nods. She explains where to find the tea and Parekh moves through into the kitchen.

'Did he suffer?' Ms Coles asks. There's a tremble in her voice now; a crack in her hard veneer.

No doubt, thinks Dom, but he shakes his head. She might be a bit frosty, but he can see she's hurting. The specifics aren't going to help her. Better that she has a little comfort. 'He was injured before he got to ground level, but when the vehicle hit him it would have been very quick.'

'Well that's . . .' She grabs a tissue from the box on the side table and sniffs into it. 'Can I see him?'

Dom keeps his voice gentle. 'I don't think that's wise. The cab was travelling quickly. The identification was confirmed by his dental records.'

She sits motionless then, just as Dom's about to ask if she's OK, she lets out a sob and buries her face in the tissue. 'I can't believe he's just . . . gone. What will I tell the girls? They . . . I don't . . .'

Parekh hands black tea in a dainty china cup to Ms Coles. 'Is there anyone you can think of who would want to harm your husband?'

Ms Coles shakes her head. 'No one specific, but he was a banker. These days everyone seems to hate them.'

True, thinks Dom. 'When did you last see him?'

She takes a sip of her tea. 'It must have been yesterday evening, pretty late, around ten, but I didn't see him, just heard his door bang shut. The basement is his domain – when we split, we had it refurbished into a self-contained apartment. It meant he could still see the kids and we could both stay living here.' She shakes her head. 'We married young, but it was the cancer that killed our relationship. After he'd gone through the rounds of chemo and went into remission, it was like he felt he was being held back by having had a family. He said he needed space, time to have adventures. At first, I hoped we'd get back together when he'd got the "adventures" out of his system. We'd been through so much together, you know? But as time moved on I realised it wasn't going to happen, he'd changed, grown more distant. I had too, probably.' She looks down at her tea. 'I didn't stop loving him, though.'

13
CLEMENTINE

Albert has gone, but I decide not to return to the faculty. It's mid-afternoon and this desk, stacked high with notebooks, encircled by a collection of mugs and an overflowing ashtray, has always been the place where I do my best work. Especially as there's no Wade here, breathing down my neck. Wanting more from me than I'm able – willing – to give. Before, when I felt numb, sex was one of the few ways I could make myself feel something. The dramatic high of the climax could chase away the nothingness, just for a little while. It was sex. Urgent, frantic, sex. I thought Wade knew that. I thought he was one of the very few people who understood me. Now I'm not so sure.

Turning my attention to my laptop, I access my university email and see David has sent me another link to the urban explorers site and the video that he showed me this morning. He says getting together with the whole group might be tricky straight off, but he's trying to set up a meeting with one of them. If that goes well, they can introduce me to the rest.

I click the link to the video and watch the action unfold again – the four balaclava-wearing figures in the forest, the crowbar to the door, the plastic sheeting, the flashes of light, red and silver, then the running and the clown heads. There is one moment I'm searching for and it comes seconds before the end. I pause the video, and stare at the face on screen; the cameraman, Jedx, his features close to the fractured lens of the camera.

Lighting a cigarette, I inhale strongly. I've looked death in the face, I know what that fear feels like. From the expression on this man's face, I know he was looking at it too.

There's a ping, and a message box appears in the right-hand corner of my screen:

GhostAvenger posted in True Crime London: Who Killed Robert Starke?

I click the box before it disappears, and my web browser opens to reveal the blood-splattered microscope logo of the CrimeStop website, home of the True Crime London group. This specialist social networking site for true-crime fans was one of my only links to the outside world just a few months ago. Initially I saw them only as subjects for my PhD research into crowdsourced crime solving, but through integrating into their group, I've become a little more comfortable in the company of others. And by working with them, I succeeded in catching the Lover. Our Lover investigation group is deleted now, but I only use one sub-group within the site. It's a new one, a secret one. I hope, again, that we'll be able to catch a killer.

Typing in my password, I ignore the blue icons at the top right of my screen that show I have over a thousand notifications, and the icon beside it showing my personal inbox has nearly six hundred direct messages. I click through to the secret area of the website. At the side of the screen my avatar appears – the aquamarine iris of my eye, in close-up – beside the name of my alter ego, The Watcher.

GhostAvenger to True Crime London: Who Killed Robert Starke?
I've got the USB stick, thanks @TheWatcher, and have run some basic repair programs. Although they've done enough to let me see there are hundreds – maybe thousands – of files on this thing, they're still not readable. I've contacted a tech friend of mine who's written a program I think could help. They're US-based, and I'm waiting for them to come back to me.

It took me a while to ask the group for help investigating the death of my father, Robert Starke, but in the end it was that or admit defeat. Dom and I had become close following my final confrontation with the Lover, supporting each other in the aftermath of what had happened. Then, a few weeks on, he'd pulled away.

He was refusing to talk to me now, and Albert wasn't making progress. The memory stick, with its cracked casing and the word COBALT written on a sticker on the side, belonged to my father. It was one of the things that was rescued from the fire, and I'd kept it in the wooden box on the mantel ever since, along with his medals and an old picture of him in uniform.

Ghost Avenger works in a mortuary for his day job, but he's also a bit of a hacker. He's already done far more than I could. The files on the USB stick could give me valuable information about what my father had become entangled in. It could be connected to his work undercover.

I click the comments field and type a message.

The Watcher: @GhostAvenger Thank you! I know it's a long shot.

More replies come almost immediately.

Robert 'Chainsaw' Jameson: We all have skills. Anything else we can do?
The Watcher: Kind offer @RobertChainsawJameson — right now the USB stick is our best lead. So it's a bit of a waiting game.
Crime Queen: @TheWatcher When we've figured this out, you'll let me have the exclusive on this for my blog, won't you?
The Watcher: @CrimeQueen Of course.
JusticeLeague: You know we love a good challenge!

They might be a collection of oddballs, but they've come through for me before. I consider telling them about the video, but I hold myself back. Something makes me want that investigation for myself.

Opening a new browser window, I type the words *'murder death hendleton studios'* into the search engine. Scanning through the results, I see nothing relevant. There's plenty of nerd blogs about the films that were made there, and a long list of conspiracy theories and forum discussions about the owner's mysterious death – alleging that everything from aliens to M15 were involved – but nothing posted is more recent than two years ago.

I walk up to the research web on the wall. Reaching out my fingers, I circle the pin that holds my photo, subject zero, in place. I think about the video, and the look on Jedx's face as he tried to escape that building. It wasn't a hoax. Perhaps finding the truth behind it could be a new element to add to my web. I'm not sure about that, but there is something I am clear about.

My stomach flips at the thought. My mouth goes dry. My breath becomes shallow.

I have to tell Dom.

14

DOM

Back at the office, Dom sets up the murder board in the boxy incident room at the end of the open plan. He gets to work while he's waiting for Parekh and Abbott to join him, writing THOMAS LEE in capital letters at the top of the whiteboard. Below it he adds: *murder / accident.*

The door opens and Abbott comes in. There's an odd look on his face; wary and anxious. His hands are clenched into fists, his shoulders tense. He glances back towards the door before he speaks. 'You all right, guv?'

Dom frowns at him. 'I'm fine.'

'You sure? Only you seem pissed off with something.' Abbott clears his throat. 'And if I'm honest, it seems to be something to do with me.'

Dom tightens his grip on the marker pen. He turns to face Abbott. His tone is harsher than usual. 'And *are* you honest?'

Abbot tilts his head to one side. Looks confused. 'What do you mean?'

'What do I mean?' Dom takes a step towards his sergeant. Tries to swallow down the anger. Keep control, even though he really wants to punch the baffled expression off Abbott's face. 'I think you know *exactly* what I mean.'

'I . . . really, no.' Abbott rubs his eyes. He looks tired, his already slim face more gaunt than usual, and his eyes bloodshot. 'I'm in the dark here.'

If Dom didn't know the truth, if he didn't have physical evidence about the tricks Abbott's been playing, he'd almost believe he's innocent. 'Spare me the bullshit, yeah.'

Abbott puts his hands up as if in surrender. 'But, Dom, just tell me what it is that . . .'

The door handle clicks down.

'Not now, *Taylan*.' Dom spits out Abbott's first name like it's poison. He refuses to get into it like this, with Parekh about to walk in. He'll have things out with Abbott, but on his terms, his timescale. Let Abbott sweat. He knows what he's done. He knows the rules he's broken.

Turning away, Dom sticks a copy of the photograph Ms Coles gave them in the top left corner of the board. He takes a deep breath, trying to recompose himself. Right now, they have a killer to catch.

The photo shows Thomas Lee was a good-looking man with a neatly trimmed beard, who wore his dark hair fluffed forward to hide a receding hairline. They know he had testicular cancer three years ago and was in remission. That he ate a raw-food diet, was teetotal, worked out regularly, and shared childcare with his ex-wife. He worked for a private bank in the City and enjoyed adventure holidays. None of that seems to reveal anything that helps them understand why he died.

Dom draws a line in black marker pen from Thomas Lee's picture to a photo of the initial crime scene at ground level; his body sprawled on the tarmac, the cab twisted at an angle from the kerb. He moves on quickly, drawing another line to Alice Klevie, the Transport for London employee, bulleting the key points from her statement: the way Thomas Lee was stumbling, looking around at the crowd, not responding to her when she called out.

The next line is to the cab driver's name, Derek Webster. Dom turns, nods at Abbott. 'What did the cabbie say?'

Abbott looks awkward, flushed. He doesn't meet Dom's gaze. 'He was in pretty bad shape, but seemed lucid. He said Thomas Lee just kind of lurched into the road. The thing that shook him the most was that as Lee hit the windscreen, he was staring straight at him. Webster said he'll never get that image out of his head.'

'The station's external CCTV confirms that, guv.' Parekh's perched on the table opposite the board, scanning through her notes. 'It's shows him weaving from side to side as he exits the foyer, so it's easy to see how Alice Klevie might have thought he was drunk, and as he approaches the road he's looking over his shoulder. He just steps into the traffic, no warning.'

'Can you see who he's looking at?' Abbott says.

Parekh shakes her head. 'It's too busy and the angle is wrong.'

Shit.

The final marker line is to the ex-wife, Ms Coles. Dom remembers the way her frosty manner had fractured at the news of Lee's death. He makes notes on the board as he summarises what they know. 'Thomas Lee lived in the same property as his wife, in a self-contained basement apartment. She remembers hearing him go out last night, around ten o'clock, and didn't see or hear from him after that. A search of the apartment didn't yield much; nothing that links to the abandoned underground station or to anything like the dagger, but we found his phone and laptop so the techs are taking a look.'

Parekh nods. 'There's no joy from the techs on the laptop yet, but they've got into the phone. It's mainly work-related stuff. No mention of what he was doing last night. No calls incoming or outgoing after 7.18 p.m. No entry in his diary for last night, either.' She closes her scratchpad. 'I've requested his phone and financial records.'

Dom notes what she's said on the whiteboard. 'What else?'

'I was wondering if he had a life insurance policy,' Parekh says.

Abbott turns to her. 'You suspect the wife?'

'Not especially, her alibi checks out. But it might be a motive and she could have hired someone.'

'Yeah, look into it,' Dom says. He doesn't think the wife's involved, but they need to be thorough. 'Abbott, anything else from you?'

'I've spoken to Thomas Lee's employer. He was a good employee, did his job well and got on with everyone. They said that he was personable but private, he tended not to socialise with colleagues outside of work.'

Dom writes this on the board, glad it gives him an excuse not to look at Abbott. 'OK, so that brings us to the trail of blood through Holborn station, the issue of what he was doing in Aldwych station and why he was stabbed with what looks like a ceremonial weapon. That dagger is key evidence. Finding out where it came from needs to be a priority.'

Abbott clears his throat. 'The CCTV at Aldwych was going through a software update last night between midnight and one o'clock. There's no record of anyone breaking in or going into the building. TfL didn't realise the place had been broken into until this morning when they got the call from Jeff Timber. When they replayed the tapes, they realised the lock to the access door of the second entrance – the one on Surrey Street – had been cut during the period the system was offline.'

Dom raises his eyebrows. 'So, if Thomas Lee was the one who broke in, he knew about the security update?'

'Looks that way.'

Dom thinks back to the tunnel that morning. 'He wasn't alone in Aldwych. The larger pool of blood we found was on the track but, from the splatter pattern, it looks like he was stabbed on the platform and then fell, or was pushed, onto the rails.'

'And then left there?' Abbott asks.

Parekh nods. 'With those wounds, down there with no easy way of escape, the killer probably thought he was as good as dead.'

Dom runs his hand through his hair. 'There are more maybes in this theory than I'd like, but I'm inclined to agree.' He takes the last two pictures off the table and fixes them to the board – one shows the small diamante in a pool of blood, the other the thick-bladed dagger with its jewelled hilt and strange rune-like icons carved into the metal. He taps the pictures. 'We need to find where the murder weapon came from. The dagger's unusual. Parekh, dig into it and see what you can find.'

'Yes, guv.'

'So, we're officially treating this as a murder?' Abbott says.

'The visual evidence confirms that the cabbie hitting Thomas Lee was accidental, but it doesn't look like the stabbing in Aldwych station could be anything other than attempted murder,' says Dom.

'I've had a trawl through social media,' Parekh says. 'There's a bit of interest, mainly on Twitter. The usual stuff about congestion and road safety, but there are a few pictures and videos as well.'

Dom frowns. 'Pictures? Of what?'

'The bashed-up cab on the street and the forensics tent, that sort of thing. Luckily so far there's no mention of the blood trail. As he was wearing dark clothes and it was so busy in the tube station, people didn't seem to notice he was bleeding, or if they did they ignored him. We saw on the CCTV that even those he bashed into barely glanced his way.'

Abbott turns to his phone and brings up Twitter.

The whole mass voyeurism that social media promotes makes Dom sick. 'A man died and these ghouls are posting videos?'

Parekh shrugs and looks unfazed. 'It's how people share information. It's better than the news – more immediate, unbiased.'

Better is a matter of opinion, Dom thinks. 'Anything we can use?'

'There's a new picture.' Abbott angles his phone towards Dom so he can see it. 'Looks like the moment Lee was hit.'

Dom squints at the photo. The focus is better than the CCTV, the colour image more compelling. Thomas Lee has stepped off the pavement, he's looking over his right shoulder, the cab is just inches from impact. 'How the—'

'The new photo's trending,' Parekh says, also on her phone. 'They're using hashtags #killercabbie and #deathbycab.'

Dom curses. 'Get the social media people on it. Tell them to ask people to DM us their photos. There could be something useful among all this shit.'

Parekh raises an eyebrow. 'DM? Yes, guv. You know some of the jargon then?'

'I'm not that much of a dinosaur.' Dom frowns. He just never imagined scavenging social media for evidence would become standard police practice. He looks at Abbott. 'Chase up the lab and find out when the PM is scheduled. I want to know about the stab wounds and if they can confirm our theory about his fall. If he fought back, there could be forensics we can use.'

The DS nods. 'I'm assuming it'll be tomorrow, they're stacked up at the moment.'

With all the budget cuts, wasn't that the truth. A death like this wouldn't be at the top of the pile. Although the circumstances of Thomas Lee's death were strange, without it suggesting the imminent threat of a serial killer or terrorist attack, there's no leverage for them to get it higher up the priority list. Maybe they should tweet about that.

He looks at the picture of Thomas Lee smiling down from the top of the murder board. The bloke might have had his issues, but he'd beaten cancer and was trying to live his life. Dom thinks about Ms Coles, and her two daughters who'd be growing up without their father. They deserve to know what really happened to their dad. Everyone should know the truth.

Everyone deserves justice.

15

SASS

Sass isn't in the mood. Drinks at Belton Tap had seemed a good idea as she was leaving work; anything was better than going home to her empty flat and being alone with her memories of what she'd seen on Saturday night. But now that she's here, two glasses of pinot in, and surrounded by colleagues sharing work gossip, she's regretting it. There are really only two options – leave or get hammered. She doesn't want to leave.

Downing the rest of her wine, she stands up. Ellie, Mark and Lisa look at her expectantly. She forces a smile. 'More of the same?'

They whoop.

As she heads towards the bar, the smile dies on her face. All around her people are laughing, talking, having fun. She can't imagine ever feeling happy enough to have fun again. Not after witnessing last Saturday's sickening scene, now imprinted on her mind.

Sass shudders. Blinks away the memories of the rotten wooden floor, the blood spreading across it, mingling with the debris. She tries not to think of it but still the images come; the blood leaking out from the weird wooden contraption – an implement of torture literally right out of a horror film. The naked woman strapped inside, her body limp, her face covered by white-blonde hair. And the knives – so many knives – embedded in her flesh. Blood, everywhere.

Grabbing the bar, Sass steadies herself and takes a deep breath. She isn't cut out for this. Unlike the others, she didn't get into urbexing for the thrills, all she wanted was to see places forgotten by humans, the places nature was reclaiming for itself.

'Yeah?' The hipster barman is looking at her. 'You being served?'

She shakes her head. 'Bottle of merlot, and two large glasses of pinot, please.'

He nods. As he fixes the drinks, Sass remembers the first abandoned place she discovered. They'd come across it by accident. She'd been with Nanna walking in the grounds of an old mansion. In the woodland they'd found an ornamental rose garden; huge cast-iron gates ajar, a chipped mosaic path overgrown with creepers, leading to a summer pavilion. The domed ceiling of the pavilion had been painted with a fresco of birds and clouds, faded but still beautiful. Around it the roses, once cultivated, had run wild. It felt like they'd found an enchanted, secret garden. It was the most beautiful sight she'd ever seen.

All she'd ever wanted was to find that kind of magical place again.

'There you go.'

The barman's words bring her back to the present. The drinks are lined up in front of her. She taps her card against the machine without looking at the amount. Somehow it doesn't seem to matter. Nothing does. There's no magic in the world any more, only horror. She downs one of the glasses at the bar then moves back towards her colleagues.

One of her phones beeps in her bag, and her stomach lurches. The message isn't on her regular phone, the one registered in her real name. It's the disposable which only three other people have the number for.

Putting the bottle and wine glass down on a table, she reaches into her bag and takes out the phone. It doesn't have any numbers programmed into its memory. No names either, not even the fake ones. She thinks it's safer that way. No real names, and no speaking about the group to outsiders; those are two of their rules. With the stuff they do, secrecy is essential. The penalty for breaking a rule is severe.

It's Jedx. Footage from Aldwych is aces and getting a great reaction. Sass – how are you? Come explore with us tomorrow. We missed you!

She stares at the group message. Wonders if *he* misses her. She thought he'd have messaged her privately before now. It could be that when she said she was done, he thought that meant they were over, as well.

Beaker: Yeah you have to be with us tomorrow night Sass.
We need you!

It's tempting, she loves exploring with the guys, but after Saturday it feels wrong. How could they seem so oblivious to it?

Sass: Maybe.

Jedx: You know the plan is to do this place . . .

Jedx: [click link to view map]

She knows the location. It's a new-build behind the façade of an old building, bang in the middle of town. It's still under construction, so a real challenge to access, but if they're successful it could be a fascinating photography subject.

Sass: I want to, but I still think we should go to the police about Hendleton.

She takes a gulp of her wine and stares at the phone, waiting for one of the guys to reply. She can see from the three round icons alongside her message that Jedx, Beaker and Cap have all read it. It's odd Cap's not getting involved in the conversation, but maybe he's with his kids, he often doesn't answer then.

'You OK?' Ellie's voice beside her makes her jump.

Sass turns. Ellie's smiling, her eyes are over-bright from the wine they've already drunk, and her often haughty tone is softer, uncharacteristically kind. Sass nods. 'Yeah, I just . . .' She can't tell her what she's doing. Ellie might act like your best friend, but she hates not to be the centre of things. Angling her phone so Ellie can't see the screen, she says, 'One of my friends is having a crisis.'

Ellie smiles sympathetically. 'One of them? Tell me about it. I have a friend who's a total drama addict. Drives me crazy.' She picks up the bottle. 'Look, I'll carry this back to the table, and keep the troops happy. See you when you're done.'

Sass forces a smile. 'Thanks.'

She turns away from Ellie and looks back at the chat thread.

Beaker: We can't. I don't want a criminal record, OK? It'll bugger us up for life – our jobs, everything – we'll all be totally screwed.

Sass pauses, her finger hovering over the phone as she thinks about what Beaker's said. If she gets charged, she'll lose her job. It happened to one of the other PRs a few months back after they'd been convicted of being drunk and disorderly. Breaking and entering was way more serious. Shit. Maybe Beaker *is* right. Perhaps she should sleep on it, think everything through when she's sober. Things always seem worse when she's had a drink. Yes, she decides. That's what I'll do. I'll think about it in the morning.

Sass: OK. Assume I'll be there tomorrow.

Dropping the phone back into her bag, she takes another big gulp of wine and heads back towards her colleagues. The room seems out of focus and she blinks a few times to clear her vision. The step is higher than she remembers and she catches her toe and stumbles, only just managing not to drop her wine. She giggles as she slides back onto the bench seat beside Ellie. As Ellie drapes her arm around her, Sass starts to feel more relaxed.

At last, the wine seems to be kicking in.

16

CLEMENTINE

I am loitering with intent. Leaning against a wall next to a bus stop around the back of Earls Court. My chin's tucked into my scarf, my beanie hat pulled low over my fringe. It's freezing cold and six buses have come along in the time I've been here. But I'm not waiting for a bus.

In the inner pocket of my parka I have my mobile phone with the urban explorer video downloaded. Across the street in front of me is Dominic Bell's apartment building. It's one of those modern ones, all pale brick cladding and glass. I've been here before. I know what floor he lives on and the number of his flat. I know he has a small feline called Black Cat, but otherwise lives alone. I could go to the intercom and buzz him right now, but something is making me hesitate.

I never used to hesitate. When I was numb I did what I wanted in any given moment, not thinking about the consequences of my actions. Not caring either, because nothing really mattered anyway. Right now, though, this matters.

I want Dom to listen to me. I need him to see the video.

Taking out my phone, I dial his number. It rings twice unanswered before he picks up on my third attempt.

'Dom?'

He doesn't speak, but I can hear him breathing.

I grip the phone tighter. 'I know you're there. I need to see you.'

'Not a good idea.'

'I have something you need to—'

'I can't do this again, Clementine.' His voice breaks as he says my name. 'I'm sorry.'

'But it's been six weeks.' After the few weeks we'd been close, following what happened with the Lover, Dom had pulled away from me. The two of us had been sitting opposite each other at one of the metal café tables outside Coffee Bean in Clerkenwell. Dom was drinking espresso, I had a green tea. I was laughing, talking about the strangeness of our relationship; how it was something different to the norm, because it had been forged through shared trauma. I was struggling to define it, saying that it wasn't purely friendly, yet it wasn't sexual either. It was when I called us symbiotic that Dom had freaked. The way he acted threw me. I tried to make him see that he needed me; that I would always be there for him. But he pushed me away and I got upset, then angry. I flung the cold dregs of my tea at him. Made a scene. 'You said you needed space, isn't six weeks long enough?'

He sighs. 'I can't do this. You're too intense. It's exhausting.'

'But, I need to—'

The call disconnects and he's gone.

I stare at the phone. My hands are trembling.

Whether he likes it or not, we have a connection, Dom and I. He held me, naked and shaking, as the drugs the killer had given me forced my body into shock. Dom has seen me at my most vulnerable *and* my most powerful. He has seen *me*, the real me. He's the only person who has seen me as I truly am.

His words repeat in my mind. He thinks that I'm too intense. I am too much for him.

Emotion surges through me making me breathless. I put a hand on the wall to steady myself and focus on the coldness of the brick, the roughness of the texture; anything to stop myself thinking about Dom. It takes a minute to get myself under control. As soon as I do, the urge to flee is overwhelming.

Turning to leave, I shove my phone back in my pocket then halt as I remember the urban explorer's video. That look of terror on Jedx's face as he stared into the fractured lens of the camera; it means something. I can't let this go. Dom has to see it.

I exhale and my breath clouds around me, mingling with the freezing night air. I can't take no for an answer. I look up at Dom's apartment building and step towards the road. Push my hands deeper into my pockets and rehearse my next moves in my mind.

Go to the building.

Press the intercom.

It's right there. Do it now.

17
DOM

After Clementine's call, he tries to block out all thoughts of her. He just can't handle talking to her; she's so dramatic, far too intense. It does his head in. When the buzzer goes the first time he hopes it's just kids mucking around, but the second blast is longer and more insistent somehow, so he moves Black Cat off his lap and onto the couch and gets up to answer it. 'Yeah?'

'It's me.'

Fuck. The voice of someone he's not seen in a while. Not the voice of someone he's wanted to see. 'What do you want?'

There's a pause, followed by a tight laugh. 'Are we really going to have this conversation through the intercom?'

He thinks for a moment, his finger hovering on the door release. He'd rather not have the conversation at all, but now that she's here he supposes he should let her in. They were close once. He'd thought that he loved her. 'All right, come up.'

His kitchen seems too small for the two of them, but Dom doesn't want to take Therese into the lounge. He'd half thought it might be Clementine ringing the buzzer, trying again to force him to talk to her, and feels oddly disappointed that it wasn't. Tense too, because the last thing he needs is Therese coming back into his life. He doesn't want her getting too comfortable and staying long. As soon as she stepped inside the flat, he regretted letting her in. He's pissed off she's here. It feels like an intrusion. Still, he attempts to be civil. 'You want a drink?'

Therese props herself against the counter by the cooker. Smiles. 'Sure.'

'What, then? Coffee? Whiskey? I've got some mango juice in the fridge I—'

'Whiskey. You remember how I take it?'

He nods. He knows. He remembers a lot of things from when they were together. Taking the whiskey from the cupboard beside the sink, he pours generous measures into two glasses, tops hers up with a splash of water, and adds Diet Coke to his. He hands her a glass. 'So, what's this about?'

'Can't it just be that I wanted to see you?'

'Is it?'

Therese shakes her head. 'Same old Dom. Always so suspicious.'

He takes a sip of his whiskey. It's been two months since he last saw her. She'd just been discharged from the hospital after getting shot during the Operation Atlantis raid. She'd looked pale and far too skinny. Now she seems her usual self again – her dirty blonde hair cascades around her shoulders, her skin has a slight tan to it, even though it's winter, her eyes are as beautiful and mischievous as ever. The short black jersey dress she's wearing under her leather jacket shows her athletic figure is back in shape, too.

She catches him checking her out and smiles again. 'It's been too long.'

Dom looks away. Doesn't want to get sucked back into anything. 'So why did you want to see me?'

'I miss you.'

'Yeah?' He'd like to believe it, but he can't, not now he knows she'd been off shagging behind his back. 'Last time I saw you it was pretty clear you'd moved on.'

She takes a gulp of her whiskey. Changes tack. 'Have you heard anything about the IPCC investigation?'

'Like what?' Dom keeps his tone unhurried. Watches Therese's reactions. 'As far as I know it's still ongoing.'

'I heard a rumour they'd found something. New evidence.'

Dom shrugs. Trying to act casual even though his heartbeat's racing. 'Who said?'

She waves the question away with her hand. 'I thought if anyone knew, it'd be you. Holsworth updates Jackson, doesn't he? And you and Jackson are tight – you've always been like the son he never had.'

Dom doesn't deny it. His own dad died when he was fresh into the force, and his mum took her life soon after. Jackson knew how tough it'd been for him; suddenly becoming the breadwinner and taking on responsibility for his younger sister, Chrissie, who'd been a wayward teen at the time. The DCI mentored him and, in many ways, became a surrogate father. 'Why the interest? We'll know when they've got something concrete.'

Therese plays with the diamond pedant around her neck, pulling it back and forth along the chain. 'I'm just impatient, that's all. Whoever tipped off Genk that night blew the operation and got me shot. It's not too much for me to expect that they get what they deserve, is it?'

Dom holds her gaze, trying to get a read on her. 'I guess not.'

She exhales hard. 'You still think I was involved somehow, don't you?'

Maybe, Dom thinks. 'What do I know? I got knocked out, remember?'

'But you look at me differently now. You don't trust me any more.' She keeps staring at him. 'That hurts, you know.'

Dom downs the rest of his whiskey. Sets the glass back on the counter with a bang. 'I think you should go.'

'So soon?' She moves closer to him. Puts her free hand on his chest and looks up at him in that seductive way of hers that always gets him going. 'Why can't you trust me, Dom? We were good together, weren't we?'

Dom clenches his fists. They had been good together. He'd thought they had something special. He'd told her he loved her, and she'd brushed away his feelings like they were nothing. Said what they had was just a bit of fun. He glares at her. 'You still fucking Lindsay?'

Therese steps away from him. Pouts. 'Don't cheapen this. You're better than that.'

'Yes, I am. I'm not the one who shagged around.'

'But you are the one acting like a child.' She shakes her head, her expression sad. 'I stopped seeing him after that time you found us together. I haven't seen him since, and I don't want to. But you . . . I miss *you*, Dom.'

He holds her gaze. 'You knew how I felt. You made your choice.'

Therese exhales softly. Putting her empty glass in the sink, she turns to leave. Glancing back at him she says, 'You know, everyone makes mistakes.'

Yeah, thinks Dom, as he shuts the door behind her. Especially me.

18

CLEMENTINE

She beat me to it; walked right past but didn't see me. I recognised her – the dirty blonde hair and angular features. She's the one Dom said had been injured in the police operation they'd partnered on. The one who he told me had been more than just a friend.

The woman reappears in less than thirty minutes. On the surface, I'm frozen. My cheeks are numb, my fingers and toes feel rigid and brittle. Inside though, the jealousy burns blisteringly hot, intensifying with every glimpse of her. Engulfing me from within. It's in danger of getting out of hand, this rage, and I wonder if I will be able to control it.

And so I follow her.

The pavements are busy, which makes them the perfect place to hide. In London on a cold night like this, everyone is walking briskly, heads down, focused on getting home or to wherever they're going for the evening. No one so much as glances at the people right beside them. She is the same, more interested in what's on her phone than where she's walking. I use that to my advantage.

We walk. Miles, I think. Her steps are purposeful, brisk and rhythmic. She has a destination in mind and what started as my urgent need to calm the feelings boiling up inside me, becomes focused on finding out where her purposeful steps are taking her. I want to see where she's going. So I allow her to stay a whisker in front, a half step. I like that I'm getting close to her. Enjoy that she's unsuspecting. As I walk, the rage and jealousy changes into something else, something more pleasurable – the thrill of the chase.

And then, she's gone; disappeared into a pub, the Black Horse. I frown as I recognise the name. Before, when Dom was still talking to me, he told me he often used to drink after work with his colleagues. There were two pubs they'd go to. One was the Princess Victoria. The other was a place called the Black Horse. This time I don't hesitate. I push open the heavy door and step inside.

It's a traditional pub that's been badly modernised. The wood panelling has been painted yellow, the smoked glass overwritten with pseudo-literary quotations. I notice one from Yeats has the wrong wording, and I try not to let it irritate me. No one else seems to care, too busy with their pints and shouty conversations.

The woman now stands across the bar from me, beside a table in the far corner where two men are seated on mismatched chairs. The blond, in an armchair, faces the door, while the dark-haired one on a stool has his back to it. I wonder who they are, and how she knows them. I move to the bar for a better view.

'Gin and soda,' I say to the barman.

He fixes my drink with a quick efficiency born of repetition, places it in front of me and takes the cash, then moves on to the next customer. The space around the bar is busy, and I'm too far from the corner table to hear what's going on. I wait until the woman takes a seat with the men, then carry my drink across to a table two away from them, sitting down without a further glance in their direction.

At the table next to me a man and woman sit in silence. His eyes are on the television screen on the wall where there's football playing with the sound muted. She just looks bored. I pity her, but the apathy of their relationship is perfect for my purposes. Getting out my phone, I pretend to take a picture of my drink as I listen in on the conversation at the corner table. The woman I've been following doesn't sound happy.

'He was evasive, defensive. He kicked me out.'

The dark-haired man squirms on his stool. I can't see his face, but his shoulders are tense and high, his back muscles rigid. 'I knew this wouldn't work—'

'He knows something.' My target picks up the blond man's pint and takes a gulp. 'He thinks he's good at masking his reactions, but I saw it on his face when I asked him. The rumours are true, there's new evidence.'

'If he knows, why didn't he tell you?' The blond man sounds authoritative, as though he's the one in charge. I sneak a glance. He's classically attractive but his pale eyes are cold, hard. I sense the ruthless spirit of a predator.

'Because he doesn't trust me any more, he suspects me.' She gestures towards the two men. 'All of us probably.'

'He's not bothered about you.' The dark-haired man shakes his head. 'It's me he's avoided since it all happened. He suspects *me*. Probably told the IPCC as much. I don't bloody blame him.'

The blond glares at the other man. He reaches out and clasps his shoulder. 'Don't bottle it now, or things won't end well for you.'

The dark-haired man recoils, but the blond keeps hold, his knuckles whitening as he increases the pressure on the guy's shoulder.

The woman gives the blond man a warning look. 'Simon, don't.'

He ignores her and moves closer to the dark-haired guy. 'You don't get to just walk away.'

The dark-haired man shoves his stool back, yanking away from the other man's grip. 'Don't threaten me. It's because of you I'm in this—'

'Keep your shit together, or . . .' The blond gives a shake of his head. He looks like he's about to square up to the guy, the lanyard and ID card around his neck swings forward and I catch sight of the name beneath his photo: Simon Lindsay.

The woman puts her hand on Lindsay's arm. 'Leave it.'

'And don't you just sit there like it's nothing to do with you. You're worse than him,' the dark-haired man points at the woman, his voice rising in pitch and volume. People are starting to stare, sensing a fight could be in the offing. 'You used me. Now you're trying to use Dom, too.'

The woman fixes the dark-haired man with a hard stare. 'Calm down, you're causing a scene.'

'A scene? You're worried about a scene? I'm going to hang because of you, because of following *orders* – my career is over! And, what, now you're threatening me because I don't want to lie about—'

She moves fast. I'm as surprised as the dark-haired man when she slaps him. His hand flies to his cheek as he recoils from her. His mouth opens, and it looks as if he's going to say more, but then he changes his mind. As he turns, I see the shock on his face turn to anger. Shaking his head, he walks away.

Simon Lindsay and the woman watch him go.

Fifteen minutes later. Outside, in the alleyway behind the pub, they are fucking; the blond man – Lindsay – and the woman. It's drizzling now, but it's still so cold it feels as if it could turn to snow. They are oblivious. Shoved up against the back wall of the pub, hidden by the almost darkness, they are frantic, animal. Gropes and thrusts. Grunts and gasps. Her dress hitched up over her hips, his trousers pulled down just far enough.

Not interested in watching them for a voyeuristic thrill, I turn away. I hide in the shadows, behind the industrial rubbish bins that shield me, and wait for them to finish.

I hear him groan her name as he comes. 'Therese.'

As their panting subsides, the thoughts and questions whirr inside my head. They're trying to cover something up and manipulate Dom, and I feel the anger building in me. I cannot let them do that. They're dirty, just like the coppers who framed and murdered my father. I have to fight against them, for my father and for Dom. Dirty coppers have to be taken down. Narrowing my gaze, I watch her smooth her dress as the blond man zips himself up. I crouch lower, staying cloaked by the shadows as Therese struts past my hiding place. She's so wrapped up in Lindsay that she is oblivious to me.

I think of Dom, and the hurt behind his eyes when he spoke of his relationship with this woman. I won't let her hurt him again.

TUESDAY

19

DOM

Chrissie's text had surprised him, her request to meet even more so. Now he's perching on a high stool at one of the long benches in Starbucks, waiting. Nervous. Bleary-eyed after another sleepless night; images of blood sprayed across the tube platform, that ceremonial dagger, the memory of Therese's visit, and the ever-present struggle to keep Clementine at arm's length, refusing to rest easy in his mind. He's irritated at himself for feeling nervous about meeting his own sister.

A woman in a violet tweed skirt suit puts her coffee and handbag on the table and gets up onto the stool next to him. Her hair is swept back into a chignon, and her skin has the sort of shiny aura only perfectly applied make-up can give. Beside her, he feels even more dishevelled.

All around him there's chatter; commuters grabbing coffees to go, people meeting for breakfast. Sometimes he wishes he could mute London, the noise and the people. It grinds you down and wears you out. He feels nearer fifty than forty. The city ages you. He shakes his head. No. It's the job that ages you.

'Dom.'

He looks round, and there she is. Her brown curls have grown long and been tamed into soft waves. The sweep of freckles across her nose makes her look younger than mid-twenties. He feels the instinctive need to protect her, as he's always done. 'Chrissie, I . . . can I get you a coffee?'

'No, it's OK. I'm not staying long.'

He frowns. Unsure what to say next.

She remains standing. 'I don't . . . I haven't forgiven you.'

Dom glances at the woman in the violet tweed. She's pretending not to listen but he knows that she is. He looks back at Chrissie. 'Then why did you want to meet?'

She exhales. 'Darren heard a rumour from one of the old team about there being a break in the IPCC investigation. I thought you might know something about it.'

Dom clenches his jaw and wishes he could tell her the truth, but remembers Jackson's warning and knows that he can't. 'Sorry, I don't.'

Chrissie shakes her head. Gives a sad smile. 'You're lying, bro. I can always tell. You've got no kind of poker face with me.'

'I'm . . .' He hates lying to her. Can't do it. 'Look, I'm not able to say. I wish I could, but I just can't.'

Her eyes dart side to side, searching his face for information. 'Is it bad? About Darren?'

He looks away. Says nothing. The noise of the coffee shop seems to crescendo around him.

'Oh shit. It is, isn't it?' Chrissie's voice is low, panicked. 'You have to tell me. We're family, and Darren's a good man, he'd never do anything to hurt us.' She clutches her hand to her chest. 'I know he didn't jeopardise that operation.'

There's something in her expression that Dom can't read. It's not just that she's upset with him for being evasive about the new evidence in the Operation Atlantis investigation, there's something else. He puts his hand on her arm. 'Are you OK, sis?'

'He's clean, all right?' There's a tremble in her voice. 'I know he isn't dirty.'

'But?'

She curls a strand of her hair around her index finger, winding it tighter. 'Something's different. I know he's on suspension, and that's stressful. And he feels betrayed by you. *I* feel betrayed by you. I mean it's your witness statement that put him in the thick of the action when he was never inside that building. *You're* the reason he got suspended.'

Dom knows it's true. He has no words. He'd reported what he saw in good faith, but also knowing the 'truth' wasn't what he'd seen.

'But he's different now, more anxious, and it's getting worse. Recently there have been these calls to his mobile. Darren doesn't

96

answer if I'm in the room, but sometimes I walk in on him and he's on the phone talking in whispers. He always hangs up when he sees me but it's like . . .'

'What?'

She frowns. Thinking a moment. Finding the words. 'It's like he's afraid of someone.'

20

CLEMENTINE

When David called earlier inviting me to meet him and one of the urban explorers at Costa Coffee, this isn't how I envisaged things going. It began normally enough, with us standing in line to be served. But that was because he waited until the woman had got her coffee before accosting her. It's obvious that he didn't set up a meeting, he just knew where to find her. Now she's glaring at me. She's about my age, with shoulder-length blonde hair. Her expression is anger mixed with fear. 'What do you want from me?'

I glance at David. He's beetroot red and visibly sweating.

'I asked you a question.' She's staring at David. Shaking her head. 'How did you know I'd be here? How do you know my name?'

David looks panicked. 'I . . . I . . .'

'I've seen you in here before. Were you following me?' She starts gesticulating at him, her voice rising. 'Are you some kind of stalker?'

This isn't good. She's drawing attention to us. The shop is rammed with pre-work coffee buyers. People are staring. It's only a matter of time before someone recognises me. I step towards the woman. Keep my voice calm. 'Sass? It's OK. He's here because of me. I wanted to meet you, your urbexing group, actually. I'm a researcher at the university and I'm studying—'

'I'm not interested.' She holds her hand up, palm out, to stop me. 'How do you know my name?'

'Dink told me.' David's voice is hesitant but clear. 'Said you'd be here.'

The colour drains from her face. 'Dink? How did . . .'

I don't know what's going on here, but I sense that whatever it is will interest me. I gesture for David to give us some privacy, and he moves to a table. 'Tell me about Dink.'

'I can't.' The woman looks like she's about to bolt. 'I can't talk to anyone about anything. It's against the rules.'

I hold my ground. 'Not even about the Hendleton video and what really happened?'

'Our identities are meant to be secret.' Swearing under her breath, she grabs my arm and drags me out of the crowd to the side of the shop. 'What the hell do you know about that?'

'Enough.'

Up close, she looks pale and hungover. Her eyes are bloodshot and even the thick layer of foundation she's wearing can't disguise the dark patches beneath them. 'You saw her?'

I nod. Don't say anything. Sass must think the video shows more than it does – a woman – and I want to know more. I hold her gaze, waiting to see what she says next.

Her lower lip starts to tremble. 'She's dead, isn't she? I told the others we shouldn't have run. I *told* them. Are you going to report us?'

I don't answer. Instead I extract my arm from her grip. 'As I told you, I'm a researcher at the university – Clementine Starke, you might have heard of me?'

She stares at me for a long moment. 'The true-crime specialist? The one who solved a murder?'

Close enough. 'Yes.'

Sass glances towards the door, a panicked expression on her face. 'Oh God, you *are* going to tell the police, aren't you? I never meant . . . I didn't know what to do. We were just exploring, right? Not prepared for finding . . . that. The place had been empty forty years. It *should* have been empty.'

I was right. It doesn't sound like the video was a hoax, Sass believes she saw a murdered woman. I have to know more. 'So why didn't you report it?'

She glances at the people around us and shakes her head. Turning, she moves to a table, beckons me to follow. She leans close to me, her voice hushed. 'The rules mean we only share video. We keep our identities secret, nothing can connect to our real lives.'

'Not even murder?'

Sass flinches at the word. 'It sounds ridiculous, I know, but going to the police has to be a group decision. We have a responsibility to each other – what we do is illegal, if we're charged with breaking and entering we could all lose our jobs.'

Her loyalty to the group is impressive. She's able to justify not reporting a possible murder because they don't want to deal with the consequences. Her level of psychological compartmentalising both fascinates and horrifies me. I need to gain her trust, get her to confide in me more, and find out exactly what she saw at Hendleton. 'So why do it?'

She glances from me to David, checking that he's still out of earshot. Keeps her voice low. 'It's like society wants to make us compliant. We're all forced into being the same. Wear the same fashions, like the same bars. Exploring is different. It's unique.'

'Yet on your videos you use fake names, and keep your real identity secret?'

'Part of what makes the experience special is that it's secret.'

'Is that part of the thrill?'

'Exploring isn't about thrills, not for me. It's about going into forgotten places, buildings stuck in time, and capturing their beauty as they evolve.'

I don't want to talk about beauty. I want to know more about the woman Sass thinks could be dead. But I have to build rapport, keep the conversation flowing, so I can lead Sass to fully open up. 'Tell me how you feel as you enter a new place.'

'Excited. Nervous. Sometimes the anticipation is so strong I feel a little bit sick.'

'They're all feelings associated with heightened adrenaline. A buzz, in other words.'

She takes a sip of her coffee as she considers my words. Nods. 'I get a buzz from it, yes. Stepping inside places no one's been for many years gives me a kick. I love seeing the way time has changed them, and photographing those changes. I'm always in awe of the power of nature to reclaim spaces, the way the organic mixes with the man-made. It's like a kind of sympathetic magic.'

'Is that how your explorer friends see it?'

She frowns. 'Most of them.'

'But not all?'

'No.'

'Does that create friction in the group?'

'Not really.'

'So there is some friction?'

'Occasionally, I . . . look, it's more that you need to know your own limitations. Some people can be a bit "I'm invincible" once they've done a few explorations and they think it's time to start hanging off high buildings or whatever. That doesn't help the group. To stay safe, you need to be able to rely on your partners. If they lie and make out they're cool with something – tight, dark spaces for example – it can be a problem. You don't want to be four hundred metres into a cave system or tunnel only for them to have a panic attack.'

'Has that happened to you?'

'I don't go into tunnels, it's not my thing.'

'You didn't answer my question.'

'I know.'

I sense she's going to pull away and I know I have to circle back to the key question. I hope the connection I've built with her is strong enough. 'Are you going to report what you saw on that sound-stage?'

Sass holds my gaze. Shakes her head as she stands. 'The others say there's no point. She was already dead, reporting it won't bring her back. I have to abide by the group decision otherwise it's all over.'

I watch her leave, coffee in hand, slightly unsteady on her feet. I don't try to stop her. Reaching into my pocket, I tap stop on my phone's voice recording app. David was too far away to hear what she said, but I heard and now I know. The video wasn't a hoax or a fake; to Sass it was very real.

She believes she witnessed a murder.

21

DOM

Abbott's hunched over his desk, eating a bacon sandwich and typing things into Google when Dom arrives. Ignoring him, Dom throws his jacket over the back of his chair, and picks up his mug, ready to go and make a coffee. The conversation with Chrissie is weighing heavy on his mind.

There's a Post-it note stuck to his computer screen. Peeling it off, Dom reads the message: *Thomas Lee PM this afternoon, prob late.*

He looks across the desks at Abbott. Holds up the sticky. 'You took this call?'

'Yeah. They phoned about an hour ago.'

'All right, cheers.'

'Guv, I think I've found the origins of the dagger.'

Dom frowns. 'Didn't I ask Parekh to follow that up?'

Abbott looks embarrassed. 'Yeah, but I was here early and I thought—'

'So what did you find?'

Abbott angles the computer screen so Dom can see it. The window is open on the IMDb film website. He points to an image of a film poster. '*Death by a Thousand Daggers*. It was made back in the seventies but has something of a cult following with classic horror buffs.'

'How does it relate to our case?'

'OK, I did an internet image search using that new piece of software we've got, and it came back with a strong match. The dagger you found almost exactly matches the style of those used in the film. The markings along the handle are identical.' Abbott toggles to another window, opens an image of a dagger. 'This is one of the film's original daggers. It's a prop, obviously, so made of hardened rubber, and not dangerous. They sell on eBay for good money these days.'

'They?'

'Apparently there were a lot of them made for the film.' He grins. 'I mean, the clue's in the title, isn't it?'

Dom just looks at him. Doesn't smile.

'Anyway, the dagger you found in the tunnel can't be an original from the film – it's real not fake – but if you put the two images side by side it definitely looks like a copy. The design of the daggers was created especially for the movie, apparently.'

'So what are you implying?'

'Nothing at the moment. It could be a coincidence, or it could be linked. I need to do some more digging.'

Dom nods. It's good work, but he can't bring himself to praise Abbott. Seeing Therese last night has convinced him he needs to clear the decks, get rid of the people around him who've abused his trust. He's got evidence of what Abbott did, and he's let it slide for too long. 'I need a word. Let's use the box.'

The box is a small office in the corner of the open plan, a space for impromptu meetings, just like this one. It's not popular, though, because the seal along the large window on the outside wall is dodgy, so there's one hell of a draught. As a result, it's usually not in use. Dom opens the door, and they go inside. It's much colder in here than in the open plan. Outside, the rain is getting heavier, battering against the window like it wants to break the glass and force its way inside.

They stay standing, facing each other. Abbott looks stressed; a muscle above his left eye is twitching.

It's time.

'You've been playing away. Selling information.' Dom takes the printed emails from his jacket pocket. They show the exchanges between Abbott and Glen Eastman, the journalist who got close to the serial killer in their last case and ended up being one of his victims. They detail not only the confidential case facts Abbott revealed to him, that put him in the serial killer's path, but the money that exchanged hands, too. 'You as good as got Eastman killed.'

Abbott bows his head. Takes the emails but doesn't look at them. 'Shit. I . . . I fucked up.'

'Yeah, royally.'

His DS stays silent, mouth set in a thin line.

Dom's voice is gruff. 'Why did you do it?'

Abbott exhales hard. 'Money. Stress. Without my wife's income, we're barely able to manage the basics. Babies are so damn expensive, childcare's a nightmare. I didn't want to worry her. I had to do something, and then Eastman approached me. The first time it seemed like such a small thing, just one name that didn't even link to our lines of inquiry. It got worse, of course, he wanted more. Threatened to name me as a source if I didn't keep playing along.' He shakes his head. 'I just didn't want to lose the house.'

What a mess. Dom rubs his forehead. He feels the slight depression where his skull absorbed the force of a baseball bat during Operation Atlantis. The old injury is beginning to throb.

'You should report me,' Abbott says.

'Yeah, I should.'

They stand in silence. Rain pours down the window like heavy tears.

Abbott glances at Dom. 'What will you do?'

He'd got it all planned out before; confront Abbott, then report him to Jackson. He'd expected denial, anger, perhaps a bit of coercion to try and get him to stay quiet. Not this sad acceptance, this fatalistic lack of anything. It seems as if Abbott's given up. He looks deflated, like there's no fight left in him.

Dom turns away and opens the door. 'I don't bloody know, mate.'

Back in the open plan, Dom strides to his desk and grabs his mug. Parekh's arrived and is switching on her computer. He nods good morning but keeps walking to the kitchen. Doesn't want to talk right now. Needs to get his head straight.

As he's spooning coffee into his mug, his mobile rings. He checks the screen: *Darren Harris* and curses under his breath. He doesn't want to speak to Darren either. He'll only try to guilt him into giving details of the new evidence in the IPCC investigation. Staring at the phone, he lets it ring until Darren eventually hangs up, then puts in back in his pocket and makes his coffee.

'Go on, be a gentleman.'

Dom turns, and sees Parekh standing behind him. Smiling, she holds out her mug. 'Strong, with a touch of sugar please, boss.'

'Sure.' He takes the purple mug and does as she asks. 'Where are you up to?'

'Well, Abbott's taken the dagger line of inquiry, and will chase the financials, so I'm going to follow up with the contacts on Lee's phone – see if he had plans with anyone the night we know he was in Aldwych station.'

'OK, good.' Dom hands her the coffee. 'And pull any street level CCTV around Aldwych. Let's see if we can catch him on camera before he broke in.'

'Will do.'

As he follows Parekh back to their bank of desks, his phone vibrates. Pulling it out, he sees it's Darren again, this time a text: We need to talk. Call me?

Damn, he's persistent. As he stares at the message, Chrissie's worries about Darren's erratic behaviour come back to him and he wonders, could Darren actually be the one, not Lindsay?

Taking a gulp of coffee, Dom deletes the message. He doesn't want to talk to Darren. Let Holsworth and the IPCC find the truth. Until then he wants nothing to do with any of his old colleagues. He glances across the desk at Abbott. Shakes his head. There's only so much shit he can handle. And then there's Clementine, but at least he's been able to cut himself off from her. He can't get mixed up in that emotional nightmare again.

22

CLEMENTINE

I'm in the faculty office but my mind is elsewhere. I messaged Dom as soon as I left the coffee shop, but I still haven't heard back. I have to get hold of him, there's so much to tell him. He needs to hear me out. He has to know how his ex-colleagues were plotting against him after that woman, Therese, went to his flat. And the urban explorers' video could give a glimpse of a murderer's kill room. I can't sit by and let a victim lie undiscovered. They have a right to justice. A right to have their story pieced back together. A right to have the puzzle of their death solved.

As I'm thinking about my next move, an instant message from Wade appears in the bottom right corner of my screen: We need to talk.

I ignore it, and am careful not to look over the divider at him. If Dom isn't responding to my messages, I think the best way to get his attention is with the video. Opening my email, I type a short note:

Subject: Murder!
Look, Dom, I know you don't want to see me, but this is important. I think there's been a murder. Watch this video and see
for yourself, then call me. I've spoken to one of the people who
was there. You have to investigate this. Cx

I cut and paste the video link from David's earlier email, and press send. As I do, another instant message pings onto my screen:
Clementine?

I type a reply: I'm busy.

In my peripheral vision I see Wade staring at me across the desk. I don't want to talk right now, so I keep my gaze on my screen and hope he'll get the hint. The office is almost empty, only one of our colleagues is at their desk. Sitting next to Wade,

Brian Clapperton is an earnest senior lecturer with an impressive beard. I know Wade won't speak openly while Brian is within earshot.

A message appears in my inbox; my email to Dom has been returned undelivered. That's strange. I copy it and resend. Again, it bounces back.

This has never happened when I've emailed him before. I don't understand why it's doing so now. I type Dom's details into Google and find him listed on the Metropolitan Police's website. I compare his email address against the one I've used and, just as I thought, they match.

I check my phone. The iMessage I sent him earlier hasn't been read but it's turned from blue to green – meaning it's been sent as a text rather than a message. That's never happened before either. A terrible thought comes to mind.

Opening another window in my browser, I type '*How to know you've been blocked*' into the search engine. My stomach flips as I read the list.

Your email will bounce back undeliverable.

Phone calls will ring once then divert to voicemail.

Texts will appear to deliver but will not be read. iMessages will fail to send, then resend as texts. They will show as delivered but not read.

Papery moth wings flutter in my throat. So far, I have had two of the three happen, I need to try the third.

Dialling Dom's number, I hold my breath. It rings once and goes to voicemail. The moths swarm in my throat, their sharp wing edges slashing at my flesh.

He has blocked me. Deleted me from his life.

I toggle back to my Google search for him and click on one of the images. Sitting as still as a statue, I grip the seat of my chair tightly, my hands clawed, and stare at Dom's picture. He's forcing me away. Discarding me like I'm nothing and I won't stand for it. He needs me, and I will make him see that. I bite my lip. Tell myself this is temporary, that I'll make him see sense. But still I can't stop howling inside.

I hear the office door bang shut. Looking up, I see Brian's chair is empty.

'Clementine?'

Reluctantly, I turn and meet Wade's gaze.

He holds up a piece of paper. 'We need to talk about the conference invitation.'

'I'm working right now.'

He looks at my screen. 'That's not work, it's the bloody detective.'

I don't respond.

'The last time you got close to him you were lucky to escape without a criminal record. If he found out what you did to get information on the Lover, he'd . . .'

Wade is referring to when I broke into a crime scene. I found important evidence the police had missed, and I'd do it again. I turn in my chair. Keep my voice low like a growl. 'Don't try to threaten me.'

'I wasn't.'

'You were and you shouldn't.'

We glare at each other. It feels as if there are sparks igniting the air between us, setting flames running up my arms, over the scars from the skin grafts. Wade wants me, I can see it in his gaze, feel it in the energy between us. After Dom blocking me, rejecting me, the strength of Wade's desire is alluring.

He shakes his head. 'I'm worried for you, Clementine. You get so obsessive, it's not healthy. Is this detective your latest infatuation?'

'I'm not infatuated with him.'

'You need to focus on *our* partnership.' Wade brandishes the conference invitation for HUMTEC at me like a weapon. 'We should accept this. You know it makes sense.'

'OK.' I close the window and Dom's picture disappears. I understand that Wade's jealous. I know he's angry because he feels shut out by me, but I cannot tell him the truth, how these emotions collide inside me until it feels as if they might rip me apart. Wade is only about logic, he could never understand. I lower my lashes, then look up at him. 'I don't want an argument.'

His breath catches in his throat. 'What do you want?'

To be desired, to forget Dom's rejection, and get lost for a moment in the dramatic high of a lustful climax. That's what I want. There's no one else here in the office, and I can use that to my advantage.

Smiling, I take Wade's hand and lead him towards the photo-copying room.

23

DOM

The day drags on, bringing no new breakthroughs. Pulling out his phone, Dom looks at the main social media sites. Speculation about Thomas Lee's death has died off on Twitter. New hashtags are trending – yesterday's news forgotten in the thirst for more incidents to sensationalise – a child abduction out in the sticks somewhere, a gang-related shooting over in east London. Dom just doesn't get it, the way these tweeters treat death and tragedy like it's the latest craze, their theories and conspiracy rumours spreading like wildfire. These days public opinion broadcast in 280 characters seems to have more validity than facts.

It makes him think of Clementine, made a social media star overnight for her role in stopping the Lover. He wonders what her take on Thomas Lee's death would be. On impulse, he taps out a message to her, then immediately deletes it, unsent. He can't get back in contact. It'll all start again if he does. She's too impulsive, and unpredictable. Her obsession with him is more than borderline unhealthy.

Guilt hits him in the chest. Because unhealthy as it was, he enjoyed her company, at least at first. He hates to admit it, but a part of him misses her. He thrusts his phone into his pocket and shakes the thoughts of her away. He needs to focus on the case.

'Guv? I've got something.' Abbott's voice is animated, excited. 'I think I could have found the origin of the dagger.'

He looks across the desk at the sergeant. 'Where?'

'I was searching online and I found an image of an exact replica of ours, posted by a guy who specialises in recreating props from films and television – swords, daggers and the like – in metal.' He taps the screen, on the picture of the dagger. 'It's listed as sold.'

'Address?'

Abbott nods. Scribbles it onto his notepad. 'Scorpion, on Camden High Street, so not far.'

Grim-faced, Dom stands and grabs his coat. He's still thinking about what to do with Abbott. He'd rather not work one-to-one with him right now, but the lead is his so this time it's unavoidable. 'Come on then. Let's see what they have to say.'

The shop's easy enough to spot. Several hundred model scorpions are fixed to its mustard-coloured façade making it look like they're swarming over the outside of the building. The name 'Scorpion' is emblazoned in silver capitals across the black awning below.

Making their way past the racks of T-shirts featuring old film posters, Dom and Abbott duck beneath hanging mobiles of skeletons and skulls, and continue through the shop. Glass cases house memorabilia covering tastes from Betty Boop to the *Scream* films. On top of them jewellery and talismans are displayed on black velvet boards decorated with feathers. The tall bookshelves around the walls are crammed with second-hand books and graphic novels. The place smells musty, with an undertone of leather and weed.

Abbott nods to a display cabinet at the very back of the shop containing daggers, swords and guns.

Dom picks one up. He's surprised by its lightness. It's warm to the touch, unlike metal. He passes it to Abbott. 'It's a fake. Rubber or something.'

Abbott raises his eyebrows. 'Realistic though.'

'Yeah, very.'

A young woman with green hair and a lot of facial piercings sits on a stool behind the steel counter. She looks up from the graphic novel she's reading, glancing from Dom to Abbott. 'You looking for something specific?'

Abbott puts a photo of the dagger on the counter and pushes it towards her. 'Do you have any of these? In metal?'

She cocks her head to one side. 'Nah. Not in the shop.'

Dom shows her his warrant card. 'Your website said different.'

Turning on her stool, she nudges the wall behind her, opening a concealed door. 'Taz. There's police here.' She looks back at Dom. 'He's the owner, talk to him.'

Moments later the door opens and a short, paunchy bloke in a Hawaiian shirt, with straggly brown hair and round glasses, peers through. He nods to Dom and Abbott. 'What's this about?'

Abbott taps his finger on the photo. 'Did you sell this dagger?'

The man peers at the close-up image and nods, no hesitation. 'I did more than sell it. I made it.'

'Can you tell us who for?'

'Of course. I'm legit, I keep all the records required by law. I'll need to check the ledger.' He opens the door wider. 'Come down to my workshop and I'll take a look.'

They follow him down the narrow stairs to the basement. Given the clutter upstairs, this underground space is bigger and tidier than Dom had anticipated. Recessed spotlights line the ceiling making the room brighter than the shop above. Aside from a small desk and shelving unit in the corner, the only furniture is a large workbench in the centre of the room. On it, a curved samurai sword is held in position by two iron clamps.

'My latest commission – the hero's sword from *Until Last Breath*,' Taz says. 'For an American collector.'

Dom doesn't know the film. 'Was the dagger a commission?'

'It was. One of my biggest.'

Abbott frowns. 'Your biggest?'

Taz pulls a large hardback journal from one of the shelves above the desk and starts flicking through the pages. He stops, tracing his finger along one of the entries. 'Yes, here it is. Definitely my biggest commission so far.' He hands the ledger to Dom, pointing to the line. 'Twenty daggers, direct copies of those used in *Death by a Thousand Daggers*. It might be old, that film, but it's still popular.'

Dom reads the entry. 'Did you meet the buyer – A. Driscoll?'

Taz shakes his head. 'Everything was done online. The order was very specific – twenty daggers made in steel, exact copies of those in the film. It was a rush job too, quick turnaround, I had to work long days to get it done in time.'

'Do you know what they wanted them for?'

'I didn't ask.'

'Why not?'

Taz shrugs. 'The way I look at it, it's none of my business. A lot of my clients are collectors, movie buffs. I'm used to strange requests. I fulfil the order and send them out. Then it's done.'

Dom gestures to the photo of the dagger that Abbott's holding. 'That one was used in a stabbing. The victim died. We're going to need the contact details for your buyer.'

'Ah, well I . . .' Taz looks shocked, then shifty, avoiding Dom's gaze. 'I can give you the address I sent the merchandise to no problem, but it's a PO Box.'

'We'll need their credit card details then – we can get their address from that.'

'The thing is, I don't have any card details for them.'

Dom frowns. 'How did they pay?'

Taz is silent a moment. He glances from Dom to Abbott. 'They sent me cash. Used notes, in a Jiffy bag.'

'Thought you said you were legit?' Abbott says.

'I am, taking cash isn't illegal.' Taz looks offended. 'I put it through the books properly. Declared every penny.'

Fucksake. If the buyer used a PO Box, and sent cash in the post, Dom's money is on the name they gave being a fake. Whoever ordered the daggers didn't want to be traced.

24

CLEMENTINE

The sex is fast and urgent; me bent over the photocopier, Wade hammering into me from behind. The buzz of the afterglow doesn't last long. I know Wade is counting it as a victory, but he's wrong. The sex was for me, not him. The more he tries to cage me here in the faculty office, the fiercer becomes my urge to roam.

Wade will never understand that there are more important things than journal publications and impact factors. For him the hunt is about the glory at the end. For me the hunt and capture is everything. And the underlying need to know who killed my father, and bring those responsible to ground.

Dom is the same. That's why I have to make him hear me; he has to be told what the urbexers saw. The more he pushes me away, the more I think I should investigate myself – go to Hendleton and see what I can find – but if I embroil myself in another murder case, I know that Dom will never forgive me. I don't want us to be enemies, and so I fight my instincts. I have to get him to listen. And not just about that.

I scroll through the mentions of him that are thrown up from my Google search. Other than those discussing the Lover case, the most recent are about his failed raid, Operation Atlantis, and the IPCC investigation that's under way. Several officers are named in connection to it; one of them is Simon Lindsay. Was that what they were talking about in the pub?

Maybe there's another way. If I can show Dom I'm on his side, no matter what, he'll let me back in. I think about last night, the woman, Therese, and the men she was with in the pub. They're up to something, something led by Simon Lindsay, and whatever it is will be bad news for Dom. If I can find out more about what

Lindsay's up to, confront him myself, then I can help Dom and get him to trust me again.

I type '*Simon Lindsay*' into my search engine and an address for his work base comes up as south of the river. Jotting it onto a Post-it, I grab my coat and head for the door.

25

DOM

They finish the day around the murder board. Dom's written in the details of Taz at Scorpion in Camden, and the order of twenty daggers for A. Driscoll, but otherwise the board is unchanged since this time yesterday. He exhales, frustrated. 'Abbott, tell me you've found A. Driscoll.'

Abbott shakes his head. 'The PO Box was paid for in cash, no forwarding address. I'm working my way through the A. Driscolls in the area local to the box but nothing yet. To be honest, I think it's a non-starter and the name's a fake, like we thought.'

'What about computer forensics – can we find out the IP address of the computer used to place the order?'

'I've got the techs working on that now, but the word so far is that it was bounced through a network of servers, they're not sure we're going to get anything useful at the end.'

Shit. 'Parekh, have you got anything?'

She flicks through her scratchpad. Shakes her head. 'It's all background really, nothing actionable.'

He waits for her to continue.

'So I've been through Thomas Lee's financials, but nothing especially stands out. He's got a few credit card debts, but there isn't much left on the mortgage for the house, and his credit's good. I checked and he did have a life insurance policy. It was for half a million. He had it amended at the time of the split, instead of going to his wife he changed it to be put into trust for his children until their eighteenth birthdays.'

'It's not that surprising,' Abbott says. 'From what you've said of their relationship they were only in contact because of the children and due to him living in the basement flat.'

Parekh nods. 'True. I've also been calling his phone contacts. So far they've all given a similar story – he had a bit of a midlife crisis after the cancer, but was basically a good guy. One I spoke to, Kevin Yeoh, had been due to meet up with him on Sunday night – they often went to a local bar to watch live music on Sundays – but he says Lee cancelled earlier that day saying he couldn't make it.'

'Did he give a reason?' Dom says.

'No, just that something had come up. I looked into Kevin Yeoh and his alibis check out.' She closes her pad. 'I've got the Aldwych street camera footage now, so I'll be making a start on that next.'

Dom notes her findings on the board. Then turns back to Abbott and Parekh. 'OK, keep pushing, yeah?' He looks at Abbott. 'Dig deep into this A. Driscoll angle. And, Parekh, that camera footage is your priority.'

As they leave the incident room in silence, Dom glances up at the picture of Thomas Lee smiling from the top of the board. He shakes his head. Looks at the crime scene photo below, Lee's crumpled body in a heap in front of the battered face of the cab. Shit. They're nearly thirty-six hours into the case, and their leads are going nowhere fast. They need something new, quickly, before the trail turns completely cold.

He feels a vibration in his pocket. As he heads back towards his desk, he pulls out his phone and looks at the screen. Damn. It's another text from Darren Harris.

Dom, we need to talk. They don't want me to talk but I need to tell you. It's bad. I've been a fool. I don't trust the IPCC. I want to tell you. Face to face. Can we meet? Tonight? Not at your place or mine, somewhere in the open. I'm scared. I'm scared for Chrissie. Robbie, too. I'm scared about what they might do to them.

He rereads the last line. Feels his pulse accelerating. The site of his head injury starts to throb again. He can't let his sister, Chrissie, and, Robbie, her young son, be at risk.

Leaning on the back of his chair, he stabs out a text:

What the hell have you done? Why is my sister in danger?

'You OK, guv?'

He glances up. Sees Parekh looking at him with a concerned expression. He nods. 'Yeah, I'm fine. Look, you get off home, OK? We'll get stuck in again tomorrow.'

His phone vibrates.

Parekh looks uncertain but nods anyway. 'If you're sure?'

'Yup,' Dom says. He looks at the message from Darren. Exhales heavily.

I know what happened during Operation Atlantis. They don't want me to tell. I can't lie about it any more. Meet me in forty-five minutes. Embankment Pier. Don't tell anyone.

26

DOM

It's dark, it's pissing down, and Darren Harris isn't here. Dom checks the time on his watch again; 7.26. He pulls out his phone; no messages, no calls. It looks like Darren's bloody stood him up. Not for the first time, he wonders why the hell Darren wouldn't just come to his flat. It seems that whatever's going on has made him totally paranoid, unless . . . unless he wanted him out here for some other reason.

Dom scans the area, but there's still no sign of Darren. He leans on the railings and stares out across the water. In the moonlight it looks like liquid tar. The lights from the buildings at the side of the river reflect off the water. In the distance, the London Eye is slowly turning. He glances back at his watch and decides he'll give Darren until half past, just in case. He's drenched already; a few more minutes won't make much of a difference. He's tried calling a couple of times but it's gone straight to voicemail. He figures Darren was either on the tube or driving, or at least he hopes so.

Another minute passes. One of the party boats cruises along the Thames, loud dance music lingering in its wake. Shaking his head Dom gets out his phone and checks the screen. Still nothing. He's just about to put it back in his pocket when it rings, making him jump. The caller's name flashes on the screen: Emily Renton.

Dom answers. 'You all right, Doc? Working late?'

'No rest for the wicked, Dom, surely you know that by now? Thought I'd get the autopsy on your guy done before heading home.'

'That's good of you. Find anything I can use?'

'Well as you'd expect, in addition to five sharp force injuries – the stab wounds – he has damage consistent with being hit by a moving vehicle. However, the cause of death is less clear-cut.'

There's a plop out in the water. Dom glances over but sees nothing. Thinks it was probably a fish. 'The collision didn't kill him?'

'You're always so impatient, Dom.' Emily gives a little laugh. 'It's rather more complicated than that. Obviously his facial injuries were significant, and there are a number of fractures – right femur, right scapula, and a hairline to the pelvis. Given we have camera footage of him walking and looking relatively unbattered facially before the accident, it's safe to conclude these occurred as a result of the collision.'

He grips the phone a little tighter. 'What then?'

'Both the stabbing and the collision contributed to the cause of death. He died of hypovolemic shock.'

'Blood loss?'

'That's what I said, isn't it? He'd lost over forty per cent of his blood volume, largely from the stab wounds. Before stepping in front of that cab he would have already been highly compromised from peripheral hypoperfusion.'

Shit. 'Being in shock would explain why he stepped straight out into the road.'

'Indeed.'

'Is there anything else?'

'Nothing that's going to give you new lines of inquiry I'm afraid. The puncture wounds are consistent in length and depth with the weapon you found at the scene, but that's about it. No secondary forensics to speak of. I'll get the report in your inbox by morning so you can have a proper look-see.'

'Thanks, I appreciate it.'

'No problem, but that's me done for the day. Speaking of which, there's a good woman and a glass of wine with my name on it waiting at home, so I'll be getting off now.'

Dom smiles. Emily's wife, Jacquie, is a semi-professional comedienne. She's been away on tour for the past month, and although Emily hasn't talked a lot about it, he knows she's found the forced separation tough. He's glad Jacquie's back. 'Romantic night in?'

Emily laughs. 'If you call a bottle of Pinot, takeaway Thai, and a binge on Netflix romantic, then yes.'

'Sounds good to me.' And it did. It's been months since Dom shared a night in with anyone. Shit. Clementine Starke would have been the last person. 'You and Jacquie have fun.'

Dom hangs up. It's almost quarter to eight now; Darren's definitely not coming. Fucker. As he steps away from the railings and back towards the tube, Dom considers calling him, but decides against it; right now he's too angry. He's shoving the phone back into his pocket when it rings again.

He answers without looking at the caller ID, expecting it to be Darren. His tone's harsh, ready to tell Darren where to stick it. 'Yeah, what?'

The caller doesn't speak, but he can hear irregular breathing. Sobbing.

'Hello?' Dom takes the phone away from his ear. Looks at the screen. His breath catches in his throat. 'Chrissie? What is it? What's wrong?'

More sobbing.

What the hell's going on? 'Talk to me, sis. I'm right here.'

'It's . . . Darren. He's . . .'

'What's happened? Tell me.'

'There's . . .' Chrissie's breath is coming in gasps. 'There's been an accident.'

27
CLEMENTINE

Simon Lindsay wasn't in his office, or at least that's what the officer at the front desk told me. I didn't leave a name or a message, wanting to retain the element of surprise, but I wasn't ready to admit defeat. So I came back here, to the Black Horse, the pub that I followed Therese to last night. I remembered Dom telling me that during Operation Atlantis they'd sometimes gone to this pub after work, so I took a gamble, hoping Simon Lindsay had continued *his* habit of after-work drinking and favoured this place over the Princess Victoria.

He wasn't here when I arrived, but I tried to be patient, waiting well over an hour, and now it has paid off. He arrived a few minutes ago, ordered a pint from the barman and carried it across to the same corner of the pub as last night, alone. He's now sitting in the seat facing the door. His attention isn't on the room, it's on his phone as he taps away at the screen. I bet he thinks he's king of this place, the alpha. He doesn't realise that I'm onto him.

Downing the last of my gin and soda, I stand and make my way between the tables towards him. The people here, chatting and drinking, making the most of having got out of work at a reasonable time, don't give me a second glance. I clear my throat as I get to him, but my voice comes out like a growl. 'Simon Lindsay?'

He glances up from his phone. Looks me up and down. 'Who wants to know?'

I tilt my head to one side and force a smile. Keeping my tone friendly I say, 'Weren't you here last night with Therese?'

Lindsay smiles, and leans back a little. He's taken my bait and thinks I'm interested in him. Smug bastard. 'You were here?'

I sit down opposite him and put my hands on the table. 'I was.'

He shrugs. 'I don't remember you, love, sorry.'

'You were deep in conversation,' I say, giving him a wink. 'Plotting.'

His shoulders stiffen, but his expression doesn't change. 'Oh yeah?'

I lean forward. Keep my voice low, no playfulness in my tone. 'I know what you're doing, you and your friends.'

A muscle pulses in his jaw. He doesn't blink. 'And what's that?'

'You're dirty. You use your colleagues and leave them to hang. You frame others for your dishonesty.'

His smile looks strained. 'I've no idea what you're talking about. You must have me confused with someone else.'

'I'm not confused. I know the truth about Operation Atlantis.'

The smile disappears and he scowls. 'Then you're in a dangerous situation.'

I keep my eyes on his. Don't look away. He's an alpha but so am I. 'I'm on to you and I'm going to expose what you did.'

He looks me up and down again. Shakes his head. He reaches across the table, slides his hand around my neck and yanks me towards him. His face is just inches from mine. 'Walk away while you still can.'

I don't flinch, don't react, even though he's so close I can feel his breath on my face. I feel the overwhelming urge to lash out with my claws and silence him. 'Let. Go.'

'You have no idea who you're dealing with.'

Glaring, I snarl back. 'Nor do you.'

I see a flicker of doubt cross his face and he releases me. I smile. He's rescinded ground. I am dominant here.

We stay silent as a woman in black jeans and shirt collects the glasses from a nearby table and wipes the surface with a cloth. As soon as she's out of earshot, Lindsay points at me. 'I know you.' His tone is low, menacing. 'You're the girl who caught the Lover.'

I say nothing. I didn't come here to talk about me.

'Did Dom send you?'

I curl my top lip.

Lindsay grimaces. 'He's a bloody idiot.' He leans closer. 'Tell him that he can't win. The more he fights back, the worse things will be. We're untouchable.'

I stare at Lindsay. My fingers start to tingle and I dig my nails into the wooden tabletop. The anger, the need to protect Dom, comes through so strongly I fear it will overwhelm me. I have to walk away before I do something regrettable.

'No one is untouchable.' Pushing back my chair, I stand and stride to the exit, battling to contain my rage. I concentrate hard on putting one foot in front of the other, trying to ignore the image in my mind's eye, and what every fibre of my body is urging me to do right now – to fling myself across the table and rip open Lindsay's throat.

But I have his scent. I won't let him harm Dom.

This wolf is baying for blood.

28

DOM

He jumps in a cab and gets to the hospital as fast as he can. Darren's in surgery and has been for well over an hour. Dom finds Chrissie in the relatives' waiting room; a windowless box as depressing as hell, decorated in faded pastel colours. There's a tired-looking box of toys in the corner. Chrissie's young son, Robbie, is half-heartedly playing with an armless Barbie.

His sister looks up as Dom enters the room. Her eyes are red and her face is blotchy from crying. She doesn't smile. Hospitals hold so many bad memories for them both; their dad dying of bowel cancer, their mum confirmed dead on arrival after taking her own life. Now Darren.

Dom rushes up to Chrissie. She doesn't get up. After their conversation this morning he feels awkward and unsure what to do. He stops a couple of feet in front of her. Kneels down and puts his hand on her shoulder. 'How's he doing?'

She shrugs him away. 'Broken jaw, fractured pelvis. He dislocated his shoulder and knackered his elbow. His face is a real mess from the air bag.'

'I'm so sorry.'

'Yeah, sure you're sorry, like that's going to help.' She turns away. Looks at Robbie as she blinks back tears.

Dom hates that she's so angry with him. Doesn't know what to do. He stands up. Shifts his weight from foot to foot. 'He called me today, you know? Wanted to talk about Operation Atlantis.'

She turns back to look at him, surprised. 'I didn't know . . . what did he say?'

'I couldn't answer. I was on a—'

'On a case? Yeah, that sounds about right.' Her voice gets louder. 'You never change, do you? Even after everything that's happened, even after what I said this morning, you carry on just the same, tunnel vision, the job comes first and screw everything else.'

'I didn't know something like this would happen—'

'No, how could you?' Chrissie's tone is angry, hurt. 'Since when did you actually act like you give a crap?'

'Look, I arranged to see him. We were due to meet at Embankment Pier tonight.'

'Why there?' Chrissie looks confused. 'Why drag him into town?'

It was a good point. Chrissie and Darren live out in Twickenham, nowhere near Embankment. 'I don't know, it was Darren's choice.'

'That must have been why he was driving. He didn't even tell me he was meeting you, just said he was popping out.' She inhales sharply and lets out another sob. Her brown curly hair flops forward across her face and she brushes it back, tucking it behind her ears.

He keeps his voice gentle. 'Where did it happen?'

'About ten minutes from home.' She hugs her arms across her middle. 'The eyewitnesses say he was speeding, that he got to the end of the street and just didn't turn, or brake. He ploughed straight into the tree. Head on.'

'I'm so sorry, Chrissie.' He glances over at Robbie. 'If there's anything I can—'

She holds up her hands. Tears streaming down her face. 'Don't, OK, don't try to make out that you cared about Darren, about any of us.'

Dom steps closer and tries to put his arms around her. 'Of course I bloody care.'

She lets him hold her, just for a moment, before shoving him away.

'Prove it,' she says, her eyes blazing. 'Find out what happened. What made him do this?' Her voice cracks. 'Do something, *anything*, to make it make sense.'

29

SASS

Gasping and sweaty from the climb, they stop on the fifth floor of the construction to catch their breath. Getting past security was easier than their earlier recon had suggested. Now they're up here, sitting on one of the outer steel girders that form the skeleton of the new building, looking out through the windows of its original Victorian façade, the view across Soho and the West End is incredible.

'So we're at the top now,' Sass narrates, as Jedx unclips his iPhone from his chest rig and slowly rotates the camera three-sixty from their vantage point. 'As you can see, this level hasn't been fitted out yet so you can get a proper sense of the huge space of the original building. Once the renovation is complete, this whole place will be apartments.' She points out of the window. 'I reckon you'd have to pay several million for this view.'

'Wow' emojis float across the screen. The viewer total has risen to over seven hundred.

DavidSees: So in awe of you. How does it feel being up there?
Pinnyhip078: Lovin' your feed!
LiveWildRock: That was a hell of a climb. All those ladders. Props!
Koso: You're very high. Easy to fall . . .
Upyeah99: The lighting is better on this feed. Thanks.

Jedx flips the camera to face him and gives a thumbs-up to the viewers. 'OK folks, that's the first part of this explore done. So stoked you're enjoying it. We're taking a moment to catch our breath, and will be back live in ten, when we'll be going down to the lower floors and giving you a proper look-see at what those apartments are going to be like.'

He switches off the live upload. Pulls off his balaclava, grinning. 'Tonight's feed is going crazy. Nearly double the live viewers we've had before, and new subscriber notifications are off the chart.' He puts on his movie voiceover voice. 'Team, we're hitting the big time.'

Beaker laughs.

Sass forces a smile. Although the building is every bit as cool as she'd hoped, she's not feeling it tonight. She's carrying too much guilt. 'It's a shame Cap didn't make it.'

'Yeah, I wonder where he's at. You think he got cold feet?' says Beaker.

Jedx shrugs. 'He seemed all right when we left him at Aldwych, still up for it enough to do a bit more exploring on his own. And he's read the messages detailing what time tonight and everything. Guess there's somewhere else he had to be.' He scoots along the girder, closer to Sass. Reaches out his hand so their pinky fingers are touching. 'I'm sure he'll check in with us later.'

They sit for a moment. Sass wants to push her hand into his, feel his warmth, but the memory of Hendleton Studios still seems a barrier between them. She hasn't told him about the woman, Clementine Starke, who accosted her that morning. The guilt of betraying the group is heavy on her shoulders. She has to get Jedx and Beaker to see sense before Clementine or that weird guy, David, reports them. 'I really think we have to go to the police you—'

'No police, we decided.' Beaker looks away from the message he's tapping on his phone and holds her stare for a beat, looking more intense than she's ever seen him. Then he gestures to Jedx's chest rig. 'How's the new kit?'

'Not bad for a cheap fix.' Jedx turns towards him, moving his hand away. 'It seems solid enough, not as good as the GoPro, but it's keeping the feed stable.'

As the guys talk about Jedx's insurance claim for the camera lost at Hendleton, and how he'll have to fake it because he can't say he was somewhere he wasn't entitled to be, Sass raises her digital SLR and takes a few shots of the modern London cityscape framed by the aged bricks of the old building. She's trying to stay calm. Knows she won't change their minds by being emotional. She has to keep working on them.

'Shit.'

Sass looks round to Jedx. 'What is it?'

He's staring at the screen of his phone. 'We're getting trolled.'

Beaker doesn't look bothered. 'That's normal though, right? It was always going to happen as we get more popular.'

'This is weird, though.' Jedx angles the screen so Sass and Beaker can see the most recent comments under the video they've just been live-streaming.

DavidSees: Got myself a beer. Ready to see the apartments now.

Upyeah99: Come on! Surely you've got your breath back!

Koso: Four are now three. One of you won't get out alive. Who dies next?

Sass shivers. 'They're threating us. It's karma.'

Beaker's shaking his head. 'Someone's just messing, seeing that Cap isn't with us this time. It's probably some sad twelve-year-old kid in his bedroom.'

Jedx looks unconvinced. 'I thought that the first time, but then—'

Sass peels up her balaclava. Frowns. 'The first time?'

'They started commenting during the Hendleton explore. Nothing too bad, just telling us to keep out, basically. I reckoned it was jealousy or one of the XB100s mucking about. You know they're still hanging onto the hate after what happened in the autumn. But earlier I saw this.' He passes the phone to Sass. 'It's on the Aldwych upload.'

Koso: Curiosity killed the Cap. It's going to kill you all.

Sass's mouth goes dry. She feels sick. 'Killed Cap? What are they—'

'Stay calm, all right,' Beaker says. 'He was alive and well when we left him at Aldwych. It's a hoax. Has to be.'

'Does it?' Sass scrambles to her feet. 'We thought it was strange Cap didn't show tonight, maybe he's . . .'

'He's read the messages,' Beaker says, his irritation clear in his tone. 'He's fine.'

'Well, I'm not staying here. Whoever wrote that is watching the live-stream – if they know London, it won't take them long to work out our exact location. If they want to hurt us, they can just—'

Jedx looks from her to the screen. Frowns. 'But we can't go. Our viewers are waiting to look around the building.'

'Seriously, you're putting the viewers ahead of our safety? *My* safety?'

He stays silent and looks away, snapping the phone back into his chest-mounted rig.

'Wow. Guess I know where I stand in your priorities, don't I?' Her voice is louder now. Angry. 'Tell you what, I'll make things easy. We're done, OK? Spend all your time on your precious videos.'

They don't try to stop her leaving, and her hands are shaking as she climbs down the ladder to the fourth floor. She thought Jedx was different, that they'd had a connection, shared a passion, but if he can't put her safety over viewer figures, then it's all bullshit, she realises that now.

She continues down, passing through the hole in the floor between levels four and three – the ladder in place of where the lift shaft will be in the finished building – and steps off on the third floor. This level is more finished than the ones above; the inner walls are up, giving the impression of a vast maze. She heads along the corridor, making her way to the opposite end where the stairs have been fixed into place.

Bloody Jedx. She'd thought it weird that he didn't want her to go to his place, and he always came to hers. Now she wonders if he lives with someone else, and she'd never really mattered to him. Maybe she was just a convenient bit of fun.

Sass bites her lower lip and tries not to think about him, or the message on the live-stream page. She hurries faster along the corridor, her footsteps echoing off the concrete floor slabs as she searches for the stairwell.

She should never have come here; Jedx is always different when he's with Beaker, and there's something about that guy that creeps her out. She should've listened to her instinct and gone to the police about what they saw at Hendleton. She should have stayed away tonight. And why hadn't Cap shown up? All around her the building seems alive with creaks and groans. She flinches at every sound. Needs to be out of here. Gone.

With her heart pounding, Sass breaks into a run.

WEDNESDAY

30

DOM

Everything's fucked up. He can't sleep. One minute he's too hot, the next he's too cold. Every time he shuts his eyes, the events of the evening repeat over and again.

He left the hospital just after midnight. Darren was out of surgery but still deemed in a critical condition. Chrissie was preparing to take Robbie home. The doctors told them to rest; they can't do anything else now but wait. Getting through the next twenty-four hours is up to Darren. Whichever way the doctors told them the odds, the outlook seems pretty damn bleak.

He promised Chrissie he'd find out what happened and he's going to keep his word. The traffic police might be treating the crash as an accident but Dom isn't so sure, he's asked them to keep him informed of any developments. So far they seem to be willing to extend that professional courtesy.

He keeps wondering what Darren wanted to tell him, what he knew about Operation Atlantis that he'd been threatened not to tell. He said *they* didn't want him to speak about it, and he was sick of lying. Dom needs to find out who *they* are.

Dom hasn't told Chrissie that Darren thought he was in danger but there's someone he does need to talk to about it. He'll call this morning, first thing. He closes his eyes, tries to get comfortable and force sleep to come, even though his mind is buzzing.

On the bedside table, his phone vibrates. He rolls over, taking care not to squash BC who is snoozing on top of the duvet beside him, and answers, 'This is Bell.'

'We've got another one, guv.' Parekh's voice sounds distant and tinny. 'A young woman has been found by construction workers over near Leicester Square.'

Dom rubs his eyes. His skin feels dry and tight. His mind is groggy. 'Why've they called us?'

'She's been stabbed with what looks like another ceremonial dagger.'

Dead aged twenty-four; what a waste of a life. Dom asks for a few moments alone with the body of the female victim. He wants to get a feel for how she died. He needs this time. It's as though the contract between him and the dead is written and sealed in these moments. The dead can't speak, can't get justice for themselves. Dom knows it's up to him to do that.

The scene in front of him is really bloody depressing. The victim was found here, on the third floor, in the en-suite bathroom of the apartment closest to the stairwell. The room is part fitted; a huge designer spa bath, double sink vanity unit and toilet have been installed, but the floor is rough concrete and littered with plasterboard off-cuts and dust. The walls haven't yet been tiled. The feature lights, two ornate miniature chandeliers, hang bulbless and impotent from the raw plaster ceiling. Instead, the room is lit by four powerful spotlights set up on tripod stands by the CSIs. The light they give is harsh and unforgiving.

The young woman is slumped on the toilet. She's wearing maroon Converse and dressed in black running tights, and a black fleece over a grey T-shirt. Her face is covered by a balaclava with diamante around the eyeholes. Some of the gems are missing. One arm hangs limp at her side, the other is draped over the edge of the vanity unit. Her head is resting on her arm, her face angled down. Blonde hair sticks out from beneath the balaclava.

Someone so young dying anywhere is tragic, but breathing your last in this soulless, lonely space seems especially pitiful. Dom moves to his right and steps closer to the woman. Sees the jewelled hilt of the dagger sticking out from the back of her neck, the now familiar runes etched into its metal part-covered by blood-soaked blonde hair.

He stands very still. Inhales the air, dust-laden and gritty on his tongue, and takes in the smell of sawn chipboard and adhesive sealant mixed with bodily fluids.

Somewhere on the floor below, someone's hammering. Outside on the street a truck is reversing, its automated warning beeping continuously. Dom scans the room. There's extensive blood splatter, isolated to the area closest to the victim. She must have remained still as the blade sliced into her flesh. He wonders why she didn't struggle.

Turning, he calls to Parekh who's standing just outside the door.

She joins him. There's pity on her face. 'I'm sorry about your brother-in-law.'

'They're not married.' Dom's tone is harsher than he intended, but he doesn't want to think about Darren and the crash right now, doesn't want it distracting him from this crime scene. It's not Parekh's fault though, he realises she's only trying to be kind and immediately feels bad for being a dick. Softening his tone, he gestures towards the body. 'So what do we know?'

Parekh faces the victim. 'According to her driving licence she's Ruth Kemp. Twenty-four years old. Lives out near Harrow.'

'Who found her?'

'One of the plumbers who works here. Four of them started on-site at six this morning, he found her just before quarter past. Yelled for his mates and they called it in.'

'Has he made a statement?'

'Yes, but it pretty much says what I've just told you. The guy's in shock, he can't stop shaking.' She looks up at Dom. 'I searched her pockets with the CSIs. Aside from the driving licence, she had forty quid in notes and a house key, no phone or purse.'

'But with cash still on her it wasn't likely to be motivated by theft.' He stares at Ruth Kemp. 'Any sign of sexual assault?'

'The doc hasn't had a proper look yet. She's just arrived.'

'We shouldn't leave her waiting.' Dom glances out into the corridor. 'Is Abbott here?'

Parekh looks flustered. 'I haven't called him yet. Wasn't sure you'd want me to, but I can do it if—'

'Don't worry, just get him to notify the next of kin and arrange the ID. Then you get onto finding out as much as you can about Ruth Kemp. Like why the hell she was in this building for starters. Pull CCTV from around the area, and get Abbott to find out from her next of kin where she worked and the names of any good friends we can talk to.' He points to the dagger embedded in Ruth's neck. 'Why does the murder weapon look like the one used to stab Thomas Lee? Find out if they knew each other.'

As Parekh moves away, Emily Renton joins Dom. They stand together looking at the scene in silence, before moving back to allow the photographer to take the close shots.

Emily gestures towards the dead woman. 'Not the best wake-up call to have after my romantic evening.'

Dom nods but doesn't answer. 'How soon will you be able to get her on your table?'

'Soon. It should be longer, but because it's you, I'll bump her up the order.' Emily steps closer to the body. 'To answer your earlier question, I'll need to have a proper look at her to know for sure. What I can say is that whoever did this knew exactly the location and angle for death to be almost immediate.'

'Very different to how Thomas Lee was stabbed.'

'Yes.' Emily nods, her expression thoughtful. 'The direct opposite to the way his stomach and chest were slashed. His wounds were done to cause maximum pain before he died. With this murder, it's as if the killer wanted to spare the victim distress.'

Dom turns to look at Emily. 'You think the killer knew Ruth Kemp?'

'That's your domain, Dom. I wouldn't want to hypothesise. What I can tell you is that the victim was upright when the wound was inflicted.' Emily gestures to an arc of blood across the plasterboard above the victim at shoulder height. 'The blood spray here is uninterrupted. On the floor in front of her the splatter is most dense but voids are present. The killer must have been either in front of her or partially to the side, thus causing these voids in the blood pattern. She was stabbed while standing. Then, the trajectory of the spray and the reduction in density, suggests she stepped backwards and sank down to sitting. Death would have been rapid, she'd have needed support to end up in this position.'

'You're saying the body is staged?'

'I'm saying whoever killed her wanted us to find her sitting on the toilet like this.'

Dom checks the CSIs have got what they need with the body in situ, then reaches forward with his gloved hand and removes the balaclava, handing it to a CSI for bagging. 'We have that diamante found in Thomas Lee's blood on the platform at Aldwych. Let's get the diamantes on this tested and see if they're a match.'

He stares at Ruth Kemp's face. Her eyes are open wide, as if in surprise. Beneath them, her mascara has run dark rivers down her cheeks, and her red lipstick is smeared across the right side of her mouth.

Dom has a sick feeling in his stomach. In just seventy-two hours he has two victims, both wearing dark clothing and found in places prohibited for entry by the general public, and both attacked with replica ceremonial daggers. The order made and dispatched to the untraceable PO Box by Scorpion in Camden was for twenty daggers.

He very much hopes this isn't a serial killer just getting started.

31

DOM

Dom gets the call from Hawkins – the officer in charge of the investigation into Darren's crash – when he's en route to the PM, and he knows he has to take a short diversion. The doc will need to prep for the PM, so Dom figures he's got time. He *needs* the time. He can't let Chrissie go through this alone. He has to be the one to tell her the news.

The hospital is a hive of activity. The corridors that were dimly lit and virtually deserted the previous night are now bustling with doctors and nurses, patients and relatives. Nervous energy and the smell of disinfectant, mingled with sweat, permeates the air. Dom strides through the halls to emergency care. He finds Chrissie and Robbie in the relatives' waiting room.

Chrissie is slumped in a chair opposite the door, staring into space. She's make-up-less, with dark circles beneath her eyes, and Dom thinks it's unlikely she's had any sleep. Robbie is hunched over a superhero colouring book, his tongue poking out between his lips as he concentrates on keeping his red crayon within the lines.

Robbie looks up when he hears Dom close the door, and grins. 'Uncle Dom!'

'How are you doing there, champ?'

Robbie glances at his mum, then back to Dom. 'We're waiting for Darren.'

Dom smiles and ruffles Robbie's mop of unruly curls. 'Hopefully you'll be able to see him soon.'

As Robbie goes back to his colouring, Dom steps closer to Chrissie. 'And how are you doing, sis?'

She hugs her arms around her. Exhales. 'I'm going out of my mind. All this waiting, it's . . . they say I'll be able to see him soon. They're doing some more tests.'

'Is he conscious?'

'No, not yet. They're hopeful but . . .' She shakes her head.

'He'll be OK.'

'You don't know that, no one does.'

Dom stays silent. He knows his sister's right. This waiting, it makes him feel helpless, impotent. The way he felt when their dad got sick, the way he felt after their mum took her own life. He wishes he could *do* something, but right now, the thing he has to do, is tell her the news. 'You were right, I should have talked to him before.'

'Yes, you bloody should have. I begged you, I . . .' She stops, glancing at Robbie.

'I'll make this right. I promise, sis.'

Chrissie sighs, like she's heard it before and doesn't believe him.

'I can come back after I've finished work. I could—'

'I don't want you here, Dom, not now. It's too . . . it's just . . . just find what happened. Find out why Darren was acting weird, and what caused him to crash. Then we'll see.'

She doesn't want him. His own sister, the only family he has left, has no confidence that he'll give her support. It's making him put off telling her. He doesn't know how she'll react. 'I just want to help.'

Chrissie stares back at him, holding eye contact. 'OK, look, the police questioned me earlier. They were asking if Darren had any enemies, they wanted to know if he'd fallen out with anyone recently, or had threats, or trouble outside of work. Why were they asking me that? Have they found something?'

Dom's phone vibrates in his pocket, making him flinch. It could be the doc telling him she's ready. He moves to take the phone from his pocket.

Chrissie's still talking, her voice is rising in pitch and volume. 'I can't believe you're going to check your phone while I'm talking to you. You just got here. Are you listening to me? Why did you bother coming if you're not going to listen? You should just go and—'

'Hold on a minute, OK, there's something I need to tell you. I've just got off the phone with the lead guy investigating Darren's crash.'

'What? What is it, tell me, I need to—'

'It wasn't an accident.'

141

Chrissie inhales loudly. There's a tremble to her voice as she says, 'How do you—'

'The inspection of his vehicle found the brakes had been tampered with, the steering column, too. Someone meant for him to crash. It was attempted murder.'

'Who?'

Dom clenches his fist. 'Someone he used to trust.'

'You know who did this? You have to tell—'

'I've got a hunch but no proof.'

Chrissie's words come out in a rush. 'You need to get some. You need to tell the investigating officer. You need to . . . what if . . . is he still in danger? If they tried to hurt him and failed will they try again?'

If they knew Darren was going to squeal on them and want him silenced, Dom is almost certain they'll try again. But Chrissie doesn't need to hear that, not right now, so he says, 'I don't know.'

'You need to find out, Dom. *I* need you to.'

'I'll do what I can.'

'Promise you will. This is important. They almost killed him.'

He grits his teeth. 'I know.'

'Can you get an officer to stand guard here at the hospital? These people, if they attack him there . . . I need him safe, I couldn't cope if—'

'I'll see what I can do.' Dom will, but he also knows that putting a uniform outside the room won't necessarily make Darren safer. How could it, when the most likely suspect is one of their own. Maybe Holsworth is someone who can help protect them.

In his pocket, his phone vibrates again. This time he checks the screen; it's the doc telling him that she's starting the PM. He looks at Chrissie. 'Sorry, sis, I have to go.'

'OK.' She's trying to be strong, but he can see her lower lip quivering. 'Don't forget us, Dom. Get the bastard who did this. Don't let me down.'

'I won't, I promise.'

His words sound hollow, meaningless. They taste like ashes on his tongue.

32

CLEMENTINE

Dom still hasn't replied. I've left voicemails, sent emails and texts, but nothing's getting through; he must still be blocking me. Short of visiting him at work or his apartment, there's nothing more I can do. Correction. There is more I can do, it's just I promised him that I wouldn't do it again. He'd reacted so badly when I told him about breaking into a crime scene, that I said I'd never investigate a live case again. I'd promised never to put him in a situation that might compromise him. If I go back on my word now, I'll have no chance of him ever trusting me again. I know accosting Lindsay was taking things close to that line, but what I found out can help Dom, not hinder him, so I'm pretty sure it'll be OK. But the more I dig into the world of this urban explorers group, the more anomalies I find. It could become a live case, a murder investigation. But if Dom continues to ignore me, what else can I do? How can I just walk away, especially after the comments I've read?

I saw them first on the most recent video uploaded by the group. Jedx, Beaker and Sass are exploring a construction site where a new block of apartments are being erected within an old Victorian shell. Beneath the live-stream, the voyeurs watching it type comments to interact with the group. But the comment that catches my eye is more of a statement.

Koso: Four are now three. One of you won't get out alive. Who dies next?

No one from the group acknowledges the comment, but when they come back online after a short break to catch their breath only Jedx is visible on camera. I replay the video again from that point.

Jedx is narrating as he climbs down a ladder. 'So Sass had to leave, she's got an early start tomorrow, but don't worry there's still a whole bunch of stuff we're going to explore. The lower levels have started getting fitted out, so let's take a look at what's going on there first.' He steps off the ladder and walks down a dark corridor. There's a light coming towards him. 'Beaker?'

'I've found a way,' Beaker says. He sounds excited, almost breathless. He looks into the camera. 'We came in through the interior of the building, but we're going to climb down the exterior.'

I watch as Beaker leads Jedx through a maze of portioned walls and partially fitted rooms, to the right of the corridor. They reach the external wall and step out onto the scaffolding. I stop the video as they start their descent. I've already seen it to the end. Unlike Beaker, Sass doesn't rejoin Jedx. There are no further comments from Koso.

I call David. It takes him eleven rings to answer. 'Have you seen the comment on the live-stream?'

'What?' He sounds groggy. 'Who is this?'

'It's Clementine. Aren't you up yet?'

'I . . . had a late night.'

'So have you seen it?'

There's a crash at his end of the phone followed by loud rustling. 'I . . . no, what comment are you talking about?'

'I thought you were some kind of super fan. How have you not noticed it? On last night's JedUrbXTM live-streamed video there's a comment from someone using the name "Koso", threatening the group.'

'It's not a big deal. Trash talk is normal. It comes with popularity, all the groups know that.'

'But who is Koso?'

David exhales. 'I've not heard of them before. Probably some kid.'

'Could they be a friend of Dink?'

'How would I know? I've no idea who Dink even is, I just made up that Dink told me where to find Sass so she didn't scream "stalker" at me in front of everyone in that coffee shop.'

Shit. I can't help but be disappointed. 'How did you know where she'd be, then?'

His voice is more hesitant. 'I was trying to find out who the group were in real life. One of the live-streams they did was near where I live, I went down there, and watched them leave.' David coughs. Sounds embarrassed. 'I followed Sass home. Started learning her routine, that's how I found out about her always getting coffee there.'

I can't believe he thinks that's OK behaviour. Even I can see it's wrong. 'So you're what, just some creepy stalker?'

'I was going to research each of them,' David stammers. 'I just wanted to know all about them. To be part of their world.'

'I thought you were part of their world.'

'I know a lot about it, but I'm an observer, not a participant. I thought if I introduced them to you, a celebrity researcher, and you helped raise their profile, then they'd let me into their inner circle.' He sighs. 'But I'm still on the outside, I don't have access.'

I sigh. Shake my head. I need to know more about the group, and how this mysterious Dink that Sass seemed so wary of fits into everything. 'Then find me someone who does.'

33

DOM

Emily seems unaffected by the early start, despite a late night, but maybe it's the half packet of chocolate hobnobs she munched before starting that is helping her power through. Dom finds an autopsy a hard thing to witness at the best of times, but even worse with no sleep and a banging headache.

When she's finished the wet-work she beckons Dom over to join her by the gurney. A sheet now covers Ruth Kemp's modesty. In this sterile environment, under the harsh lighting, her body looks paler and more fragile than she appeared at the crime scene. Dom shakes his head, sickened by the pointlessness of her death. A stainless steel counter is no place for a young woman to end up.

Emily scans through the notes her assistant made as she dictated her findings. She uses a voice recorder too, but doesn't like to rely on it. Prefers a traditional paper record. 'So, as I said, she's a well-nourished twenty-four year-old female with an above average level of fitness and muscle tone. Cause of death was a single stab wound to the neck. In layman's terms, the dagger was thrust downwards from just below the base of the skull, hitting the carotid artery and jugular vein, and also severing the windpipe. She would have lost consciousness almost instantly from the sudden drop in blood pressure, and bled out within less than half a minute.'

'Could she have screamed?'

'Maybe at the point of impact, but it's unlikely. There are signs that her mouth was forced closed.' Emily points to bruising around Ruth Kemp's lips. 'These are fingermarks. Whoever stabbed her, clamped their hand over her mouth to prevent her calling for help.'

'If they were that close they would have got covered in her blood.'

'Yes, and the voids we saw in the blood splatter at the crime scene would suggest they did.'

Dom remembers the way Ruth Kemp was sitting on the toilet, slumped sideways over the vanity unit, her back to the wall. 'How do you think they did it?'

'Well, I don't like to guess, but from the evidence I'd say they were facing her – the voids were in front of her rather than behind – and then moved to the side as they put her into position.' Emily pauses, thinking for a moment. 'An angle like that though, it's a strange choice. It wouldn't have been easy.'

'To inflict the damage, they'd have had to be very close to her.' Dom frowns. 'They'd have been staring straight into her eyes as the blade went in.'

Emily nods. 'Maybe that's what they wanted.'

DCI Paul Jackson looks at Dom over the top of his glasses. 'And you're telling me they made twenty replica daggers?'

'That's what the owner of Scorpion told us. We've confirmed the dagger from this latest murder as the same batch.'

'Shit.' Jackson crosses his arms. 'But the MO for this second murder is different, you say?'

'Death was quicker. It felt more personal.'

'Any leads?'

Dom shakes his head. 'A few lines of inquiry but nothing concrete. The PO Box where Scorpion shipped the daggers was set up with fake documents, the trail's cold. We're still waiting on CCTV and forensics, but there's nothing yet.'

Jackson slumps down in his throne-like chair and sighs loudly. 'We don't want this getting out, Dom. Having another serial killer on our patch, it's not going to—'

'They're not a serial killer.'

'Not yet, perhaps,' Jackson says. 'But if there are eighteen more daggers they could have bigger plans.'

The DCI is right of course. That's precisely why Dom needs the information to stay secure. 'We can't have the press getting wind of this. It'll be a total shit-storm. The panic they'll create will be—'

'Agreed.' Jackson leans forward in his chair, elbows on the large paper blotter. 'Catch this bastard, Dom. Don't let this turn into a circus. You've got some credits with the brass after getting the Lover, but it won't last, and the press are still out to get you.'

Dom knows his boss is telling it like it is. His relationship with the media is antagonistic at the best of times. He hates the vulture-like bastards – always looking for a dodgy angle to sensationalise a headline, with no regard for the real people, the victim's loved ones, whose lives are left shattered by the crimes he investigates. The journalists always punish him when he won't pander to them. 'I'm doing all I can.'

'I need you to do more, Dom. We can't let this carry on. If it comes out we knew about the daggers and still couldn't find this monster, it'll make us look really bloody incompetent. Stop this now. Push hard.'

I always do, Dom thinks, but he says, 'Yes, Paul.'

'Good man.' Jackson turns back to his computer screen and Dom takes it as his cue to leave. He's almost at the door when it opens and Jackson's assistant pokes her head into the office.

She smiles at Dom, and then looks at the boss. 'DI Lindsay's here. Shall I send him in?'

Dom freezes. Lindsay is here? He's never known him come this side of the river to talk to Jackson before. He turns back to the DCI. 'Do you want me to stay?'

Jackson shakes his head. 'No, no, you carry on, Dom.'

Stepping past Jackson's assistant, Dom moves into the waiting area outside the office. Lindsay is sitting in one of the chairs flicking through a magazine. He gets up as Dom approaches. 'All right, chap?'

Dom wants to punch the smile off the bastard's face. 'What the hell are you—'

'Come on in, Simon,' Jackson calls.

'Sorry, duty calls, no time to chat.' Lindsay points towards the DCI's door. As he passes Dom, he leans close and, keeping his voice low so that only Dom can hear him, says, 'Call your bitch off.'

Dom frowns. 'What are you talking about?'

'Don't play innocent, you know exactly what I mean,' Lindsay says. He glares at him, the threat implicit in his cold stare. 'She comes at me again I won't hesitate . . .'

34
DOM

Back in the office he calls a team meeting. He's trying to keep his shit together. He's suspected Lindsay was guilty of corruption for a while now, he just needs Holsworth to prove it. But rather than acting worried because the IPCC are still investigating Operation Atlantis, Lindsay's behaviour is getting more obvious, it's like he thinks he's untouchable. And Dom doesn't get why Lindsay's here talking to Jackson, or what the hell he meant about 'calling his bitch off'. He's worried Lindsay meant Chrissie. Dom shudders. He hopes she hasn't done something to put herself in danger.

In the incident room they now have two murder boards; one for Thomas Lee, another for Ruth Kemp. Despite the early start, Parekh looks her usual enthusiastic self. Abbott is more subdued, slouched down in his chair as if the weight of the world is on him. Dom feels like it's on him, too. His body's tense, his mind feels scattered, and that's not bloody good enough. The victims deserve someone fighting their corner. Getting them justice. And it's meant to be him. The whole reason he went into the police in the first place was to fight for those unable to fight for themselves. He needs to pull himself together. He tries to focus. 'What have we got?'

Abbott shakes his head. 'The sale of the daggers are a dead end, so I'm going to take another look at the film to try and understand their significance. I've worked my way through all the A. Driscolls and the only one who doesn't alibi out for the time of Thomas Lee's attack is a ninety-four-year-old man who can't walk unaided. Computer forensics haven't had any luck either. The IP address was cloaked by bouncing through so many different places, the closest they can get is a server in Venezuela.'

Shit. Dom can tell Abbott's trying, but he's damn passive compared to normal. Dom's confirmation that he knows about

Abbott's extra-curricular activities must be preying on his mind. They need to have another conversation, but Dom's got to decide what he's going to do first. He knows he should report Abbott, as far as procedure goes it's a no-brainer, but he's a bloody good officer and he's always had Dom's back before. Dom can see he's in a tough position with his wife and new kid, Macey, and their money problems; he's obviously been teetering on the edge for a while.

Dom's well known for seeing things in black and white, not tending to recognise the shades of grey. It's weird, Dom thinks, because right now he's internally debating the grey areas of what Abbott has done. Everything that's happened in the past couple of months seems to have changed Dom and he doesn't know how to get back to the way he was before. All he can do is try to focus on the case they have. Everything else needs to wait, including Abbott. He can sweat it a bit longer. 'Anything from the CCTV?'

'I've been pushing for the footage from the streets outside the construction site where Ruth Kemp was found,' Parekh says. 'It all came through about twenty minutes ago, so we can get started on it once we've finished here.'

'How about the pictures from social media for Thomas Lee?'

Parekh shakes her head. 'Nothing useful.'

'That's pretty much the whole situation with the Thomas Lee case,' Abbott says, without making eye contact.

Dom exhales hard. 'Get going on the CCTV. We need something otherwise we've totally stalled on this. There has to be footage of Thomas Lee approaching the station, and Ruth Kemp near that building – it's impossible to be on the streets in this city without showing up on a camera somewhere.'

'I'm on it,' Abbott says, slumping back onto his chair and looking anything but 'on it'.

Dom rolls his shoulders, trying to release the tension, and moves across to the second board. Fixed to the top is the large photograph of Ruth Kemp – she's on a beach with palm trees in the background. Her blonde hair is pinned up on top of her head, she's make-up free and smiling at the camera. The crime scene picture alongside it, showing her bled out in the part-fitted bathroom, is a stark contrast. Dom turns back to Abbott and Parekh. 'We've had confirmation from the doc that a single incision killed Ruth Kemp. The dagger severed her carotid and jugular, and pierced her windpipe.' On the board he writes: *single stab wound: fatal.*

He nods to Abbott. 'Where are we at with the next of kin and formal ID?'

'It's done. Mr and Mrs Kemp are relatively local, living in Maida Vale. They're understandably upset. I took a basic statement, but Mrs Kemp had to be sedated. We'll need to revisit them tomorrow. Until then I left them in the hands of the FLO, Gary Ekman, he's a good sort and will give us a shout if needed.'

'OK, good.' Dom looks towards Parekh. 'What else do we know about Ruth?'

'She worked for a small PR firm – YSL Associates – as a junior account manager. I've spoken to the office manager who said Ruth was a happy, popular person. She enjoyed her work and loved travelling.' Parekh sounds far more animated than Abbott as she reads from her scratchpad. 'But over the last couple of days apparently she hadn't seemed her usual self. She said Ruth was increasingly withdrawn and spending a lot of time on her phone. They went for team drinks the night before she died, and her colleagues said she was drinking far more than normal.'

Dom makes a note on the board. 'Have we any idea who she was talking to?'

'Not at the moment,' Parekh says. 'I've requested the phone records but they're slow in coming, and I've been trying to access her bedsit, but so far I've not managed to get hold of the landlord.'

'Keep pushing, OK?'

'Yes, guv.' Parekh looks thoughtful. 'One thing that's weird is she doesn't seem to have any social media accounts.'

'None?'

'No, not even Facebook. Apparently she operated the Twitter feed of YSL Associates, and has done a fair bit on Instagram for them, but there's nothing I've found so far in her own name.'

'Strange for someone her age,' Abbott says.

Dom nods. 'Yeah. Keep looking, people have all manner of odd user names on social media sites, could be she's not used her real name. We have to find a connection between Ruth Kemp and Thomas Lee.'

Abbott frowns. 'There's nothing to say that they have to be personally connected.'

'Of course they are,' Parekh says. 'The daggers are from the same batch, ordered by the same person. They were both targeted by the killer.'

Abbott sneaks a look at Dom. He looks sheepish, repentant. Dom gives him a nod but doesn't smile. 'I'm with Parekh on this. These murders are very specific, not random opportunistic attacks. That suggests that the killer purposely went after Thomas and Ruth. If nothing else, they're connected through him. The question is, how?'

Abbott checks his notes. 'So far there's nothing to suggest Thomas and Ruth had ever met. They didn't share social circles, their workplaces were miles from each other and their routes to them different.'

'There's the diamante.' Parekh steps up to Thomas Lee's murder board and taps the crime scene picture of a diamante in a pool of blood on the Aldwych platform. 'This one was dropped at the scene of Thomas Lee's stabbing.' She moves across to the board for Ruth Kemp, and points to a photo of one of the bagged pieces of evidence. 'This balaclava was worn by the victim at the time of her death. It has diamante around the eyeholes, and some are missing.'

Abbott looks unconvinced. 'What, so you think Kemp stabbed Lee, then a couple of nights later stabbed herself?'

'No, of course Ruth Kemp couldn't have done that to herself. I'm saying if the diamantes are from the same source it gives a potential connection between the victims. If we assume they entered the places where they died of their own free will, then they were both trespassing before the killer struck. Maybe they were trespassing with the killer.'

She's right, although Dom isn't sure what the connection could mean. 'What would make them want to go into these places?'

Parekh shakes her head. 'I don't know, guv.'

Nor does Dom, but he thinks Parekh could be onto something. 'Have we got anything back from the lab on the diamantes?'

Parekh shakes her head. 'Not yet. I'll add it to my things to chase.'

'Keep looking for connections. The killer had twenty daggers made and they've only used two so far. We have to find something that connects why they targeted Thomas and Ruth.'

Abbott and Parekh both nod.

Dom feels pressure building in his chest, a sure sign that the frustration is getting to him. He clenches his fists. Needs to get out of here. Needs some air and some answers. He steps towards the door. Looks at Parekh. 'And keep trying to get hold of Ruth Kemp's landlord. We have to get into Ruth's flat, I want to get a sense of who she was outside of work and who she spent her time with.'

'The office manager said her closest work friend was another account manager, Ellie Webster. She went home sick after learning about what happened to Ruth.'

'OK, get in touch with the friend and arrange for us to meet her.' Dom stands. His mind flashes back to his earlier encounter outside Jackson's office. He doesn't think Chrissie would have spoken to Lindsay, but if not her, then who did Lindsay mean? Shit. There's someone Dom knows who ignores boundaries and flouts rules. He'd been wondering why Clementine had been trying to get hold of him again. Could she possibly have something to do with it? 'Call me once it's set up, I'm heading out for a bit.'

'You want company?'

'No,' says Dom. He instantly regrets his sharp tone. Not Parekh's fault, it's because he's ashamed of what he's planning. 'I need to do this alone.'

35

CLEMENTINE

All his text said was: Meet me in the Two Brewers. We need to talk.

I got here in twenty minutes. A few minutes later I'm watching him arrive, striding through the doorway of this over-lit, trying-too-hard gastro pub, scanning the faces of the people sitting at each of the wooden tables. He's scowling, and his expression doesn't change when he sees me, but he heads in this direction.

It's obvious that he's stressed; it's in the furrow of his brow, the tightness of his jaw, the squint of his eyes. I want to reach out and smooth the stress away with my fingers. He sits down, perching on the stool opposite me, but doesn't take his coat off. He looks at me but doesn't speak. His gaze makes me feel self-conscious. My delight at seeing him starts to fade.

'Are you fucking interfering in my work again, Clementine?'

His words hit me like a slap. I stare at him, shocked by his anger. All the carefully learnt strategies I used to employ to fake emotion have deserted me now that I feel things for real. I give into my natural instinct and snap back at him. 'I've been trying to get in touch with you. Why aren't you answering my messages? Why do my emails bounce back?'

'Shit.' Dom shakes his head. He looks tired. There are shadows beneath his eyes, and his dark curly hair looks greyer and more dishevelled than usual. 'You were pissed off at me so you went to Lindsay? What the hell, I'm in the middle of a case, my sister's partner's just been in an accident, and now . . . I don't need this shit.'

I reach out and put my hand on his arm. He flinches beneath my touch, but I don't move my hand away. 'I'm trying to help you.'

His voice is bitter. 'How the hell are you helping?'

I rub his arm with my fingers. Feel the rough fabric of his jacket beneath my skin and a jolt of electricity vibrates through me from the contact. 'When I called you the other night I was outside your apartment building.'

Dom shifts back in his seat, forcing me to remove my hand from his arm. 'You what?'

The group at the table next to us burst into laughter. The noise is out of kilter with the conversation we're having. I block them out, keeping my eyes focused on Dom. 'I'd gone there to see you, but I called before pressing the buzzer and you said you didn't want to see me. As I was leaving, I saw a woman buzz your flat and then enter your building.'

He clenches his jaw. 'So, what, you spied on me and Therese? Fucksake, that's crazy.'

I feel a flash of anger at the mention of her name. Anger mixed with a side order of jealousy. 'No, I followed her.'

He rubs his forehead. Looks confused. 'Wait, you what?'

'I followed her afterwards.' Dom is looking at me with a shocked expression. I fight the urge to clam up, knowing I have to tell him this, it's important that he knows. 'She went straight from your place to a pub – the Black Horse – and met two men there. One was called Lindsay, the other Darren. I sat at a table nearby and listened in on their conversation.'

Dom's just staring at me, frowning.

So I continue. 'They were arguing. Darren told them he wanted out, but the blond man, Lindsay, said he didn't get to walk away and that if he bottled it now it wouldn't end well for him. Darren spoke about how he'd only been following orders, but he was going to lose his job anyway.'

Dom grips the table. 'What else?'

I hesitate before I answer. Dom looks angry now, furious. He gestures at me to carry on, hurry up. 'Tell me.'

'Things got physical, the woman, Therese, slapped Darren and he left. Then . . .'

'Then?' Dom's voice is granite cold. The psychic void between us is widening.

I take a breath. 'Lindsay and Therese went outside. They fucked against the wall in the alley.'

Dom swallows hard. He's looking at my face, but it's as if he's staring straight through me. 'Right.'

I reach out and touch his arm again, but he shrugs me away. 'Don't, yeah.'

'I had to see you. I discovered something else you have to look into, it's a video with—'

'Stop.' Dom holds up his hands. His tone's hostile. His face is an angry mask. 'Just stop speaking. I can't . . . I can't listen to any more of this. You were stalking me, and then you followed my ex-girlfriend? That's fucked up, seriously fucked up.'

'If I'm so fucked up why are you here with me, Dom?'

'I ran into Lindsay. He told me to "call my bitch off",' Dom's watching me carefully. I can tell that this is a test; that he's looking for a reaction. 'Lindsay made threats about what he would do if this "bitch" doesn't back down. Did you speak to Lindsay?'

I don't answer. Take a gulp of my drink, not looking at him.

'Clementine?'

'He needed to know you had someone fighting your corner. He's planning something, Dom. He's dirty and—'

'I never asked you to get involved.' Dom flushes red. His voice is raised, angry. 'You should have just—'

'Let it go? Let them fuck you over?' I slam the glass down onto the table and it shatters. I stare at the fragments, shocked at what I've done. Emotions – anger at Dom's hostility; fear that I've lost him; desire to protect him – swirl in my chest. 'You can't let dirty coppers win. They can't win. Not again . . .'

'Again?'

I shake my head. I don't want to talk about my father right now. Rather than answering the question, I reach into my jacket pocket and pull out my phone. Opening the voice recorder app, I find the latest recording and hold the phone out to Dom. 'I recorded my conversation with Lindsay. Listen, then tell me you don't need me.'

He mutters under his breath but plays the recording anyway. Listens to me challenging Lindsay, and Lindsay threatening me. When it's done, Dom hands the phone back.

'I'm not afraid of him,' I say firmly.

'Maybe you should be. This isn't a game.'

'That's why you need me.'

'You're putting yourself at risk.'

'I can look after myself.'

Dom holds my gaze. 'You sure about that?'

I don't look away but stay fixed eye to eye with him. I know that expression, the slight twitch of his brow; he's worried about me. He cares, even though he tries his damnedest to fight it. He told me I was too much for him the last time we met, but I've analysed the timeline, and I've pinpointed the moment things changed. It was before that day, when I told him I'd broken into one of the Lover's crime scenes and taken a piece of evidence his CSIs had missed. That was the moment he decided he couldn't trust me. He's seen me take care of myself though, he should trust in that. 'You've seen that I can. Maybe I should kill him for you.'

'What the . . .?'

'It was a joke.' I reach towards him. Grab his fingers and cling onto them tight, but he's already recoiling.

He yanks his hands away. 'No. I can't do this, OK? You need to back off. Leave me alone.'

Shoving his chair back, he jumps up and strides away. I watch him push his way out through the door, and hear it bang closed. He's gone. The people sitting at the tables around me are staring. There's some whining love song playing over the speakers, taunting me. I keep my gaze down. My heart's pounding in triple time. My face is flushed with embarrassment and I feel as though I'm about to vomit.

He's gone, and I'm left howling.

36

DOM

He can't believe Clementine followed Therese, and that she'd threatened Lindsay. Her words ricochet around his mind as he takes the tube to Ellie Webster's place to meet Parekh. Therese is betraying him, lying about still seeing Lindsay just as he'd suspected, and Lindsay's guilt seems certain now. But him learning this information from Clementine, what the actual fuck? Clementine is unhinged, properly messed up, and yet he still can't stop thinking about how she'd put herself in danger for him. No one has ever fought his corner like that before. Shit. She's borderline obsessive, unpredictable, yet, if he's honest, part of him enjoyed seeing her.

He shakes his head. He can't let her back into his life. She's already compromised him once and she doesn't even understand that. She's too unpredictable. He has to put her out of his mind.

Their relationship, whatever else it is, is seriously fucked up.

It's barely afternoon but Ellie answers the door with a glass of red wine in her hand and wearing what look like her pyjamas – pale blue shirt and plaid trousers with fluffy boot slippers. Her black bobbed hair is dishevelled and unbrushed, and her face is blotchy from crying. She leans against the doorframe as if she's too frail to stand unaided.

Dom glances at Parekh. He's already feeling bad because of what Chrissie's dealing with, as well as processing the total mind-fuck with Clementine and what she's told him. Now he feels even more of a dick for intruding on Ellie when her friend's just been murdered. But it's his job, he has to prioritise the case. Without Ruth's phone records, and no leads from social media, so far Ellie is the only person they know of who was friends with Ruth. He wants to take things gently, though. 'If this is too much, we can come back?'

He's relieved when she shakes her head.

'No, if it'll help find Ruth's killer, let's do it now.' Ellie waves them inside, and points to her wine. 'Can I get you a drink?'

Dom and Parekh shake their heads.

'No thanks,' Dom says. 'We won't take much of your time.'

Ellie shows them into the living space. It's all varnished oak floors and designer furniture – good stuff, not like his own self-assembled units from IKEA.

She notices him looking. 'It's not mine. Kitty, who owns the place, is loaded. She doesn't need lodgers, but she doesn't like living alone – so here I am.'

'Have you been here long?' Parekh says.

'I moved in about eight months ago. The others were already here. They advertised for a new flatmate and I answered first.' She gestures to the corner sofa. 'Please, sit.'

He and Parekh sit on the short side of the sofa. Ellie flops down in the middle of the longer part and hugs a fluffy cushion to her stomach. She takes a gulp of wine.

Dom keeps the file he's brought on his lap. He tries to keep his body language casual and reminds himself to put her at ease with small talk. 'It's a nice place.'

'I was . . . lucky.' Her voice breaks. She looks down. Takes a breath. 'Sorry.'

'It's OK. Take your time.'

There are four candles burning on a round silver tray in the centre of a low table. The candles are different sizes; two pillars, a short one in a glass and a tea light. There's a strong aroma, like sage and something musty. It's making his eyes water.

This doesn't seem right. Dom feels like they're intruding on her grief, on what should be a private time. But they can't go. They need to know more about Ruth. 'Can I . . .?'

She looks back at him. Her glance falls to the folder on his lap. 'What was it you wanted to know?'

'The office manager at your work said Ruth seemed distracted in the days before she died. Were you aware of anything bothering her?'

Ellie looks at both Dom and Parekh. 'I guess she was rather preoccupied. I asked her about it when we were out for drinks on Monday night, and she said one of her friends was having a crisis. I got the impression she was a bit fed up with them.'

Parekh leans forward. 'What made you think that?'

'She said something about them being a bit of a drama queen.'

'Do you know the name of this friend?' Dom says.

Ellie shakes her head. 'Sorry, no, she didn't say and I didn't want to pry. I didn't think it was important . . . I . . .' She sniffs loudly. Grabs a tissue from the box on the glass side table and dabs her eyes with it. 'I wish I'd asked her now.'

Parekh gets out her scratchpad. 'Can you give us a list of her other friends?'

'I'm sorry, I can't. I mean, I don't know her other friends. We were colleagues, friendly, but not best friends or anything.' She hangs her head. 'Sorry to be useless.'

'I know this is tough, but you're doing great.' Dom says, his tone gentle. 'Aside from the friend in crisis, had Ruth mentioned anything else worrying her?'

Ellie blows her nose. 'No, not that I can think of.'

Parekh catches Dom's eye, and jumps in with a question. 'We've been trying to find her social media accounts but not had any luck. Do you know what she used?'

'She doesn't . . . didn't use anything. Ruth was all about living in the moment. She didn't like social media.'

They're not getting anywhere fast. Dom tries another approach. 'What about hobbies, what sort of things did she do in her spare time?'

Ellie looks confused. 'Hobbies? How's that relevant to—'

'It helps us get a better sense of her, the sort of person she was, and the type of friends she had.'

'Why are you asking about her friends again? Do you think one of her friends killed her?' Ellie pulls the cushion to her tighter. 'Does that mean I'm under suspicion, DI Bell, do I need a lawyer?'

'No, not at all, we're trying to work out what led Ruth to being on a construction site in the middle of the night. Any information you can give about her personal life could be helpful.'

Ellie takes another gulp of her wine, and then sets the glass down on the low bench. Her expression is unreadable. 'I see.'

Dom wonders why the question has stumped her. Maybe it's grief, or the amount of alcohol she's drunk. He watches her carefully as he asks again. 'So, do you know if she had any hobbies?'

'Like I've said, we were colleagues, Detective, and friends, yes, but mainly through work. I can tell you all about her client list and her projects, the ones she liked and the ones she was bored of. The only hobby we both shared a passion for was photography.'

Dom nods encouragingly. 'Tell me about that.'

'We both enjoy . . . enjoyed, photography. She had a thing for places, you know, old buildings, parks, that kind of stuff? I'm more about people.'

He nods. Noticing she's more at ease when she's talking about photography, he gestures to a large photo on the wall above the fireplace. In it a teenager is looking wistfully into the camera. 'Is that one of yours?'

'Yes. He was my sixth-form sweetheart.' She gives a sad smile. 'All ancient history now of course, but it was the first portrait I took that I was proud of. It was an old SLR camera – film not digital – I still prefer the old ways.'

'It's a great shot.' Dom waits a moment, observing her. She seems more relaxed so he moves the conversation back to Ruth. 'So you and Ruth went out taking pictures together?'

Ellie picks up her wine and takes a sip. 'No, not really, we mainly swapped tips, but we did go to the park at lunchtime a few times last summer and take a few shots.'

Dom opens the folder and removes a photograph. He holds the picture towards Ellie; it's the diamante balaclava Ruth had been found wearing. 'Do you recognise this?'

Ellie takes the photograph from him. She stares at it a moment, then looks back at Dom. 'I'm sorry, I don't know what this is.'

'Ruth was found wearing it.'

'Why would she . . .?'

'You said Ruth liked to photograph old buildings,' Parekh says. 'Were you aware of her trespassing to take pictures?'

'Trespassing?' Ellie's eyes widen with shock. 'No, not that she ever told me.'

Dom takes the picture from Ellie and tucks it back into the file. 'You and Ruth, did you talk much about men?'

Ellie looks confused. 'That's a strange question. I . . . well, not really. Ruth played her cards close, if you know what I mean? She didn't talk about guys, not to me.'

Dom watches Ellie for a moment. She acts relaxed but her shoulders are tense, her jaw rigid. He has the feeling she's holding something back, it's as if he can't get a proper read on her. 'Did she have a boyfriend?'

'I don't think so, not recently. I mean, there was some guy she mentioned a few months back, but she never told me his name. I assumed he was married.'

Thomas Lee was married. 'How well would you say you knew Ruth?'

Ellie flinches. Tears stream down her face. 'What are you saying?'

'I'm just asking a question.'

Parekh shoots Dom a warning look.

'Look, sorry.' He puts his hands up, palms out, trying to soothe Ellie. Reminds himself that she's grieving, and he's distracted. He's still thinking about Darren, about Chrissie, and what Clementine just revealed to him. It's screwing with his intuition, messing with his head and making him clumsy as fuck. He needs to think clearly, concentrate. He clenches his fists and tries the question another way. 'I just need to know if there is anyone else you think she might have confided in, or who might have wanted to hurt her?'

'Why would *anyone* want to hurt her?' Ellie grabs another tissue from the box beside the sofa. 'Ruth was well liked, she got on with everyone, but she was a private person. How she felt about social media was the way she lived her life – she didn't share personal things.' She wipes her eyes. 'I don't think she ever let anyone close enough to see the real her.'

37

DOM

On the drive back to base from Ellie's Shepherd's Bush apartment they have a debrief on the interview. The temperature has plummeted and Dom's glad to be in the car and out of the icy wind. Not that they're getting very far. The traffic's as good as stationary.

Parekh turns to Dom. 'Do you think Ruth was sleeping with Thomas Lee?'

Dom shrugs. 'It's possible and it would explain why she didn't tell Ellie his name, although if we're only talking a few months ago he'd already have been separated from his wife.'

'The divorce wasn't final then, and from the way she was when we interviewed her, it's obvious his wife still had feelings for him. I was thinking a relationship with Ruth would've given her motive.'

Dom remembers how Ms Coles took the news of her ex-husband's death. Unless she's an Oscar-worthy actress, he doubts she had anything to do with it. 'She alibied out though.'

Parekh drums her fingers on the steering wheel. 'Maybe she hired someone to kill him and Ruth?'

'And had them order twenty daggers for the job? That's a pretty wild theory.'

Parekh glances at him. 'You got anything better?'

He doesn't at the moment. 'OK, follow it up. Talk to the wife again, but tread gently.'

'Will do, guv.'

Dom's phone starts vibrating. He pulls it out, and sees he has six missed calls. The caller ID is flashing on the screen: *Chrissie*. He answers immediately. 'You OK?'

'I've been calling you for ages.' She's talking fast. 'Where are you?'

'I've been interviewing a—'

'It doesn't matter, listen, he's talking, Dom.' Chrissie's voice is full of emotion. 'Darren's able to talk. He told me he was being followed, that they were trying to force him off the road.'

'Who's with you now?'

'No one, I wanted to talk to you first but you weren't answering your phone.'

Shit.

'Call Holsworth.' Dom recites the number. 'Tell him that Darren's awake and wants to tell him what happened.'

'The IPCC interrogator?' She sounds confused. 'I don't think—'

'Do it now. Darren could be in danger, you all could be, but you can talk to Holsworth. This is bigger than Darren. It's bigger than me. Holsworth can help. You have to trust me.'

'OK, yes, I do trust you, I . . .'

'Where's Robbie?'

'He's here with me. Why are you asking? Dom, you're scaring me.'

Dom grips the phone tighter. Once Lindsay hears Darren's talking he's going to want to silence him. Dom reckons he won't make any mistakes the second time. 'Just call Holsworth, and things will be OK. But do it *now*, Chrissie. Promise me?'

'I'm hanging up. I'll do it now.'

'Stay at the hospital and keep Robbie with you. I'm on my way.'

Parekh drops Dom at the hospital. Darren's been moved to a private room and although usual visiting hours are over they've allowed Chrissie and Robbie to remain. It's quieter than when he was last here, and most of the nurses are gathered at the nurses' station. The air of restfulness is at odds with how Dom's feeling. He hates hospitals at the best of times. Right now, the antiseptic smell of the place is making him want to heave.

'Dom?'

He turns and sees his sister walking towards him, a plastic cup of coffee in her hand. 'How are things?'

'I made the call like you said. The IPCC are on their way.'

Good. 'How is he?'

'Come and find out for yourself.' Chrissie opens the door and enters the room. Dom follows. The antiseptic smell is stronger inside, made worse by the additional stench of lilies and stale sweat.

Darren's propped up in bed. There are a lot of wires attached to him, his eyes are closed and he's deathly still, but the heart rate monitor beeps steadily. Curled in the chair beside the bed, with his head resting against Darren's hand, is Robbie. It looks like he's asleep.

Dom feels suddenly awkward, as though he's intruding on their family reunion. He stays standing at the end of the bed while Chrissie moves around it to be with Robbie and Darren. She puts her hand on Darren's arm. 'Look who's here . . .'

Darren opens his eyes. He smiles at Chrissie. This disappears when he sees Dom.

Dom isn't sure how to play it, then decides neutral is best. 'All right, mate?'

Darren says nothing. Chrissie looks from him to Dom. Leaning down, she scoops Robbie into her arms and says, 'Seems you two need some space. I'll take Robbie down to the—'

'Stay.' Darren gasps out the word. 'Please. You need to hear this too . . . no more secrets.'

'OK.' She sits down on the chair beside him. Hugs Robbie to her tightly.

Dom picks up the other chair in the corner of the room and puts it next to Chrissie's. Sitting down, he says, 'OK, mate. Tell me what you did.'

Darren's silent, hesitating for a while. 'I took the comms offline during Operation Atlantis.'

Dom nods. He's not surprised. Darren had the access and the skills. 'Why?'

'He threatened me.' Darren looks at Chrissie. His voice is strained, his breathing increasingly laboured. 'He threatened you and Robbie. That's why I did it. What was I supposed to do? They're police, and there are more of them than I know the names of . . . from him all the way up to the top brass.' He exhales hard. 'I didn't know who I could trust, so I trusted no one.'

'You could have trusted me,' Dom says.

'Could I? How did I know that you weren't in on it with them? You were seeing Therese and she was shagging Lindsay . . .'

They all knew, Dom thinks, everyone except me.

He doesn't look at Chrissie, doesn't want to see the pity. Biting back the pain, he tries not to let his feelings show. 'The fact they twatted me around the head with a baseball bat could have been a clue.'

'It could have been a decoy, to put you in the clear. He said if I told, they'd hurt Chrissie and I'd never see Robbie again. They had pictures of Robbie at pre-school, in the car with Chrissie, and the pair of them together at the park.' Darren looks down. 'I couldn't risk them being hurt.'

'I get that.' Dom tries not to judge him; it was an impossible situation, he can understand that. 'So why the change of heart, why call me and ask to meet?'

'They wanted me to do more. Lindsay has a hair up his arse about you. He wants you to take the hit for what happened in Operation Atlantis. Said I had to admit to my part.' He pauses for a moment, trying to catch his breath. The heart rate monitor's beeps are sounding faster now. 'I mean, Holsworth was onto me, I was going to hang for what happened anyway, so Lindsay figured he could use that to his advantage – have me offer to give evidence on you in return for a deal.'

'And?'

'I refused.'

'Why?'

Darren looks at Chrissie then back to Dom. 'Why'd you think? You're family.'

'And taking down the comms is all you did?'

'Yeah.'

'What about entering the house during the raid and talking to Genk?'

The beeping of the heart rate monitor accelerates even more. 'That wasn't me, but I know why you'd think it could have been.'

Dom stays silent. Waiting.

Darren closes his eyes a moment. His face is pale, his skin almost grey. He lets out a long breath, then opens his eyes and stares at Dom. 'Lindsay took my boots. Said he needed to be sure I was balls deep in it with them. *Lindsay* met Genk, and he did it wearing my boots. He wanted you to see them and knew it would be all you'd be able to make out from where you were. He wanted you to turn against me.'

It was all staged for my benefit, Dom thinks. They had it all figured out, *me* all figured out. They played me like a sucker. 'And Therese, was she part of it?'

Darren looks away. 'I'm sorry, mate, I'm not sure how much Therese did herself. All I know is that she's shagging Lindsay.'

Dom isn't convinced he's telling him everything he knows, but, for now, he lets it pass.

There's a brisk knock on the door a moment before it opens. Holsworth enters. He's got Donald O'Byrne with him; one of the two investigators who tag-teamed Dom during his Operation Atlantis interrogation.

Holsworth nods at Dom, then fixes Darren with his piggy eyes. 'I hear you've got something to tell me, DC Harris?'

Dom stays with Chrissie and Robbie until Holsworth is finished. Lindsay is still out there; he doesn't want Chrissie left alone before those responsible for the failure of Operation Atlantis, and the attempt on Darren's life, are arrested. Lindsay is ruthless and, if he's in business with Genk, he's lethal. Genk is the worst kind of criminal – smart, organised and able to get to people anywhere. Dom won't take a risk on his sister's safety.

It's gone four o'clock when Holsworth and O'Byrne are finally done. As Chrissie and Robbie go back into Darren's room, Holsworth asks Dom for a word. There's a new uniform on the door now. Someone Holsworth really trusts. So Dom agrees and follows Holsworth and O'Byrne out past the nurses' station and a little way along the corridor.

O'Byrne keeps walking, but Holsworth stops and turns to Dom. 'We've got enough to get Lindsay. I need to run a couple of things past legal, but it'll be fast.'

'You believe Darren?'

'There's evidence from the crash investigation that corroborates his story. The street camera footage shows he wasn't alone, a vehicle was following him. Before he turned on the street where he crashed the other vehicle was driving aggressively. It didn't pursue him into the side street, but it stopped level with it and watched the crash. It stayed in that position for . . .' Holsworth consults his notebook. 'Sixty-three seconds.'

'What do you know about the vehicle?'

'It was a black Merc . . . Charlie-Kilo-One-Eight-Three-November-Tango.'

Dom clenches his jaw. He knows what comes next.

'Registered to Simon Lindsay.' Holsworth looks at Dom a long moment. 'He's being arrested as we speak.'

'Good.' It seems like an understatement, but Dom's battling to process the emotions he's feeling – relief there's evidence so Lindsay can be charged, mixed with fury at the audacity of the man for so blatantly trying to destroy his family.

'I'm telling you this as a courtesy. And as a warning.'

Dom frowns. 'A warning?'

Holsworth gestures back towards Darren's room. 'Lindsay tried to kill Darren, but from what he's said, it sounds like Lindsay also meant to frame you, DI Bell. This is a heads-up – you need to watch your back.'

I always do, Dom thinks. 'Surely once Lindsay's in custody the threat goes away?'

'We can't be certain of that. It sounds like he's only a small part of the problem. Lindsay has been careless and arrogant in the way he attacked Harris. He knows he has powerful people behind him, maybe he forgot the rules still applied to him. Whatever the reason there's a long way to go here. You're on Genk's horizon now, along with whoever else is involved higher up the food chain. I doubt that target on your back is going to go anywhere fast.'

38

CLEMENTINE

I'm back at the faculty office, but my mind isn't on my work. I'm angry with Dom. Angry at myself. Furious that the connection we once had is now destroyed. I need to decide my next move.

Why couldn't he see I was trying to help and protect him against Lindsay, against their corruption? Then there's the mystery of what Sass and her group saw at Hendleton Studios, and the messages in the comments section of the urbexer's live-stream. Dom has to know what I've found, it could be a murder. But I can't force him to listen. That leaves me with the decision of whether I investigate what happened alone. I also only have ten days left to interview other urban explorers and finish this phase of my research.

As the possibilities whirl in my mind, I work through my emails. There's still nothing new from David. It's just more of the same – conference invites, university strategy bulletins, fan emails and dick pics. I click through, deleting them all, until something different catches my eye.

In the subject line are the words: *DON'T TRUST HIM.*

There's no message, only an attachment, so I open it. It's a photograph of Wade.

It shows him outside the faculty building, walking across the lawn of the quad. The shot is in profile, but his head is turned in the direction of the camera, his attention on something slightly over to its right.

Looking over the divider between our desks, I compare the picture to the man. The clothes he's wearing are identical. His shirt is new, blue with fine yellow checks. I've never seen him wear it before, meaning this photograph must have been taken today.

It's not the fact that the photographer was here at the university that bothers me, or the fact that they've sent me a picture of Wade. It's what they've written across his body in thick black font that I don't understand. The word: *DANGEROUS*.

39

DOM

Chrissie eventually persuades him to go by promising to stay at the hospital until Lindsay is in custody. Dom's reluctant, but he can't neglect the cases he's working any longer. Parekh collects him from the front of the building. She's been unsuccessful in speaking to Ms Coles to test her theory the ex-wife could have a motive and be behind the murders. But she's had more luck with Ruth Kemp's landlord. He's agreed to let them into the flat this afternoon if they hurry.

Parekh manoeuvres her Fiat 500 back into the flow of traffic as soon as the door of the passenger side is closed. 'You need to call Abbott.'

Dom finishes fastening his seatbelt and looks across at Parekh. Her face is flushed and there's a gleam of excitement in her eye. 'Why?'

'He's seen something on the CCTV. He's back at base, still working on it, but here's what he's found so far.' She hands him her smartphone. 'Wake the screen and you'll see the video.'

Dom takes the phone.

'It's from the camera on the corner of Strand and Surrey Street,' Parekh says.

Dom taps on the screen and the video opens. The timestamp is 11.42 – about an hour before the approximate time the doc gave for Thomas Lee's stabbing. He sees two figures of average height and build, most likely male, approaching the corner. Their heads are bowed, and their beanie hats pulled low over their brows. As they get to the corner, one of them reaches into their pocket, takes out a couple of cigarettes and lights up, passing one to the other. They turn away from the camera. 'It's interesting they're careful not to look towards the camera. Has Abbott managed to get a clear view of their faces?'

Parekh shakes her head. 'Not yet, but keep watching.'

Dom does as she says. A taller man, slim with a long stride, joins the pair. He's wearing a beanie and has a rucksack slung over his shoulder. 'Thomas Lee?'

'That's what Abbott thought.'

He watches Lee accept a cigarette from one of the others. Then a fourth person appears, walking up Surrey Street with their back to the camera. Shorter and petit, their beanie has something shiny along the brow. 'Ruth Kemp?'

'It could be. She doesn't stay long though.'

On-screen, Dom sees Ruth talking to Thomas. Her body language is defensive, hugging her arms around herself. One of the other men says something and she takes a step backwards, away from him. 'They're arguing.'

Parekh indicates left and takes a short cut through one of the side streets. 'Yes.'

On the video, Dom sees Ruth shake her head, then she turns and retreats back along Surrey Street and away from the view of the camera.

Parekh glances across at him. 'Abbott picked her up again on a camera in Temple Place and tracked her back to Temple tube.'

'Good work.'

'You should tell Abbott that.'

Dom clenches his jaw. 'What about the three men?'

'They go into Surrey Street at 11.59 and as the Aldwych cameras were updating from midnight to one o'clock there's no footage of them. Thomas Lee doesn't reappear at all, but then we know where he was. The other two get picked up on the same camera walking back along the Strand at 12.54. Abbott's tracking their onward route now.' Parekh points to the envelope sitting on the dashboard. 'In there's the best quality image Abbott's managed to pull from the video. It's got the four of them together.'

Dom picks the envelope off the dash and tucks it into his jacket pocket. Then he restarts the video, pausing it at the moment the two men start smoking. Stares at them as a hit of adrenaline spikes in his bloodstream. 'One of these men, or both of them could be our killer. They know Thomas and Ruth, and they exited Aldwych when Lee never made it out.' He looks across at Parekh. 'They're clever to avoid the camera. We need to find out who they are. Top priority.'

The balding landlord wears a grubby T-shirt that stinks of stale cigarette smoke. He's not best pleased to have to open Ruth Kemp's second-floor flat for Dom and Parekh, and grumbles about police liberties and wasting taxpayer's money as he finds the right key and unlocks the door.

When he moves to go inside, Dom stops him. 'We'll take it from here, mate.'

'Suit yourself.' The landlord sniffs loudly and buggers off back to his own flat downstairs. Dom waits until he's out of sight before he steps over the threshold.

The Edwardian house would once have been grand, but the layers of paint on the woodwork, and grey carpet with threadbare patches, show the landlord only does the minimum upkeep. The flat is spotlessly clean and tidy, though. Ruth Kemp may not have been able to afford anything more upmarket, but she took pride in her home. Six steps take him into the main living space, a lounge of sorts, with a kitchenette at one end and a small bistro table with one chair jammed close against the wall. The cabinets are farmhouse style, well used but serviceable. On the shelf that runs high above the counter are patterned china plates and a blue flowered tea set. As he moves closer, Dom notices one of the dainty porcelain cups has been broken and fixed back together with glue.

On the low wooden unit opposite the sofa is a small flat-screen television and a proper record player, original not a reproduction. On the floor below it are two boxes filled with vinyl. Dom leans down and pulls a few out – The Beatles, Pink Floyd, Eric Clapton – all albums that would have been released years before Ruth was born.

Putting the vinyl back, he looks up at the wall. It's covered with a patchwork of framed photographs. There's Ruth on a cycling holiday, her bike parked alongside a huge lake surrounded by forest, several of her hiking in mountains, another of her drinking cocktails from a red bucket at a full moon beach party, and one of her on a narrowboat with what looks like her parents. Happy moments in her life captured permanently as memories on film. Now they're all that's left of her.

Pulling a pair of latex gloves from his pocket, he turns to Parekh. 'Look for anything that might connect to the men on the video. We need names, details.'

Parekh frowns. 'This isn't my first time, guv. I know how to do a search.'

He nods, admonished. After Clementine's weirdness, and the stress of Darren's accident and Chrissie's angst, he feels exhausted. Drained. Usually a discovery like the men on the CCTV would spark a new surge of energy, help him power through, but right now the sadness of this young woman's death is getting to him. *Everything* is getting to him. He needs to sort his head out. 'Sorry, yeah.'

He leaves Parekh to search the living space and walks through to the bedroom. The bed has a wooden frame and the grey linens have been made with the precision of a maid in a top hotel, hospital corners and everything. On the bedside table is a stack of books. Five of the six are on photography, the sixth is a romance novel. There's a half-drunk glass of water beside them, and a Post-it note. He steps closer and reads the note: *don't forget to give Karl £10 (again)*.

He wonders if Karl is one of the men on the CCTV and why Ruth owes him a tenner. He's been in victims' bedrooms many times before in the course of his work, but there's something about being in this young woman's bedroom that makes him feel uncomfortable. Maybe it's the degrading way in which she died, or the fact that she was so young and should have had so much more time to live her life, but being here feels as though he's snooping. A voyeur. Resisting the urge to call Parekh to join him, he turns away from the bed and scans the rest of the room.

In the corner is a wooden desk painted grey, with a photo printer and a stack of photographs on it. At the top of the pile is a picture of someone he recognises: Ellie – Ruth's friend from work. Ruth has taken a photograph of Ellie taking a photograph of a statue of a photographer in a park. Very meta, thinks Dom. Maybe it was on one of their lunchtime excursions that Ellie talked about. He looks through the other photographs. There are a few cityscapes, but most of them are of inside spaces, old buildings; a close-up of a collapsed ceiling, the plaster hanging in tendrils around a dusty chandelier, a spiral staircase with ivy growing around the banister, a room with a broken window and a row of rusty iron bedsteads, a theatre that looks untouched since the fifties.

He looks around the room but sees no sign of a camera. Pulls open the desk drawers, but finds only notebooks and pens, an old bank card with the expiry date long past, a stack of Manila envelopes. Moving across to the wardrobe, he opens it and checks inside. Everything is neat and ordered, the clothes hung on the rail with similar colours batched together. Bending down, he searches for the camera, but finds nothing.

'Guv? I've got something.'

Closing the wardrobe, Dom hurries back to the living space. Parekh is standing next to an open kitchen drawer. She gestures to the smartphone on the counter. 'This looks like Ruth's mobile, but there's another one in the drawer.'

'Maybe she's just upgraded.'

'I thought that, but then it beeped.' Parekh lifts out the phone using her gloved hand. 'The screen's locked, but you can see the message if you touch one of the keys.'

Dom takes the phone. Reads the message.

We need to talk. Don't go to the police.

40

CLEMENTINE

It's getting late but I'm still in the faculty office when the second email arrives. Like the first, this one has no message. The subject line is: BE CAREFUL.

I recognise the sender's email address from the first email: afriend@gmail.com. Are they a friend? I'm not so sure, but I open the email and the attachment it contains anyway.

I gasp, and rock back on my chair. This picture is different, more personal. The photograph contains my father. Staring at the screen, I take in all the details. I've seen this image before. It's the same as the copy Father kept with his medals in the wooden box on the mantle.

Father is in uniform, young again. He's posing for the picture with four fellow officers. They're holding up certificates but the picture is too grainy for me to read any of the names. There are other words written on this photograph though, scrawled in capital letters with a thick marker pen.

My father stands second from the right. Across his body is the word: *FRAMED*.

The man to Father's right, the tallest of the group, has his hand on my father's shoulder and his face slightly angled towards him. They look like they're friends. Written across him is the word: *KILLER*.

My heartrate accelerates.

I could be staring at a picture of the man who killed my father.

I scan the rest of the words. The man on Father's other side, standing in the middle of the group, has *TRAITOR* written across him. The blond officer with a beard on his left is captioned *THIEF*.

The last word, written on the figure standing to the far left of the group, isn't a judgement but a statement. All it says is: *ME*.

I stare at the picture. This could be a vital clue in the mystery behind why my father was framed, or it could be a hoax. I don't know what to think. But I need to consider the facts logically, and I need to know more. Pressing reply, I type a message.

Who are you?

The reply comes quickly: A friend. I used to work with your father.

I shake my head. Not good enough.

That doesn't answer my question.

There's a pause. Two minutes later a reply pings into my inbox: Gerry Matthews.

My stomach flips.

I remember that name.

41
DOM

He left Parekh at Ruth Kemp's place waiting for the CSIs. It's gone six o'clock, but the tech guys have already taken Ruth's phones and are making a start on them. They were getting closer to breaking the case, Dom could feel it, and for a moment exhilaration pushed away the exhaustion.

Then Holsworth called and told him the news.

Dom's at the police station now. He shouldn't be, he knows that, but the duty sergeant is an old mate. He says he'll give Dom five minutes.

Lindsay's lying on the bunk, his arms behind his head, eyes closed. He's wearing his usual black suit, characteristically smart, with a deep blue shirt and silver cufflinks. He looks out of place in the cell and for a moment Dom gets the overwhelming sense that this must be some huge mix-up, or a badly played practical joke. Then he remembers the evidence showing what Lindsay did to Darren, the threats he made against Clementine, and all Dom suspects he's done for Genk, and tells himself that whatever happens to Lindsay he shouldn't fucking care.

Dom closes the door behind him. There's a faint smell of residual body odour and through the wall he can hear the occupant of the cell next door vomiting. 'Lindsay?'

Simon Lindsay opens one eye. Grimaces. 'Why are you here?'

It pisses Dom off, the way Lindsay looks at him like *he's* the shit. He tries to ignore the fact that they were once mates, and keeps his tone neutral and no-nonsense. Focuses on getting the information he needs. 'Holsworth told me they'd brought you in.'

Lindsay eases himself up to sitting. He doesn't look at Dom and concentrates on smoothing out the wrinkles in the grey blanket covering the bunk instead. 'Figures you were the snitch. You were working with him all along then?'

'Not all along.'

'Yeah right.'

'Why'd you do it?'

Lindsay stays silent.

'Come on, talk to me, Simon.' Dom hates this. Feels powerless. His time will be up soon and he's getting nowhere. He fights the urge to pace, shifting his weight from foot to foot instead. Tries again. 'Why Therese, tell me that then? You knew how I felt about her.' Dom can't hide the bitterness from his tone. 'I thought we were mates.'

'What the fuck is this, your way of trying to guilt trip me into a confession?' Lindsay turns his face away. 'Spare me the Romeo and Juliet bullshit, OK. Just sod off.'

'You don't give a crap about her, do you? She was shot that night, because of you, but you're still fucking her, and using her to do God knows what.' Dom's tone is hard, angry. 'And the whack to the head I took could've put me down permanently. You sold me out.'

'I was following orders.'

'Yeah, right. Genk's orders, you bloody Judas.' Dom shakes his head. 'Was it worth it? Did he pay you well?'

Lindsay narrows his gaze.

Dom tries a different approach. 'Look, mate, wouldn't you rather tell me than one of the IPCC lot what happened? Don't you feel like you owe me after everything you've done?'

Lindsay scowls. 'I'm not talking. They can't hold me long, there's no evidence of—'

'You're wrong, they have more than enough to convict you for running Harris off the road – Darren's statement, CCTV, forensics, the lot.'

Lindsay hesitates, then sneers, almost trying to reassure himself. 'That's not possible, it's been buried.'

Dom stands over him. Lindsay's trying to tough it out, but there's no hiding the look of panic in his eyes. If someone was supposed to get rid of whatever linked him to the crime, they didn't deliver. 'Who didn't clean up, Simon? Did Genk promise you something?'

Lindsay looks at him, holding his stare. 'No, not Genk, someone much more powerful.'

'So tell me. Let me protect you.'

Lindsay laughs; it's a forced and bitter sound. 'No one can protect me, Dom. Especially not *you*. Their people are everywhere. The force is riddled with them.' When he meets Dom's gaze, there's pity in his eyes. 'Maybe they're done with me, that's why I'm here. I've served my purpose and now they've chucked me on the scrapheap for the crows to pick my bones dry. But you, Dom, you need to be very careful.'

His stomach flips. 'Why?'

Lindsay shakes his head. He laughs again and lies back down onto the bunk.

'Tell me, Lindsay. Why do I need to be careful? Who's behind this?'

Lindsay says nothing. He just closes his eyes and starts to whistle.

Dom bursts out of the station and into the street. His heart's banging. He feels sick. It's freezing but he thinks he's burning up. He strides fast, his fists clenched. Trying to make sense of it all.

Lindsay has rattled him big time. The logical part of him knows that he's probably just trying to mess with him, to mind fuck him, playing him as he always has done. But the rest of him feels that there's more to this, that what he's discovered Lindsay was involved in is only the tip of the iceberg.

He needs a friend, someone he can talk things through with. But Chrissie's busy with Darren and Robbie, and Abbott's a no-go at the moment, so there's no one, not at this time of night. Correction. There's one person who'd listen to him. Clementine. But it's risky if he lets her back into his life. She's obsessive, unpredictable.

He keeps walking.

Keeps hearing Lindsay's whistling in his mind.

The anger keeps building. His head's pounding. He can't think. Needs to get his head straight. Needs to talk to someone who won't judge him.

Clementine's proved that she's looking out for him. She might take things too far, but in her own peculiar way she's in his corner. Maybe he was too hasty earlier, should've given her more of a chance, heard her out. Although she talks a good game there's something sad, broken, about her. Something he recognises because he sees it in his own eyes, in the lines of his face and the grey appearing in his hair, every time he looks in the mirror. He hates to admit it, but he's realising he's drawn to her as much as she is to him.

Raising his arm, he steps out from the kerb and hails a cab.

He needs to see Clementine.

42

CLEMENTINE

He's standing on my doorstep. Wet, the dishevelled curls of his hair damped down against his skull, and the shoulders of his three-quarter-length navy coat are darker than the rest. I'm pleased to see him. The emails from Gerry Matthews have left me feeling unnerved, unhinged, and uncertain how to proceed, eclipsing all other concerns. Maybe Dom can help, he's police after all. Despite the heat of our conversation earlier, his presence here still calms me.

I stare at him before he says, 'Can we talk?'

'OK.' Stepping aside, I let him enter and close the door behind him. He wipes his feet on the mat, waiting for me to go up the stairs first. The last time he was here he forced his way in, desperate to stop the Lover from claiming me as his next victim. Dom's resolve gave me the opportunity to overcome my would-be killer.

Dom speaks as soon as we're inside my flat. 'Were you really coming to see me the night you followed Therese?'

'Yes. I saw this video and I wanted you to—'

'Clementine, look . . .' He steps closer. Puts his hands on my shoulders. Appears as if he's going to hug me. 'I know I was harsh earlier.'

I'm frozen. I don't know what to say or what to do. When I'd put my hand on his arm in the pub, he'd flinched as if I'd burnt him, when I took his hands he was desperate to shake me off. Now he seems to want me to hug him. It's confusing. I'm unsure of what we are: friends or enemies, partners or rivals. He's looking at me expectantly, waiting for me to make a move.

I can't.

I pull away, uncomfortable with the closeness. 'Why are you here?'

He frowns. 'I just . . . needed to talk to someone. Things are . . .' He scans my living space, probably realising nothing much has changed since he was here before, aside from the new sofa. His gaze stops on the end wall, on the spidery collage of my investigation map. He moves towards it. 'What the hell?'

'That's my work, I'm—'

He turns back to me. His expression is furious. 'Why is there a picture of me on your wall, Clementine?'

I hug my arms around myself, feeling exposed. 'I'm researching—'

'No, don't give me that shit.' He looks back at the wall. Traces his fingers over the strings connecting the subjects, and the themes. Stops at the word OBSESSION. 'What the fuck is this?'

I stand my ground. Have to brazen this out. 'It's my *work*, like I told you. I'm researching the nature of obsession, using thrill-seekers and voyeurs as subjects, and participating actively in the research myself, as you know I've done before.'

'Yeah, yeah.' He runs his hand through his hair and leaves it sticking up in wet spikes at odd angles. 'I know *all* about what you did before.'

I step towards him. 'Dom . . .'

His tone is sarcastic. Bitter. 'So have you broken into any other crime scenes yet for your research?'

'Not yet, no, but I have a video of one, from a group of urban explorers. I've been trying to tell you about it, but you never listen to—'

'You have a video of a crime scene?' He shouts me down. Raises his hands to quiet me. 'You said you were done with true-crime. You told me you wouldn't get involved in another case.'

'And you told me that you'd help me. That you'd be there for me.' I glare at him. Can't hide the hurt from my voice. 'I guess everybody lies.'

THURSDAY

43

CLEMENTINE

I stand motionless at the window as the early morning light filters through the grubby glass into my flat. I haven't slept, and although exhaustion makes my limbs feel heavy, adrenaline is keeping me alert. My world has been turned on its axis, and I have yet to understand the full implication – my father, Wade, Dom – all these men and my relationship with them has been thrown into question in the past twenty-four hours. I am a lone wolf, but I do not wish to be alone.

That's why I turn back to the group and confide in them. I've never been good at sharing, always calculating the probable outcome, and only engaging others when I can manipulate them to my will. But I'm different now, and they're already helping me investigate the cold case of my father's murder. Maybe they can provide a useful sounding board on the decision I have to take.

The Watcher to True Crime London: Who Killed Robert Starke? Advice needed: I've been contacted by someone who claims to know things about my father. They've sent me two pictures [attached]. They've told me their name, and I recognise it. I don't know if they are genuine, of course they could be anyone as I only have an email address for them, but I need to know more. If they have information, I need it. I'm thinking of asking to meet them. Thoughts?

Even at this time in the morning, the replies are fast in coming.

Robert 'Chainsaw' Jameson: What name have they given you?
Crime Queen: Are the photos genuine?
Ghost Avenger: Sounds dodgy. Are they not just another crackpot fan of yours?

Justice League: Meeting them sounds risky. What if they're a weirdo?

They all make good points.

The Watcher: Gerry Matthews. I remember my father talking about him, he was one of his colleagues. I might have met him once, I can't remember. I think the photos are genuine, but I don't know if the allegations written on them are. I need to find the truth.
Crime Queen: Will meeting this person help you get to the truth?
Robert 'Chainsaw' Jameson: Will they meet you?

Another good point. I haven't replied to their last email yet. I think it's time that I did. Toggling to the window with my university email account, I type a reply to afriend@gmail.com: You've got my attention. Tell me what you know.

I sit and wait for a reply, hoping it will be instant. Twist my butterfly ring around my index finger. A response pings into my inbox four minutes and twenty-nine seconds later.

Not on email. Face to face.

I reply: OK. When and where?

0900 hours. This location.

I click on the link and it takes me to Google Maps. The location is a residential address in an OK neighbourhood, but I know from experience that appearances can be deceptive. I flick back to True Crime London and add an update into the replies beneath my post.

The Watcher: I'm going to meet them at nine at what looks like a home. I'm posting the location here. If you don't hear from me afterwards, please investigate!
Ghost Avenger: Do you want company?
The Watcher: @GhostAvenger No, but thank you. I have to do this alone.

44

DOM

He's waiting outside the gym as it opens at five but even a workout doesn't help quiet his confused mind. Replays of the previous day's conversations – the words of Darren, Lindsay, Clementine – haunt him, taunt him.

He gets into the office before seven. The open plan's virtually deserted, just Abbott there, tapping away at his computer. It's dark outside, and only the MIT area has the lights on. Dom heads to his desk. His muscles are aching; there's heaviness in his legs from the two hundred squats, weariness across his shoulders from the hundred-plus pull-ups. Fatigue dogs his movements, but not his mind. Reaching his workstation, Dom grips the back of his chair. Pushes all thoughts away that are not connected to the investigation. Thinks about Thomas Lee and Ruth Kemp; forces himself to focus.

'I've been going through the CCTV, guv. I've found more.'

He looks across at Abbott. The DS looks tired, his eyes blood-shot. 'What is it?'

Abbott gestures to his computer screen. 'Footage of Ruth Kemp arriving at the construction site. It looks like she's with the same two men she met with Thomas Lee in Surrey Street.'

Dom leans over the desk divider. 'Show me.'

Abbott plays the video. Three figures, all wearing beanies, the shortest with something shiny lining the brow of theirs, approach the building. They walk briskly, but not so fast as to draw attention, duck through a gap in the safety fence and disappear into the building. 'She doesn't look under duress.'

Dom nods. 'True.'

'Ruth doesn't reappear, but the two men return just over an hour and a half later.' Abbot switches to another piece of footage and presses play. The two guys emerge from around the side of the building and go out through the gap in the fence. Their heads are bowed, but they appear to be in conversation, relaxed. 'The images of them aren't great. If I try to enlarge their faces it gets too grainy and distorted to be any use, but as far as I can see there's no blood on them. If they'd killed Ruth, they would have got covered in it.'

'They could have covered up or switched clothes, but why do it, and why here?'

'Beats me,' Abbott says. 'The CSIs didn't find anything in the building, and they're not carrying stuff.'

Shit, Abbott's right, they're not carrying anything. 'Can you go back to the first clip and play it again?'

'Sure.' Abbott replays the footage.

'There, look,' Dom says, pointing towards Ruth on-screen. 'She's carrying a camera. There wasn't a camera with her when she was found, and neither of the two men have it. We'd be able to see something of that size on them.'

Abbott frowns. 'You think the killer took it?'

'Someone did.'

Abbott stares at Ruth Kemp's image, paused on the screen. He rubs his hand across his forehead. 'I don't get why she'd even take a camera if she was planning to break and enter, especially a big one like that.'

'Because taking photos of abandoned places was her thing.' Clementine's words come back to Dom suddenly. 'I think these people could be urban explorers.'

As soon as Parekh arrives they gather in the incident room. They need to re-evaluate what they have. Dom sits on one of the tables. 'So, we know that Thomas Lee and Ruth Kemp were involved with a group that broke into buildings. From the footage we've got, it seems neither of them were put under duress to do so. At Ruth's flat we found pictures of derelict buildings. That seems to have been her motivation – taking photos. Why Thomas Lee and the other two men were doing it isn't as obvious.'

Parekh nods. 'I've googled urban exploring, and they fit the profile. Urban exploring, or urbexing, has had a massive boom in popularity. There are loads of videos being posted online – some of these groups have large followings, virtually cult status – and run their own channels. It's big on Instagram, too.'

'Is there money in it?' Abbott asks. 'Could it be motive for murder?'

Parekh shrugs. 'Maybe. I need to dig more, but it seems the popular urbex sites have big sponsorship deals – clothing companies, equipment and the like. They run advertising too, which could earn them a lot, given how many subscribers some of their channels have.'

Dom nods, then asks, 'Have the techs had any luck cracking Ruth's second phone? We need to find out who Ruth was contacting on that. I want to know who sent her that message.'

Parekh shakes her head. 'Not yet.'

Abbott clears his throat. 'Thomas Lee's phone records came in late last night. In the past months he had mainly work calls plus a few to his elderly mother, and one to his ex-wife. Nothing that helps us.'

'Ruth Kemp's smartphone records are the same,' Parekh says. 'All the usual stuff – family, work, a couple of friends from where she grew up – but nothing to Thomas Lee.'

Dom frowns. 'They must have communicated somehow.'

'You think he had a second phone, like Ruth Kemp?' Abbott says.

'If I was a betting girl, I'd put money on it.'

'Where is it then?'

Good question.

'There are questions to resolve about where Ruth's camera is, and how the killer could get away without being covered in blood, but from looking at the CCTV there's a clear pattern. Each time a group of three enters a building, only the two unidentified men come out. It happened with Thomas Lee at Aldwych, and with Ruth Kemp at the construction site. We've been assuming we're looking for one killer but . . .'

Parekh inhales hard. 'But we could be looking at a duo.'

'Precisely. If our assumptions are correct, we have to have those details from Ruth's second phone to uncover the connection between Ruth and Thomas, and understand what their relationship was. It could help lead us to the other two.'

Parekh nods, and makes a note on the murder board. 'I'll push the techs again.'

Dom turns to Abbott. 'We'll take the still you pulled off the CCTV footage, when the four were together on Surrey Street, and see if Ruth's parents recognise any of the others.' He looks at Parekh. 'Go back and visit Ms Coles, show her the image too and ask if she knows who they are.'

Abbott and Parekh nod.

They're getting somewhere. Abbott's done good work, he must have been at it most of the night to get through all the CCTV footage. He's an asset to the team; reliable, steady, until recently anyway. The more Dom thinks about it, the more he sees what happened with Abbott and the journalist as a case of momentary bad judgment. Maybe Abbott deserves another chance. It's time to decide.

Dom clears his throat. 'Abbott, stay here a minute.'

'Sure.'

Parekh shoots him a look, raises her eyebrow. Dom waits for her to exit the room, closing the door behind her, before he speaks. 'You've been a twat, yeah? What you did was bang out of line.'

Abbott looks away, can't meet his gaze. 'I know, guv. I . . . I wanted to stop but the guy kept blackmailing me, threatening to expose me as his source. So I—'

'Threw me under the bus instead.' Dom says bitterly.

Abbott flinches. 'I never meant to cause you any . . .'

'Yeah. I noticed that when that arsehole journalist wrote the assassination piece about my incompetence and Operation Atlantis.'

'I'm sorry.'

'So you've said. But those are just words, aren't they?' Dom inhales. Decision time. Break the rules or stick with them. 'You're a bloody good detective. It's a damn waste for you to be terminated.'

'Yes, sir.'

'I'm not going to report you. But if you ever pull something like that again, I'll make it my personal mission to take you down, even if I end up going down with you, you understand?'

'Yes, guv.' Abbott swallows loudly. Blinks. 'I really . . .'

Abbott looks like he's going to get emotional. Dom turns away before he does, reaching for the door handle. 'Come on, we need to speak to Ruth Kemp's parents. Get your coat, you're driving.'

As they walk out into the open plan, Dom hopes to hell that he hasn't just made the biggest mistake of his career.

45

CLEMENTINE

I stand on the pavement looking at the twenties-style house in front of me. It's Gerry Matthews's place, according to the location he sent me. It wasn't hard to find, just a ten-minute walk from Boston Manor tube. It's strange, even though I'm still in London it feels different here; the road is wider and the houses have more space around them. Even in the peak of rush hour it doesn't seem to have the same manic bustle of the city. It makes me feel more exposed somehow, but maybe that's because of what I'm doing.

Pushing open the wooden gate, I walk up the path to the front door. The small patch of lawn is cropped close to the ground, and the flower border around the fence is weed-free. I step up onto the spotlessly clean front step and press the bell.

My heart thumps in my chest. I'm light-headed, giddy, with both exhaustion and adrenaline. Through the mottled glass I see a person moving towards the door. Moments later it's opened by a tall man with receding blond hair. He looks at me intently, his expression giving away none of his thoughts. Then he smiles, and pulls me into a bear hug. 'My God, little Clemmy! The last time I saw you, you must have been all of about nine years old.'

I freeze. This isn't how I expected it to go. I'm not completely sure that I have met this man before and, as with Dom, I don't know how to respond to his intrusion into my personal space. So I stay stiff and awkward, holding my breath until he releases me from his embrace, trying to hide my revulsion at being touched by him.

He doesn't acknowledge my discomfort. Laughs. 'You can't remember me, can you? Don't worry, we only met briefly. Your dad was called in when he was off-duty, but you were home for the weekend and he didn't have a sitter. I offered to entertain you for a few hours.'

'You and my father were close then?'

'We were good mates – colleagues first, then friends. He talked so much about you.' Gerry gestures inside the house. 'Well, don't just stand on the doorstep, come in. Do you want a cup of tea or something?'

I'm still unsettled by the hug. I don't want him to touch me again, but I can't go now. He knew my father, and he sent the weird photos. I have to know what he meant by them. 'Yes, please. Tea would be great.'

Gerry steps aside so I can enter. I'm on hyper-alert as I follow him along the carpeted hallway to the lounge. It worries me that I can't remember this man. Aside from the fragments of memories from the day Father died, I've always had a good memory.

'Have a seat. I'll put the kettle on.'

I do as he says, sinking down into the cream sofa that's so saggy I fear for a moment it's going to swallow me whole. I scan my surroundings. The room is spotlessly clean, but everything in it is a bit shabby; between the sofa I'm sitting on and its mirror image opposite is a wooden coffee table. The surface is scratched and the corners battered, and the old-fashioned sideboard and bookcases lining the walls are in similar condition. In the corner of the room, to the side of the large bay window, there's a large flat-screen TV. On the shelf of the cabinet below I notice a video player next to the DVD player. I wonder why everything's quite so dated.

'It was my parents' place,' Gerry says, as if reading my mind. He sets a tray with two mugs of tea, sugar, milk and a packet of bourbons down onto the table, then sits on the sofa opposite me. 'I split from the wife six months ago. I think the realisation that she'd be stuck with me 24/7 when I retired was too much for her. It was easiest for us both that I moved in here.'

'You live with your parents?'

'No, they're dead. My dad passed years ago. Mum held on until the start of last year.'

I never know what to say in these situations. 'I'm sorry.'

'Thanks, love, she had a good innings.' He adds milk and two sugars to his tea and takes a slurp. 'I only retired a month ago. It already seems like I've been out the game for ages.'

I nod politely. In his faded jeans and yellow jumper, he doesn't look much like a copper, or much of a threat, but I'm getting a strange vibe from him that I can't put my finger on. I tell myself that I don't need to be afraid of this man – I have beaten a killer, I can look after myself. But it doesn't seem to help. Still, I try to act normal, pick up the remaining mug of tea from the tray and take a sip. 'It must be strange, being retired after so many years in the service.'

He holds my eye contact. There's something odd in his expression. 'Yes and no.'

I wait for him to continue but he doesn't. His expression unnerves me, as well as the fact he seems not to blink. The urge to run crashes through me like a wave but I fight it. I have to get the information I came for. 'Why did you send me the photos?'

'I thought you should know the truth.'

I lean forward. 'So tell me.'

Gerry frowns. 'I knew your dad pretty well back in the day. We started around the same time and went up the ranks together. He was a good man, one of the best. He always had my back, and didn't get involved in all the political crap. He was a really straight-up guy.'

'But he was found guilty of fraud and corruption. He—'

'I never believed it and you mustn't either. I think the evidence they had on him was fabricated, and they framed him because he got in the way.'

'Whose way?'

'Ah, well that's a harder question to answer. I don't know. You see I hadn't seen him in a while. He was on one job after another, deep cover stuff, which meant no ties back to us.' He shook his head. 'He tried to speak to me though. The day before he died he called me. I was away on holiday so he got the answerphone. I didn't hear his message until I got home the following week.'

'What did he say?'

Gerry rubs his hand over his chin. 'I can't remember exactly, something about meeting up, but it wasn't so much what he said, more the way he said it that bothered me. Your father was always laid-back. Even when everything was going to shit, he had the ability to stay calm. But he wasn't calm on the message, he sounded agitated . . . afraid even.'

'Did you tell the people investigating his death?'

He doesn't meet my eye. Shakes his head. 'I couldn't.'

'Why not?'

'Look, Clementine, you've got to understand, if this was an inside job then he was framed by powerful men within the force, they didn't want his death looked into too closely.' He sighs heavily. 'I couldn't put my family in danger.'

I clutch my mug tighter. Feel rage building inside me. 'My father burnt to death, and you, his friend, didn't even care enough to tell the truth?'

'I've always felt bad. That's why I reached out to you.'

'Twelve years later, yes, what did you expect that to achieve? Why now?'

'I thought you deserved to know the truth. I saw you in the media and have been following your progress. You solved that serial killer case, made quite a stir, maybe you can get to the bottom of this, too.'

Taking copies from my bag of the pictures he'd emailed me, I place them on the table beside the tray. I hope he doesn't notice my hands trembling. 'Tell me everything you know.'

He puts his hand on the picture of my father and four men in uniform. 'Well, you know who I am, and you recognise your dad. This guy in the middle is Jon Garrett, another undercover officer and someone I believe your dad confided in, not that it did him any good. The man to his left with the beard is Alan Holt. Your father told me once that Alan had taken evidence from a secure locker, but he had no proof to back up his claims. And this man.' Gerry taps his finger on the tall man on the far right of the group with KILLER written across his body. 'This is the man I believe is responsible for getting your dad killed.'

'He killed him?'

'No, no, I didn't say that. But they worked closely together, Paul Jackson and your dad, so whatever happened to your dad, Jackson has to know more than he let on.'

Disappointment floods through me. Gerry Matthews doesn't know who killed my father. This is all conjecture and bullshit. Conspiracy theories cooked up to try and ease his guilt. 'So you don't actually know who framed and killed my father?'

'No, love, that's why I sent the pictures to you like this, to get your attention. You and that true-crime solving collective need to look into it. Maybe you can succeed where no one else did.' His expression is kind, but I'm angry with him. He'd labelled each figure in the picture so confidently, but he had no evidence for any of it. I move on and point to the other photo. 'What about this, why send it?'

Something flashes across Gerry's face, but it's gone before I can place the emotion. 'You need to be very careful with that man, he's dangerous.'

'He's my boss, he has nothing to do with this.'

'Are you sure about that?'

'This is ridiculous.' Gerry Matthews is just a lonely man, filled with guilt and bored now that he's retired. 'Wade never knew my father.'

'Wait here.' Shaking his head, Gerry gets to his feet. As he pads out of the room I notice he's wearing moccasin slippers with a lining of grey fur, like wolf pelt, and I fight another urge to flee. From a nearby room I hear the sound of rustling papers and something falling to the floor, then Gerry reappears holding a piece of paper. He hands it to me. 'You're wrong, Clemmy. Very wrong.'

Shit.

My heart's pounding. The picture Gerry has given me was taken inside my flat. From the furniture, I can tell it was some years ago. It's a relaxed shot, the focus is a little blurred, but one of the figures in it is obviously my father. His appearance suggests the picture must have been taken not long before his death. He's laughing with another man. Their body language is friendly, comfortable. It's clear that they know each other, and they look more than casual acquaintances. 'Did you take this photo?'

'A long time ago.'

'Do you know this man with my father?'

He shakes his head. 'No.'

But I do. My breath catches in my throat. Heat rises up my neck and to my face.

No.

It can't be.

I peer closer. Need to be certain. It feels as if the room around me is spinning.

I recognise him. I *know* him. His tall, athletic build is familiar. His black quiff is sculpted just the same as usual. I know the line of his jaw, the angle of his brow. I know the feel of him naked inside me.

My stomach lurches and I push away my chair, barely registering the clatter as my mug and the tea tray are knocked to the ground. Ignoring Gerry's cries, I stagger to the front door, and shove my way out into the street.

My legs are unsteady. My vision is kaleidoscoping in and out. I gulp at the air, but still feel as if I'm drowning. Doubling over, I struggle for breath as the realisation circles like a tornado in my mind.

Gerry said that he's dangerous. Told me not to trust him.

Now I understand.

He has deceived me all this time. To me he was a stranger, but he knew my father and never told me. He kept it a secret, and there must be a reason why.

How did Wade know my father?

46

DOM

Ruth's parents live in a first-floor apartment a couple of minutes' walk from Maida Vale tube. It's a nice part of town, tree-lined streets and majestic old buildings. The Kemps' two-bed apartment must be four times the size of Dom's place. It's all high ceilings, sash windows and beautifully restored original features – cornicing, ceiling roses and cast-iron fireplaces. But the most striking feature is that every wall is adorned with framed photos of varying sizes, like a continuous mosaic throughout the living space. It reminds Dom of the similar, though smaller, arrangements he'd seen on the walls of Ruth's bedsit.

He and Abbott are sitting opposite Mr Kemp, as Mrs Kemp busies herself in the kitchen making tea. Mr Kemp is silent. He sits ramrod-straight, with his hands on his knees, staring past them at a spot on the wall behind their heads. The silence is uncomfortable.

When Mrs Kemp bustles back into the room the contrast between her and her husband is extreme. She's short and round with a kind face and eyes red raw from crying. Her voice is rich and honeyed, with a touch of West Country lilt, as she asks them if they'd like milk and sugar.

Dom says yes to sugar. Abbott declines.

Mr Kemp remains silent. He's reed-thin to the point of gauntness and has a deathly pallor that verges towards green. Dom wonders if that's his usual state or one brought on by grief. He knows from experience everyone reacts differently to loss. People never know how they'll respond until the worst happens.

He thanks Mrs Kemp for the tea and looks at Abbot. He's letting him take the lead on this one. Abbott came here before to do the death knock, so he's already built up an element of rapport with the Kemps.

Eager to fill the silence, Mrs Kemp starts talking. 'We've been here nearly five years now. We sold the Surrey house after Ruthie moved out. We just rattled around in it after she'd . . . gone.' She takes a breath. 'So it seemed to make sense. We bought this little place, closer to her and so convenient for the shows and galleries, plus somewhere out in France.' She glances at her husband. 'I've no idea what we'll do now . . .'

Abbott uses the pause between her words to gently interrupt. His voice is relaxed and friendly as he says, 'Thank you for letting us visit you this morning. We've just got a few questions to try and find out a bit more about Ruth as a person.'

'Of course,' Mrs Kemp says. Dom can tell she's trying hard to suppress the quiver in her voice. The over-talking is a nervous reaction, he's seen it many times before.

Mr Kemp nods once. Still doesn't make eye contact.

Abbott continues. 'We have evidence that links Ruth to a man called Thomas Lee he—'

'The poor man who was run over by a cab?' Mrs Kemp clasps her hands to her chest. 'No, like we said to you before, Detective, Ruthie didn't know that man, we're sure of it.'

Reaching into his pocket, Abbott takes out the grainy image pulled from the Surrey Street camera. 'We have CCTV footage of her with Thomas Lee and two other men that was taken a few days before her death.' He points to the tall man. 'We believe this is Thomas Lee. Do you recognise the other two?'

Mrs Kemp puts a hand to her mouth. 'It . . . why would she be dressed like that? Why is she with these men in the middle of the night?'

'We think she was involved in urban exploring.' Dom leans forward, keeps his voice gentle. 'It would really help if you could have a good look at the men. We need to locate them urgently.'

'I'm sorry, I've never seen them before.'

Dom looks at Mr Kemp. 'Sir?'

He shakes his head.

Abbott takes the photo from Mrs Kemp. 'Perhaps sometimes Ruth mentioned people, friends, that you didn't know?'

'No,' says Mrs Kemp. 'I can't think of any time she did that. She always told us about her friends and what they were getting up to. We're a very open family. We talked about everything, shared everything.'

Not this, Dom thinks. 'Urban explorers break into abandoned places or sites not open to the public. Had Ruth ever done anything like that before?'

Mr Kemp rears backwards on his seat. Mrs Kemp reaches out to him but he brushes her hand away. Leaping up he paces across the room to the window and stands with his back to them, staring through the glass. His shoulders start to shake.

'We . . .' Mrs Kemp glances at her husband. Keeps her voice hushed. 'We don't really talk about it.'

Dom keeps his voice low. 'And why is that?'

Mrs Kemp sighs. 'It was just too painful for such a long time, for all of us, and then later, when it was almost bearable to speak about, we just couldn't find the words. I know Ruthie wanted to, especially when she was a teenager, and she kept trying, but we just couldn't.'

Dom doesn't say anything, waiting for her to elaborate.

'It started after Sara died. Sara was Ruthie's twin. She passed just before their fifteenth birthday. She wasn't strong enough for the world. Her heart just . . .'

Shit. Dom looks at Abbott. He's chewing his bottom lip, looks a bit troubled. His sergeant should be leading this interview but Dom realises that he's taken over. 'I'm sorry for your loss.'

Abbott picks it up again. 'You were talking about what Ruth did?'

She bites her lip, then continues. 'After Sara died, Ruth was in a bad way. She got into a little bit of trouble, but nothing serious. It was a phase, I mean, people were very understanding about it, what with it being just after Sara . . . Anyway, it all stopped when she went back to school in the autumn.'

Dom glances over towards the window. Mr Kemp is still staring out of it.

'What sort of trouble did she get into?' Abbott says, an empathetic look on his face.

'Sometimes she broke into places. There was an old Victorian swimming baths about a mile from us. It'd been closed for, gosh, at least ten years and was about to be demolished. She got inside. Stayed there for hours until the security guards found her. She went back a couple more times, too.'

Abbott nods encouragingly. Keeps his tone soft. 'Did she do any damage?'

Mrs Kemp gives a strangled laugh. 'No, of course not! All she did was draw pictures of the place, if you can believe that. Took a few snaps on her mobile phone, that's about all. No vandalism. She wouldn't do that, she was a good girl . . .'

'She called it a magical place.' Mr Kemp's voice is unexpected, and louder than before. He moves back to the sofa and sits down again. 'She hated that it was being levelled for a new shopping centre. Said that it was a piece of history and should be preserved.'

'She did love beautiful things,' Mrs Kemp says.

They sit in silence. Dom looks at all the pictures on the walls. Most of them have Ruth in them, there's no sign of her twin, Sara.

'You've got a lovely home.' Dom gets up and moves towards the mosaic of pictures on the wall behind the sofa he was sitting on. 'And so many photographs. Which one of you is the photographer?'

Mrs Kemp looks at her husband. His lower lip trembles and for a moment it looks as if he'll say something again, but he just nods.

'Roger has always loved photography. Ruthie had his eye too. We thought she might go to art school at one point, but—'

'She got talked out of it by that idiot career counsellor.' Roger's voice is back to not much more than a hoarse whisper, but there's no mistaking the anger fuelling it. 'They told her she should do something with social media because it's the *future*. She had this thing about having to pay her way, even though we offered to help her. She rented that God-awful flat and took that PR job. Just look where it got her.'

'You think her death is connected to her job?' Dom asks.

'If she'd never got that stupid bloody job she wouldn't have been in London at all, and . . .' He wheezes, coughing as he tries to catch his breath, then stares back at the wall.

Abbott glances at Dom, concerned.

Dom looks to Mrs Kemp. 'Did you have any reasons to suspect she was in danger?'

'No, but well, it's just you can't help thinking what would have happened if she'd taken a different path, can you?' Mrs Kemp hugs her arms around herself. 'I mean, isn't it normal to think what could have been?'

'Of course,' Dom says. He can understand Ruth's parents torturing themselves with 'what ifs' and 'what could have beens'. They'd lost one child almost ten years before. He can't start to imagine how you carry on after losing two.

Tears start to trickle down Mrs Kemp's face. 'I always thought she could take it up seriously again – the photography – when she was older, you know, if she wanted to? Now she'll never get the chance.'

47
CLEMENTINE

Going into the office is the last thing I feel like doing, but I have to know why he hid the truth from me. As my computer powers up I glance around the faculty office and wonder if I can continue in this job. With what I know now, it seems unlikely that I can.

Wade looks surprised when I request a private meeting with him, insisting we speak in the meeting pod at the end of the faculty office rather than in the open plan.

I shut the door and remain standing as Wade sits down. I clench my fists tightly, trying to keep the emotions raging inside me under control. Wade crosses his legs. He rubs his hand across his jaw, looking as calm and well groomed as ever as he waits for me to speak. He's relaxed with me now, since our last encounter. It seems his thoughts of the keynote address invitation and frustration with my desire to work at home have been eclipsed by sexual satisfaction. I'm about to change all that.

My voice is so laden with anger I barely recognise it myself. 'You lied to me.'

Wade looks surprised but not worried. 'About what?'

He's so casual, so unaware that I know his secret, which just makes me madder. I dig my fingernails into my palms. Use the pain to try to keep the rage contained. 'You. Knew. My. Father.'

Wade says nothing.

I step closer to him. Keep my eyes on his. 'It's true, isn't it? Admit it.'

He looks away. Guilty.

'Tell me.'

He sighs. 'How did you find out?'

My legs feel weak and I battle hard to stay upright, stay strong. It *is* true. He has deceived me these past four years. 'How could you not have told me?'

He shakes his head. Doesn't speak. His lack of reaction is infuriating.

'Talk to me, don't hide behind silence like a coward.' I'm shouting now. Pointing at him, my fingers jabbing against his chest. 'How could you lie? Why didn't you tell me?'

'You're losing it, Clementine.' He reaches for my hands. 'You need to—'

'Don't touch me.' I jerk away from him. 'You said I could trust you and you . . . you . . .'

He stands up and moves closer. 'You *can* trust me.'

I put a hand out, warning him to stay back. 'How? When you've lied to me the whole time I've known you.' I shake my head. 'I slept with you, and . . . did you know me as a baby, as a little girl? Why didn't you say that you'd—'

'I never met you before you came to the university. I hadn't seen your father in years.'

My body's shaking. I feel dizzy, uncoordinated like the world has shifted on its axis and I can't get my balance. Needing support, I prop myself against the table. Glare at Wade. 'Tell me how you knew each other.'

He holds my gaze, then nods. 'There isn't much to tell. It was a long time ago, back when I was an undergrad, your father too. We rowed together for a time, had a few drinks now and then. We got on well, shared similar thinking on things, but we didn't see each other after graduation, not until one catch-up for old times' sake many years later.'

I narrow my gaze. His explanation seems so easy, so pedestrian. As if him knowing my father is nothing at all. 'Why didn't you tell me?'

Wade moves towards me again. His voice is gentle, smooth as silk. 'Do you remember what you were like when you first started as my PhD student? You didn't speak to people unless you had to, you refused point-blank to come into the faculty, you wouldn't engage in any student activities, you said you didn't trust anyone. I was the only person you seemed to connect with. I thought about telling you, really I did. Then I remembered the way you reacted in your interview when I asked you about your family; the look of fear and anger on your face. It was obvious that you and your father didn't have a good relationship – I thought mentioning a connection with him would be a bad move, and you were so fragile, so afraid of everything. I didn't want to spook you.'

'So you screwed me instead?'

He looks sad. 'Don't play the victim, Clementine. We're both adults.'

'Yes we are, but in the narrative you've put around our relationship I'm portrayed as the victim, the poor fragile girl, but I am *not* that person.'

'If you say so.' His brow is furrowed, and the look on his face is one of hurt. If I didn't know the truth, I'd think he was the one who'd been wronged. 'Look, I'm sorry I didn't tell you about knowing your father, but I can't do anything more than apologise.'

I glare at him. I want to yell and tell him to go to hell, to stomp out of here and slam the door in his face, but I also want to know more about my father. Wade can tell me things. In the end my curiosity starts taking over. 'Tell me more about your relationship with my father.'

Wade shakes his head. 'I've told you. We were young, at university, it was before he met your mother. Before you.'

'Why did you stop seeing so much of each other?'

'As I said, we grew apart.'

I don't believe him. 'Why?'

Wade doesn't answer for a moment. 'Look, your father was an idealist, he was far more suited for academia than the police force. I told him that. He disagreed, didn't want to hear it. We had a falling out.'

'And that was it?'

Wade turns away from me, a haunted expression on his face. I could go now, get out of the office while he's distracted by the memory of whatever happened between him and my father, but I stay. I need him to tell me more.

Eventually he says, 'I tried to speak to him, offered an olive branch a few times in fact. But it was only once, a couple of months before he died, that he agreed to meet.'

'And what happened?'

Wade swallows. 'It didn't go well. Your father told me not to contact him again.'

I wonder if it's true. Wade is not usually an emotional man, but now I can feel the angst and regret leaching out of him. I believe they did fall out but there's something in his expression, the way his eyes dart from side to side as he's thinking, that makes me wonder if he's telling me everything. 'And that's it?'

'He was a good man, Clementine. Always up for an adventure – hiking, climbing, swimming. He was an idealist too, said he wanted to change the world, make it happier and safer.'

'And you. What did you want?'

Wade gives a sad smile. 'I wanted to help him.'

48

JEDX

He runs, but it doesn't help. Getting active has always done the trick before when he's feeling tense, but not today. This is too fucking weird. Off the scale messed up. They're being hunted. It's obvious. He has to do something. *They* have to do something, what's left of them anyway.

Jedx glances at Beaker, loping along beside him. There's no need for masks today, they're not recording, but it seems odd somehow to be without them. They've not run together before, although he knows Beaker lives somewhere locally. He was surprised to see him waiting outside his flat when he left this morning. He'd mentioned his usual running route and time to the group before, but this is the first time anyone's joined him.

It's not that that's worrying him. What bothers him is there's something strange about Beaker today – he's barely spoken – and Jedx can't figure out why he seems so unconcerned about Sass. Personally, he can't stop thinking about the comment from Koso, the troll on the live-feed: *One of you won't get out alive. Who dies next?*

Jedx tries again, the emotion distorting his voice. 'She's dead. They said they'd kill one of us, and they killed her.'

Beaker still doesn't speak. Quickens his pace. The sound of their trainers on the pavement seems as loud as a thunderclap.

Jedx can't bear the silence between them. They're mates, kind of mates anyway. 'They said in the paper she'd been stabbed.'

'How do you know it was Sass? Could have just been someone who looks like her.' Beaker's voice sounds strained. 'Do they know about the group?'

'No. I recognised her name. We saw each other a few times, just the two of us . . . hooked up, you know?' Jedx glances at Beaker. 'She told me her real name.'

Beaker's expression is hard to read. 'You broke the rules.'

'We liked each other.'

'How you liked all the others?'

Jedx looks away. Keeps running. He isn't proud of the way he is, but he needs something to take him out of the monotony of everyday life. He's been his mum's primary carer since he was eleven years old, a month after her diagnosis; the day his dad went to the pub for a pint and never came home. Back then, when she'd had a bad day he'd go out and jack a car or lift something from a shop. Now he lets off steam urbexing, and when it all gets too much he finds comfort where he can. 'Sass was different. I really liked her.'

Beaker shakes his head. 'You always do.'

'I'm going to the police.'

'No.'

'What do you mean, no?'

'We agreed. No cops. We'd get done for all the break-ins, you know what we do isn't legal. That worried you before.'

'Things are different now!' He knows he's shouting but he can't understand why Beaker's so reluctant. It makes no sense. He thinks back to Hendleton, to the figure chasing them out of the sound-stage; its grotesque skull mask with red lips grinning while it bellowed at them to leave. He'd been at the back of the group as they'd fled; was the only one who got a good look at that thing. 'They're hunting us down. Cap's gone AWOL – what happened to him? Sass is dead. That Koso is picking us off one by one, just like he said he would. It must be the whack-job in the mask.'

Beaker doesn't look at him. Speeds up a fraction. Pumps his arms faster. 'We don't know for sure.'

'Who else could it be? We saw what he was doing at Hendleton, using that fucked up contraption to kill the woman. He commented under my video, warned he was coming for us. Now the others are dead.'

Beaker says nothing.

They make a left turn and start the climb up the long slope of the street parallel to the heath. It's a quiet road, minimal traffic.

Jedx keeps watching Beaker. His expression is impossible to read. It's like he's not even listening. 'Look, I'm going to tell the police everything.'

Beaker turns to him. 'And what about our ratings? What about the hopes we have for—'

'It's not worth it! If they could get to Sass, they can find us.' Jedx lengthens his stride up the hill, his stamina better than Beaker's. 'I've got my mum to think about, I'm all she has. If the police charge us, I can hope for a suspended sentence or community service or something. But if I'm dead there'll be no one to care for her. I can't let that happen. There was even a new comment last night. It said *Two down, who's next*?' Jedx watches Beaker again, desperate for more of a reaction. Misjudges the kerb and catches his toe. Stumbles. He feels like he's about to be sick. 'It's you or me next. We have to do something.'

Beaker doesn't answer. He keeps running, staring ahead at the road.

Jedx doesn't understand. This is crazy. He's all for adventure but this is serious shit. 'I don't get why you're so afraid of the police. Is having a criminal record worse than dying?'

Beaker ignores him.

They continue up the hill, then duck right through a gap in the hedge and onto the heath. The frigid air whistles around Jedx's face. His teeth ache from the cold. He pushes on to the top of the hill, the still frosted grass crunching underfoot. Beaker matches him pace for pace.

He glances at his friend. There's a weird look on his face.

It's quiet here on the heath; the only sound comes from bird-song and the distant traffic. There's no one in sight. Jedx doesn't know what's going on with Beaker but it's starting to freak him out. He slows, jogging on the spot. 'Look, I'm done, mate, I'm not discussing it any more. I'm going to the police.'

Beaker stops. He shakes his head. There's a dark expression on his face. 'You know, I really wished it wouldn't come to this.'

49

CLEMENTINE

I won't fuck him again. I don't know whether Wade is dangerous as Gerry Matthews suggested, but he's hidden the truth from me for four years and I will never trust him.

I'm outside the faculty office, standing in the smoking square outlined with green paint on the concrete of the quad. It's colder today. The sky is bright and the pale clouds are high above me, but they seem threatening all the same. It's that dry kind of cold that chills the blood and makes it feel as if snow is coming. The wind is bitter, and I turn away from it to light my cigarette before opening the browser on my phone and logging into the CrimeStop website. I go straight to True Crime London. The first thing I see is notification from Ghost Avenger about the USB stick.

> **Ghost Avenger** to The Watcher: The US tech has sent me the advanced repair program and I've set it running. It's complicated, might take a day or so to complete given the high volume of files. I'll update you when I have more.

I hope this program works. Maybe there's something on those files that will link with the things Gerry Matthews told me. I think for a moment, then type a new post.

> **The Watcher** posted in True Crime London: Who Killed Robert Starke?
> Update: Gerry Matthews was good for background but has no tangible evidence. I have learnt something though – my boss, Professor Wade, knew my father. This is a fact he has hidden from me the whole time I've known him. When pushed, he said that they met at university but lost touch. However, they did

meet a few months before my father's death. Could someone see what information you can find related to their friendship?

I take a drag on my cigarette and wait for someone to respond. I jump as my phone starts to ring instead. 'Hello?'

'Clementine? It's David.'

'David.' Gerry Matthews's photographs, and his allegations against the people who'd known my father, had turned my focus away from the urbexers and their videos. 'What have you got, do you have any urbexers willing to speak to me?'

'I can do better than that.' David sounds pleased, proud. He clears his throat. 'I can introduce you to one of them right now.'

We meet in a backstreet cafe a few roads over from the university. It's basic and smells of cheap frying oil, but it's clean and busy enough that no one bothers to look at who's coming and going. David is already there, sitting poker-straight on a stool at a high table in the corner by the window. Next to him is another man.

On the phone, David told me the guy he'd introduce me to is called Karl and that as an urbexer, he is something of a hero with a reputation for extreme exploration; he sees abandoned places as adventure playgrounds, and off-limits construction sites as outdoor gyms. He thrives on danger and pushes himself to the limit, and knows almost everyone on the UK urbexing scene. He also has one of the biggest egos.

I need to get past his ego to find out more about Sass and the group. With his connections, this guy could know what made Sass so fearful of Dink.

I take my tea from the server, carry it across to David's table, and hop up onto the stool beside the stranger. 'Hi, David. Karl? Thanks for meeting me.'

Karl turns his face to me. He sits still on the high stool, but I can almost feel the energy pulsing from him across the table.

I smile, hoping to break the tension, but it doesn't work. 'David says you're an expert on urbexing. Have you ever explored with a group called JedUrbXTM?'

'I know them,' Karl says. His accent is London with a hint of West Country. 'Did something a while back. Pretty tame.'

'Have you seen their more recent live-streams? The exploration of Hendleton Studios looked far from tame.'

He waves my question away.

'I'd like to know more about—'

'Tell me.' His stare is intense from beneath his shaggy black hair and, oddly, his interest in me seems as great as mine in him. 'Have you ever done it?'

I frown. 'And I thought I was the researcher here. Did David tell you why I wanted to meet? I'm studying thrill-seeking and obsession and wanted to—'

'Sure he did. But if you've never experienced the feeling yourself, I doubt you'll understand my answer.'

I hold his eye contact. 'Try me.'

He shrugs. Pushes his long fringe away from his eyes. 'Suit yourself. The thrill of UE is about getting close to death and cheating it. It's the proximity to disaster that makes the rush so intense. Heights work best – an abandoned Ferris wheel, a semi-built high rise, a disused crane – climbing to the top and dangling your feet over the edge for a picture. It's doing the impossible and not dying that makes you feel truly alive.'

I nod. Pull out my phone and make a few notes. 'I see. Do you think that's what the JedUrbXTM group did at Hendleton – get close to death?'

He ignores my question. 'But you don't see do you? How can you possibly understand? You talk about thrill-seeking but you can't *feel* the thrill, you aren't inhabited by obsession. You never will, if you always wrap yourself in the safety of a white coat, theorising rather than doing. You've got to break out. Otherwise you'll die never having felt a thing.'

I narrow my gaze. 'I can feel.'

'Spoken like a true drone.' He laughs and leans back in his chair.

'You're wrong. I've felt it.' I hiss. 'I've been closer to death than you could possibly imagine.'

He smiles in triumph. 'So tell me about it.'

I close my eyes a moment and remember how it felt as I slammed the needle into the Lover's eye and depressed the plunger. My words are slow whispers. 'I nearly died. It left me hypersensitive to the moods of others and my own emotions. Every feeling is like an explosion repeating through me, even when it belongs to someone else.'

He leans forward. Pats his hand against his chest. 'And in that moment, how does it *feel* in here?'

'Like I'm experiencing every sensation all at once – the ultimate euphoric high, the most horrific darkness, and everything in between.'

He nods. Satisfied. 'You do know, then.'

It's a mistake, revealing this much about myself. David is staring at me wide-eyed. I feel exposed, vulnerable, but I'm curious too. Karl has experienced sensations and emotions like I have. 'Know about what?'

'That once you've felt that high, it's like a drug. You crave more, but to get the same feeling again you have to find greater danger, harder challenges, the stakes always need to be bigger.'

'Until?'

He exhales. 'Until it kills you.'

I try to look unconcerned. Take a sip of my tea. 'That's ridiculous.'

I hold Karl's gaze and change the subject. It's clear he doesn't want to be drawn on the group, so I try a different approach. 'Tell me what you know about Dink.'

He shakes his head, causing his hair to fall across his face again. 'Well that's a name I haven't heard in a while.'

'Why?'

'Story is Dink got cast out of the JedUrbXTM group.'

'Was it because of the situation with the UB100s?' David says.

Karl turns to look at him as if he's just realised David's still here. He nods. 'Something like that.'

I narrow my gaze. 'And what did happen with the UB100s?'

Karl whistles, shaking his head. 'So JedUrbXTM and the UB100s are rivals, but the UB100s were around first and they're more of a collaborative group than most, so they suggested a joint explore, both groups coming together, with the idea they'd post pictures to followers and cross-promote each other.'

David nods. 'This was last autumn, before JedUrbXTM started live-streaming.'

'True,' says Karl. 'So they're down in the cave system, and the explore is going well, when Dink pulls the stunt.'

'What stunt?'

'No one knows for sure, not even Topski. All he remembers is one minute they're on track, crawling through the narrow section of the tunnel on all fours, with their torches lighting the way, and the next it's pitch-black and he's falling. He snapped his ankle in two places. It took hours to get him out.'

'Shit.' I shake my head. This doesn't add up. 'But why was Dink blamed?'

'Because it wasn't an accident. Dink had the main torch and, just as the light went out, Topski is convinced that Dink kicked him in the face and took out his head-torch.'

'Dink meant to hurt him?'

Karl nods. 'Yeah, the UB100s think it was a play to take one of their most popular players out the game for a while, and they're probably right because it worked. JedUrbXTM are bigger now, they have a much larger following than the UB100s.'

'And what happened to Dink?'

Karl shrugs and takes a slurp of his coffee. 'Who the hell cares.'

50

DOM

Back at base, the news isn't good. As Parekh gets off a call with the techs, she's unable to hide her disappointment; her usual upbeat energy is rather deflated. 'The memory of Ruth's second phone was deleted. There's nothing – no call log, texts or even saved numbers. The techs have tried recovering the data, but no luck. All we have is the message that arrived when we were searching her flat.'

Dom thinks back to the message: *We need to talk. Don't go to the police.* 'Who sent it? We need that information urgently.'

'There's no name,' says Parekh. 'I tried calling the number but it's switched off, and there's no voicemail service.'

'Have you tried tracing it?'

'Techs are doing it now, but they're having problems.'

Shit. Ruth's second phone could have been the key to finding the identities of the two men who knew her and Thomas Lee. 'Get on to the phone provider at least. Now you've got the phone details you can request Ruth's call history from them.'

Parekh nods. 'I'm on it.'

Jackson said he wanted an update, but so far all he's talked about is involving the media more and working in partnership – a phrase that makes Dom want to heave. Still, he tries to keep a neutral expression as his boss bangs on. He thinks he's just about managing it.

'. . . and yes, we've been releasing partial information to the media, as you know, Dom. But they're demanding more, not satisfied with the scraps any longer. We need to do a press conference, or an appeal or something.'

'I've told you why I don't want to share the more sensitive details. If we talk about the daggers it won't take the media long to connect the dots like we did – they'll track them to Scorpion and the details of the order will come out. There'll be hysteria on social media.'

'Then release the photo, the one from the CCTV.'

Dom shifts in his seat. 'If we release the picture to the public it'll give away one of the only proper leads we've got.'

Jackson looks at him over his glasses. 'Except it's not really a lead, is it? We don't know who the other two men are.'

'We're working on it. Uniforms have the image, analysts are watching the CCTV feeds, it's just a matter of time.'

Jackson grimaces. Rubs his thumb against a coffee stain on his desk blotter. 'A few days ago, I thought Thomas Lee would be a quick case. Now we've got daggers and break-ins and a second body. The thing's spiralled into what's looking like another bloody serial killer on our patch. We need to get the media onside now. The longer we delay, the more brutal they'll be when it comes out.'

'We're making progress, Paul. But I need longer.' Dom leans forward. Knows he has to get Jackson onside. 'We have proof that Ruth Kemp and Thomas Lee knew each other, and we believe they shared a hobby: called urbexing. They were urban explorers – people who break into abandoned or off-limits spaces, but they kept their activities secret from their families. Thomas Lee's ex-wife and Ruth Kemp's parents didn't know what they were doing and that's making the other people they were doing it with hard to track. We believe the other two men in the photograph are part of their team. From the message we've managed to pull off Ruth Kemp's phone we know that she and at least one of the others had knowledge of something that could be of interest to the police.'

'What?'

Dom shakes his head. 'I don't know yet, and we're not sure if the two men in the photo are friends of theirs. It's possible they are behind Ruth and Thomas's murders. Until we uncover more, we need to treat them as suspects. If you release that image, you could be forewarning the killer.'

'But the press are seeing no progress.' Jackson waves his hand towards his computer, the screen open on an online news website.

'There's mutterings that you've lost your edge, that you're not up to leading a murder inquiry, something to do with PTSD.'

Dom looks away from the screen. 'That's crap and you know it. This is real life, not a TV show – it takes longer than a couple of days to catch a killer.'

Jackson watches him a moment. Then nods. 'I have to give them something.'

'Tell them we're continuing the investigations. Following a number of leads. Promise a briefing in a few days or something. Just give me a bit longer to work this.'

'You think you can close this in a couple of days?'

No, thinks Dom. 'Maybe. We've got some new information.'

'Tell me.'

'She might have deleted the memory, but the phone company will have a record of activity on Ruth Kemp's second phone, and we're waiting for them to provide it. Our working assumption is that this was how the urbexers kept in touch. If that's right, we'll get the contact details for the other group members from Ruth's call and text history.'

Jackson pushes his glasses off the bridge of his nose and rubs the skin beneath. 'And if the phone company can't help?'

Dom stays silent. The gold carriage clock on the shelf behind the DCI seems to tick louder.

'Let's hope to buggery that they can, then.' Jackson's expression softens. There's kindness in his voice when he speaks. 'This thing with your sister's partner is a nasty business. Holworth told you what happened with Lindsay, I assume. You doing OK?'

Dom clenches his fists. 'I suppose now Lindsay's locked up I should be able to relax, but it makes me sick just thinking about it. I thought he was a mate.'

'It's tough, I know. Been through it myself, back in the day.' Jackson looks at him, concerned. 'A thing like that shakes your faith in humanity.'

'I'll be fine. I'll keep trying to support my sister and get on with the job.'

Jackson nods. 'Good man.'

Dom wonders whether to tell Jackson about the threats Lindsay made, and his claims that the corruption goes high up in the force. Jackson's been like a father, a mentor, to him. It could help to talk about the danger he could be in, to get Jackson's take. Dom's about to speak when his phone buzzes. He glances at the screen.

Shit.

Parekh's message is brief and to the point: We've got another body.

51

CLEMENTINE

I take my time in the faculty kitchen. It's just me and Wade in the office at the moment and I'm sick of the way he stares at me over the divider between our desks. As I stir the tea bag around in my blue mug, I hear the door open. It's Wade.

He stands in the doorway. I don't look at him, concentrating instead on taking the tea bag out of the mug, dropping the bag into the fishy-smelling bin and wiping away a splash of tea from the wooden laminate counter.

'Clementine?'

I don't respond. Instead I wash the teaspoon under the tap and put in on the drainer. Wade deceived me. I've trusted very few people in my life, but he was someone who I always believed was on my side, however suffocating I found it. Now I realise that was never true; the relationship we had was a sham, built on a lie.

'You can't just ignore me.'

I can, though. And I do. Abandoning the mug on the counter, I push past him, and stride back across the office to my desk. What I've learnt has made me feel unstable; as if the foundations I have built my world on have been eroded and my sense of self is crumbling and threatening to topple over at any moment. I have always prided myself on being able to read people, on catching them in the lies they tell and the secrets they keep. Since the fire changed me, I studied the people around me so that I could mimic their emotional reactions, their truth and their lies, to camouflage my own lack of feeling. And I was good, very good; almost a perfect facsimile of a fully functioning human. So how is it that I didn't realise Wade was hiding something? I never suspected *him* of lying.

I cannot stay here with him watching my every move. Switching off my computer, I shove the papers I'm working on into my bag.

I can continue my research at home. Location doesn't matter and I work better there anyway.

There's more urgency in his voice now. 'Clementine, what are you doing?'

I don't respond. Keep walking.

Wade hurries around me and blocks my exit. I flex my claws. Tense my muscles ready to lash out. If he gets any closer, I might rip him apart.

He's looking at me with concern. 'Where are you going?'

'I'm not staying.'

He towers above me, over a foot taller and physically dominant. 'You should.'

I press my back against the noticeboard and feel the pins from the flyers and posters digging into my back. 'I need some space. I can't stand you—'

'We've spoken about this.' His voice is gentle. 'Reclusiveness isn't good for you. It's far better if you participate in the faculty.'

He talked about that. *He* thinks I should join in. It was a lecture, not a discussion, and one I didn't agree with, especially now. 'I'll be in on Monday.'

Wade looks disappointed. 'Lack of engagement won't serve you well when your case goes to the promotions committee.'

'I'm not looking for promotion.'

Wade takes a step closer. 'I'm on your side, Clementine. I'm worried about you.'

'Don't be.' His proximity makes my hackles rise. I don't trust him, and I do not forgive him. 'I don't need your concern.'

Something flashes across his face, anger perhaps, before being replaced with his usual unreadable mask of neutrality. His jaw is tighter than before, though, and his posture's more rigid. I can hear the jealousy in his tone. 'This isn't just because I knew your father, is it? It's still got something to do with that detective.'

'No.'

Wade shakes his head. 'Infatuation isn't healthy, Clementine. You know very well that you're prone to fantasy. Whatever you think you're feeling for him, it simply isn't real.'

I hug my bag to me more tightly. 'Me leaving isn't because of him, it's about you lying to me.'

He sighs. 'I never lied.'

'Whatever words you use to dress it up, you hid the truth. I'll work from home until Monday, maybe longer.'

'Clementine—'

'No.' I hold up my hand to stop him talking. I don't want more excuses. I just want to leave. 'Keep away from me, OK? I'm going.'

Back in my flat, high above St John Street, I update my research web by running another red thread from the photograph of Father to the three pictures Gerry Matthews gave me. There was something strange about Gerry that I still can't put my finger on, but even though he has no evidence to back up his claims, he's given me new information; names of people who worked with my father. I write them on the photograph of Father and his four colleagues: Gerry Matthews, Jon Garrett, Alan Holt, Paul Jackson.

I have questions about these men. I want to know what their relationship with my father really was. Perhaps one of them knew about my father's undercover work, maybe he confided in one of them. I need access to the police databases and more information on the cases my father worked. But I have no leverage, not on my own.

Setting down the spool of thread on my overflowing desk, I open my laptop and wake the screen. I toggle webpages until I get to the one open on True Crime London. I type into the status field and press return.

The Watcher to True Crime London: Who Killed Robert Starke? @GhostAvenger do you have an update on the USB stick?

As I wait, I pick up the spool of thread again and go back to the research web. I stare at the central word – *OBSESSION*. Think about the Hendleton video and possible murder scene.

Adrenaline fires through me. I run two more threads from the central word, add new pins, then list the details of my two new subjects, the first of my thrill-seekers – spoke number nine, *Sass*, and spoke number ten, *Karl*. Based on my conversation with Karl, it's clear the online audience element of adventuring adds to the adrenaline buzz of thrill-seeking for some. I wonder if the need for followers and likes becomes as much of an obsession as the thrill of the activity. Maybe the thrill for some is the social kudos, and they need increasingly dramatic live-streams to pull in viewers. I remember Sass's worry about going to the police, and how the other group members pressured her not to. Could one of them be so obsessed with getting viewers that they'd commit murder?

I add a third pin, unravel more thread to meet it, and attach a piece of paper with the number eleven and *Dink?* I don't know who Dink is, but I can tell that they're important. Sass used an analogy of someone freaking out underground when she was talking about ego and group trust; Karl told a similar story about the UB100s and Dink. I think Sass was talking about Dink. Was Dink cast out of the JedUrbXTM group? Is Dink holding a grudge? Have they been leaving comments on the group's live-streams? Maybe they know Koso.

I take a breath. Try to calm myself. I'm onto something, I know it.

Dink could be the key. I have to find them.

Grabbing the Post-it pad on my desk, I scrawl myself an action to check through the comments on the group's other videos. It's important, and I'd been about to do it before I got diverted by the emails from Gerry Matthews. Beneath the first action, I write a second. I need to speak to Sass again and I need to persuade her to tell me *everything* about Dink.

There's a ping from my laptop. I look at the screen and see a notification from True Crime London. I click it and read the message.

Ghost Avenger to True Crime London: Who Killed Robert Starke?
USB stick update: the repair is at 81%. Another day and we should be able to take a look at Robert Starke's files.

52

DOM

Hampstead Heath is a nightmare as a crime scene. Open-air sites always bring out the rubberneckers and freaks. The media are drawn to them, like vultures circling carrion, and if they take to the air – cameras in helicopters – it's almost impossible to stop key details getting out. He looks up through the tree canopy. So far there's nothing. He hopes to hell it stays that way.

Ducking under the outer cordon, Dom and Abbott turn off the path and pick their way through the long grass and undergrowth, following the common approach. It doesn't feel like the city here, and it smells different – earthier – the air less polluted. Everything is damp. It's impossible not to get caught by the brambles. By the time they round a large tree with a yellow number marker to the right of it, Dom's trousers are drenched from the knees down and his socks are squelching inside his shoes with every step.

'The body's over the ridge,' Abbott says, pointing to a short rise ahead. 'But as they were cordoning off the area, uniform found what they think is material from his clothing up here. Footprints too.'

Dom's thankful Parekh circulated the CCTV image to uniforms, asking them to be vigilant. The first responder is convinced the body they'd found matches one of the men.

He stops by the number marker. The undergrowth is flattened around the area, briars snapped and broken. Caught on a thorn is a scrap of black fleece.

Sidestepping away from what he assumes was the victim's exact direction of travel, Dom moves forward with caution, scanning the surroundings for clues. The scrub is too dense here for footprints, but as they move to the top of the ridge, the groundcover has been cleared. In the orange-brown soil he sees one distinct set of footprints, and one trail that's been scuffed over, extinguishing any details.

'You can see where he landed,' Abbott says. 'They're excavating a new water feature. The groundsmen found him when they started work this morning. So far we've had no witnesses come forward – no one saw him jogging, not even a dog walker.'

Dom moves to the edge and looks down into the freshly dug pit. The body lies at the bottom, about ten feet below. The soil is loose around the edge, so Dom can't get too close, but he can see the poor bloke's neck is twisted at an implausible angle. There's dried blood crusted across his face, but the worst of the damage is obvious even from a distance. His torso is covered in blood. There's a gaping wound running from his chest to his belly, and a dagger sticking out from where the man's belly button would have been.

Shit.

In a paper suit that looks at least a size too big, Emily Renton approaches the body. As if sensing Dom's eyes on her, she squints up and waves when she sees him.

He raises his hand and shouts, 'I'm coming down.'

Leaving Abbott talking to the CSIs about what they've found so far, Dom slides down the bank and joins Emily beside the body. 'What have we got?'

Emily gestures to the man's torso. It looks like the killer used the dagger to try and gut him like a fish. 'Aside from the obvious, there's blunt force trauma to the head, evidence of strangulation and in all likelihood a broken neck. As you can see there are some facial lacerations which could indicate signs of a struggle. There's secondary matter beneath his fingernails, most likely from him trying to fight off his attacker. I'll get his hands bagged and should be able to tell you more once I've got him back to base for a proper look.'

He stares at the victim's body. Shakes his head. 'This is different from the last two, more excessive. Why strangle him and cut him open?'

'At this stage, from the clinical signs observed, I'd say he was partially asphyxiated, possibly to weaken him prior to making the incision with the dagger.'

'Poor bastard.' Dom crouches down to take a look at the victim's face. The first responder is right, this bloke is one of the unidentified men from the CCTV image. 'How soon will you be able to do the PM?'

'Tomorrow maybe, if I jig things around.'

Abbott's walking towards them, picking his way across the sodden earth.

'Phone? Keys?' Dom says.

'No phone but they found a wallet and keys. His name's Ian Lowe, lives a couple of miles from here.'

Dom gestures to the earbuds and cord lying near the body. 'Looks like he had a phone or iPod.'

'Must have been taken.'

Dom looks at Emily. 'I really need a DNA match from those fragments under his fingernails. This bloke is the third person murdered of a group of four urban explorers. The fourth guy could be the killer, or he might be in danger.'

Emily looks from Dom to the body. 'You know Jacquie goes back on the road tomorrow, don't you? I've booked leave for this afternoon.'

'I wouldn't ask if it wasn't critical.'

She sighs. 'OK, fine. But you owe me, and I expect chocolate. Fancy stuff, no value shit.'

'I appreciate it.'

'I'll call you as soon as I have anything.'

Dom looks down at the man lying broken in the dirt. Thomas Lee's wounds were inflicted to prolong his death, Ruth Kemp's were done to make hers as painless as possible, but this seems more sadistic – as if the killer wanted their victim to see the dagger going in and their body slit open, but powerless to stop it.

As he's staring at the body, a pounding starts to build in his chest. He feels the wind in his hair, and he knows what's coming.

Looking up, he sees two vultures circling above. The helicopters getting as low as they can. Their cameras point at him and the body. Dom turns to Abbott. 'We need a forensics tent out here now. Get this place screened off from these fuckers.'

But even as he says it, he knows it's too late.

53

CLEMENTINE

While I wait for Ghost Avenger to report another update on my father's USB stick repair, I trawl through JedUrbXTM's live-stream page. I've been at it a while when I make the discovery. Koso began commenting on the videos much earlier than I thought. The words were barbed at first; a snide comment about Jedx's inability to hold the camera steady, a nasty remark about Sass being too heavy to make a jump. It wasn't until the Hendleton Studios live-stream that their tone became more threatening. They'd typed a warning for the group not to go inside just before they broke in, then warned them not to go further as they entered the sound-stage. But they still just seemed like a troll, as David had said they were. It wasn't until the Aldwych tube station video that things became more serious.

The station exploration wasn't live-streamed but filmed on bodycams, edited together with audio narration from Jedx, and uploaded the next day. Most of the comments beneath the video praise Jedx, Beaker and Cap. Koso's stands out in stark contrast.

Koso: Curiosity killed the Cap. It's going to kill you all.

It's a sinister coincidence when Cap then doesn't appear on the next video, taken two nights later, as Jedx, Beaker and Sass explore a building under construction. That was the video I first saw Koso comment on. It was during the first part of the live-streaming as the group entered the building and climbed up to the top floor.

Koso: Four are now three. One of you won't get out alive. Who dies next?

I read the comment again and feel chilled to my bones. Pulling the fleece throw around me, I try to get warm, but still I start to shiver. I have the feeling that Cap is dead.

There are more comments on the video now; voyeurs have continued to watch it after the fact. Scrolling down to the bottom, I find Koso's original comment, then begin scrolling up, scanning the new ones to see if they wrote anything more.

Pinnyhip078: Freaking awesome guys.
UrbexUncovered: Old and new combined. Great explore.
NanExp7856: Thanks for sharing!
Upyeah99: You got safety harnesses there? You should, man.
LiveWildRock: Love this. More please!
UrbXclub2018: Weird vibe in that place. It's like someone ripped out the building's insides.
Perkypete11: Great capture.
HookedOnHitchcock43: What no more clown heads??
Koso: I'm not far behind you. Watch out in the dark.
TattyMPug: Fun.
RookieUx87: Respect.
Aarroynnnl33: Kings!
Koso: Goodbye, Sass, and good riddance. Sorry about the blood.

I shiver harder. These comments don't sound like a kid mucking around. They're dead serious. Grabbing my phone, I call David.

He answers on the fifth ring. 'I haven't got you anyone else to interview yet, just bear with me, OK, I'm doing my—'

'No, David, I'm not calling about that, it's about the videos. Get onto JedUrbXTM's video page and look at the comments from "Koso" beneath each of them. They're different to all the others, it's like they're toying with the group, boasting about catching them. It's as if they're being hunted.'

As I say the word *hunted* I realise that's what bothers me most. Koso is playing a game of cat and mouse, prey and predator. I recognise the pattern. I'd use it too.

Koso is a predator.

I hear David typing on his keyboard and clicking a mouse. 'Shit. No, this is . . . weird. I haven't seen trolling like this before, usually it's more that commentators call groups out for faking and hoaxes.'

This doesn't look fake. These comments have been escalating with each video posted. There's a queasy feeling in the pit of my stomach. Opening a new window, I type 'murder London female blonde' into the search engine and press return. I've been so busy I haven't checked the news recently, now I realise that was an error.

The fourth news item is accompanied by a picture.

David's still prattling on, but I don't want to hear it. I end the call, dropping the phone onto my desk as if it's on fire, and stare at the woman's picture on my screen.

I remember how David confessed to following Sass home, to learning her routine. To being obsessed. A question pops into my mind and I shudder. It's not one I've considered before, but in hindsight I think I should have. What might an obsessive voyeur do to a thrill-seeker?

I think the answer could be murder.

54

CLEMENTINE

Looking away from the picture, I read the news article. It says Ruth Kemp was found on the second floor of a building under construction. There aren't many other details, aside from the fact she'd been stabbed and that the time of death was late the previous night. There is no explanation as to how she came to be in the building.

I stare at the photographs accompanying the article. The picture of the victim is unmistakable. 'Sass' was the urban exploring alter-ego of Ruth Kemp. The time of death fits with the timestamp on Jedx's live-stream of his, Beaker's and Sass's exploration. Sass's death confirms the threats and gloating comments made by Koso.

I was right, and in this situation, I hate that. But I'd never thought that David could be involved. I've seen his comments made using his online name; DavidSees. I never considered that he could have two identities.

The second picture is an exterior shot of the crime scene, blue and white police tape cordoning off the entrance to the building. There's a man behind the tape, his face is half turned towards the camera, and there's an express of anguish on his face.

Reaching out, I trace the curve of his jaw with my finger. So, he's the officer in charge of this investigation. I know how hard each murder case that he works on hits Dom. Why hadn't he listened to me before? I wish he would let me help him. Our cases are the same!

Taking a deep breath, I toggle back to the urbex live-stream page, and continue scrolling up the comments on their last video.

Jedx82UBR: Why are you doing this? What do you want?
Koso: You should never have gone to Hendleton. I warned you, now it's too late. Run, Jedx, run!

I've been right all along; the Hendleton video is important. Dom needs to know. He has to get someone to the studios, find what these people discovered there that made Koso decide they must die. And he needs to interview David.

I have to make him listen to me.

I dial Dom's number. It rings four times, then goes to voicemail.

I keep scrolling through the comments.

PippinZander: @Koso stop the trolling, dude. Not cool.
Koso: Poor Beaker – he was too slow! Guts everywhere! This is almost too easy.

Now they've killed Beaker? Three of the four explorers are dead. I feel sick, guilty that I got distracted and should have done more to prevent this.

As I reread the last comment, a new one appears.

Koso: Jedx, it's time! I've planned something special.
Koso: You. Die. Next.

I redial Dom's number and hear it start to ring.

'Answer, come on. Answer,' I mutter under my breath.

It rings out to voicemail again.

Shit.

I call again, and again, but every time I get the answerphone. After my sixth attempt I leave a message. 'Dom, it's me. This is urgent, about your case. I know who the next victim will be, and I think I know why they're being targeted. Call me.'

I wait. Ten seconds. Thirty. One minute. I can't take it any longer; I can't *wait* any longer. I cannot sit here and do nothing.

Grabbing my red parka from the back of the door, I zip up my knee-length boots and stuff my phone and purse into my pockets. I leave the flat at a run, hurtle down the stairs and rush out onto the street. The traffic is already building in the lead-up to rush hour. Raising my hand, I step into the road and flag down a cab.

The cabbie winds down his window. 'Where to, love?'

I give him the address and urge him to hurry. He mutters about the weather and the traffic but says he'll take the backstreets.

As the cab pulls a U-turn at the lights, I try Dom's number again, but it goes straight to voicemail. Again. I curse him under my breath and will the cab to go faster.

Most wolves hunt in packs and I've had enough of being alone. I'm going to find Dom and this time I'm going to make sure he listens.

A man's life depends on it.

55

DOM

Abbott stays at the crime scene and Parekh drives Dom to Ian Lowe's address. The London traffic is terrible, not helped by roadworks causing everything to back up even worse than usual. The address isn't far – just a few miles from the heath – but it's taking an age to get there. The people on the pavement are walking faster than those driving. Dom exhales loudly. He doesn't have time for this.

'The forensics came back on the diamantes found in the blood on the Aldwych platform and the balaclava that Ruth Kemp was wearing – they're a match.'

'OK.' It's as they expected, and confirms the connection, but there's something about it that bothers Dom. 'From the CCTV it looked as if Ruth Kemp never entered Aldwych, so how did diamantes from her balaclava end up in Thomas Lee's blood?'

'No idea,' Parekh says, inching the car forward. 'And if she did get inside and killed Lee, then who killed her and Ian Lowe?'

Fuck knows, Dom thinks. Boosting himself up, he tries to see over the line of traffic ahead. It's jammed. They're not going anywhere fast, that's for sure. He turns to Parekh. 'Use the bus lane.'

'Guv?'

Dom gestures left. The bus lane is relatively clear. 'Do it, yeah. We can't waste any more time.'

Parekh indicates left and does as Dom says. As they pull into the lane a taxi blasts its horn at them.

'Quick as,' Dom says. 'Tick tock.'

He drums his fingers against the leather seat. Hates the waiting.

'We're almost there,' Parekh says. 'Should be the next turn on the right.'

A few hundred metres further and she takes a right onto a narrow residential street. The houses are old, Victorian or Edwardian. Some are freshly painted, the original windows replaced with UPVC, and their fronts made attractive with smart window boxes and little bay trees either side of the front door; others are tatty-looking, paint peeling from the render, split bin bags heaped by the front steps. Number 83 is tidy but in need of a repaint.

Parekh parks on the double yellow lines. They hustle across the pavement, and up the front steps. Dom has the keys, but he presses the buzzer for flat C anyway. He doesn't know if Ian Lowe lived alone.

There's no answer.

Dom pulls on a pair of latex gloves and removes the set of keys from the evidence bag. He inserts the Yale key into the lock and opens the door.

Inside, the house is split into four bedsits, two on each floor. Bizarrely, flat C is on ground level. Dom knocks on the door first. Waits, but hears nothing. If there was someone inside they'd have heard, so he uses the second key to unlock it.

Dom goes in first, and Parekh follows. It's a studio flat, one large space and a tiny shower room. The place is a mess; the pull-out bed is unmade, and there are heaps of clothes on the floor. There's a pile of pizza boxes stacked on the worktop beside a sink full of dirty crockery. The air has a chewy staleness about it.

Dom turns to Parekh. 'Look for anything that'll give us a lead on the group and the fourth man.'

They start searching. There's dust on every surface except one; a square table to the right of the bed. On it sits a laptop and a box of tissues, on the floor between the bed and the table is a heap of scrunched-up, used tissues. Dom moves towards the table. The lid of the laptop is up but the screen is in darkness. Using his gloved hand, Dom touches the trackpad. The screen illuminates. There's no password needed.

He inhales sharply. His phone starts vibrating in his pocket but he ignores it.

Parekh steps closer and peers at the screen. 'Is that them?'

'Looks that way.'

The video is paused. On the screen there are three people, all wearing balaclavas.

Dom moves his finger across the trackpad and presses play.

He'd been surprised to get Beaker's text message. Beaker had been so angry when they'd argued about going to the police this morning, continuing to yell after him even when he was walking away from him on the heath. Jedx doesn't know what made him change his mind, but he's relieved he has. They agreed to meet at three-thirty and go in together. The police have to take them seriously if there are two of them, surely. Jedx needs them to take this seriously.

He hurries along the pavement, head down, bowed against the cold. He avoids making eye contact with others on the street. Flinches as a passing bus lets off its air breaks. Shit. He needs to get a handle on himself. Needs to calm down. He's almost at the police station.

In a few minutes everything will be out of his control. His urge for thrills might have ruined his life, and his mum's. It's messed up, this whole thing. He should never have got involved. When he first got into exploring it'd seemed so harmless, and yet he'd still been able to feel that rush, experience the thrill of doing something dangerous. It let him forget, just for a while, that his mum's condition was getting worse, that it couldn't be cured, and soon he'd have to find a way to pay for more nursing care. The passion for filming he'd developed had surprised him, he loved doing the live-feeds – the camera stuff and the narration. It felt like it was meant to be. Right up until it went bad.

He shudders at the memory; the blood, and those damn clown heads that made him drop his camera. His only proper camera; far better than the one on his phone. It was a real item of beauty, the thing that mattered most to him after his mum; lost. He shook his head. Given what he was about to admit to, he supposed it didn't matter – once the police charged him with breaking and entering, he'd never be able to risk urbexing again.

Reaching the police building, he looks around for Beaker but there's no sign of him. It's unlike his friend to be late, Jedx knows he's usually the one who holds them up. Keeping his back to the wall, he hunches down, tucking his chin into his scarf. It's so damn cold.

He glances back down the road towards the tube station and sighs. He wishes Beaker would hurry up, now he's here he wants to get this over with and face up to what's coming. A tapping on his shoulder makes him jump. He turns.

'Hey. What are you doing here?' She's smiling, happy to see him, unlike the last time.

'I . . .' He doesn't want to tell her. 'Why are you here?'

She looks sad as she gestures towards the police building. 'I wanted to talk to the lead detective on Sass's case.'

Jedx tries not to look surprised. 'You're helping them?'

'Yeah, course.'

He looks away. This is awkward. He hopes Beaker gets here soon.

There's a pause, then she says, 'It's OK, you know, I forgive what you did to me.'

Jedx glances back at her. Remembers the screaming and the crying. The way she punched him when he told her the group's decision. 'I'm sorry, Dink, we didn't—'

She gives him a half-smile. 'It's ancient history. What's more important is finding out who killed Sass.'

He's impressed by the determination in her voice, but then she never did do anything by halves; that had been the problem. When he speaks, his own voice sounds weak in comparison. 'It's because of Hendleton.'

'I don't think so.'

'But we saw a murder, a killer, now they're trying to silence us, hunting us down like animals.'

'I know what you think you saw.'

'How . . . what do you—'

238

She puts her finger to his lips. Smiles. 'Sass told me where you'd gone, what happened, and showed me her pictures. Straight off, I was sure she'd got things wrong. Didn't she tell you guys?'

'No.' Jedx doesn't quite believe her, Sass hadn't mentioned showing her pictures to anyone. But then she was freaking out, she could have done anything. 'Wrong about what?'

'The woman you saw, the one Sass told me was dead. I don't think it's true.'

'What?' Jedx doesn't understand what she's talking about. 'She looked dead. There was so much blood. It was—'

'Fake.'

'How can you be so sure? You weren't there, you didn't see it like we did.'

She puts a hand on his arm. Squeezes. 'You always were a sucker for special effects. Look, the place was a film studio, right? One of the biggest films they made was *Death by a Thousand Daggers*, it's a cult classic.'

The film's name rings a bell. He's heard it before. 'Sass told us that.'

'Yeah, and if you google it, you'll see what I mean.'

He frowns. Moves his arm, trying not to react when she grips it tighter for a moment before releasing him. 'Google it?'

'Yes.'

Getting out his phone, he looks up *Death by a Thousand Daggers*. 'And then?'

'Check out the images.'

He taps the screen. 'Shit.'

'What you saw were the props used in that film. Not a person getting murdered.'

'But the film's over forty years old, the props would be long gone. And the body, it was real, I'm sure it was . . .' But as he starts thinking about it, trying to remember, the memory seems blurry, the glimpses of the body not enough to see if it was a person or a dummy. He scrolls through more of the Google images. 'In these pictures the victim's brunette, the person I saw was blonde . . .'

'If you say so.' She shrugs. 'Well, that's my theory. I came here to tell the detective what I know, but he's not there. He's at another office today, I've got the address.'

'You're going to talk to him?'

She laughs. 'Bloody hell, you're slow today. Yes, I'm going to talk to Dominic Bell, the lead detective. You can come if you like.'

Jedx looks around. There's still no sign of Beaker. Where the hell is he? It must have gone three-thirty now. 'The thing is, I'm meant to be meeting someone here.'

'OK.' She looks unfazed. Shrugs. 'No worries then, see you later.'

He watches her turn and start walking away. He feels partly relieved, but also as though he's missing a trick. What if it was a fake body at Hendleton? If that's true, then this Koso threatening them isn't necessarily the person they saw there. Maybe Koso is just a troll, and Sass's death was an unhappy accident. Could be that he's connected them, put two and two together and made five. Shit. He needs to get his facts straight for the police to believe him. If they doubt what he's saying it could make things worse, increase his punishment. His stomach flips at the thought.

But if he goes with her and they talk to the police together that might be easier. Dink could tell them her theory about the body at Hendleton and maybe put them in the clear. The police could then concentrate on catching the killer, and he and Dink would have helped. That'd count for something, surely – maybe he could barter with the detectives, persuade them not to prosecute him for breaking and entering after how helpful he'd been. Or at least make certain he isn't thrown in jail – anything to make sure he'd still be able to look after his mum.

He runs after her. 'Wait up!'

She turns, one eyebrow raised.

'I changed my mind.'

'All right,' she says, and loops her arm through his. 'Let's go.'

57

CLEMENTINE

We're just metres from the police building when I see him. He's standing on the pavement at the bottom of the steps to it, in conversation with a woman. She's short and petite and wears a navy beanie over her hair. I don't know who she is, but I recognise the name she calls him – Jedx – the cameraman from the urbexer group in the video. The person Koso said would be their last victim.

My cab is still stationary at the side of the road. I open the door again and keep listening to the couple's conversation.

The driver turns in his seat. 'You changed your mind, love?'

I nod, but I don't speak, not yet. I'm watching, listening hard. Trying to work out what they're saying.

The cabbie taps on the glass divider. 'Miss? Did you hear me? Do you want to go somewhere else? I can't sit around all day.'

I keep my eyes on the pair. 'Wait a moment.'

He tuts. 'I'm trying to earn a living here.'

'Start the meter running then.'

'More money than sense.' He huffs under his breath as he switches the meter back on. 'You're on the clock again then, love.'

'Thanks.' Their voices are softer now, and I can't hear them above the traffic noise, but I can see from Jedx's body language that the woman is saying something he doesn't like. He's shaking his head and she's moving closer to him. It looks as if she's trying to convince him of something, I can't hear what.

As I wonder why Jedx is here and whether he knows that he's in danger, I watch the woman put her gloved hand on his arm and rub his sleeve in what looks like an intimate gesture. I see him pull back from her. She tightens her fingers around his arm and leans closer, whispering. Then she turns and walks away.

I wonder what's going on. Jedx had commented to Koso on the thread beneath the last video, so he must be aware of the danger he's in. Perhaps the woman knows it too, and that's what they were discussing.

I watch the man's expression change from uncertainty to hope, and then hope to determination. He calls after the woman and I lip-read him say to her, 'I'm coming with you.'

As he hurries to catch her up, the woman steps towards the road and flags down a bright pink cab. She climbs inside, and Jedx follows. He must trust her, but what are they doing, and where are they going? I glance around us. Relieved that at least there is no sign of David.

If Koso has killed three of the four urbexers, Jedx is in danger. The killer could strike at any time. I think of the anguish on Dom's face in the picture of him taken outside the crime scene where Ruth Kemp's – Sass's – body was discovered. I know the turmoil it would cause him if he failed to catch the killer before Jedx became the fourth victim. Dom has tunnel vision in his determination for justice, and there's something so very admirable about that; something so incredibly compelling. It's one of the reasons I want to be closer to him, and strengthens our affinity. He deeply feels the need to catch criminals and prevent crime, just as my father did.

I remember Wade's words, his jealousy as he accused me of being infatuated with Dom. Am I infatuated? I wonder. Perhaps. But it is a healthy infatuation, a friendly infatuation, one borne of two broken souls connecting in a moment of extreme trauma – because killing the person who is trying to murder you is an extreme situation, and being the person who helped save me makes Dom special, too.

I dial his number again, and again it goes straight to voicemail.

The door of the pink cab closes. I have to make a decision. I owe Dom my life. And I know that saving Jedx will be important to him. It's important to me too, and I will do all that I can to help him succeed. I'll keep Jedx safe within my sights until Dom can take over.

On my phone I switch to the video of the urbexers and copy the link. The first time I tried to send it it failed, but I have to try again. I paste it into a text message and send it to Dom: Watch this. Read the comments from Koso. I think this is your killer. I'm following Jedx. He's with a woman. Call me.

Then I jump into the cab and tap the glass divider. The cabbie turns around at looks at me. 'Where do you need me to drive you now?'

I force a smile. 'Sorry to be a pain, but . . .' I point towards the pink taxi on the opposite side of the street. 'I need you to follow that cab.'

58

DOM

Dom presses play on the video on Ian Lowe's laptop for a second time. Parekh is standing next to him, writing down the names she hears – Cap, Beaker, Jedx. Dom gestures towards the screen. 'This is definitely Aldwych station.'

'The camera angle is weird, below face height. Looks like the footage is from a bodycam.'

'Yeah, could be.'

'Do you think he filmed it without the others knowing?'

Dom pauses the video. Points at the screen. 'No, look here at this guy.' He taps the chest of the man they know to be Thomas Lee, but who is being called 'Cap' on the video. 'He's wearing a bodycam too. Maybe they all are.'

Parekh frowns. 'We didn't find a bodycam on Thomas Lee.'

'True. Just like we can't locate Ruth Kemp's camera and Ian Lowe's iPod.'

She looks at him. 'You think the killer took them?'

'Yeah. Could be trophies, or something else . . .'

'Like?'

'I'm not sure yet.' He presses play and they watch as the three urbexers run towards the tube station entrance. They cut the locks and crowbar the concealed emergency exit door open. It takes them less than twenty seconds to get access. 'They're fast. They must have been doing this a while.'

It's dark inside. The three men, with their head-torches now switched on, run along an unlit corridor. They take a right, the beams of their torches briefly highlighting an old-style tube map on the wall, and run through what looks like a wood-panelled lift with both its doors open.

'They know exactly where they're going,' Parekh says. 'They've put time into preparing for this.'

Dom nods. Watches as the figures race past a ticket office and take a left down some stairs. It's dark but ahead of the torch beams there's luminous paint by the side of the treads, shining like beacons down the spiral staircase. The guy whose bodycam they're watching lags behind. Up ahead, the one who isn't Thomas Lee is talking, but the sound isn't good enough for Dom to hear what he's saying.

'Why do you think Ruth Kemp didn't go with them?' Parekh says.

'They looked like they were arguing on the CCTV footage from Surrey Street. My guess is that it could be something to do with that text she received, and whatever it was referring to. It sounded like she knows about or saw something criminal, maybe they all did.'

'More criminal than what they're doing?'

'Maybe.' On-screen the three explorers are walking along a deserted platform. Dom catches glimpses of old posters, the Transport for London sign for Aldwych, and the rails running along the track below the platform. Up ahead the tunnel continues away from the station, the wall lights illuminating it up to the first bend. 'It's platform one – where Thomas Lee was found.'

The guy narrating is talking about the movies that have been filmed on the Aldwych platform – *V for Vendetta*, *Patriot Games*. When the bloke wearing the bodycam, whose footage they're watching, tries to interrupt he can't get a word in. They hear him mutter under his breath. 'Fuck you, Josh.'

Parekh notes in down. 'So this Jedx is really called Josh?'

'Seems that way. They're calling Thomas Lee Cap, and as the other one's called Beaker, I'd say none of them are using their real names.'

'Making it much harder for us to trace them.'

Dom nods. He watches as Thomas Lee and the guy called Josh get further away. As the pair continues along to the end of the platform, the guy with the bodycam turns off into an exit tunnel, plunging the view into darkness with only his head-torch and a strip of luminous painted bricks along the bottom wall of the tunnel as a guide.

Dom frowns. 'What's he doing?'

The guy has stopped. He's leaning over, his breathing quickening. As the camera angles downwards, his body is illuminated in the beam of his torch. His right hand is down the front of his trousers and he's rubbing himself vigorously.

Parekh inhales. 'What the . . . is he having a wank?'

Dom looks at the balled-up tissues on the floor of the flat. 'Could be he gets off on this sort of thing.'

Parekh removes her hand from the edge of the table she's been leaning on and pulls a face. 'I'll get Abbott to send the CSIs here next, and have the techs search the laptop. Maybe there's something on it that'll help us identify the fourth man.'

Dom nods. His phone vibrates again for the umpteenth time. Irritated, he pulls it out and checks the screen.

Missed calls (19)

Voicemails (4)

Messages (2)

All are from Clementine.

59

JEDX

It's warm inside the cab. They're bunched together on the back seat. It feels cosy, comfortable. Dink passes him her flask and he takes another sip of the hot chocolate. He offers it back to her, but she waves it away.

'You finish it, you look freezing.'

He takes another sip. Feels grateful. He's been afraid for almost a week, but now for the first time since they broke into Hendleton he thinks things might work out. He feels less helpless because they're doing something. Taking charge. He smiles at her. 'I've missed this.'

She smiles back, but it looks a little forced. 'Really? We hooked up twice, then you seemed to move on from me without a second thought.'

'No . . . I . . .' He rubs his face. His skin feels odd, kind of rubbery, must be from the cold. 'I've often thought about you. I'm just not good at relationships.'

She raises her eyebrows. 'I noticed that when you texted me it was over, and I never heard from you again. It's not easy to get closure when things end like that.'

Closure. He tenses at the word as he remembers Dink's angry texts; long tirades using capitalised words and multiple exclamation marks. He'd blocked her immediately, just couldn't cope with the volume – a hundred a day sometimes, maybe more. Dumping her by text *was* cowardly, he knew that, but he'd had a reason. Although now, as he tries to recall what happened, he can't really remember. Dink had been part of the group before Sass; had been there when they decided to do regular live-streams. Actually, doing that might have been her idea, but she'd left before they filmed the first one.

He'd liked her but even before they'd had sex she'd always wanted things her way. Every exploration location had to come from her list. After they shagged, she'd wanted him to take her out on dates to fancy places, expensive places. She didn't care about his mum. He'd tried to do what she wanted, but there was so much pressure not to disappoint her. He'd felt as though he missed the mark – his clothes not quite right, the place he'd taken her to not cool enough.

That'd brought back the memories, the ones of not being cool enough at school, having to wear unfashionable stuff because Mum's budget didn't stretch to new clothes, and of never getting to hang out after school with the few friends he had because of his chores. He loved his mum, but he'd had a childhood crammed with feelings of inadequacy compared to his peers; he'd wanted to escape that in adulthood.

Jedx shifts his weight across the seat away from her.

She senses him pulling away. 'You OK?'

He nods. 'Hot, that's all.'

They travel on for a few minutes. Jedx peers through the cab window. It's almost dark outside. He can't make out much more than the road in front. 'Where are we?'

'Close. It's not far.'

He nods. Feels sleepy. Leaning forward, he opens the window a couple of inches. There's a brief icy blast of cold air and he wonders why the lead detective on Sass's death is working at an office so far from London.

Then Dink reaches across him and closes the window. 'It's freezing out there.'

'Yeah, sorry,' he mumbles, feeling like a disappointment again. He drinks down the last of the hot chocolate. Can't remember the thought, the question that had occurred to him a moment earlier.

He's drowsy. His eyelids are getting heavier. Dink's talking, but his brain's all mushy, and he can't understand what she's saying. He tries to speak, but he can't summon the energy.

His head rocks back against the seat as the darkness closes in on him.

60

CLEMENTINE

I have no idea where I am. Dom still hasn't called me back. The sun is dropping lower in the sky with every minute, and at the same time the pounds are mounting up on the cab's meter. The driver keeps glancing at me in his mirror. I'm sure he thinks I'm a crazy person, but I do not care. I keep my eyes focused on the pink cab in front and wonder where the hell they're going.

We're not in London any more. Our surroundings aren't even urban. We've travelled out of the city on the motorway, then turned off through country lanes. The driver is staying well back from the pink cab. I'm not sure if that's intentional, but I'm thankful for it; two cabs in convoy out here would look more than a little strange.

We enter a village. The houses are huge and set well back from the street. They line one side of the road with their neat lawns and new cars on the driveways. On the other side is a river. Everything looks like a rural version of the Stepford wives, and I feel a pang of longing for the familiarity of central London, with its crowds and grime and pigeons, and all the alleys and places to hide. In London it's easy to skulk in the shadows. This place, with its wide open spaces, makes me feel on edge. Exposed.

Up ahead I see the pink cab's brake lights flare. It indicates left and pulls into the kerb. 'Keep going a bit,' I say to the cabbie.

He nods and follows the car in front past the pink cab and along the street.

Twisting in my seat, I peer out of the back window and see the man and woman getting out. I turn back to the cabbie. Point at a side street coming up on our right. 'Turn here, please. And I'll get out.'

'Here, love?'

The couple are moving away from their taxi, the woman leading the way. I can't lose them. 'Yes, please. Hurry.'

'All right.' He turns across the road and stops. Presses the meter and looks back at me. 'Let's call it a round one-fifty.'

'Fine.' Anxious to pay and get going, I put my credit card into the machine and follow the instructions. 'Thanks,' I say, and jump out into the freezing-cold street.

I jog back around the corner, scanning the pavement ahead for signs of the pair, but they're gone. My heart bangs in my chest. I was too slow. I've lost them.

I run faster, sprinting along the pavement until I reach the spot they got out of their cab but there's still no sign of them. I stop. Turn and scan the area around me. Look towards the huge houses set back from the road and wonder if they're inside one. The places have secure gates and camera entry systems. I'm thinking about the best way to talk myself inside when I hear a splash, and muffled talking.

Spinning round, I hurry over the road towards the river. The noises came from this direction. I step across the verge and down the slope to the edge of the bank. The grass is crispy beneath my feet, already freezing from the cold. The sun has almost set, its dying rays streaking orange across the horizon and so, although the light is fading, I can just make them out, silhouetted against the sunset. They're in a boat.

There's no motor, just the rhythmic drop of oars into water. With each stroke they're putting more distance between us. As I squint at them through the encroaching darkness, it begins to snow.

Stepping back from the edge, I stay low and run along the bank, following the direction they're going in. They're faster than I am, the flow of the river helping them speed along quicker. I stumble on the uneven ground, catch my toe on a divot, lumpy and frozen hard, and almost tip into the water.

They glide on. The snow falls faster.

The river takes a right turn and loops away from the residential area. The bank is much steeper here, so much so that it's hard to stay upright. The sun is completely set now and the moon is hidden behind a veil of cloud. Without street lights, it's increasingly hard to see anything. I could use the torch app on my phone, but then they'd see me. So I stay shrouded in darkness, clambering along the bank as best I can. Up ahead, they use torchlight from the front of the boat to light their way.

A few minutes more and they start slowing. I'm almost level with them now, and as they manoeuvre the boat towards the bank on the other side, I sink back against the icy grass and stay still, silent. Watching.

They tether the boat to the mooring with a rope, and then step onto the bank. The woman goes first. I hear her encouraging the man to follow. Flashes of torchlight illuminate their movements and I see that he's unsteady on his feet. He's leaning heavily on the woman, her arm is around him, and as they climb up the bank he falls several times to his knees.

The woman laughs, the noise carrying over the gentle lapping of the river, and I hear her say, 'We're here, come on.'

They scramble up the bank and disappear into the darkness of the trees. I'm alone on the bank and it's freezing. But I can't let them get away, not when I've come this far. I have to find a way to follow them.

Pulling out my phone, I press the maps app, and tap '*find my location*'. The map takes an age to load, the signal down to a weak 3G. I grip the handset tighter. I need to know where they're going. What's across the river?

Slowly the map appears. I zoom in closer to my location. Wait again as the image reloads. 'Come on, come on.'

And then the map renders and their destination is so obvious that I laugh out loud I hadn't guessed it before. I know where they're heading. It's through the trees, on the opposite side of the river, half a mile downstream. Hendleton Studios.

I have to tell Dom.

61

DOM

He listens to the voicemails first, one after the other.

'*Dom. We need to talk. Call me.*'

'*It's Clementine. Look, call me, OK. I need to tell you something.*'

'*Dom, come on, stop ignoring me. I know you're pissed off because of what I did, but this is important, it's about your case, you need to listen to me. Call me.*'

Clementine sounds annoyed in the third voicemail, but there's something different about her tone in the fourth; she's angry, but she sounds nervous too.

'*Fucksake, Dom. Call me back. I have to tell you what I know.*'

Parekh raises her eyebrows. 'Girlfriend trouble?'

Ignoring the look she's giving him, Dom gestures to the laptop. 'See if there are any more videos, yeah?'

He steps away. Dials Clementine's number.

Voicemail. Shit.

He goes to his messages and opens the first one. Clementine sent it a few minutes after her last voicemail.

Watch this. Read the comments from Koso. I think this is your killer. I'm following Jedx. He's with a woman. Call me.

Dom clicks the link. It opens in full screen. The video is paused. It's night. Four people wearing balaclavas are running through trees. The shortest figure has diamantes sewn around the eyeholes of their balaclava. He presses play.

'Oh shit,' Parekh says behind him. 'I've found something.'

Dom turns, still watching the video. He sees the group entering a derelict building. Hears excited chatter as they break into a sound-stage. Watches them pushing through plastic sheeting. The camera jerks and he catches glimpses of what they see; bright lights, blonde hair, daggers, and blood. Then they're panicking, running. The camera drops to the floor and clown heads scatter around it, grinning. There are footsteps as boots approach the camera. A gloved hand reaches towards the lens and Dom feels himself draw back, away from the video. Then there's nothing. He scrolls through the comments beneath the video and realises what Clementine had been trying to tell him when they'd met the previous day. Why she'd been so insistent that he stayed. How he'd got things so totally wrong.

His head pounds. His mouth goes dry. He opens the second text.

You're not responding and I can't sit by and do nothing. I've followed Jedx and a woman to Hendleton Studios. I'm not sure what they're up to but I'm going to find out. You need to get here. Please, Dom. Just trust me.

'Fuck.'

'Guv?'

He looks at Parekh. Her eyes are wide, her expression serious. On the laptop, the same video is playing.

She points at the screen. 'This looks like they found a kill room. It could be what Ruth was being warned off going to the police about.' Sliding her finger along the trackpad, she rewinds the video to the beginning, and freezes the frame on the name over the stone door surround. She looks at Dom. 'We need to go to Hendleton Studios.'

62

JEDX

It's easier by boat, she'd said. *It's easier to get in by boat.*

But how can she know that? She didn't come with them last week. How can she know it's easiest to get into Hendleton going across the river rather than through the woods? And why are they even here? He thought they'd been going to an office to meet the detective. His thoughts jumble into a confusing swirl.

He peers at Dink through the falling snow. 'Why are we here?' She stays silent.

Jedx rubs his forehead. Can't think straight. Maybe she'd suggested they visit Hendleton when she was part of the group. He can't remember if it was one of the locations on her list. His head's spinning and he feels like he might throw up. It's the river, bound to be, he always gets seasick. He should have told her that, and said he'd rather go through the woods. Now it's too late.

He looks at her, facing him as she rows the boat backwards towards the bank. Snow has settled on the hood of her jacket, her knees and her feet. She doesn't seem to feel the cold though, or if she does she's ignoring it. Her jaw is set, her expression determined. No, he decides, there was no point telling her about getting seasick, she'd have insisted on using the boat anyway, it was right there waiting for them.

Right there. He blinks, trying to hold onto the thought. How did she know about the boat moored down the bank from where the cab had dropped them off? He leans forwards. Asks in a voice that sounds strangely distant. 'Whose boat is this?'

'Does it matter?' She keeps on rowing. Doesn't make eye contact.

'I just . . .' The thread of the conversation is gone from his mind. All he can hear is the splash of river as the oars enter it, the lapping of the water against the wooden hull. 'Don't like boats.'

She smiles. 'Don't worry, that part's over. We're here.'

There's a dull thud as the boat hits the bank. He watches her spring into action, securing the boat to the mooring, and laying the oars down flat inside the boat. The nausea is getting worse. It must be because of the way the current is pulling at the boat, trying to drag it further along the river, away from the mooring. When he thinks about where they're going he wishes that it would. 'We could just—'

She laughs. 'Not giving up so soon, are you? Isn't this a bit of a thrill? You're going to discover what's really going on here at Hendleton Studios. See who's doing the killing, maybe even unmask them if you get lucky. And I know how much you enjoy getting lucky, Jedx.'

He blinks. His face feels weirder, the skin numb from cold, and his mind is sluggish, but there's something about what she just said, something that they didn't tell anyone and wasn't on the video – the man in the mask. 'How do you know there—'

'You forget. I know a lot about this place. It was me who found it, remember? I pitched it as a location to the group. Not you.' Then her hands are on him and she's pulling him from the boat. Chiding him for being clumsy.

He stumbles up the bank. The snow is slippery and his legs won't work properly. He feels light-headed, dizzy. Falls to his knees. Once, twice.

Each time, she helps him up.

He's wary now though. She shouldn't know about the masked man.

After what seems like an age they reach the top. The trees aren't as dense here and there's no wire fence. He's glad. There's no way he'd manage to climb anything right now. He feels her hand around his shoulders and he leans on her, thankful for a moment for the support. Then he pulls away.

'Can you see it?' she says.

He peers through the snow and the trees. Swallows hard, then nods. He sees it well enough; the ghostly outline of the Hendleton Studio buildings.

'Good,' she says, as she pushes him forward through the snow. 'Come on.'

He tries to speak, but no words come. He feels frozen all over and not from the snow. There's something more than irritation in her voice now, something different to frustration in her expression. He turns to her and feels again like he's about to be sick.

This is all wrong.

Now all he sees on her face is glee.

63

DOM

He's angry with himself for not listening to Clementine before. If he hadn't walked away from her, if he'd heard her out, discovered what she knew, then they might have figured this out before Ruth Kemp and Ian Lowe were killed.

He's been so angry with her, but all she's done is try to help him – finding out what Lindsay was plotting and seeing if she could help with his case. She might interfere in things she shouldn't and make him feel claustrophobic, out of control, but her motivation comes from a good place. A fucked-up place, but a good one.

Shit. He knows he's acted badly, and that pushing her away made her worse rather than better, but when she'd told him that she broke into a crime scene during the Lover investigation and took evidence missed by the CSIs, he'd been furious. The way she'd said it, so casually, as though she didn't care that her revelation compromised him professionally, pissed him off. Looking back, he realises she trusted him with a secret, and he punished her for it.

Fuck. If he'd been more tolerant and listened to her about her theories on this case he'd probably have solved it after Thomas Lee died.

He swears again, under his breath. Getting to Hendleton is taking forever and Dom has no idea where the fuck they are. He peers out of the windscreen as Parekh indicates left and takes the turning off the motorway. Minutes later they're twisting through snow-covered county lanes at barely thirty miles an hour. There's no street lighting, and with the heavy snow the visibility is almost non-existent. 'Can't you go any faster?'

Parekh's hunched forward over the steering wheel. She doesn't speak for a moment, instead she switches on the windscreen wipers, trying to keep the worst of the snow from settling on the glass. 'It's not exactly ideal conditions.'

Dom feels like a twat. 'Yeah. Sorry.'

The waiting is getting to him. They need to find Jedx before anything happens, and now they have a location, the time getting there is agonising. He tries not to dwell on the fact that they only know for sure where Jedx is heading due to Clementine. He hasn't told Parekh, just went along with her suggestion of going to Hendleton after she saw it on the video. That's what they told Abbott too, when they called him and instructed him to bring backup. They should be on their way by now.

He glances at Parekh. He knows he's keeping Clementine's information from her, but it's better this way. It means he doesn't have to fill out any paperwork naming Clementine as a source. If he did, the link between them would be reinforced and stored on permanent record. But, although he might not be acknowledging her involvement, the fact she's tracked down the fourth member of the group before them makes him uneasy. She's good, very good. Better than most detectives.

'It shouldn't be too much further, guv.' Parekh squints through the snow at the road ahead. 'Just a few miles or so, I'll tell you when to keep an eye out for the entrance. If the place has been closed over forty years, I doubt it'll be that obvious.'

'Which side of the road?'

Parekh glances at her smartphone on the dash. 'Should be on the right.'

'OK.'

He tries texting Clementine's number again, but the message remains marked as undelivered. Clenches his fists. He needs an update. Has to know what the hell is going on at the studios. He's worried about Jedx, and he's worried about the case. But, he realises, most of all he's worried about Clementine staying safe.

And he worries about what that means.

64

CLEMENTINE

I need to get across the river. Using the map on my phone I search for a place to cross. There's no sense in me heading back towards the road. Although the light is better, the nearest bridge is almost two miles away. The closer option is about half a mile along the towpath, where there's what looks like a footbridge. It's my best shot.

Switching my phone's torch on, I shine the light down onto the stony path and sprint in the direction of the bridge.

The path is uneven, the freezing air feels like a thousand tiny needles puncturing my lungs with every breath, but I keep sprinting. I have to find Jedx and the woman. I have to protect Jedx until Dom gets here.

Up ahead, the iron structure of a bridge looms out of the shadows. I jump up the first step, and slide on the metal tread. Falling, I lunge for the handrail. I miss and plummet down onto the ice-covered steps.

The metal edge of the step slams into my hip. Pain vibrates through my bones, but I ignore it, the adrenaline overriding the blow. Pulling myself up, I grasp the rusty handrail, and continue up the steps. I have to get across.

Using the torch, I illuminate the narrow bridge. Its surface is a sheet of ice. I proceed with caution, sliding my feet across the ice and gripping the handrail to stay upright. It's slow progress, too slow. Anything could be happening at the studios.

My breath comes fast and shallow as I force myself to move more quickly.

The snow is coming down rapidly now, heavier. It's settling on everything; the ice, the handrail, me. My hands are numb, my fingers frozen into half-flexed claws. I lose my grip on the rail and cry out as I fall onto one knee.

The ice cracks. My phone falls from my grasp and I watch it plunge down to the water, disappearing with a splash into its murky depths. I have no light now. No way of contacting Dom. I am alone.

But I know where Jedx and the woman are going, and I remember the route to get there. Clinging tightly to the rail, I slide the last few feet across the bridge and make it down the steps onto the other side.

I'm breathing heavily. My hip and knee are throbbing, my hands ache from cold, but I won't give up. The studios are a half-mile back from here, through the woodland. The snow is getting thicker with every moment. Still, I refuse to be deterred. Looking up, I see the moon coming out from behind her veil. Lighting my way.

I will find them.

Following the path now lit by moonlight, I head into the forest. Running.

The fence stops me. It's tall and made of heavy squared wire; just as I saw it on the video clip. I gaze up, my breath pluming into the air around me as I work out the best way in. There are no trees hanging over the fence, so climbing one won't help. And there are no obvious gaps in the wire. Searching for one will take too long. It seems ages since I lost sight of Jedx and the woman as they left the boat, I can't waste time. I have to find them. I've promised Dom that I will watch Jedx until he gets here.

There's a sign attached to the wire. On it is a faded picture of a dog, and the words: TRESSPASSERS WILL BE PROSECUTED. SECURITY PATROLLING.

Given the amount of undergrowth on both sides, I doubt security have patrolled this perimeter for a long time. I put my hands on the fence and shake it. It seems secure enough, robust. So I decide up and over, like Sass and her group, is the best option I have.

Retreating a few steps, I take a couple of deep breaths, and sprint towards the fence. I leap up, reaching for as high as possible on the wire, and fold up my legs, my toes seeking gaps from which

I can boost myself up. The fence shakes with the impact and, for a moment, I almost fall back. Then I'm climbing, up to the top, swinging my legs over, and dropping down to the ground on the other side.

I'm in.

The studio buildings sprawl all around me. A few are squat, wooden-clad boxes but most are brick-built and higher – four or five storeys high at least. Some look like vast aircraft hangars, others more like offices or apartments – their structures silhouetted in the moonlight. I wonder where Jedx and the woman are. I wonder if Dom has read my messages and watched the video. I hate that I have no way to contact him.

I'm warm from the run. I can't feel the cold any more, I feel alert, ready. Standing still, I listen hard, waiting for a sound, a clue of where Jedx might be.

I hear nothing.

Turning away from the perimeter fence, I jog along a gravel pathway between two buildings. Grass and nettles have grown up between the gravel and they catch at my feet as I run. At the end of the buildings the path joins with a wider, tarmacked road. Looking to my left I see that it leads out of the buildings to a high gate with a sagging wooden hut beside it. The original road access I assume. I see no cars parked there; no sign that anyone – Dom – has arrived here.

I am still alone.

I have to find Jedx. I can't let any harm come to him.

Next to the large two-storey building in front of me I see a white signpost. There are multiple arrow signs; all have names painted on them. The letters are faded, some are too weathered to be legible, but I recognise the one at the top: *Sound-Stage One*.

That's the place the urbexers broke into to explore. There has to be a chance that's where Jedx and the woman have gone. But why would they come back here in the first place, if they are aware of the danger?

Turning right, I follow the direction of the sign, along another pathway. The snow-covered undergrowth has been flattened down;

people have been through here recently; a good sign. Hopeful that I am on the right track, I sprint faster.

The front entrance is just as I remember it from the video. The arched stone doorway is mouldy and the render between the stones is crumbling, but it's still imposing, rearing upwards into the dark night sky, double the height of a normal doorway. Carved into the stone are the words HENDLETON STUDIOS: SOUND-STAGE ONE.

Ripped and faded 'Keep Out' notices are plastered across what remains of the plywood cladding that once blocked the doorway, but most of the wood is heaped around the mouth of the building, splintered and useless after the urbexers' assault with the crowbar. A few more steps and I'll be inside.

But I hesitate. This is the way in, I remember the corridor from the video, the door to the recording area at the end. But I also remember that the way onto the sound-stage is through heavy plastic curtains. Plastic like that is noisy if moved. Using this way will give me limited opportunity for stealth. I don't know why Jedx and the woman have come here. I've been rushing to help protect Jedx, but for all I know either of them could be the killer. Or maybe David is Koso. Or maybe they're working together and have lured Jedx here. There are too many possibilities and not enough information to be sure. Until I can assess the situation better, I need to stay hidden.

Stepping off the path, I move across the frozen grass and around the building. My pulse is pounding in my ears. Every fibre of my being is on high alert. The intensity of it makes my hands tremble. Logically, I know I'm here to keep Jedx safe, but there's something else, I can feel a buzz building inside me; the high of a chase. In this moment, alone in the moonlight, I feel a thrill of anticipation and it's so sweet I can almost taste it.

That's when I hear the noise.

A thud.

I halt. Listening hard. Waiting for another sound.

A few seconds later I hear it again.

Thud.

There's a gap of three seconds, and then it happens a third time; thud.

Up ahead, I see a soft glow shining through the windows of the building. I sprint forward, and raise myself up on tiptoes to peer in, but the windows are too dirty, I can't see anything. Using the sleeve of my coat, I wipe the glass, careful not to make a noise. After a few rubs, the glass is smeary but there's a small circle that I'm hopeful is clear enough to see through.

There's another thud.

A woman cries out.

I have to see what's happening.

Rising onto my toes again, I grip the narrow metal windowsill and press my face to the glass, trying to see the sound-stage. The light inside is dull and all I can make out are packing containers and boxes stacked high. I press my face closer. Clench the window-sill tighter.

Thud.

The spotlights switch on, bathing the whole stage in bright white light, and I gasp. At the edge of the light, in the gap between the props area and the stage, on the rotting and filthy floorboards, is a naked body. Her white-blonde hair is fanned out around her head, obscuring her face. She's half curled, half lying. Her limbs are bent back at impossible-looking angles, as if she's been dumped there, no more important than a prop or piece of scenery.

The light is so bright. Her skin so pale. The crimson splatter across her body and the floor beneath her is as vivid as blood on snow.

I drop down from the window and continue around the building. I need to know more, see more. I need to see if she's dead, if I can help her, get help. I need to get closer.

I have to get inside.

65

DOM

They miss the entrance the first time and need to turn round. As Parekh crawls along the lane, trying to find a place to turn that won't put them into deep snow, Dom texts Clementine's number, but again the message remains undelivered.

Eventually there's a break in the overgrown hedges lining the lane, and Parekh stops. She reverses into a field gateway, the wheels spinning as she tries to pull away. Dom leans forward, willing her Fiat on. The snow thuds under the car, the wheels sinking deeper.

'Hold on.' Dom climbs out and steps through the snow to the back of the car. 'OK, go.'

Parekh tries again. The wheels spin, and for a moment Dom thinks the whole thing is futile. Then they get traction and the car lurches forward, onto the lane. Dom jumps back in. 'Had me worried there.'

'Yeah. This snow's getting worse by the minute.'

Half a mile later and Parekh stops opposite a driveway-sized gap in the hedge. She squints through the snow into the darkness. 'According to the sat nav this is it, but I'd have thought there'd be a sign or a gate or something. If I take us down there and the snow gets any deeper, I don't think we'll get back out.'

'It's been abandoned for years, the sign probably fell down. We can't waste time, let's go for it.'

'OK.' Parekh turns in through the gap, steering the Fiat along the snow-covered path between the trees.

The woodland continues on for a few hundred metres. Dom checks his phone again; still nothing from Clementine.

Parekh stops the car. 'Guv?'

Dom looks up from his phone. The view in front of him looks straight from a horror film. Huge black wrought iron gates with spikes along the top block them from getting any closer. Through the bars he can see the imposing frontage of what must have once been a small stately home – a stout, white stone mansion with huge pillars either side of the front entrance, what looks like battlements on the roof, with lines of big rectangular windows, all boarded up. It looks dark and forbidding in the gloom.

Pulling the door release, he climbs out. His feet sink down into the snow. It's deep, almost a foot already, and he can feel the cold leeching into his bones. He glances at Parekh over the top of the car. 'This place looks like the setting for a bloody Stephen King film.'

She nods, fastening her hood. 'Perfect for the horror they made here.'

Dom wonders what horrors they're going to find tonight. He steps up to the gates. They're fastened in place with a newish-looking galvanised steel chain and padlock. 'We're not going to get through these.'

Parekh scans the area around them, then pulls her gloves on and undoes the bottom two buttons of her coat. She nods towards the gates. 'Come on then, you'd better give me a bunk-up.'

The gates must be ten feet high. The wall they're attached to is the same height, but it doesn't have the potential footholds of the gate. Dom does as she asks, and watches Parekh climb nimbly to the top and carefully navigate the spikes. As she drops down onto the other side, he follows. He's not as nimble or as fast, but he makes it to the other side without injuring himself. Right now, that's all that matters.

He pulls out his phone, but the signal is non-existent. The site looked huge on the map, and until he can find a signal there's no chance of getting in touch with Clementine. He hopes she's OK and that she's still got Jedx in her sights.

'Look,' Parekh says. 'There are some tracks here.'

He hurries over to her and checks out the footprints. They're recent, not yet covered by the snow, and seem to come from the treeline. He follows them back a few metres and finds the spot they begin. The person came over the high wire fence at the perimeter.

The prints are small, female he reckons, and alone. Clementine.

Dom breaks into a run. 'Come on.'

He just hopes they're not too late.

66

CLEMENTINE

The fire exit door is battered and the edges crusted with rust from being open to the elements for so many years. I don't try to open it wider for fear it will make too loud a noise. Instead I press myself up against the crumbling doorframe, and slide through the gap.

It's dark inside. The huge cavernous space of the sound-stage is unlit, aside from the spotlights directly focused on the central stage. Back here, in the shadow of what seems to be the props storage area, I am hidden. But I can't stay, I have to see what's happening with Jedx and the woman. And I need to check for sure that the girl with the white-blonde hair is dead. Confirm my assumption is correct that she's the woman glimpsed in the video.

Inching forward, I skirt around the stacked crates and heaps of mouldering fabrics, taking care not to knock into the freestanding stage scenery – fake bushes and trees – and huge structures covered with wallpaper and paintings that must have once made up set interiors. Everything is dust-coated and damaged.

The further inside I go, the thicker the air seems to get. The musty stench of decay is all around. My mouth feels dry, and I worry I'll cough and give myself away. Swallowing, I continue on, my eyes focused on the edge of the pool of light and the broken-looking body of the girl.

She is so still.

The floorboards around her are rotten and broken. I slow my speed, sliding my feet gently across the wood, trying to be quiet.

I hear voices. Halt. Listening.

It's a woman and a man; I'm assuming it's Jedx and the woman, though I cannot be sure. Their words aren't clear, but the woman's tone is angry. She's doing most of the talking. Jedx sounds barely able to get a word in, but his voice is relaxed, too relaxed, and slowed down as if he's talking at half speed.

I move closer to the girl's body. Her back and legs are covered with dried blood that looks almost black in the gloom. It's crusted in the dips and hollows of her body, and pooled beneath her on the dusty floor. I can't see any wounds; no knife slashes or gunshot injuries. The more I stare, the uneasier I feel. Something seems strange about her. I don't understand how there is all this blood.

Kneeling, I reach out and touch her arm and in that moment, I know. She's dead cold, but her skin is rubbery, inhuman. I roll her onto her front, sweep her white-blonde hair back from her face and look into her lifeless eyes. She's not dead because she was never alive. This woman is a life-size doll, a mannequin, a facsimile of a human. It's easy to see how I was fooled though. She's extremely lifelike – her features are realistic, her skin almost identical to the real thing even this close up. In the gloom she passes for a human well enough.

I look at the blood dried across her pale skin; she's like the victim of a frenzy killing, but that makes no sense. If she wasn't alive in the first place, why go to all this trouble to "kill" her? She looks too modern to be a stage prop from when the studios operated forty years ago. Whoever did this brought her here more recently.

From the stage I hear Jedx shout out and the woman reply. Standing, I step over the mannequin and inch closer to where they are. I cannot tell how the stage is set, but I'm thankful for the cover provided by the high plywood structures of the stage backdrop.

I notice a hole punched out of the wood a few feet along at waist height, and move towards it, trying to fit myself between the prop boxes and the structure. Old rat droppings crunch beneath my feet. A floorboard squeaks and I freeze, listening to see if I've been heard.

No, it's OK. Jedx and the woman are still arguing, their voices continuing to rise in pitch and volume. As I get closer, I start to make out some words.

'. . . you caused this . . .'

'I never meant any . . . what do you . . . please, don't . . .'

'This was mine . . . you took it . . . ruined it . . . you had no right . . .'

I need to see what's going on. Crouching down, I put my eye to the hole and peep through. The light is so bright that I'm momentarily blinded. Blinking, I try to focus as my sight adjusts. There's only one voice now. I hear them laugh and I look in the direction of the noise.

My breath catches in my throat as I see what they have done.

It's twisted. It's horrifying.

I cannot look away.

67

JEDX

He just wants to go to sleep. But *she* won't let him. Every time his eyes start to close she pinches him or pokes him, forcing him to stay awake. He feels groggy, his mind sluggish, like he's had far too many beers. At least she's let him sit down but the floor is hard, and this place smells damp, rotten. He supposes it's better than trudging through the snow.

'Don't get too comfortable.'

Her voice is nearby, but he can't work out exactly where. He turns his head, looking for her, but everything's a blur and he feels suddenly like he might be sick. 'Where are—'

'I'm just getting things set for you. Nearly ready.'

He wonders what she's getting ready. They did come here for a reason, he's pretty sure, but he just can't remember what it was. No, they were meant to be meeting the detective, telling the police about Sass and this place and what they found when they broke in here. He'll be arrested for breaking and entering, locked up, and his mum will be on her own. It's all a mess. He feels like he might cry. He's so tired. Even sitting is too much of a struggle; he doesn't have the strength. He rocks back, letting himself sink to the floor. Closes his eyes. Starts to drift off.

A sudden pain explodes in his stomach, jerking him awake. He rolls onto his side, coughing. Clutching his belly, he looks up at Dink. She's glowering at him, her hands on her hips. 'Why did you—'

'No more sleeping, or I'll kick you again. I didn't give you enough sedative to make you pass out.' She's taken her beanie off and her bobbed hair is tucked behind her ears. There's menace in her voice. 'I need you awake. It's time.'

He eyes her warily. Tries to scoot backwards away from her

but he can't coordinate his limbs. He flounders on his back like an injured beetle. 'For what?'

She smiles, but there's no joy behind it. 'What you deserve.'

Even through the haze in his mind the fear is instant. Flight or fight – he has to get away. He turns over onto his hands and knees, crawling, but progress is slow. He feels so weak. It's all too much effort.

Her footsteps follow him. He turns, sees her black Doc Martens just inches from his face, and knows that he can't escape.

She sighs. 'So you want to do this the hard way? Fine.'

He tries to raise his arms to shield himself as he sees what's coming, but they are so heavy, so he cowers, helpless, and watches her raise the brick. Feels the blow vibrate through his skull and into his body.

Then everything goes dark.

Jedx opens his eyes. Blinks. It's bright, so bright. Above him he sees eight orbs, shining down. Black spots dance across his vision. He blinks more, tries to turn his head but he can't. The lights are blinding him. He's unable to place where he is. Can't remember what he's doing here. He wonders for a moment if he's dreaming.

That's right, he must be dreaming. He inhales. Then the pain begins and his surroundings come into focus. Rope. Wood. Blades. The side of his head is throbbing. His body feels like it's on fire. He hears laughter. Remembers where he is, who he's with, and that's when he knows for sure that this isn't a dream; he's in a nightmare.

He can feel bindings at his wrists and ankles, his waist and his throat. All around him he sees the wooden frame of the contraption she's bound him to, the one he saw when he was here before, the one he recognises from the images on the Google search. He strains against the ropes, but it's no use. They keep him secured to the wooden planks that hold his weight. But it's not the ropes that are making him shake with fear. The cause of his terror comes from above.

Daggers, seventeen of them, all point vertically down. The last time he glimpsed this torture instrument a blonde woman was trapped inside it, blood everywhere. He'd turned and run, all four of them had. He can't let that happen to him. Jedx strains against the ropes. Tries to cry out but there's tape across his mouth. He breathes heavily through his nose, can't get enough air. Panics.

His vision's still hazy, but he squints upwards into the light, trying to work out how the frame holding the daggers is secured. It looks like some kind of elaborate pulley system, medieval shit. If the rope holding the frame of blades loosens they'll drop and impale him. Game over. He heaves and tastes vomit in his mouth. Swallows it, grimacing. He has to get free. Thrashing harder against the ropes, he prays that the blades don't fall.

'They're real.'

Her voice is close and to his right. Jedx tries to tilt his head so he can see her but there's a wooden rail blocking him. He wants to speak, but his mouth is held shut by the tape.

'I'd forgive you for thinking they were fake, you know, the original ones were.' She steps closer. Runs her finger along the flat outer surface of one of the daggers, tracing the rune markings, and circling the jewels along the hilt. She presses her index finger against the point of the blade until a bead of blood appears, then sucks the blood off her finger, all the time keeping eye contact with him. 'I replaced the fakes with the real thing for this. Just like I've replaced the doll with you.'

The memory of the previous Saturday night replays in Jedx's mind. Breaking into Hendleton Studios. Sass telling them that sound-stage one was the ultimate challenge to explore. Opening the plastic curtains, the bright lights shining down on the centre of the stage, seeing this strange wooden contraption, and the blonde woman covered in blood.

She smiles down at him and rips the duct tape from his mouth.

He gulps the air. 'The woman we saw, she wasn't dead?'

'Of course not.' She laughs again. It sounds sinister, evil. 'There were only four people I wanted to kill.'

He stares at her as the words sink in. 'You . . . *you* killed Sass?'

'And Cap and most recently Beaker, but then you probably don't know about that yet. I waited until you'd trotted off before I got him.'

'But Cap's been reading his messages, he—'

She laughs as she pulls a pair of phones from her bag. 'This one is Cap's, and the other is Beaker's.' She grins. 'You really are gullible. It was me who arranged to meet you at the police station, Beaker was already dead.'

Jedx stares at her. Frozen. He tries to think it through but his mind's foggy, can't connect the pieces to make her actions rational. They're not rational. This can't be true. 'I don't get it. You were our friend. We . . . you—'

'No, of course you can't understand. You've no concept of loyalty, have you? You and your stupid fucking friends. You wanted me at first, but in the end you were all just like my first boyfriend. I never told you about what happened to him did I? His *accident* just after we broke up. Such a shame.'

There's a manic look on her face. I *have* to get free, thinks Jedx. If I keep her talking, maybe I can loosen one of the ropes. 'Why are you telling me this?'

'Because the anticipation is the best bit, isn't that right? Delayed gratification, that's what you told me you get off on; doing all the planning and reconning the place, all building up to the moment of breaking in and exploring. Well it's like that for me, so I'm going to prolong every moment.'

He tastes bile in his mouth again. Terror makes him clumsy, but his left hand feels like it's got more flexibility. Curling his fingers up, he starts to work at the knot joining the rope around his wrist. His fingers ache. They fumble at the rope, but he keeps trying. Has to keep her talking. 'So what . . . what happened to your first boyfriend?'

'He was hit by a bus. They said it was so sad. We were walking along together having just made up. It was a foggy evening, and the number twenty-nine had just loomed out of the fog towards us.' She gives a rueful smile. 'The next minute . . . bang.'

Jedx inhales. Feels sick again. 'You killed him?'

'Well, really he killed himself. He hurt me. Rejected me. And I wanted to hurt him back, make him feel powerless just as I did.' She shakes her head. 'You know I hardly shoved him at all, I don't even know if I meant to kill him, but as he stumbled into the path of that bus, and I heard the delicious thump as it mowed him down, I realised taking his life was the ultimate act of revenge.' She pauses and takes a large breath. 'Still, I cried when the nice police officer took my witness statement. I told them I'd tried to stop him, but the stress of exams and coursework made him feel he couldn't carry on living, and they, like fools, believed me.'

Jedx works the knot harder. Feels it loosen slightly.

'And the adrenaline high, the rush of it, wow . . . I'd never felt more powerful. I vowed in that moment no one would take away my power again. Ever. And no one did. Until you and your friends.' She smiles down at Jedx. The glow around her head makes her look like an angel. Now he knows she's anything but. She puts her hand on his stomach, slides it under his shirt and caresses his skin. 'It's a real shame I have to mess you up.' She looks sad. 'But it's your fault, you understand that now, don't you? You caused this. All four of you brought this on yourselves.'

Her touch makes him want to hurl. He recoils and lets go of the knot he's been working on. Panics. Struggles against the ropes, feeling them bite into his flesh, but it does no good. He's her prisoner. 'But what did I do to—'

Her cheeks flush red. Her voice is raised as she says, 'How is it that you even need to ask that? You left me, Jedx. The four of you went off and had adventures without me. Of course you and Sass had a more personal adventure too. You know, I toyed with the idea of framing her for Cap's death, I took a few sparkles from her balaclava and sprinkled them in his blood, but afterwards I realised that wasn't enough punishment. You all needed to pay the same price, because none of you would have been anything if it wasn't for my ideas. *I* put you on the urbexing map. But were you grateful?' She's shouting now. Spitting fury. 'Oh no, you took *my* ideas, and *my* location list, and then got rid of me as soon as you could. You banned me from adventuring with you, from getting the adrenaline hit I loved.' She jabs her finger into his chest. 'How do you think it made me feel when the four of you decided you didn't want me any more?'

He grapples for the knot. Fails to grasp it. Needs more time. 'You were reckless, Dink, it was a group decision, after what happened in the caves with . . . you didn't care that guy got injured, you never even said sorry . . .'

'It was their own fault, but you listened to them and blamed me. You were supposed to be my friends.'

'We never meant . . .'

'It felt like a thousand daggers to my heart.' She gestures to the blades suspended above him. 'So this is an appropriate punishment, don't you think?'

She's crazy, Jedx thinks. 'This isn't punishment, it's murder.'

She shrugs. 'Maybe. But you deserve it. You all deserved it. When you discarded me, you stopped me getting my fix, my drug of choice – the thrill – and when the supply is cut off the cravings can make a person do terrible things. I learnt back with my first boyfriend that nothing is more thrilling than taking a life.' She caresses his cheek. 'Because isn't being able to play God the ultimate thrill?'

He tries for the knot again, but his fingers are numb, he can't grip the rope hard enough. 'Please don't do this.'

'What, you're begging now?' She laughs. 'God, you're pathetic. You always were weak, you and the rest of them. You never understood that I wasn't reckless, I was brave. I *am* brave.'

His head's pounding. He has to talk reason into her, somehow. 'We thought you'd joined a different group. I thought you were happy.'

'Happy?' She laughs again, a single *ha*. 'I was biding my time, waiting for you to decide on Hendleton as your next explore. Sass still spoke to me. I convinced her sound-stage one was the most important part of the studio, and she kept me updated on your plans. Once I knew the night you'd picked to break in, it was easy.' She gestures at the contraption he's held prisoner within. 'I set up my display on the stage and waited for you to arrive. At first I was going to trap and kill you all together.' She smiles. 'But then I changed my mind.'

'Why?'

'Because it was too easy, I needed a bigger challenge.' She steps closer, her voice getting louder, her expression more angry. 'And all four of you betrayed me. You needed to pay, one by one. Cap died an agonising death alone, Sass looked into my eyes as I stabbed her and finally realised that I wasn't her friend, I hated her. Beaker died lying in the dirt with his guts hanging out.'

'I don't . . .'

'Revenge. It's called revenge, Jedx.' She picks up a rope attached to the winch holding the frame of daggers in place. The frame wobbles. 'In this world, it's survival of the fittest, isn't that what Cap always used to say?' Her grip tightens around the rope. The frame holding the daggers in place swings from side to side. 'Well, I'm the fittest, and I'm going to survive all of you.'

'You . . . I . . .'

'No, that's enough talking. Now, I know how much you like to be on camera, so filming your death in the style of *Death by a Thousand Daggers* will be the perfect way for this to end. I'll upload it to your webpage. You'll be a star, Jedx. It's just rather a shame for you that you'll be too dead to know it.' Removing the roll of duct tape from her pocket, she tears off another piece and sticks it over his mouth. 'Hush now.'

He cries out, and thrashes against his bindings. Feels his bladder release.

Ignoring him, she walks away towards a camera set up on a tripod. He can barely see her in his peripheral vision as she picks up a piece of black material from the floor and puts it over her head. She pauses to adjust the camera angle, before taking hold of the rope connected to the frame of knives. Then she turns, and he sees the mask that's haunted him since the previous Saturday; a grinning skeleton with red lips.

He tugs against the ropes. His screams muffled by the tape.

'Smile, Jedx.' She laughs, the mask's material moving as she says, 'It's time for your final close-up.'

68

DOM

Fucking clown heads. They're all over the place and it's almost impossible to see them in the gloom. He and Parekh move along the corridor, towards Sound-Stage One, as fast as they dare. Dom doesn't want to alert whoever is inside to their presence; he wants to keep the element of surprise.

The air is musty and rank, the floor beneath their feet is rotten and littered with debris. Cables hang from the half-collapsed ceiling, and he can hear the dripping of water somewhere above them. The red beacon next to the door is flashing – there's a recording in progress. This is it. The room from the video.

As they reach the door, he turns to look at Parekh and raises his eyebrows in a silent question: you ready? She nods.

Taking hold of the handle, he opens the door. It's stiffer than he'd anticipated, and he has to put his shoulder to it. They enter an anteroom. The way onto the stage is blocked by floor to ceiling plastic sheeting, thick and black. As Dom peels it back, bright light floods through the gap.

How can there be that much light? The place has been derelict for over four decades, surely the utilities were cut off years ago. Maybe there's a backup generator.

Dom pulls the plastic away. Parekh's close behind him, and as soon as the gap's open wide enough she slips through into the sound-stage. Dom follows.

He halts.

What the . . . ? He tries to process what he's seeing.

Parekh's a few feet ahead, also immobile. She's on the edge of a circle of light that's illuminating the centre of the vast building, staring at the stage; at the contraption.

What the actual fuck *is* that?

The middle of the stage is bathed in light from eight huge spotlights and in the centre is a strange wooden contraption. There's a bloke inside it, held in place by ropes around his arms, legs, waist and head. Suspended above him, a rack of blades point down at his body, a complicated set of ropes and pulleys keeping it in place. It looks like a medieval torture instrument.

The man struggles against his bindings. He cries out, although the tape used to gag him blocks most of the sound. Parekh rushes towards the trapped guy before Dom can stop her.

'Stop where you are.' He can't see where or who the voice is coming from. It's distorted, almost rendered machine-like from the voice-changer the person's using. 'Any closer and he's dead.'

Parekh stops a few feet from the contraption and peers out towards the side of the stage, blinking in the blinding light. Dom has a better vantage point from the shadows. He sees movement, a small figure, all dressed in black, shifting behind a tripod-mounted camera.

'We're police,' he says. 'Come out with your hands where we can see them.'

The figure turns towards Dom. Puts their hands on their hips without a hint of fear. 'I know who you are. You should smile, you're on camera.'

Parekh takes a pace closer to the wooden contraption. Then another.

'I said stop.'

Using Parekh's diversion, Dom moves fast towards the camera. He steps lightly. He can make out the figure on the other side more clearly now. There's something over their head, obscuring their face. In their left hand they're holding a rope. He sees the rope lead from their hand, onto the stage and around the back of the contraption to where it attaches above the daggers. Shit.

The man in the contraption cries out.

'Stay still,' the masked figure shouts at Parekh.

But Parekh takes another pace forwards, while Dom moves closer to the figure. Another few steps and he'll be able to grab them, and the rope.

His mobile rings in his pocket. Fuck.

The hooded figure turns. Their mask is a ghoulish skeleton with red lips and a cruel smile. Shaking their head, they tug the rope hard.

There's a snap high on the contraption and a chain reaction is set off. The ropes twang, pulleys tighten and release. The man thrashes against his bindings.

The blades plunge down.

They cut off the man's muffled scream abruptly, brutally, as they find their target.

Dom sprints towards the masked figure but they're too fast. Pulling the camera from the tripod, they kick it into Dom's path. He trips, pushing it away, but the figure is already running across the stage.

Parekh blocks them. They try to dodge around her, but she mirrors their movements and lunges. She grabs their hood, pulling them down. They fight back hard. Hit her with the camera.

Dom sprints towards them. Hears the crack as the camera smacks into Parekh's head. Watches her stagger sideways, reeling from the blow. The hood is in her hands. She pulls.

The figure tries to twist away but Parekh clings on tight. They thrust the camera into Parekh's stomach and, as Parekh falls to the ground she pulls the hood with her, unmasking them.

Wild-eyed, with her bobbed hair falling forward over her face, the woman kicks Parekh away from her, and turns to glare at Dom.

Fuck.

He reaches out to grab her. Misses. Yells after her as she runs. 'Ellie?'

69

CLEMENTINE

I see everything. Every dramatic beat of the narrative this woman – Dink – has created. The slaughter of Jedx, the beating of the female detective, the choice for Dom; chase the killer, help his colleague, save the victim. I knew Dink was connected from the moment Sass mentioned her, and now I see all that she's created, and how she intended for it to play out. It's theatrical, over-the-top murder. Unwarranted, selfishly motivated, murder. I cannot let that to go unpunished.

But just as I'd been about to step in, to stop her, Dom arrived. I couldn't reveal myself to his police colleague, it would compromise him if she found out I've been helping him with this case, and with what's happened before I couldn't risk that. So I've stayed hidden, witnessed all that's happened. None of them have seen me here behind the wooden scenery prop, watching.

Dink hurtles past, her eyes focused towards the exit that she must know is in the corner of the building. Dom won't know it's there, but I do. I glance at him; he's crouched over the female detective who's sprawled on the floor, his hands on her shoulder, checking if she's OK. This is his case, but he's letting the killer go free. I can't let that happen.

Springing up from my hiding place, I clamber over the crates, pushing the debris aside, to get to the exit. Dust fills my nostrils. My feet slip on the floorboards, and some crack beneath the sudden movement of my weight.

She squeezes around the door and, through the safety glass, our eyes meet. Then she grabs the handle and tries to yank the door shut, but she fails. It's too warped, too disfigured, to move. And that helps me make ground on her.

Wriggling through the gap between door and frame, I jump down the steps outside, onto the frozen ground. She might have a head start but the snow is thicker now. Good for me, less so for her. The snow makes the night seem lighter; it's easy to follow her footsteps.

I track her across the grass and along a pathway. The snow is thinner between the buildings, but there are enough prints for me to know I'm on her trail. We pass the main entrance, and I see a car on the other side of the gate, but her prints swing left along the fence line, back towards the woodland.

She must be heading for her boat. I have to catch her before she gets to it. Once she's in the water I will have no chance.

I push myself harder. Move faster; legs pumping, eyes on her footprints, and I'm sure that I must be gaining on her.

Then the footprints stop.

Where is she? She can't have disappeared.

Breathing hard, I scan the ground around me looking for footprints or scuffmarks; anything that will give a clue as to where she's gone. The snow around is virgin and crisp. If the woman is heading for the boat it's by a different route, she has not sought the cover of the trees.

I clench my fists. How is this possible? How can there be no sign of her?

No one can vanish into thin air.

Air.

I look up. And that's when I see her. There's a metal ladder attached to the side of the hangar on my left. It's rusty, and the bottom section has sheared off so it doesn't start until about two metres from the ground, but it runs all the way up the side of the building and onto the roof. She's almost at the top.

I leap up, and grasp the first rung of the ladder. The rusted metal flakes beneath my grip, and the painful cold of the rung registers after a delayed moment. I know that if I'm going to make it to the top, I must act fast.

Using all my strength, I pull myself higher, pressing my feet against the side of the building until I'm able to get my boots onto the rungs. I move as quickly as I dare. The ladder feels precarious; much of it is corroded, and parts of it lift away from the side of the building as I ascend. I don't care. I have to catch the woman. I continue climbing.

She's at the top now; I caught the flick of her feet over the edge in my peripheral vision, and when I looked up she was gone. I don't know if she's seen me, but she must have felt the movement from me starting to climb. It doesn't matter anyway. All that matters is that I reach the roof.

I keep climbing. My thigh muscles burn from the effort, my fingers are stained red by the rust and numbed from the cold. The snow is falling faster. The wind is stronger up here, it swirls the flakes into mini tornadoes. The snow gets into my eyes and sticks to my lashes, blinding me. I shake my head. I can't give up, I just can't. Dom needs my help. I won't let him down.

I force myself to continue. One hand in front of the other; rung by rung. Until I reach the top. The handrails rise up over the edge, but they've broken loose from the building, corroded where they were once welded tight. So I throw myself forward into the snow, and swing my legs up and onto the roof, rolling clear of the edge.

My breathing is heavy, but I can't rest. Scrambling to my feet, I use my hand to shield my eyes from the worst of the blizzard and scan the vast roof for signs of the woman. The moon seems brighter up here, and the light is reflected back from the snow.

I see her.

Across the roof, she's moving slowly, zigzagging across the space. Every few steps she stops and reaches down into the snow, then continues on. She's looking for something.

Standing, I surge forwards into a run. I'm thirty feet away and closing fast when she sees me. Her mouth opens, a shocked expression on her face, then she turns and sprints away.

'Stop,' I shout.

She ignores me. Doesn't look back. Hurtles towards the edge of the building, accelerating rather than slowing.

I see what she's going to do. 'No!'

She leaps from the building, and disappears.

Shit.

Running to the edge, I skid to a stop and peer over, expecting to see her body on the ground below. But she's not there, she's sprawled in the snow on the roof of the next building. It's a few feet away and about five foot lower.

She smiles at me. Thinks she's free and clear.

She's wrong.

I curl my lips into a snarl. She will not outsmart me, nor outrun me. I have caught a murderer before and I can do it again. I'm not afraid.

I was born to do this. Hunting is my nature.

With her in my sights, I fling myself off the roof.

70
DOM

Dom wants to chase Ellie but he has to check on her victim and Parekh. Hurrying to Parekh, he drops to his knee beside her. 'Narinda? Talk to me.'

There's blood running down the side of her head from a deep gash in her hairline. One eye is already swollen and closing. 'I'm OK . . . just . . . the guy?'

Dom glances towards the contraption and sees the man impaled by the knives, a red stain spreading across his shirt. His eyes are closed, but he still seems to be breathing.

Dom rushes over to him. He's losing a load of blood. The knives are embedded in his flesh, blood draining from the wounds, but there's no arterial spray, and it looks as if they've missed his heart; there's still a chance they can save him. Dom pulls the duct tape from the man's mouth and presses his hands against some of the wounds. 'Parekh, I need you over here.'

The man's eyes flicker open. He whimpers. 'I . . . what, I . . . she . . .'

'It's all right, you're safe.' Dom tries to look reassuring. 'Hang in there, mate.'

The bloke opens his mouth, trying to speak. Then his eyes roll back and he passes out.

Parekh looks pale and groggy, but she's on her feet.

'Call it in, get an ambulance straight away and find out where Abbott is with our backup, they should be here already. Then press here,' Dom says, indicating where his hands are. 'We need to slow the bleeding.'

Parekh takes out her phone, dialling with her right but already putting her left hand against the worst of Joshua's wounds. 'What are you doing, guv?'

'I'm going to find Ellie.'

*

Dom races across the stage and into the darkness. It's some kind of storage space, cluttered with junk. He jumps over crates and debris, following the path he saw Ellie take. The dust flies around him, making him cough. There's no sign of her; nothing back here but old film props and the stench of decay.

Where the hell is she?

Where did she go?

He spots a chink of light in the far corner. Fighting his way through the mess, he makes it to the light and sees that it's coming from a half-open fire door. Squeezing through, he steps out into the freezing night. The snow is coming down thick and fast, and he's glad of that. Prints embedded in the snow show him exactly where Ellie went.

He follows them. Head bowed against the snowstorm, eyes focused on the footprints, sprinting between the buildings. His shoes slip on the snow. His feet are drenched, his soaked trousers weighing down his legs. He's starting to tire. Where the hell is she, he thinks again, she can't have got far.

The trail leads towards more buildings. He runs alongside the footprints, following as they loop right, down a narrow path between two huge buildings. They're about ten feet from the end of the path when they disappear.

How is that possible?

He scans the ground, searching for a sign of where they've gone. It must be a trick, misdirection, surely? They can't have disappeared.

He runs to the end of the building. Peers across the snow-covered ground. Sees nothing. The snow is coming faster, heavier, but even so, it couldn't have covered the tracks that quickly.

There's a noise, like a shout. He looks up, but there's nothing, or if there is, the snow flurrying down on him hinders his ability to see it. He stands still. Listening. Hears something else; a clanging noise, it's somewhere above and ahead of him.

Dom runs along the length of the hangar. There's still no sign of the footprints, but he's convinced Ellie is close. He turns around the next corner, moving between one hangar and the next.

He's fifteen feet along the path when he hears a whooshing sound above. Snow pelts the ground around him like an avalanche. Skidding to a halt, he looks up.

Snowflakes rain down on him. They get in his eyes, his nose, his mouth. Then he sees her, leaping across the gap between the roofs of the two buildings; black boots, red parka, long black hair flying out behind her. His breath catches in his throat.

Not Ellie.

Clementine.

71

CLEMENTINE

This wolf is hunting. I have the woman in my sights and I see where she is heading.

The snow whirls around us as we race across the roof. The thrill of the chase is better than sex, better than anything. I'm hyper-alert, my senses at full throttle. It's exhilarating. Intoxicating.

I'm gaining on her. It would be so very easy to pounce, to go in for the kill, but I hold myself back. I can't risk harming her. This is Dom's case and he has to bring in the killer, do things by the book so he can get a conviction. I'm doing this for him, so my job is to run her to ground.

In the far corner of the roof there's a structure. A metal door, the word EXIT printed in red, still visible through the snow. She's almost at it now.

She pulls the handle and there's an ear-piercing squeal as the door opens. Darting through the gap, she disappears into the building.

I'm right behind her.

It's dark inside. There are no windows in the narrow stairwell. I have to slow as my eyes try to adjust, to feel my way.

I can hear her footsteps clattering off the metal steps. See the light of her phone as she hurries downwards, using the torch app to light her way. I have to stay close. Can't get left behind, not now. I keep moving, stepping down, and squinting into the darkness.

A shaft of light appears below. I hear the bang of a door closing.

Then everything goes pitch-black. Claustrophobic darkness. I miss the next step, stumble and almost fall. Fear hammers at my chest, and I fight to keep my breathing even. Fear cannot take me now. I have to stay on mission, on the trail of this woman.

I have to stop her, for Dom.

I force myself lower into the darkness. Grope for the handrail, but all I feel is the rough brick wall, so I dig my fingers into the mortar to stay upright. Keep moving.

Then I feel it. The change in surface from brick to wood, and I know I've reached the door. Pulling it open, I rush through. My breath comes in gasps and relief floods through me.

It's short-lived.

I'm on a narrow platform that runs around the circumference of the building. There's some light from where the moon shines through the gaps in the roof, giving a dull gloom that illuminates small areas and casts shadows across the rest. I can see enough to realise this is another sound-stage.

Far below, the stage is set for a film; the huge double-height backdrops are painted to resemble a tropical island. Fake palm trees further the illusion. The floor is deep in sand. All of it is decaying and mouldering.

The woman is closer, maybe twenty feet from me. She's running along the platform, and I see where she's heading; the staircase on the opposite side, a way down to the ground level.

I sprint after her. The wooden boards beneath my feet seem to vibrate as I run. I clench my fists tighter and hope that the platform holds. There's no safety net.

The woman glances over her shoulder. Runs faster. For a few moments it looks as though she's going to get free, then she skids to a halt.

I slow as I approach her. 'You're doing the right thing.'

She turns to face me, shaking her head. 'You know I looked at this sound-stage first, stage two it is, but I thought the tropical theme would detract from what I had planned, so I discounted it. I never got as far as looking up here in the gods.'

I say nothing and take another step forward. I see then why she's stopped. She's not giving herself up; her path is blocked. There's a huge hole in the platform where the wood has caved in. She can't get to the stairs from this direction, and she can't come back the other way because I'm blocking her path.

'It's lucky I have a good head for heights.' She tilts her head to one side. 'What about you?'

Before I can answer, she takes a few steps towards me, then turns and jumps onto a lighting gallery – a narrow wooden platform that once gave the film crew access to manually adjust the spotlights focused down on the stage. It's suspended from the roof, high above the stage, crossing from one side of the building to the other. It's rickety, unstable, and the end closest to me drops a foot lower as one of the support ropes snaps beneath her weight.

'Stop,' I shout, but she's already moving along it.

I have no choice but to follow.

The rig shifts as I jump onto it. The ropes suspending it from the ceiling creak and I wonder how secure they are, and if any others will snap from the weight of us. My knees feel weak, strange, but I grip the rail and force myself to follow. The platform sways with every step I take.

The woman doesn't seem to care. This narrow space was designed for the person operating the lighting rig, the guy who could manually adjust the spotlights. It isn't made for two, and it was never built for running. But she's moving fast, her gaze set on the opposite side, the far platform, and an alternative route to the exit. I see it now; this lighting rig is her last hope of reaching the stairs. I fear I won't catch her in time.

Then suddenly she's scrabbling to a halt as chunks of rotten boards cascade to the floor, sending the rig into a wild swing. The ropes creak, the wood groans. Clinging on tight, I hurry closer to her.

She's trapped. Ahead of her, the wooden boards are jagged and splintered. A piece of the platform has collapsed, making the gap between the rig and the solid platform too big to jump across. She must realise that.

Turning, the woman faces me. Her movement is jerky, erratic, and the rig sways more dramatically in response. To my right, I hear another rope snap and the rig tips sideways.

We don't have long.

Stepping closer, I keep my hands out to my sides, my palms facing her, and say, 'Stop running. It's over.'

She slides one foot back until her heel is on the rotten, splintered edge and smiles.

She's fooling herself if she thinks she's going to do it. If she was going to try and jump she'd have done it already. She's facing me because there's nowhere else to go.

'I heard what you said to Jedx. You killed the urban explorers because they cast you out of the group.'

'I was their friend, they should have treated me better.'

'So you picked them off one by one and killed them.'

She smiles. 'Is that a hint of admiration I hear in your voice?'

'No.' I don't admire her, I don't admire a killer.

'You sure about that?'

I stare at her. The thrill of the chase still has adrenaline coursing through my body. I can taste the victory. I take a step towards her. 'You're under arrest.'

'I don't think so.' She makes a show of glancing down, and then laughs. The noise seems to echo through the cavernous space. 'I'm not finished yet.'

'Clementine?' It's Dom's voice, far below.

I peer down. He's standing on the sand-covered stage floor, peering up at us. It's surreal seeing him surrounded by fake palm trees, but he isn't there for long. As soon as our eyes meet he's sprinting for the stairway, taking the stairs two at a time. Coming for me, and for the woman.

'You're not police, but you are familiar.' She tilts her head to one side, staring at me. Then I see the realisation hit her. 'You're that academic, the celebrity one who killed a serial killer. I've read all about you.'

Saying nothing, I slide my foot along the board a little further. Inching closer.

'You shouldn't be chasing me, you shouldn't be here at all.' She takes her hands off the rail, gesturing towards Dom. 'Are you some kind of vigilante, helping the detective clean up the streets, doing his dirty work?' She laughs. 'I bet the pair of you killed that serial killer. If he arrests me, I'll make sure I take him down with me. I'll tell them all about you – his lethal little helper. It'll end him.'

I think of my father being framed and found guilty of crimes that weren't his own. I will not let that happen to Dom. Fury flushes through me. 'He's not dirty, he's good, an honourable man.'

'You have so much loyalty to him, it's very sweet. Maybe he isn't dirty or a killer.' She laughs. Shakes her head. 'But you are, aren't you? I can see it, you know, it's obvious. You are *exactly* like me.'

I act on impulse, instinct, springing towards her.

She recoils from me, and there's a crack as the wood breaks beneath her feet. She grabs for the rail, but misses.

Her eyes open wide.

Then she's gone.

72

DOM

Ellie screams as she falls. Thrashes her arms and legs as if she's trying to reach for something, anything, to stop her descent. But it does no good. It's a straight drop from the lighting rig to the floor, there's nothing to slow her.

He's almost at the top of the stairs when she hits the ground. The noise of it is deadened by the sand, just a soft thud, but he feels the impact like a blow to the gut; another body, another person dead on his watch.

He leans over the banister staring at her, willing her to move, to have survived. But he's kidding himself. The building must be at least four storeys high; her chance of survival is virtually zero. She's not coming back from this.

It's then that Dom looks across at the lighting rig suspended from the middle of the roof. It's swaying, listing sideways at an angle. Clementine is in exactly the same spot. She's clinging onto the rail. Her eyes fixed on Ellie.

'Clementine?' Dom calls.

She doesn't respond.

The short route to the rig is blocked from where the platform has collapsed, so he sprints the long way around the circular platform. He has to get to Clementine. Needs to work out what they should do. Decide his next move. But he can't think straight, the only thing on his mind is whether Clementine was trying to grab hold of Ellie or whether she pushed her.

He pumps his arms faster, concentrates on running, on getting to Clementine, on *not* thinking about the answers; because he knows what he saw.

He just doesn't like the answer.

73

CLEMENTINE

I'm like her. She said that I am like her.

I gaze down from the lighting rig and see her broken body lying far beneath me on the sand. I see her and I feel . . . victorious.

Then disgusted.

Repulsed.

Ashamed.

I stare down at her. She's fallen in a heap; a tangle of arms and legs, her bobbed hair limp across her face. It reminds me of the way she'd dumped the blonde mannequin at the edge of the stage, although I'm too high and too far away from her to see if there's any blood.

I hear footsteps. Dom calls my name, but I can't bring myself to look at him. Nausea flips in my stomach. Bile hits the back of my throat and I retch. I did that. I killed her. This time it wasn't self-defence. Did she fall or did I push her? I don't think I know the answer. She threatened Dom, said she'd use my presence here against him. I don't even know if that's how things work, but I knew that she meant it. The overwhelming need to protect him – from her, and from me – was absolute.

I meant to push her.

Didn't I?

I don't know.

My body shakes and I grip the rail tighter, fearful that the emotions colliding inside me will make me to fall. I take a deep breath in, count to ten and release. Breathe in again and try to feel calmer, but I can't.

She said I was like her; a murderer like her.

I liked it when she fell.

The rig starts to sway beneath me. I hold on tighter. My mind is jumbled, all clogged and slow. Murder is wrong I know that, but is it so wrong to kill a murderer? I could argue it was a public service, a method of justice served. I could say that her multiple wrongdoings make mine a right.

'What did you do?'

I turn and see Dom hurrying along the rig towards me.

He's scowling. He looks horrified. 'Clementine. What the hell did you do?'

I look down at the woman. Shake my head. 'I . . . I don't know.'

'You don't know? What the . . .' He grabs my hand and pulls me back along the rig to the platform. 'You shouldn't be here.'

'She jumped.' I'm surprised how sure I sound of it. 'I tried to stop her.'

Dom puts his hands on my shoulders, clinging so tight I fear he'll stop my circulation. He's looking into my eyes, searching for something, the truth. Trying to decide whether to arrest me or believe me. 'Why did you—'

'I was trying to help you, make you listen. You wouldn't be here if it wasn't for me. I told you about the video. I followed Jedx, I texted you the location. I didn't want there to be another murder.'

He says nothing. His jaw is clenched and I fear for a moment that he *is* about to arrest me. Then he shakes his head. 'You're right, I know you were helping. But you took a stupid risk . . . I saw you make the leap across the buildings, you could have—'

'You'd have done the same.'

'Yeah, probably, but it's my job.'

'And I wanted to help. That woman killed Sass, Ruth Kemp. Ruth didn't deserve to die. She needed justice.'

'Agreed.'

I hear the distant wail of sirens. 'So what now?'

'You need to go,' Dom says. 'Go back across the roof and out through the woods. You can't be here when the cavalry arrive.'

I look down at the woman's body. 'But what will you—'

'Just go, all right?' And from his tone I know there's no sense in arguing with him. 'Now.'

And so I do.

*

I go back the way I came, through the fire exit onto the roof, and down the building using an old metal ladder. I force my body faster through the snow. Head down, face bowed from the bitter flurries, sprinting back to the wire fence and the woodland beyond. I do not rest. Keep running; lungs heaving, mouth dry, skin numb from cold.

Somehow, I manage to clamber over the fence.

I pause then, on the other side, hidden beneath the dark cover of the trees, to catch my breath and look back in the direction of the buildings. The blizzard is almost blinding, my view is severely limited, but in the distance I can see the flashing blue lights coming closer.

It's OK, though. I know things will be OK. Dom will pretend I was never here, and it's snowing so hard the flakes have already covered my tracks. The fact I was here will be Dom's and my special secret. Something we share. That binds us together.

I hope it is enough.

74

DOM

The circus is all around him. Blue lights are on the scene; ambulances and squad cars. The snow is disco-lit with them, lighting the white with their blue. They burst through the gates, driving through the snow to get as close to the buildings as they can.

Dom directs them. Sends one lot off into Sound-Stage One to find Parekh and the man they now know is called Jedx, or Joshua. He tells them they might need a fire crew to cut the poor bloke free. He leads Abbott and the second lot to Sound-Stage Two. They jog out of the snow and into the beach set, the sand crunching beneath their boots. The fake tropical setting is surreal.

Ellie is still lying where she dropped. Slumped in the sand, her body is twisted, and her head is lolled back with her eyes closed. There's some blood trickling from her mouth, but not much.

Dom turns back to Abbott and the others, points up at the rig. 'She jumped from that.'

His words are dry as ashes in his mouth. The lie feels like it might choke him.

Abbott looks up. 'She must have realised she couldn't get away with what she did.'

'Yeah.'

'Weird to go up there, though.'

Dom shrugs. No words come.

Abbott looks at him, concerned. 'You all right, guv?'

Dom looks at Ellie's body. The paramedics are checking her vital signs, to confirm she's dead. Shit. She wouldn't be dead if Clementine hadn't intervened. If he'd listened to Clementine in the first place, though, rather than shutting her out, he could have prevented this.

Guilt punches him in the gut; guilt about Ellie being dead, guilt about lying and, more than anything, guilt that he is glad Clementine got away before the blue lights arrived.

'Guv?' Abbott says.

'I just need a minute, yeah.'

Dom walks a few paces away from the rest of them. Running his hand through his hair, he tries to think things through logically, but he can't. All he can think is that what he's just done, what he's feeling, doesn't make sense. He's always been straight down the line, black and white about justice and truth and how people need to face the consequences of their actions. He can't understand why he's made Clementine an exception.

But he has, and he's lied, covering up Clementine's presence at the crime scene. And, in truth, he knows why. Clementine killing one serial killer – the Lover – was an act of self-defence in an impossible situation. But what she might have done to Ellie is a totally different ballgame. She'd be arrested, convicted of murder or manslaughter, no doubt. Internal Affairs and the media would have a feeding frenzy.

He's lying to protect her, as well as himself, and to stop this whole thing becoming a complete shit-storm.

Then there's a shout, and he realises his name is being called. Turning, he sees one of the paramedics is running back towards the ambulance, while the other remains bent over Ellie. It looks as if he's talking to her.

Dom feels a tightening in his chest. He hurries towards Ellie's body. 'What's . . .'

The paramedic has hope in his eyes. 'We've found a pulse. She's still alive.'

75

DOM

They blue-light Ellie Mitchell out a few minutes after Joshua Hartwell. She's not doing as well as her would-be victim; unconscious, weak pulse, breathing shallow. They don't think her odds are good, and Dom hates that the knowledge of this brings him relief.

He watches the second ambulance leave. Its lights illuminate the trees as it forces its way through the snow-filled driveway and out onto the lane. He's standing beside a rapid response vehicle with a paramedic fussing over him, cleaning a wound on his hand. He hadn't realised he had it until his adrenaline started to drop and he felt the dull ache of it. But it's nothing compared to the pounding in his head.

'You might need stitches.' The paramedic stares at Dom, stern-faced. 'Definitely a tetanus jab.'

Dom grimaces. He doesn't have time for faffing around. He needs to talk to Parekh, make sure she's OK. And he needs to work out what he's going to say if Ellie wakes up. 'Just slap a plaster on it, yeah. I'll be fine.'

The paramedic fixes some tapes over the wound and then attaches a dressing. He doesn't look happy. 'That'll hold you together for now, but you need to get it sorted properly within the next twenty-four hours, otherwise you could be looking at an infection.'

Dom's already moving away. He nods to the paramedic. 'Thanks, mate.'

He hurries through the snow to the last remaining ambulance. Parekh's inside, sitting on the gurney. She's got a silver space blanket over her shoulders and a bandage around her head.

'You all right?' Dom asks.

She gives him a smile. 'Bit battered but I'll live. Hopefully Joshua will too.'

'How's he doing?'

'It took a while to get him free of that freaky thing, but they did it. He kept passing out and he lost a hell of a lot of blood, but he was breathing. It's a miracle he survived. The medics say he only did because the daggers didn't drop the whole way, so they missed his vital organs.'

'Poor bloke.'

Parekh pulls the space blanket tighter around her. 'Yes, but he's not dead, so compared to his mates, he's lucky.'

'True.' Dom hopes Joshua will make it. He still can't believe Ellie Mitchell was behind this. How the hell did he get it so wrong?

'Don't be too hard on yourself, guv. She had me fooled, too.'

'She was a bloody amazing actor. Her distress when Ruth Kemp's body was found, the way she talked about their friendship . . .' He shakes his head. 'And yet she'd killed her, Thomas Lee and Ian Lowe too, all totally premeditated.'

'Revenge for humiliation; it's one of the strongest motivations, you know that.'

'Yeah, but . . .' He gestures towards Sound-Stage One. 'All those theatrics, all that effort to have the replica daggers made, and customising the film prop as a murder weapon . . . it's fucked up.'

Parekh nods, then winces from the movement. 'It is that.'

They sit in silence for a moment. It's freezing, but he's so numb now he hardly feels it. Outside the ambulance, the circus is calming down. Abbott's gone to speak with the CSIs in Sound-Stage One. Some of the uniforms are already heading off.

'What happened with Ellie Mitchell, guv?'

He keeps looking down at the ambulance floor knowing that he mustn't meet Parekh's eyes; she's sharp, quick, she'll be able to tell that he's hiding something. He tries to stick as close to the truth as he can. Feels less shit that way. 'She was running and ducked into the second sound-stage to escape. When she realised she'd got herself cornered, she jumped.'

Parekh nods. She's silent for a long moment before speaking. 'Do you think she had an accomplice?'

Dom frowns. 'I don't think so. Why?'

Parekh doesn't meet his eye. 'It's just that after Ellie hit me, I thought I saw someone else moving in that storage area. You didn't see anything?'

He takes a long inhale and tries to keep his expression neutral. 'No, sorry.'

'Really? I thought I saw a woman with long black hair. She looked familiar, like that Clementine Starke . . .'

Fuck. Dom swallows hard. He forces himself to meet Parekh's gaze. Tries to keep his voice steady, normal. 'But why would she have been here?'

Parekh holds his eye contact for a moment, then shakes her head. 'You're right, it makes no sense. Ellie has black hair, doesn't she? Maybe I was just seeing double.'

'You did take quite a hard whack on the head.' Dom shivers as the realisation sinks in; Parekh, one of his own team, recognised Clementine and he's just lied to her face. He knows he'll have to keep perpetuating the lie, and feels even shittier for it. He puts his hand on Parekh's shoulder, and forces a smile. 'Yeah, you must have been mistaken.'

76

CLEMENTINE

It takes over three hours to get home. Even the roads in London are gridlocked from the snow. The cold has seeped through my skin and frozen my bones. As I trudge up the stairs to my attic apartment I wonder if I will ever feel my toes and fingers again, but that's not all that I'm missing. Something is different. I *feel* different. I feel more in control, less threatened that I'll be over-whelmed, consumed, by my own feelings.

It's hard to explain, but it's almost as if the cold has tempered my emotions; knocked the peaks off the colossal highs and flat-tened out the darkest lows of the rollercoaster I've been riding ever since my apathy was punctured.

It takes me a while to unlock my door. To start with, my fingers are too numb to grip the key, too immobile to turn it. I succeed after many failed attempts and stumble into the flat.

I strip off my clothes as soon as the door is closed and leave them in a heap beside the washing machine. A heap – the word makes me think of Ellie, the way she landed on the sand below us. Untidy. Unintentional. Dead.

Murderer.

The voice whispers in my mind and I know it is right. I didn't cause the fire that killed my father as I'd always believed was the case, but I did kill the Lover. That was self-defence; today was different. I think back, replay the scene in my mind. Ellie was threatening Dom. I acted to protect him. I *needed* to protect him, and I find that strange. I've always been a lone wolf; I have never wanted to protect anyone before.

Walking on snow-chilled legs, I move to the bathroom. I insert the plug and twist the taps until hot water fills the tub and steam swirls around me.

What I have done is wrong, I know that, yet it is also right. I killed a murderer. Two murderers – the first a killer who preyed on vulnerable women, and today one who targeted a group of people who'd previously been her friends. Are these people a loss to society? No, they are not. Did they enrich the community of this city? No, they did not.

And so, although I know that killing is wrong, I do not feel ashamed. I feel powerful. Victorious. I helped Dom by solving another case, and stopping the murderer going free. The more I think about it, the more it seems as if I've done a public service.

I have helped make Londoners safer. And yet I cannot shake the fear that Dom will think badly of me. I remember the expression on his face as he asked me what I had done. I didn't even know myself in that moment, but I knew from the way he looked at me that he believed I had pushed Ellie. And still he protected me.

We protected each other.

I step into the bath and sink down into the water. At first, I feel nothing. Then a mild tingling starts, the very beginnings of sensation reigniting across my skin. The grafts that cover the burns on my forearms and legs are the last to regain their feeling. I stay submerged in the water up to my nostrils, revelling in the sensation. It spreads and heightens until I am defrosted and reanimated. My body is cleansed and calmed.

My mind feels calmer too.

Dom has seen my true nature, the she-wolf within me, twice now, and still he keeps the secret. I allow myself to think about this, about how it makes me feel; I'm braced for a dramatic reaction. But nothing dramatic comes. Instead I smile and I feel . . . happy.

Dom and I are bound by our secrets. We are connected through them, and that means something. It has to. And so I will lie low, let him come to me.

Until then, I wait.

FRIDAY

77

DOM

Dom gets to Accident and Emergency at 6.30 knowing that the wait will be shorter at this time in the morning. He feels stiff and aching. The few hours' rest he got after checking in with Chrissie at her flat hasn't helped much. Sleeping slumped on the sofa, still in his damp clothes after chasing through the snow, has made him feel ancient. As he waits to be seen he stretches, raising his arms up and trying to ease out the tension in his back. It doesn't work. The skin across his hand feels tight, and the wound throbs beneath the dressing. I'm getting too old for this, he thinks.

After he's been seen by the nurse, had his tetanus shot and the dressing changed, he goes to the public loos and splashes water on his face. He looks in the mirror, smoothing his hair with his fingers and trying to seem less like he's spent the night in a chair, but he's unsuccessful.

He doesn't go straight to the office. Instead he detours to the high dependency unit linked with ICU. He shows his warrant card at the nurses' station and a man tells him where to find Joshua Hartwell, aka Jedx. Glass dividers split the ward into cubicles. Dom assumes they're meant to reduce the risk of infection more effectively than curtains, and yet still allow the nurses to keep a close watch on their patients. There's no privacy though, and he imagines it must feel like being in a goldfish bowl, permanently on display.

Dom walks along the central aisle until he finds Joshua. His upper body is wrapped in thick bandages and there's a metal cage over his torso to keep the covers from resting on his skin. He seems to be sleeping. There's a middle-aged nurse in the cubicle, changing the bag feeding into his IV. She has a kind face but Dom can see the dark circles under her eyes, probably the effect of too many night shifts in a row.

As she leaves the cubicle, Dom shows her his warrant card and asks, 'How's he doing?'

She smiles. 'Not too bad. He had a bit of a rough night, but given what happened to him that's not surprising. His vitals are good. He just needs time for the wounds to heal.'

'That's good to hear. We'll need to take his statement and—'

'Like I told your colleague last night, his pain meds are very high at the moment so he's not likely to wake for a while. Come back this afternoon and we'll see, that's the best I can offer.'

'Thanks, I'll take that.' Dom glances further up the ward. Knows he has to ask. 'What about the woman who was brought in, Ellie Mitchell?'

The nurse shakes her head. 'The prognosis isn't as good, I'm afraid. She suffered extreme trauma and is showing no signs of coming out of the coma. The consultant will see her again today, but until we've done more tests it's hard to give an accurate assessment.'

'I see. Thanks a lot, you've been very helpful.'

As the nurse continues on her way, Dom walks along the ward to Ellie Mitchell's cubicle, nods at the uniform sitting on a plastic chair outside and looks through the glass. Ellie lies completely still. Her face is mottled with bruises, as are her arms. The handcuffs chaining her to the bed look barbaric, out of place against the starched white linen she lies on.

He still can't believe that he got things so wrong. He wants to look away, but he can't, not yet, not when he is responsible. Only three people know the truth; Clementine, Ellie and him. He's fucked up, lied to his own team, to people who trust him, in order to protect Clementine. Dom still can't understand why he did that.

He swears under his breath. Stands listening to the beep of the machines and watching the ventilator regulate Ellie's breathing, and hates himself for praying that she never wakes up.

When he can't take it any longer, he turns and heads for the exit. Pulling out his phone he taps out a text.

We need to talk.

78

DOM

'Clementine, are you in there? Can we talk?' It's fucking freezing outside, and he needs to see her. Can't go into work before they've talked, but he can't get her to answer her phone. 'Clementine?'

The door clunks as the bolt disengages and her voice through the intercom says, 'I'm here. Come up.'

Dom hurries inside, stomps his feet on the mat to get rid of the worst of the snow, and runs up the stairs. Clementine is waiting at the entrance to her flat, door open. Wearing a green jumper and black skinny jeans, she looks a world away from the snow-covered, wild-eyed woman he last saw on the lighting rig above Sound-Stage Two. She smiles when their eyes meet. He doesn't.

'I've been calling you,' he says as he follows her inside. 'Why didn't you—'

'I dropped my phone last night, I haven't got a replacement yet.'

'Where? Will anyone—'

'It fell into the river, no one will find it.' She turns, gesturing to the kettle whistling on the kitchen counter. 'Coffee? Tea? I was just making some for myself.'

'I'm all right.' He steps closer to her. Needs her to focus on him, to give him answers. 'Clementine, look at me. Why did you do it?'

She turns back to him, her expression innocent. 'Do what?'

He doesn't answer. Can't believe she's playing this game. She knows what happened up there on the lighting rig with Ellie Mitchell. They both know. Right now, he needs to understand why.

Clementine breaks the silence first. 'They're saying on Twitter that she's in a coma.'

Again, he has the thought that he wishes she'd died. Again, he feels guilty. 'Yes.'

'Do they know if she'll be OK?'

'It's too early to tell.'

Clementine wrinkles her nose. 'Oh.'

He swears under his breath. 'Is that all you're going to say?'

'You could have arrested me last night, I wouldn't have resisted. If you're so angry with me, why did you tell me to run?'

Dom says nothing. He's wondering the same thing.

'You *should* have arrested me. That's why you're angry, but that's not my fault, it's yours.'

'You nearly killed her, *that* was your fault.'

Clementine tilts up her chin. 'So you'd have preferred me to have done the job properly?'

The look in her eyes makes him shiver, but still he steps closer to her. He needs her to talk to him, help him understand. 'I didn't say that. Tell me why, Clementine. You owe me that surely?'

She pushes him back and ducks away from him around the sofa. 'Don't raise your voice at me.'

They stand like warring, gunslinger bookends at either end of the sofa. Eyes locked in combat. Both unsure who will fire the next shot.

'Sorry . . . shit . . .' What's happening to him? He feels like he's losing it. 'Look, just help me to understand.'

'You were right when you said I owed you. I do; after what happened with the Lover, I owe you my life. When she realised I wasn't police, that woman – Ellie – said some awful things. She was threatening you, your career. I couldn't allow that.' Clementine's voice is clear, unwavering. She meets his gaze without fear. 'I had to protect you.'

'Why?'

Clementine narrows her eyes. 'Why not?'

Dom holds her gaze briefly before looking away. There's steeliness beneath her fragility, and something else that he hasn't seen before. It worries him. 'How do you feel?'

She frowns. 'That's a harder question to answer. I'm not sure I know yet, it's a shock . . .' Looking down, she fiddles with the cuff of her jumper. Looks back at him. 'But I am glad I stopped her.'

Dom exhales. The way she's talking bothers him. She doesn't seem traumatised by the events of last night, and she doesn't seem upset that her actions led to a woman almost dying. 'Do you regret what happened?'

'Do you?'

He doesn't answer. Can't form an answer that comes close to making sense.

Clementine steps back towards him. Her voice is low, soothing. 'What did you tell them?'

The guilt from the lie smacks him in the stomach. 'I told them she was up on the rig alone, that she was trying to escape me.'

'Thank you.'

'Yeah.' He runs his hands through his hair. It feels like his brain is going to blow from all the crap going on in it.

Clementine reaches out to him. Puts her hand on his arm. Her touch is warm, gentle. 'You did a good thing.'

'Did I? Because it feels like I'm fucking up all over the place. I took an oath, I swore I'd act fairly and for justice, but in the last week I've . . .' He shakes his head. 'I've given Abbott a second chance when he should have been fired, stood by and watched you push a murder suspect from that rig, and then lied to my own team to save your skin.'

'You did what you thought was best.'

'But who was it best for? You? Me?' He rubs his forehead. 'Fuck. I've been such a self-centred prick.'

She smiles and tightens her grip on his arm. 'Well, don't worry. I've got something you can do for me that won't be at all self-centred.'

And that's when it hits him. His deception has tied them together. Whatever he does, from now onwards Clementine will always have leverage over him.

It terrifies him where that could lead.

79

CLEMENTINE

I lied when he asked me how I felt. I knew it was the only way to keep him on my side. Because how I feel is alive, in control, renewed and reborn from last night. But, a man of the law like him, I don't think he would agree with my logic about killing a killer being a valid form of justice.

He's wary of me, I can see that. His shoulders are rigid and he's watching my movements closely. I hope he can overcome it and not let his guilt and fear come between us. I need to persuade him that I mean him no harm. We could make a good team, he and I. I've always enjoyed solving puzzles, but now I know that facing up to real danger makes victory even sweeter. The stakes have to be high, and winning needs to mean something. Bringing down a murderer is the ultimate meaning. Justice is justice, whatever the method by which it gets served.

'I need your help in finding out what happened to my father.'

Dom looks surprised. 'Me? What help can I be?'

I give him a little smile. 'You're in the police. You have access to things I don't.'

'I don't think I can—'

'When the IPCC thought you could be dirty, I helped you. When your so-called friends where plotting against you, I found them out. I got you information on Lindsay and he was locked up. I have helped you a lot, Dom. Now I need your help. I have to root out those who conspired against my father to frame him. They've stayed free for too many years. They can't be allowed to get away with his murder.'

He grips the back of the sofa. 'You think it was someone in the force?'

Dirty coppers. Liars. Criminals. *They* killed my father. 'I don't know. But I know that your DCI trained with my father. He could know more about what he was involved in, maybe something about the undercover operations he worked and what got him killed. He might even—'

Dom looks shocked. 'My DCI, you mean Jackson?'

'Yes.'

He's frowning. Shaking his head. 'Jackson's a good man. He's been like a father to *me*, there's no way he'd be mixed up in anything—'

'Are you sure?' I fix him with a hard stare. 'Didn't you say he was pretty pally with Lindsay?'

Dom opens his mouth to reply, then shuts in again. He glances back towards my research web. 'This is all highly confidential stuff, Clementine. I can't just ask the DCI about classified operations with no valid basis for my questions.'

I can see that I need to ease Dom into this gradually if he's going to help me. I soften my voice. Give a little smile. 'I'm not saying you have to find it out all at once. First off, I just need you to confirm whether Paul Jackson stayed in touch with my father.' I walk across to the far wall, to my research map. I trace my fingertips along the red string that connects my father's name to each piece of information I have associated with him, over the picture of him with Mother, who Albert still hasn't had any luck in locating, and stop at the photograph of him with his colleagues. It's a fresh version – I took the copy with the words Gerry Matthews had scrawled across it down before Dom arrived – and unpin it, handing it to Dom. 'These were his friends and colleagues in the beginning. I've spoken to Gerry Matthews, he contacted me, and one thing he told me is that DCI Paul Jackson used to work closely with my father. I need you to find out if that's true.'

Dom still looks unsure. 'So what do you know about these men?'

I look at the picture, at the five men at the beginning of their careers, ones that took different paths – some to glory, some to death. 'I know their names – my father, Robert Starke, then Paul Jackson, Gerry Matthews, Alan Holt, and Jon Garrett. I don't know anything about Jon Garrett, but I know Gerry Matthews is retired, and that Alan Holt and Paul Jackson still work for the Met.'

Dom's turned pale. 'You believe one of them had something to do with your father's death?'

I hold Dom's gaze. 'I know my father is dead because of someone he trusted.'

80

DOM

By eleven he's in Jackson's office for the wash up. Dom's trying to keep his mind on the conversation but all he can think about is the shit-storm with Clementine. The DCI hasn't seemed to notice.

Jackson pushes the paper across the desk. He's looking chuffed. 'You should be proud, Dom. *HERO DETECTIVE SOLVES SERIAL KILLER PUZZLE*. It's a good headline.'

Not for me, thinks Dom. He doesn't feel like a hero, he feels like a fraud. 'It's not about headlines.'

'True enough, but it can't but help with the brass. Positive news stories are rare these days.' He points at the article. 'This kind of thing is good for us, like it or not.'

Dom knows the DCI is right. Hates it though. 'If they're so pleased they'll approve me recruiting for the DS vacancy in my team then?'

Jackson looks at him over the top of his glasses. 'We discussed this. I'm holding that spot for a trainee Detective Constable.'

Dom shakes his head. It's bollocks, but he doesn't have the fight in him to argue. He's distracted, unfocused. It's not the right time to launch into battle. He'll fight this trainee nonsense, but not today.

The DCI seems to take his silence as agreement. He changes the subject. 'Tell me about what happened. Why was she up in the roof rafters? Was she trying to kill herself?'

Dom tries to keep his tone neutral, measured. Needs to appear to be acting normal when discussing this case, even though what happened in the hangar at Hendleton was anything but. 'I don't know. She climbed up onto a lighting rig. Could have been trying to escape, but then realised it wasn't possible . . .'

Jackson frowns. 'It's such a waste. These young people, whatever makes them turn out like that?'

'It's hard to say. We found Thomas Lee's wallet, phone and bodycam, Ruth Kemp's SLR camera, and Ian Lowe's iPod in her room at the place she shared. From what Parekh and I heard her tell Joshua, it was a revenge attack, the most elaborate I've seen. She had this twisted idea of using the urbexer group's love of video-ing themselves and getting more social media followers against them. She ambushed them when they tried to explore the studio they thought was abandoned, then stalked them, picking them off one by one, before finally luring Joshua back to Hendleton so she could recreate a horror film murder scene. On her phone we found pictures of each of the group as she stalked them, and their dead bodies. From the scribbled notes we found in a notebook by her bed, her intention had been to post the pictures, and the film of Joshua's death, on the internet.'

'Bloody hell.'

'At least they're confident Joshua will be OK.'

'Well that's something.' Jackson shakes his head. 'Do they think Ellie will recover?'

'It seems unlikely.'

The DCI looks thoughtful. 'Well, maybe it's for the best. After what she did.'

Maybe, thinks Dom. But not for the same reasons as the DCI. Just because it'd be bad for him, and for Clementine, he shouldn't be wishing another person dead, no matter what they did. If he takes that view he's just as fucked up as Ellie.

There's a knock on the door and Jackson's assistant puts her head round. 'I have Mr Holsworth, IPCC, here for you. He says it's urgent.'

Jackson glances at Dom. 'OK, send him in.'

She ushers Holsworth into the office. He sits in the chair beside Dom, his expression grim as he looks from Dom to Jackson. 'Apologies for interrupting, but you need to know this. Lindsay's gone.'

Dom flinches, then glances at Jackson. 'What the hell do you mean?'

Holsworth stares at him, his piggy eyes unblinking. 'He was already dead when they found him. Hanged.'

Jackson clasps his hands together. 'That is a bad business.'

Too right, thinks Dom. He clenches his jaw. The anger rising. 'Lindsay knew you had evidence on him. He wouldn't have wanted to do time, but suicide? That doesn't sound his style.'

'He used shoelaces. But he wasn't wearing shoes with laces when he was arrested, they'd have been taken off him even if he had been.'

'So someone must have helped him?' Dom remembers the bitter way Lindsay had laughed when he'd told Dom no one could protect him, and the person he worked for had people everywhere, that the force was riddled with them. Dom looks back at Holsworth. 'Or else someone took him out.'

'Looks that way.' There's no mistaking the accusation in Holsworth's tone.

Dom glances at Jackson. The DCI's expression is grim. This is bloody ridiculous. He points at Holsworth, stabbing his finger towards his face. 'You can't seriously be thinking I did this? Yeah, Lindsay betrayed me and tried to kill Darren Harris. He threatened my sister and her son. But I wanted him banged up – serving time in jail – not this.'

Holsworth raises an eyebrow. 'Temper, Dom. Don't make me warn you again. I didn't come here to make accusations, I just wanted you in on the situation.'

Jackson gives Dom a look. Dom shifts back in his seat, trying to extend the distance between himself and Holsworth. He won't apologise for his rant. He can't believe the bastard would even imply he could be mixed up in Lindsay's death.

Holsworth continues. 'It's my job to look at every possibility. I'll be speaking to those whose custody he was in at the time. But we have to be prepared for the fact that we may never know the extent of what Lindsay was into. Of course we'll requestion everyone involved with Operation Atlantis, but in truth this investigation has just hit a wall.'

Dom clenches his fists. 'So you hadn't even interviewed him fully? You're no closer to knowing who the corrupt members of the brass are? Shit.'

'If the trail's cold, it's cold.' Holsworth glares at Dom. 'You, me and your attitude are going to need a serious talk again, DI Bell, and soon.'

'I'm ready whenever.' Dom keeps his voice steady, tries not to rise to the bait. 'I've got nothing to hide.'

But that's not true, and he knows it. In the last forty-eight hours he's accumulated many secrets; that Abbott was blackmailed by a journalist to reveal case information; that Clementine helped him with the murder investigation and pushed Ellie Mitchell from the lighting rig. With a jolt he realises there's something else. He went off the record to visit Lindsay in the cells. If that comes out he could look guilty of aiding him. He remembers the expression on Lindsay's face as he told Dom to be very careful. The way he wouldn't stop whistling.

Holsworth's gone, and Jackson's chatting away like nothing's happened, but Dom feels as though everything's falling apart. He's built his whole career on doing the right thing, striving for justice, never taking the easy route if it isn't best for the case and his team. But in the past few days he's let that all go to shit.

And now Lindsay's dead and it looks like they'll never get to the truth behind Operation Atlantis. It's a fucking nightmare. He wonders if he can persuade Holsworth to try again to get Therese to talk. She's managed to stay clean so far, but what Clementine saw, and what Darren's said, makes him think Therese has to have done something, know more than she's let on. Whatever happens, Dom is furious Lindsay won't face justice. And although things had gone bad between them, he's hurt by the loss of a man who he had once called a friend.

Jackson looks at him over the top of his glasses. 'Look, Dom, I know it's not the outcome any of us wanted, but it does spare us a trial, and the taxpayers . . .'

Dom can't listen to any more of this. He gets up to leave, then stops. This must be something like it feels for Clementine – knowing her father was framed but not knowing by whom. Despite everything that's happened, maybe because of it, he *should* help her. He reaches into his pocket for the photograph. Now is as good a time as any to ask. 'Paul, there's something I'd—'

The door opens and Jackson's assistant bustles in. She smiles at Dom and puts a brown bag with a well-known fast food company's logo on the DCI's desk. 'Special delivery. Thought I'd better wait until Mr Holsworth had gone.' She winks at Dom. 'I knew a gym bunny like you wouldn't want anything.'

Jackson thanks her and rips into the bag. Unwrapping the offering inside, he lifts it to his mouth and takes a huge bite of the egg and bacon muffin. 'God that's good,' he says between mouthfuls.

Dom stays standing. Waits.

His boss looks up guiltily. 'Don't tell my wife, will you? She's got me on this bloody low sodium, low cholesterol, no taste nonsense.'

Biding his time, Dom does his best to look sympathetic.

Popping the last of the muffin into his mouth, Jackson scrunches the wrapper into a ball and throws it into his bin. He dabs his lips with a paper napkin and looks back at Dom. 'What was it you wanted to ask?'

Dom takes the photograph from his pocket and holds it out to Jackson. 'Do you remember the other guys in this photo?'

Jackson looks at it, then looks back at Dom. His expression is strange, not pissed off exactly, more suspicious. 'What are you up to?'

I should have anticipated he'd want to know, Dom thinks. He feels unprepared.

Jackson narrows his eyes. 'Who put you up to this? Was it Susan?'

Dom's not sure what the DCI's assistant has to do with anything. 'I . . .'

'I bloody knew it. She's been going on about me having a party and inviting all my old muckers. And because I wouldn't give her a list of names she's got you trawling the archives and doing her dirty work.' He chuckles. 'Imagine it, all the old fossils back together again celebrating our long service, thirty-odd years later.'

Dom says nothing.

'Fine, fine, stay quiet, have it your way. I'll play your game.' He looks back at the photo, smiling. 'Well, of course you know Superintendent Holt on the other side. Next to him is Gerry Matthews, one of the best drugs men we had. The one in the middle, damn, I really can't remember. And next to me . . .' Jackson pauses. He stares at the picture, frowning. Takes his glasses off and wipes them with his handkerchief. 'I think his name was Robert, not sure about the last name. He went off undercover, a real hot shot – fast-tracked I believe. Don't think I saw him again after that picture was taken.'

'So he wasn't a colleague you worked with?'

'No, not since right back in the day.'

Dom feels the tension in his shoulders relax. Relieved he's upheld his promise to Clementine but that Jackson doesn't remember her father, they didn't work together. It makes it easier, cleaner. The last thing he wants is for Clementine to have any more impact on his work. He's let her do enough damage already. 'Right.'

Jackson finishes cleaning his glasses and puts them back on. He takes another look at the picture. 'Look how young we were. It's all ancient history of course, but I suppose there might be someone around here who remembers Robert's last name.' He shrugs. 'My memory's not what it was. It's only Gerry and Alan I've kept in touch with. You know how it is, you come up together and you think you'll stay tight, always have each other's backs.' He looks wistful, full of memories. Then his expression hardens, and he hands the picture back to Dom. 'But that's bullshit. When things get tough, the camaraderie never lasts.'

Yeah, thinks Dom, remembering how tight he and Lindsay had been back in the early days, don't I bloody know it.

81

DOM

Dom's at Clementine's flat and he's angry. The injustices of the past few days weigh heavy on his back like the devil. He's furious Lindsay won't face trial, and that Holsworth seems to be giving up. And afraid that what Clementine did at Hendleton will be discovered and send his life spiralling down into more shit.

They sit on the sofa, and Clementine listens to him rant. He shouldn't be here, he knows that, but he needed to see her; needed someone to talk to about this, and now, after all that's happened, and they've done, she's the only one he can be honest with.

Dom's words come faster, louder, fuelled by his rage. 'So there's nothing I can do, Holsworth thinks the truth of what happened behind Operation Atlantis is gone with Lindsay. He had the contacts, he knew how things worked inside and outside the force. Without him we're screwed. Darren might know a bit, yeah, but nothing like Lindsay did, and so far Holsworth seems to believe Therese had nothing to do with it.'

Clementine bangs her glass down onto the floor. 'That's not true, what I saw, what I heard, all indicates she was in it with—'

'Yeah, I know. But I can't tell him what you saw, can I?'

She holds his gaze. Tilts her head to one side. 'Maybe there's still a way.'

He puts his head in his hands. 'No. It's over.'

'Did you ask DCI Jackson about the photo with my father?'

Dom looks at her. Can't believe she's asking him about that now. 'Jackson said he couldn't remember your father's name, said he was Robert someone and that he'd not seen him since the photo was taken because he was fast-tracked.'

He sees Clementine clench her glass tighter. Her voice is stilted. 'He lied. He's lying to you.'

Dom doesn't need this. He needs to work out what to do about Holsworth, how to get him to reinterview Therese. He looks at Clementine. 'What do you mean?'

She grabs her laptop off the desk and taps the trackpad to wake it. 'After you left this morning, a True Crime London friend of mine succeeded in trying to repair a broken USB stick of my father's. He's only managed to recover a few documents so far, but it's enough to know that your boss isn't being honest.' She gestures towards the screen. 'This is my father's final entry in his case notes. It's dated the morning he was killed. He wasn't a dirty copper. He was working deep undercover – investigating corruption in senior officers, specifically a connection between criminal gangs and police that had been established for years. And he was close to exposing them. He mentions how he'd been pulled into the inner circle of the criminal gang he's infiltrated, that the ploy has worked.'

Dom feels a chill spreading down his spine. 'What information? Have you got specifics?'

Clementine shakes her head. 'No, he doesn't say. I need to search through the other files and see if there's more detail in them. What he does say is that through an interaction with an informant, he has some new information that could break the investigation wide open. Father wrote that he's told his chain of command and they have taken the bait.'

Dom tries to resist, but he feels himself getting drawn in by her. He leans closer, peering at the screen. It feels as if everyone he knows is lying about something. Hiding secrets. Just like he is for Clementine. 'He suspected his own boss was in on it?'

'It looks that way.'

'Who?'

She scrolls down to the bottom of the document. 'My father was told by his boss to sit tight and await further instructions. A few hours after writing this case note he was dead.' She taps the screen again. 'This was my father's boss.'

Dom stares at the name on the case document: Paul Jackson.

He rears back from the screen. This can't be right. It's like a fucking nightmare. 'Jackson told me he hadn't seen your father since the photograph of them in uniform was taken.'

'People lie, Dom.'

He thinks back to the way Jackson had reacted; suspicious at first, then overly jovial. He'd deliberated over the picture, over Clementine's father's name, then said he couldn't remember; but one thing about Jackson is that he's always had a memory like an elephant, Dom's never known him to forget a thing. Fuck. Now Dom thinks about it, analyses his body language, he seemed tense, and his slow movements as he cleaned his glasses looked oddly incongruent with the worried look in his eye.

The man has been like a father to him. A mentor, someone he could trust.

He looks at Clementine. 'I . . . that's . . . He lied about knowing your father. He fucking lied . . . And if Jackson lied about this, what else is he lying about?'

'Exactly.'

Dom runs his hand across his forehead. 'If Jackson's dirty, does that mean he's been playing both sides all this time?' He clenches his fists. 'Lindsay visited him and I never knew why . . . Darren said the orders came from higher up than Lindsay . . . what if Jackson is still involved with gangs, and he's the man who got Lindsay and Darren involved? What if Therese is still taking orders from him? Shit. Holsworth said Lindsay had been given help to kill himself, maybe he was murdered? It could have been on Jackson's instructions. He could have been pulling the strings all along.' Dom can't stay here. He has to do something. He goes to get up. 'I need to have it out with Jackson, find out what the hell he—'

'No.' Clementine puts her hand on his arm. Her voice is soft, soothing. 'We need to be smart. If my father was right, and Jackson was dirty, then he's been doing this a long time and covering up behind him. The stakes are high, even higher than when my father was working this, and he was killed for what he knew.'

Dom takes a breath. Knows that she's right. 'If they suspect we know anything they'll act against us.'

'It's a risk we can't take, not until we can prove what really happened.'

'To your father and with Lindsay.'

Clementine nods. 'I need to go through the files from the USB stick in detail, and we need more information – from the police database, from the other cases my father worked. We have to build the case against them, find out who is in control.'

'In that audio you recorded, Lindsay said they were untouchable.'

'That's what they think, we need to prove them wrong; take them all down, every last person. None can remain.'

Dom looks at Clementine. Her eyes are bright, excited, and he fears she enjoys the idea of this hunt too much. He's lied for her already, and he knows that if he helps her now, investigates his own commanding officer, there'll be no coming back. It's career suicide, a fatal alliance. But he can't let what's happened go unresolved.

He nods once. 'I'm in. Whatever it takes. This can't be allowed to stand.'

Clementine slides her hand into his. Looks into his eyes. '*We* won't let them get away with it. We'll root them out; Jackson, and anyone else who has been involved in this corruption, this evil, this cancer within the police service. We'll take them down together, and they will pay for all that they have done. We'll get justice.'

Justice. The way she says the word makes him shudder.

He's witnessed her kind of justice.

It's the kind that leaves bodies trailing in her wake.

TWO WEEKS LATER

82

CLEMENTINE

The hospital moved her to a private room just over a week ago, and the uniformed guard is sloppier now. I think he assumes that she'll never wake up and, as no one seems to visit her, his days are long and boring as hell. He takes longer on his bathroom breaks, a good fifteen minutes rather than the hurried four he took in the first few days after it all happened. The novelty of doing prisoner guard duty has worn off. It's his sloppiness that gives me an opportunity.

As always, I slow my steps as I approach, delaying the moment that I open the door, taking a minute to collect my thoughts. I don't need to rush. I know exactly how long the guard will be gone for, and even if he were to return sooner than expected, who would question a nurse going in to do observations on a patient? Because that is how I am dressed, as a nurse. I have the tunic with matching belt, the little fob watch that shows the time upside down, and the flesh-coloured tights and black flats.

I make a good nurse, I think. And I need to, because Dom is so stressed out about the repercussions if Ellie wakes up. He told me that he's not been sleeping, and his workout schedule is far too hardcore to be healthy. It's like he's punishing himself, but it isn't working. He needs to forget Ellie and move on, and I need to help him.

So I've been coming here, visiting Ellie in the moments the guard steps away, every day since she was moved to this private room. Every day I've wondered if today is the day. Every day so far it hasn't been. Maybe today will be different.

Opening the door, I step into the room. As usual, Ellie lies ghost white against the sheets. Her black hair is brushed back from her face and her eyes are closed. Her breathing is steady, rhythmical, not assisted by the ventilator any longer, but she remains in the coma she's been in ever since she fell from the rig at Hendleton Studios. This week there have been rumours that her eyelids fluttered, and that she might be closer to waking. And if she wakes, she will be able to tell the truth about what happened on the rig.

A part of me would like that. The moments just before she fell are vague, hazy, in my mind. I know how I felt in my moment of victory, but whether I pushed her or she fell, it's difficult to know for sure. Maybe she remembers.

But I cannot risk her remembering. Dom cannot risk it.

I step closer. Although she hasn't woken, the bruising across her body and face is fading from purple to green-yellow. She looks so fragile just lying there. Like she wouldn't hurt anyone, but I know that's an illusion.

She said I was like her.

I step closer to the edge of the bed and reach out to her, my fingers hover over her hand, but stop a fraction of an inch away from actually touching her. I keep my voice low, a whisper. 'Ellie, you were wrong. I'm better than you.'

I watch her face for a reaction, but there's no big fanfare, nothing amazing happens, not even the flicker of an eyelid. I frown. Maybe the rumours were wrong. At one stage, before she started breathing unaided, the doctors had been talking about switching off the life support; they said she wasn't going to wake up. Perhaps they're right, and she'll stay this way forever. But until she is gone, Dom will never be secure.

The machines beep on, rhythmic and steady, and I check my watch. Five minutes have passed since the guard left his post. I am safe for at least another ten, although I plan to be out of here much faster.

Looking back at Ellie it seems too easy. There are so many options from which to choose. I could reach out and press my fingers against her mouth and nose, stifle the breath until her life is over. Or there's the more dramatic approach, as favoured by her, a dagger to the neck, or the stomach, or the chest.

I shake my head. Daggers are so messy, and I don't like blood. There's a pillow propped up against the headboard of the bed. I could use it to suffocate her, the pillow a barrier between us, pressing the life from her. I'm still thinking about it when the mechanical IV pump clicks and gives me an idea.

I walk over to it. Run my hand over its smooth surface to the line running from it all the way into the cannula in Ellie's hand. She could die of a drugs overdose, morphine or whatever she might be on. If the pump malfunctioned and she got a huge hit, it'd be game over. But it would be traceable too, the drugs easy to find in a post-mortem.

I turn back to Ellie, and fancy that I see her right eyelid quiver. 'Are you waking up, Ellie? Because that really isn't going to work, you know.'

Stepping closer to the bed, I watch her eyelids but they seem still again now. The machines beep on. She doesn't seem awake, but then how would I really be able to tell?

Taking a pair of latex gloves from the pocket of my tunic, I slip them on, and reach for the pillow propped against the headboard. It's safer this way; for me and for Dom.

I take a deep breath, place the pillow over her face, and exhale as I press down. The beeping of the heart rate monitor becomes erratic, and I reach out, removing the clip from her finger to quiet the noise and stop the alarm sounding.

For a moment, beneath the pressure, it feels as if Ellie moves, struggles.

I grit my teeth. Push down harder.

It's time for me to finish what I started.

ACKNOWLEDGEMENTS:

I've had a love of abandoned places ever since I was a child. In fact, in *You Die Next*, Sass's recollection of exploring an overgrown country house garden reclaimed by nature is a memory stolen from my own. I have my Nanna to thank for taking me to visit the abandoned Italian gardens in the grounds of Halton House, Buckinghamshire, and introducing me to what felt like a magic world. Over thirty years later, while on a riverboat cruise for my Mum's birthday, I spotted a derelict film studios and the idea for Hendleton Studios and what happened there came to me – I guess even at a happy family gathering the mind of a crime writer wanders easily to murder and mystery!

Although the writing of a first draft is a solitary endeavour, turning it from a draft into a book is absolutely a team effort. First thanks go to my fabulous agent and all-round great guy, Oli Munson, whose expert guidance and advice is so important and I appreciate greatly.

Huge thanks to Sam Eades, my amazing editor; you have the knack of getting right to the essence of the story I'm trying to tell and helping me bring it fully to life. Working with you is such an enjoyable and wonderfully creative experience. And to the rest of the brilliant Trapeze team who get Clementine and Dom out into the world with special mentions for the dynamic Alex Layt and super creative Jennifer Breslin.

The crime fiction world is a hugely supportive and welcoming one. Thank you to all the wonderful readers, reviewers, and bloggers who've read and enjoyed Clementine and Dom so far; and huge thanks to all the crime writers who I hang out with at the scene of the crime, you guys are brilliant.

A big thank you to Andy for being my first reader, for your astute observations, and for encouraging and supporting me along the way. You are a rock star.

Massive thanks to my crime writing sisters – Susi, Helen, Alexandra, Louise and Karin – for the wine, laughs and support. You guys are fabulous! And to the wonderful City MA writing group – Rod, Rob, David, Laura, Seun, and James – WIP feedback is always fun and spot-on with you guys, in equal measure.

More thank yous to Caroline and Kirsten for the regular horsebox wisdom and coffee that helps me keep things together when I'm wrestling with plot holes and the like! And to my police adviser, Dave, and my academic adviser, Dr Chris – big thanks for helping me keep the technical bits close to the straight and narrow!

And lastly, I owe a huge debt of thanks to my hugely supportive family – Mum and Richard, my late Dad and Donna, Will, Rachael and Darcey, and my late sister Pod – thank you a million times, you are all amazing.